WITNESS PROTECTION

Other Books by Carol Kinsey

Under the Shadow of a Steeple
Published in 2013

Until Proven Innocent
Published in 2014

Greater Love
Published in 2015

Coming Soon

Renegades

Undercover
Sequel to Witness Protection

WITNESS PROTECTION

Carol Kinsey

Witness Protection

ISBN-13: 978-1546907725

ISBN-10: 1546907726

First Printing – August 2017

Cover Design: Ken Laivins, Erin Hottle

Layout and Design: Erin Hottle

Editing: Rachael Woodall

Special thanks to Keith and Erin Hottle for the use of their photos.

Special thanks to my team of proofreaders—I appreciate all your help and encouragement.

Thank you, Ken Laivins and Erin Hottle, for your amazing work on the cover!

DEDICATION

To my Lord Jesus Christ. May You be glorified.

To Von, Autumn, and Breanna. It's so much fun reading to you!
I love you.

"Whatever you do, do your work heartily, as for the Lord rather than for men, knowing that from the Lord you will receive the reward of the inheritance. It is the Lord Christ Whom you serve."

Colossians 3:23-24

Chapter 1

In the split second before his brain told him to run, Ty Westgate heard the gunshot. Pain rushed through his arm. He dropped his cell phone. No time to think. No time to pick up his phone.

Ty ran. He turned down an alley, ducked into a restaurant, hurried out the other side, and continued his flight.

A small row of condominiums came into view and he hurried toward them. He dodged across the lawn, slipped behind a row of high bushes, and hid beside the front door of a condo. No light. That was good.

Ty could barely hear anything above the pounding of his heart and his labored breathing. He listened for his pursuer, his back against the brick building, and his hand over his bleeding arm. It throbbed.

Footsteps slapped the pavement, but his pursuer didn't slow. The man rushed past without a glance at the oversized shrubs.

Thank You, God. Ty slumped further down the wall, closed his eyes, and the world went black.

■ ■ ■

It was almost midnight. Brooke Dunbar finished her cold coffee and tossed the empty cup in the trash. She'd been working for over twelve hours and was anxious to get home. She gathered her belongings and moved away from the nurse's station.

Her supervisor glanced up from her computer. "Are you leaving?"

Brooke turned to the night manager. "Yes." She restrained herself from sighing audibly. "Do you need something before I go?"

"I need you to take Elisha's schedule next week." It was an order, not a request.

"I've worked five twelve-hour shifts this week. That's one more than I'm supposed to." Brooke fidgeted with her hands. "I'm supposed to have the next four days off."

"In a perfect world yes, but this isn't a perfect world and I've already changed the schedule." Glenna shrugged. "You'll have tomorrow off."

Clenching and unclenching her fingers on her purse straps, Brooke glanced down the long hospital corridor and let out her repressed sigh. "Glenna…"

"I'll see you Friday at 6pm."

Brooke blinked. Was this for real? She walked toward the elevators. No point in protesting. She'd already tried that with this night manager in the past and it only made the woman more cantankerous. Weariness descended upon her shoulders. *There goes another weekend.*

Once in her car, Brooke pulled out her hairband and gave her head a shake. It had been a trying day. Between irritable patients and a demanding boss, Brooke barely had an opportunity to sit down.

The drive to her condominium wasn't long, but Brooke drove slowly along the dark, empty roads. Her body sagged with weariness, but her mind remained alert. She wanted to use the drive to unwind a little after her long day at the hospital.

Nursing wasn't Brooke's profession of choice. She had wanted to be an artist—still did—but her father shot down that dream.

"Art's not a real major." She could still hear the mockery in his tone. "If you want any help from us, go with something sensible, like nursing."

Brooke had complied. She always did. Choices weren't really "choices" in the Dunbar family. She was five years into nursing and already burning out.

She pulled into the carport behind her condo and groaned when she saw the overturned garbage can spilled across her parking spot. Just what she wanted after a long shift. Frustrated, she threw the car in park and got out. She moved the can back into position, bent over, and tossed an empty yogurt container and egg carton into the trash. Once done, she parked her car and collected her mail.

She hated getting home so late.

Brooke couldn't think of one neighbor she'd consider a friend. Most of them she barely knew by sight. Who had time to make friends?

Her front door was dark. Time to change the light bulb. Just wanting a long, hot shower and the soft, flannel sheets against her skin, she squinted in the dark, hunting for her house key.

A firm hand gripped her arm. "Don't scream. I'm... undercover. I've been shot. Please help me."

She froze and a scream caught in her throat. The mail fluttered from her hands. *Undercover? A cop?*

"Open the door," he whispered. "Please."

Brooke noticed his bloodstained shirt and the pained look on his face. She unlocked the door and he followed her inside.

The man turned and bolted the door. Clutching his left arm, he leaned against the wall and closed his eyes.

Though her nerves jangled, she switched on a light and turned to look at this strange man. He was refined and clean cut. His dark gray suit pants, designer shirt, and bold purple tie spoke of cultured taste and expense. His piercing eyes cried out to her for help.

She found her voice. "What happened?"

He swallowed hard. "My cover was blown."

"Who did this to you?"

The man shook his head. "I don't know."

"I'll call an ambulance."

"No," he said. "They'll find me."

Who is this man? Should I call 911? "You have a gunshot wound. By law I have to report it."

"Report it and we're both dead." Pleading blue eyes stared into hers. "I'm sorry..." He glanced out the window. "They could be watching. Please close your blinds."

She darted around the small condo, closing the shades. What had she gotten herself into? She heard a thump and ran back to the hallway. Did he faint? He was seated with his back against the wall, his face bent low.

"Listen, I'm a nurse. Let me look at your injury."

The man attempted to stand, but his knees buckled beneath him.

"Don't faint! Um…" Where should she put him? He needed to lie down. The couch? Too short for his tall frame. It'd have to be her bedroom—she had no other choice. She steadied him with her arm around his back. His face was white and his hands were like ice.

He let her help him up the stairs. She flipped on the lamp, pulled back her comforter, and settled him on her bed.

Still wearing her nurse's smock, Brooke removed his shirt. Bright red blood shone on his left bicep. His body was strong and well muscled, yet this injury was taking its toll.

"When did this happen?"

"I don't know… several hours. I don't even know what time it is. I passed out behind the bushes by your door."

He winced as Brooke examined the injury. "You're very fortunate. The bullet passed through. But I'm not a doctor. I can't tell how much damage it's done." She applied pressure to the wound. "You're still bleeding. I really think I should call for help."

"We can't call for help. Not now." He winced. "Can you stitch me back up?"

Could she? Yes, but not without serious repercussions. "You don't understand. I could lose my license. There are laws about gunshot wounds."

"I'll report it. I promise… but it's got to be to the right person." He closed his eyes. "What about a butterfly closure? Can you just get the skin together and tape it up?"

"You've got exposed muscle. Steri-Strips won't cut it." There was a significant amount of bleeding. What should she do? He was whiter than her sheets. But not just from pain. He was scared.

"Look, maybe just wrap it up for me. I'll get out of your hair…" He attempted to sit up but faltered.

Brooke licked her dry lips. "Lie back down. Let me get a few things."

She found a thin needle and a spool of thread. Quietly, Brooke hurried to her kitchen for ibuprofen, saline solution, rubbing alcohol, and other supplies.

The blinds in her kitchen were still opened. How did she miss closing these? Were they really being watched?

Her hands shook as she carried the supplies back to her bedroom. The man was lying with his eyes closed. Was he unconscious?

She cleared her throat and his blue eyes shot open.

"First I'm going to irrigate the wound with saline," she said as she worked. "I brought you some ibuprofen. Can you take ibuprofen?"

"Yeah." He took the offered tablets and sat up enough to rinse them down with water.

The man's eyes followed Brooke as she soaked the thread and needle in alcohol to sterilize them. "You seem to know what you're doing."

She blew out a nervous breath and pulled on a pair of medical gloves. *Do I though? This is crazy.* She flushed the injury with saline and attempted to steady her nerves. "This will hurt."

He nodded.

With painstaking care, Brooke stitched the man's flesh together. This was new for her. As many times as she'd watched doctors administer sutures, she'd never done it herself.

He let out a moan and clenched his teeth.

"I'm sorry." Brooke drew the long bloody thread through his skin. The process took several minutes.

Once finished, she snipped the end of the thread. She wrapped his arm with a clean bandage and pulled the flannel sheet over his chest. "You're not going to sue me if you have a scar—are you?"

"I can't sue you. You've got the Good Samaritan Law to back you up."

"Even as a nurse?"

"You're not liable for civil damages while rendering emergency assistance." He blew out a pained breath.

"You sound like a lawyer."

His gaze shifted toward the wall. "I'm a financial advisor."

"A legal financial advisor?" Brooke asked.

"An accountant."

"You've been working undercover as an accountant?"

"Something like that."

She wanted answers, but he had drifted to sleep. What in the world had she gotten herself into?

CHAPTER 2

When Ty opened his eyes, it was morning. While the shades were still drawn, sunlight streamed through the slats, casting long shadows of stripes across the wall. He glanced around at the clean, well-furnished bedroom. The large, queen sized bed was comfortable and covered in a thick, white down comforter. Where was the woman who'd attended him last night? It was all somewhat of a blur.

Water running in the bathroom told him someone was taking a shower. He closed his eyes. He hoped this wouldn't get awkward.

The events of the previous day ran through his mind like a movie. He'd finished up late at the office. No great surprise. There was no reason for rushing home without the warmth of human companionship to welcome him.

When he'd left his office yesterday, there were few people still in the building. He'd taken the elevator from the tenth floor to the lobby where he'd said goodbye to the evening guard and walked through the revolving door to the street outside.

It was a nice evening and rather than take a taxi, Ty had opted to walk the seven blocks to his apartment. It was supposed to rain the next day, and Ty didn't know when he'd have another opportunity to enjoy the fresh air.

He'd not gone far when something in the pit of his stomach told him a vehicle was following him. A glance over his shoulder had revealed a dark SUV moving slowly in the far right lane. He'd picked up his pace and searched for a quick get away location when his cell phone rang. The sound of a gunshot echoed through the streets and pain ripped through his arm.

He remembered the chase. How had he made it? How long had he been unconscious behind those bushes? He glanced at his neatly wrapped arm. The nurse. *That was You, God,* Ty prayed softly.

"Did I wake you?"

Ty turned his head toward his nurse and his mind to the present. She wore a pair of blue jeans and a sports hoodie. Long brown hair hung in wet waves across her shoulders and her dark eyes studied him.

"No. I'm not sure what woke me."

She laid a hand on his forehead. "No fever. That's good. How do you feel?"

"Like someone tore out a chunk of my flesh and then stabbed me multiple times with a sewing needle. All without painkillers."

"You're a pretty brave patient. I've seen people squirm more about an ingrown toe nail."

"Ingrown toe nails can be very painful." Ty smiled sheepishly. "I'm pretty sure there are extra nerves in the toe."

"Oh really?" She grinned. "They never taught us that in nursing school."

Ty gave a wry shrug.

"So, are you going to tell me who you are?"

Ty blew out a heavy sigh and eased up in bed.

"You should rest. You've lost a lot of blood." She placed a soft, restraining hand on his chest. "Let me get you more ibuprofen for the pain."

Ty blinked back dizziness and nodded. "My name is Ty."

"I think you owe me more than your first name. Or will that blow your cover?"

Ty couldn't tell if she was serious. "Ty Westgate." She turned to leave and he called her back. "Hey, I don't know your name."

She turned and smiled. "Brooke Dunbar." She left briefly and returned with two pills and a bottle of water. "I wish I could get you something stronger for the pain, but I'm only a nurse."

Ty accepted the medicine and leaned back on his pillow. "This is fine. I don't want to take anything that will make me groggy."

"I washed and mended your shirt." She lifted a hanger from the back of the door and showed Ty his clean white shirt. "Of course, afterwards I realized I might have just destroyed evidence. Tell me I didn't just assist a criminal."

"I'm not a criminal. I promise you that." Ty glanced with appreciation at his shirt. "Thank you. When did you do this?" He was impressed at how nice his shirt looked. She'd even ironed it.

"Last night. It was a little hard to sleep with an injured stranger in my house." She walked to the hallway and returned with his jacket. "I also found your jacket this morning." She touched the hole in the sleeve. "I assume this is yours. It has a matching bullet hole."

"Where did you find it?"

"Right outside my door behind the bush."

"Did anyone see you?" Ty's eyes grew wide.

Brooke pulled a chair up beside the bed. "I walked out to get the mail. But don't worry I scanned the area first. I'm almost certain no one was around."

Ty hoped she was right.

"I want to know what happened." Brooke studied his face. "You showed up at my house with a gunshot wound, had me close all my blinds, and you're obviously worried about being watched. Can you please tell me what's going on?"

Brooke ran her long fingers through her hair, loosening soft waves and brushing her layers behind her back. Her high cheekbones and long dark eyelashes were beautiful. She was a lovely woman.

"I'm undercover and whoever shot me yesterday meant to kill me." With his good arm, Ty reached into his back pocket, pulled out his wallet, and handed it to her. "I can't tell you much, but at least you can verify who I am."

Brooke opened his billfold and studied his driver's license. She flipped through his credit cards and passed his wallet back to him.

"I work a few blocks north of here. I was shot on my way out of the office."

"Am I in danger?" It was an understandable question.

"I don't think so. But I'm sure they're still searching the area for me."

"They?"

"One was driving a dark SUV. The other got out to chase me."

"So I need to keep my eyes opened for a dark SUV?" Brooke asked.

"It wouldn't hurt." Ty glanced toward the window. He hated that he was immobilized and didn't have his phone.

A knock on Brooke's front door drew both of their attention.

"Are you expecting anyone?" Ty asked.

"No." She rose. "Should I answer it?"

"How well can you act?" Ty wasn't sure if the person at the door was there for him or not, but it was important that Brooke not give him away.

Brooke frowned. "If it's someone looking for you, what should I say?"

"You can't let on that you've seen me."

Another, more persistent knock, told them both she'd need to see who it was. If she took too long getting to the door it would look suspicious.

Brooke took a deep breath and walked from the room.

Ty hoped she could pull it off.

■ ■ ■

Brooke wiped her sweaty hands on her jeans. She peered out the peephole and saw a man in a dark blue suit. She opened the front door. "May I help you?"

"I'm Officer Vince Gearhart." He flashed a badge. "Can I come in?"

Brooke glanced into her house and noticed the blood stain on the wall beside the door. Why hadn't she cleaned it up? "Is there a problem?" She took a step outside, pulling the door closed behind her.

"I'm looking for this man." He showed a photo of Ty. "From the bloodstains behind your bushes and along your walk, we are certain he was hiding here last night."

Brooke glanced at the bushes and her eyes grew wide. She wasn't faking her fear. She'd already seen the blood, but the fact that someone had tracked Ty here was frightening. *Was this man a police officer? Did he work with Ty?* Her mind whirled with questions. Ty told her to act like she hadn't seen him. "Last night?" She finally forced the words from her lips.

"Yes, ma'am. Were you home yesterday evening?"

"No. I worked second shift."

"What time did you get home?" he asked.

"It was after midnight."

"Did you see anything unusual?"

"You mean apart from the overturned garbage can where I park my car?" Brooke tried to let the memory restore her frustration and show itself in her expression. "There is nothing worse than coming home to a garbage can dumped out in your parking spot."

"Did you hear anything?"

"No." She shook her head. "Should I be worried? I mean… is this man dangerous?"

"He's a felon. And yes, he's dangerous."

A felon? Now she definitely didn't have to fake her look of conccrn. Should she tell this man the truth? Was the man upstairs in her bedroom dangerous? He said he was undercover. What did that mean? Was he FBI? She was so confused. "If I see him, what should I do? Should I call 911?"

"No." The officer reached into his coat pocket and pulled out his business card. "Call me directly."

Brooke took the offered card. A symbol of the police force was printed on the top right corner with "Officer Vince Gearhart" and a phone number written underneath in bold blue lettering. "I will. Thank you."

The man nodded then descended her walk. She didn't see a police car out front. Had he been walking the street?

Once inside, Brooke bolted her door. She washed the blood off the wall before walking upstairs to Ty.

"Who was it?" Ty was sitting on the edge of the bed wearing his clean white shirt, and doing his best to put on his tie. He grimaced at the effort.

"The police."

Ty glanced up.

"He said you're a felon and that you're dangerous." Brooke tried to steady her trembling hands. If Ty were an undercover cop, why would this other police officer be looking for him?

"Were there two officers?" Ty asked.

"No. Just one."

"Just one." Ty raised his eyebrows. "How often do you see just one police officer going around questioning people?"

"He gave me this." She handed him the card.

Ty scanned it. "Did he tell you to call this number if you saw me?"

"Yes. I asked if I should call 911, but he said to call him directly."

"Of course he did." Ty passed the card back to Brooke. "See the number? Is that our area code?"

Brooke narrowed her eyes. It wasn't. "But he had a badge. He appeared official."

"Brooke, I know that you have no reason to trust me. I showed up at your front door with a gunshot wound. But I promise you, I'm not a felon and that man is not a police officer." Ty rose from the bed and walked to the window. Carefully pulling back a corner of the blinds, he scanned the road for a black SUV. "Did you see a vehicle?"

"No…" *I was too busy trying to play it off like I'd never seen you.* Brooke studied the handsome, well-dressed man standing by her window. What was he running from? Who was Vince Gearhart?

She turned to go. Whoever he was, he'd need something to eat. It seemed like a good reason to excuse herself.

■ ■ ■

He was asking a lot of this woman whose life he'd just barged in on. Brooke seemed to understand the seriousness of his situation and he hoped she believed him.

How had he been discovered? *The phone call to my parents… that's what gave me away.*

Making that phone call had been the right thing to do. He'd agonized over the decision for weeks, but with his parents' ages, the best way he could honor them was to tell them about his newfound faith in Jesus Christ. His parents weren't Christians and Ty hated the thought of them passing away without him ever having the opportunity to tell them about a true relationship with Jesus.

Their response had been encouraging. His father understood the difference between a genuine believer and a religious person. His dad admitted that he'd gone to church as a child but rejected Christianity because it never felt real.

His honesty paved the way for Ty to share how he'd been drawn to the Lord and found the forgiveness he so earnestly longed for and needed.

His mother said that she'd been seeking God ever since Ty's "death." She admitted that she'd not found the peace her son spoke of and listened intently as he explained how he'd come to put his faith in Christ.

Ty only talked to them that one time. He told them his identity needed to remain a secret and asked that they tell no one they'd spoken with him.

But now his identity had been compromised. Maybe their phone had been bugged.

Would his Mom have told Olivia? Ty hoped not, but wondered if expecting his mother not to tell his sister was asking too much.

Olivia and her husband, Clayton, lived in Virginia. His mother and sister were not close, but undoubtedly they talked.

What's done is done. Being in witness protection might be keeping him alive, but telling his parents about faith in Christ was his Biblical mandate. If his mother told Olivia and somehow God used that to point Olivia to the Lord, it would be worth it.

Where should he go from here? He should notify the U.S. Marshal who attended his case. Matthew Pratt needed to know that Ty's identity had been compromised. Without his cell phone, Ty would have to do some research to find Officer Pratt's contact information.

The smell of bacon and eggs reached the top of the stairs and Ty carried his suit jacket downstairs where Brooke was making breakfast.

The dimly lit living room gave just enough light for him to make out Brooke's distinctive taste in furniture and décor. Decorated in blues and grays, everything was neat and clean. Ty walked to the wall where a unique assortment of paintings of various sizes hung over the sofa.

Ty studied the artwork. Each one had a distinct look, which set it apart from the other, but they were clearly done by the same artist. *Impressive.* Upon further inspection, he noticed the small signature in the corner. *Brooke Dunbar.*

"Your breakfast is ready," Brooke said from the kitchen.

"Did you do these?"

She nodded.

"They're well done. You're a very talented artist. How long have you been..."

Brooke turned away. "The food's getting cold."

Did I say something wrong?

■ ■ ■

Brooke pulled a pan off the stove and reached for a plate. "You need to eat something to regain your strength." As strange as the situation was, she still felt a sense of responsibility toward her patient.

"I'm sorry for putting you out. Although I confess, you're an answer to prayer." Ty accepted a plate and carried it to the kitchen table.

An answer to prayer? How do I even respond to that? She carried her own plate of bacon and eggs to the table and sat across from him. "I should make you a sling so you'll rest that arm."

He shook his head. "A sling will stand out." Ty took a bite of his meal. "This tastes great."

"I made coffee too," Brooke offered. "I didn't know if you liked coffee or not. Actually, I didn't know if you liked eggs or bacon... I don't know anything about you." She lowered her head and peered through her lashes at him, overwhelmed at the strange situation.

Ty turned his gaze to the closed blinds. "I'm sorry I can't tell you more. Once I leave this house, you can just forget about me. If anyone asks, you can answer honestly that you don't know anything."

"Where are you going to go? Aren't you afraid that those men are still after you? I mean... they obviously are. And what about your gunshot wound? You said you were going to report it."

"I am." Ty glanced around the room. "Actually, I was going to ask you if I could borrow your computer. When I lost my cell phone, I lost my contact's phone number. I should have memorized it, but I've rarely had to call him. Hopefully, he'll be able to give me some direction."

"Sure." Why not allow this total stranger access to her computer? He was already in her house, eating her food.

After breakfast, Brooke carried her laptop to the table and logged in.

Ty turned the computer toward himself.

What if he was getting into her personal information? Brooke cleared the table of dishes and attempted to clean up the kitchen without allowing herself to stress.

"Would you mind if I used your phone?" Ty closed the laptop.

Brooke handed him her home phone and walked from the kitchen to give him privacy. What a way to spend her day off.

■ ■ ■

"U.S. Marshal's office," the voice on the other end answered.

"Matthew Pratt, please."

A pause followed. "May I ask who is calling?"

Ty sighed. "I'm one of his clients. This is an urgent situation."

"Please hold."

Ty waited nervously. He'd never attempted to reach Officer Pratt using the main office phone number. He'd been instructed not to. Ty's identity had to be kept confidential and he was told to only report to Matthew Pratt.

"This is Officer Wyatt Longstreth," a voice on the phone spoke crisply. "Who am I speaking with?"

"I'm only authorized to speak with Matthew Pratt."

"Matthew Pratt is not available. I am taking all of his calls."

Ty paused. He'd not anticipated this. "I'll try later." He hung up the phone before the man could respond.

Ty stood and paced the small kitchen. He needed to get Officer Pratt's information. He glanced at the phone. Undoubtedly, the U.S. Marshals would have traced the call. How long until they called back?

"Brooke," Ty said upon finding the young woman in the living room. "I'll get out of your hair now. I appreciate all you've done for me."

"Make sure you have your arm checked."

"You did a class act job. Best nurse I've ever had stitch me up." Ty forced a grin. "I'm just going to call a taxi and be on my way."

"There's a dark SUV driving along my road," Brooke glanced up and followed Ty with her eyes. "I just noticed it a few minutes ago."

Ty peeked through the blinds. The black SUV was parked at the end of Brooke's street. It was the same SUV. He was sure.

"Look." Brooke rose from the couch. "I'm willing to help you. But I need to know I'm not doing anything illegal."

The phone rang.

Ty motioned for her to wait and glanced at the caller ID to see if it was the Marshal's office.

"Who is it?" Brooke glanced over his shoulder.

"Don't answer it." Ty paced the room.

Brooke chewed on her lower lip as the phone continued to ring.

"You've reached Brooke. I'm not home so leave a message." Ty glanced at the answering machine and waited for the reply.

"This is Officer Longstreth of the U.S. Marshal's office. We received a call from someone at this number and need to talk with you. Please call me at..."

Brooke's dark eyes grew wide. "I don't think I've ever received a call from the U.S. Marshal's office before. What's going on?"

Ty set the cordless phone down. "It's a long story."

"Are they going to show up at my house? Are you wanted by the U.S. Marshals?"

"I'm not wanted by the Marshals. They're protecting me. At least... Officer Pratt is." Ty ran his fingers through his dark hair. "I'm in witness protection."

Brooke studied him. "So, you're not a cop?"

"No."

"Why did you lie to me?"

Ty blew out a weighted breath. "I didn't actually tell you I was a cop. I told you I was undercover... and I am undercover."

"You misled me."

"I'm sorry. I'm not supposed to tell people. Anyone. You're the first person, apart from my own parents, that I've ever told."

"Why are you in witness protection?"

Ty shook his head. "I can't—"

Brooke's phone rang again. She glanced at the caller ID. "It's another blocked call."

Ty took the phone and said, "Hello?"

"Can I speak with a Brooke Dunbar?" the familiar voice at the other end asked.

"I'm the one you spoke with earlier," Ty said, knowing the call was truly for him.

"Who is this?"

"I have been told only to report to Matthew Pratt. Is he available?

"No," Officer Longstrech answered coolly. "Do you have your client number?"

"I do. But I prefer to wait and talk to Officer Pratt." Ty felt Brooke watching him.

"I'm afraid you won't be able to do that. Give me your identification number so I know who we're dealing with."

Ty edged to the window, eased aside the blinds, and noted the black SUV still parked at the end of the road. "I'll think about it and call you back."

"We have your location as Cincinnati, Ohio," Wyatt said, prying for information. "Can you tell me the reason for your call?"

"My identity has been compromised."

"Give me your identification number."

Ty hesitated. "I've gotta go." He closed the curtain and hung up the phone. "I think they're monitoring the phones. It's the same SUV that followed me yesterday evening and it's driving back down your road."

Brooke peeked through the closed blind and saw the dark vehicle slow down and park in front of her walk.

"Is there a back way out of your condo?" he asked.

"Yes. Through the laundry room on the far side of the kitchen."

Ty took a few steps toward her. "I can't thank you enough for helping me."

"I… it's fine. I was glad to help you. You're not going to try to leave with them right outside the condo are you?"

Ty shrugged. "I have no choice. I can't put you in any more danger." He hoped it wasn't too late. He took a few steps toward the kitchen.

She followed him. "But what if they see you? Should we call the police? Maybe they…" A knock on the door interrupted her words.

"It's them, isn't it?"

Ty placed a finger to his lips and motioned for her to move to the kitchen.

The knock turned into a pound.

"Where is your car?"

"Out back." Brooke's gaze flicked around the kitchen, her anxiety apparent.

"Get your keys. We've got to go." There was urgency in Ty's tone.

"We?"

Her front door shook. Ty turned apologetic eyes on Brooke. "By hiding me here, you've made an enemy."

Brooke snatched her computer off the table and threw her purse over her shoulder while Ty grabbed his jacket. They both slipped out the back door as a window crashed inside.

CHAPTER 3

Brooke's heart pounded as she ran toward the carport with Ty at her side. She glanced over her shoulder. Were they being followed?

With the click of a button, Brooke unlocked her car and hurried into the driver's seat. She tossed her computer in the back and watched Ty grimace as he climbed in beside her. With no time to spare, she started her car, peeled out of her parking spot, and tore through a few back alleyways onto the main road. "Where are we going?"

"My apartment. I need to get Officer Pratt's phone number. For whatever reason I was not able to get through to him this morning."

A police car roared past with its lights flashing.

"Are they going to my condo?" She glanced in her rear view mirror.

"They might be. The Marshal's office probably asked them to check on the address where the phone call originated. I knew something wasn't right when I called them."

Brooke steered through traffic and tried to slow her trembling heart while Ty gave her directions to his apartment.

They pulled into a parking spot beside the remodeled fire station. Ty handed her his keys. "You're going to have to go in."

"Me? Why?" Her voice shook. "I don't know what you need."

Ty sunk lower in the seat. "They might be watching my place. My apartment is on the top floor, number five. The other apartment on that floor belongs to a lady named Lydia. If you see anyone suspicious, just act like you're visiting her."

"What am I looking for?"

"Go to my desk. Open the top right drawer. There's a false bottom in it. Take everything."

"Do you need anything else?"

Ty nodded. "Grab some clothes. Whatever you can find. I'd like a clean suit…"

Brooke's eyebrows shot up. "A suit?"

"You'd be surprised what you can get away with when you're wearing a suit."

Scanning the area around the old firehouse, she reached for the door.

He touched her arm. "Just smile at people as you walk past. Act like you belong there and people will believe you do."

"You sound like you're skilled at the art of deception."

He shrugged. "You learn what you have to."

She tucked a long hair behind her ear and hurried out the door.

Walking toward the apartment, Brooke's hands grew wet with perspiration. What was she doing? She was about to walk into some man's apartment. How did she know this man was being honest about himself? What if this was all a lie and she was about to break into someone's place?

Inside the firehouse, Brooke followed the stairwell to the third floor and found Ty's apartment. She inserted the key into the lock, and the door pushed opened. It was already unlocked.

"Hello?" she called through the cracked-open door. "Hello… anyone here?" The door opened fully at her touch. An eerie emptiness emanated from the room, convincing her nobody else was there.

She stepped inside and let her eyes travel the room. It had been ransacked. Drawers were opened with their contents strewn all over the floor. Couch cushions had been tossed about and a small plant stand had been overturned. The mess was a strange contrast to the refinement and artistic creativity reflected in the furniture.

Ty must shop at only the finest furniture stores and galleries, as evidenced by a sleek, black leather sofa facing a huge window and a large over-stuffed chair nestled beside the window. Across from it, a beautiful coffee table made from railroad ties and a huge slab of rosewood graced the living room. Under normal circumstances, she would likely have found the apartment in pristine condition.

Hair prickling on her neck, Brooke found the desk already

opened. She cleared away the contents of the top right drawer to disclose the false bottom. At least this part of his desk remained intact.

The concealed space contained a small pile of paperwork, a wad of cash, a passport, and a manila envelope. Brooke scooped the items up and rushed to a closet in the bedroom. She found a travel bag inside and stuffed his important information into a pocket. Then she rifled through the racks until she located his gray suit, along with a couple of shirts and ties. Afterward, she searched for his casual clothes, toiletries, underthings, and shoes. *This man has more clothes than a woman.*

She zipped up the small suitcase and left, locking his front door behind her. No use letting everyone into the apartment.

On the way down the stairs she almost bumped into someone. “Hello,” she greeted the gentleman and allowed him to hold the door for her.

Doing her best to appear casual, Brooke threw the suitcase into the backseat of her Jetta. She closed the door and looked up to see the black SUV headed toward them.

Ty was still seated low in the passenger seat as Brooke started the car. “They’re here!” She threw the car into drive and Ty sat up and looked behind them.

“They turned around.” Ty warned.

Brooke did her best to weave in and out of traffic, listening to Ty’s well-spoken commands, but her head whirled and her hands shook. A quick glance in the rearview mirror showed the menacing vehicle still hot in pursuit.

A bullet ricocheted off the car and Brooke let out a little scream. Ty steadied the steering wheel. “Make a sharp right turn at the light!”

Was this for real? Brooke sped through the intersection, cutting the corner with a squeal of her tires. Thinking quickly, she made another turn down a small road.

The SUV was stuck at the intersection, behind a couple of slow-moving cars. Brooke made another sharp turn into a gas station and cut through to the other side where she wove through traffic and pulled onto another side street.

Her heart beat wildly and her hands were slick with sweat. “Did I lose them?” Her eyes were intent on the traffic.

He glanced out the back window. "I think so."

Brooke took a steadying breath and turned onto a busy street. She merged into traffic and stared at the cars in front of her.

"Any trouble at my apartment?"

"Your place has been ransacked." She sent him a quick glance. "But, I was able to get everything from the hidden compartment and a bunch of clothes."

"I figured they'd break in. Glad they missed the false bottom."

"Who are these people, Ty?"

"I wish I knew." He retrieved his bag from the backseat and dug the papers from the pocket.

"What should we do now?" Brooke blew out a shaky breath. "Are these people trying to kill me too?"

Ty was quiet for a moment. "Most likely."

Brooke felt like the air had been punched out of her stomach. "Why?"

"You've seen one of them and you're with me. They probably assume I've told you something."

"Should we go to the police?" It seemed logical.

"No. We need more than the local police."

She swallowed past a lump of fear lodged in her throat. "Then what should we do?"

"Are you willing to drive to New York?"

"Who's in New York?" Brooke glanced at him to see if he was serious.

"The FBI agent who worked my case. I trust him." Ty ran his fingers through his dark hair. "I'm sorry I dragged you into this."

Brooke's eyes were steady on the road. She couldn't go home. Whoever was after Ty knew where she lived. They knew her car. They probably knew her name. "Just tell me what to do."

"Head north east," he instructed. "Don't use your credit card or your cell phone."

"My cell phone?"

"Yeah. In fact… we need to get rid of it."

"Get rid of it?" Brooke narrowed her eyes and shook her head.

"Yes. At least until I find out what's going on at the marshal's office. They can track your phone's GPS."

“If you’d told me that, I would have left it at my house.” She heard the irritation in her tone, but she couldn’t help herself. Of all the terrors of this day, losing her cell phone was the one that sent her over the edge.

“I’m sorry.” He said in a soothing tone. “I’ll get you a new one.” He reached for her phone sitting in the middle console.

“There’re phone numbers on there that I need!”

“Tell me who. I can write them down.”

“My boss. I’m going to have to call in. I’m scheduled to work tomorrow.” Brooke licked her dry lips. “They’ll probably fire me for this.”

He rubbed his temples.

Brooke let out a resigned sigh. “Glenna Smith. She’s the only number I really need. I’ve got the rest on my laptop.”

Ty found the number, wiped down the phone, and wrapped it in a tissue. “Pull up here.” He pointed to a coffee shop on the left. “I’ll get us coffee and take care of the phone.”

Brooke pulled into the parking lot.

“I’m going to try to reach my U.S. Marshal contact with this phone before I destroy it. If I can figure out what’s going on, we might be able to hang onto it.”

“But if you can’t, then my phone will have even more evidence on it.”

“Right.”

Ty exited her car, and she leaned back in the seat. Her phone was the least of her problems. Would she even live through today?

■ ■ ■

Ty leaned through the opened passenger door and handed Brooke a large mocha cappuccino. Then he climbed in and buckled his seatbelt.

“Did you obliterate my phone?” Brooke couldn’t believe she was asking the ridiculous question so calmly.

“I destroyed it and threw it in the trashcan.”

“Nice.”

“I hope you like mocha.”

Brooke took a sip of the coffee. “My phone for a mocha.”

"It was time for a new one anyway. How old was that thing?" There was humor in his tone.

"It was my phone."

"You should get a smart phone." A smile tugged playfully at his lips.

"What? So the next person I help can destroy a more expensive phone?" Brooke breathed a laugh. She made her way toward the highway. "I take it you didn't get through to your U.S. Marshal contact?"

Ty shook his head. "I tried both numbers. One went right to voice mail."

"And that's not like him?"

"No. Pratt makes it his business to answer calls. He's got too many people depending on him."

Brooke was quiet for a few minutes. "So, is Ty your real name?"

"It is my legal name, though not the name I was born with."

"How long have you been Ty Westgate?"

"A little over four years." He took a sip of his coffee.

"Did you pick your name?"

"No. Not really. I did reject a name though." He grimaced. "It was pretty bad, too. But no, they pick the name. That way, anyone who knew you from your past couldn't try to find you by using a name they knew you liked."

Brooke glanced over her shoulder and moved her car to the middle lane. "So does everyone from your past life think you're dead?"

"They're supposed to, but…" He set his drink in the holder. "About three months ago I broke down and called my parents."

"Wow." Brooke blew out a breath. "I can't imagine going all those years letting your parents believe you were dead."

"It was hard," Ty confessed. "But it was my phone call to my parents that most likely exposed my identity."

"Did you tell them your new name?"

"No. I would never do that. But I called them. I told them I was alive." Ty ran his hand over his face. "I'm sure my agent will tell me I was a fool. But I had to do it."

Brooke peeked at him.

"About a year and a half ago, I became a Christian."

"Becoming a Christian is worth risking your life?"

"It was the best thing I ever did." He angled his body toward her. "Are you a Christian?"

Brooke clutched the steering wheel. "Why don't you finish your story?" She clenched her jaw.

"Okay. Um… Well, I was not raised in a Christian home. My parents are both in their sixties and all I could think about was, what if they died before I was able to talk to them about Jesus? They're my parents. The Bible tells us to honor our father and mother. I could think of no greater honor than to give them the message of salvation."

"So you called your parents to tell them about Jesus?" Brooke tucked a hair behind her ear.

"Yes. And I'm glad I did."

"But you think they disclosed your whereabouts?"

"No. They would never have done that. I didn't even tell them where I was living. But somehow, someone who is still looking for me figured it out and tracked me down."

"Why?"

Ty shook his head. "It's complicated."

"I'm driving to New York with some man I've known less than twenty-four hours. I think you owe me an explanation."

"Okay." Ty leaned back in his seat and closed his eyes. "I was a lawyer."

"So you lied to me again?" Brooke tightened her hands around the steering wheel. "That's twice!"

"No, I said I *was* a lawyer. I'm not anymore. I'm a financial consultant. Just like I told you."

"I don't know whether to smack you or laugh at you. You're such a lawyer. Look how you twisted things to make me believe what you wanted me to believe."

"I didn't mean to. Look, this whole thing—I never meant to drag some unsuspecting person into it. I didn't know what else to do."

"Just tell me the rest."

"I made some very wrong choices early in my law career. Several of my clients were high profile politicians who had much to hide. As their… unethical lawyer, I hid those things for them. I also made sure they were never found guilty when accused of…" Ty paused. "Things I knew they did."

"You were one of those kind of lawyers?" Brooke took a longer glance at him.

"I was. But, I couldn't continue to live that way. One of my clients pushed my integrity to the limit. What he'd done was so bad I couldn't let him win. I refused the case and he didn't appreciate it." Ty took another sip of his coffee. "Things got pretty ugly. I finally took everything to the FBI."

"Everything?"

"Well, initially just this case. But it turned out the FBI was already investigating me for another high profile case. My only option was to turn state's evidence."

"What does that mean exactly? I hate to sound ignorant, but legal terms are out of my league."

"It means, instead of getting arrested, I testified as a witness for the state against a team of my clients who were running some highly illegal activities within their political offices."

"So, you're a felon too? Just like that Vince Gearhart guy said."

"No, I was never arrested. The charges against me were dropped. I came clean on my own account."

"Were the men you testified against all arrested?"

"Those I worked with, yes. But the crime ring was wide, and my clients only represented a portion. Another lawyer, who didn't turn state evidence, also had enough evidence to pull down the majority, but there's still a missing piece. The FBI is working to find it. Until that time, I have a new name, a new life, and I live under witness protection."

"Will you have to disappear again?"

"Who knows?" Ty stared out the window. "I'm so tired of witness protection. I want to end this thing. I want them to find that missing link so I can live my life."

CHAPTER 4

As they approached Columbus, Ty suggested they stop to get a bite to eat. "I'm kind of a snob when it comes to food," he confessed. "How about Northeast Café? It's just off this exit."

"I've never been there. You'll have to direct me."

Ty spouted off directions and Brooke found street parking not far from the restaurant. After he fed the meter, Ty and Brooke walked toward the café. There was a small fireplace out front, surrounded by outdoor seating.

"This is nice." Brooke looked around as Ty opened the door for her.

"I've only been here a couple times, but it's good, and relatively fast."

"The food smells delicious," Brooke said as they walked toward a table.

Ty pulled out a chair for her. "Order whatever you like. I'll be back in a few minutes."

Ty asked the woman at the front counter if he could use the restaurant's phone.

She handed him a cordless phone and Ty carried it to a quiet place near the front door. It was close to five, so Ty tried Officer Pratt's cell phone. The call went to voice mail and Ty hung up without leaving a message.

In the four years he'd been in witness protection, Ty rarely needed to call Matthew Pratt. Ty kept a moderately low profile and knew enough about the system from his law studies to know his limitations.

He started out his years in witness protection as an employee of an accounting firm and eventually branched out to his own business.

He'd done well for himself while keeping a low profile. Officer Pratt contacted him once when he'd heard that Ty planned on speaking at an executive conference on financial enrichment planning, but Ty had maintained that the conference would not place him in the limelight and that he was only one of the many speakers hired to teach a workshop.

He returned the phone to the woman behind the counter.

"I still can't get through to the officer overseeing my profile." Ty sat across from Brooke at the table.

"Do U.S. Marshals take vacations?"

"If he did, he'd have left another contact number—or something."

The waiter arrived a moment later and took their orders.

"The FBI is our best bet at this point." Ty spoke softly after the waiter walked away.

"What's the plan then? Do we just walk into the FBI office and tell them what happened?"

"While they were investigating my clients, I worked pretty close with one agent in particular. Owen Vance. He's a good man and I trust him."

"Does he know you're in witness protection?"

"Yes. Although I haven't been in touch with him in almost four years." Ty glanced out the window and watched a couple walk past. "I don't even have his phone number. I'll try the FBI main office after we eat."

Brooke was quiet for a moment and brushed a long dark hair away from her face. "I still haven't called work. I'm supposed to be there tomorrow morning."

"You can make your call before we head out."

"My boss is going to be furious."

"Do you take off work very often?"

"Never." Brooke's eyes showed concern. "And to be honest, I shouldn't have to work tomorrow. I just finished working five twelve-hour days. My boss is making me take someone else's shift."

The lawyer in Ty perked up. "You're not supposed to work five twelve-hour days in a row and you definitely need more than one day to recover."

"Tell that to Glenna."

"You should tell her. That's your legal right." Ty moved his napkin when he saw the waiter bringing them their food. For one awkward moment Ty glanced at his plate and cleared his throat. "Would you mind if I pray?"

Brooke lowered her eyes and shook her head. "Go ahead."

Ty's prayer was simple. He thanked God for His provision and asked for protection for them.

Brooke was quiet after Ty finished.

"Does your boss always push you around?" he asked.

"Pretty much." Brooke let out a breath. "It's just part of life." Her voice carried a tone of defeat.

Ty raised his eyebrow. "It doesn't have to be."

Brooke shook her head. "I'm not real good at sticking up for myself."

"You get walked on a lot?" He said it as a question.

Brooke took a bite of her salad and shrugged.

Ty watched her curiously. With her long brown hair, dark brown eyes, and full, warm smile, Brooke was a beautiful woman. Why would anyone walk on her?

"I never had a voice growing up and quite honestly, I'm not sure I'd know what to do with it if I did."

Ty studied her for a moment. He'd been so consumed with his situation that he'd given little attention to Brooke's response to everything they'd been through. Had she ever protested? Had she questioned him or argued? She was incredibly obliging. "Brooke." Tenderness shone through his light blue eyes. "I'm so sorry."

"Why are you sorry?" Brooke tilted her head.

"I didn't give you a voice." Ty set down his fork and watched Brooke's facial expression intently.

Brooke shook her head. "I shouldn't have said anything." She turned away from his gaze.

"I dragged you into this…"

"I let myself be dragged." Brooke picked up a red potato with her fork and avoided Ty's eyes.

"Listen, Brooke." Ty reached across the table and touched

Brooke's hand. "When you call your boss, don't leave any room in your tone or words for her to object."

"What do you mean?"

"Try something like, 'This is Brooke. Hey, I hate to do this on such short notice but I really can't take so-and-so's schedule this week. I worked five twelve-hour days in a row and will be taking the next three days off. That's in my contract.'"

Brooke shook her head. "She'll fire me."

"She can't."

"She will."

"I may not practice law anymore, but I know the law. Nurses who work twelve hour days are required a certain number of days off." He removed his hand from hers and continued his meal.

"The hospital is short-staffed. Everyone is working more than they should right now." Brooke took a sip of her iced tea.

"Then that hospital would be a dangerous place for a patient. Would you want a sleep-deprived nurse administering your medication?" Ty couldn't imagine it. "I'm sure the environment can't be good. Overworked nurses are never happy people."

After dinner, Ty asked the woman at the front desk if they could use the restaurant phone again. "I'm so sorry about this. Neither of us have our cell phones with us and we've each got to make a really important call."

The woman handed Ty the phone and gave Brooke the once over.

Ty stepped away and made his call. He was discouraged to learn that Owen would be out of the office until Wednesday and they wouldn't give Ty the man's private contact number. He hung up the phone, without disclosing information to the receptionist at the other end, and ran his fingers through his hair.

His only other option seemed to be Wyatt Longstreth. Ty carried the phone to Brooke and gave her arm an encouraging squeeze. "You can do this." He watched her dial the number and carry the borrowed phone toward the doors.

He wondered if he should wait until Wednesday and talk to Owen or call Officer Longstreth again. He had no idea who the man was. He knew Matthew Pratt. He knew Owen Vance. Living under witness protection, Ty had been given specific instructions for the protocol of contacting the officer in charge of his file.

"How'd it go?" He noticed Brooke walking toward him.

Brooke shook her head. Her expression said it all.

"Fired?"

"Yes."

Ty blew out a frustrated breath. "How is that possible? You have every right to take time off."

Brooke lowered her eyes and Ty motioned for her to wait for him while he returned the phone.

Brooke stood waiting by the door and they walked to her car together.

"I saw a grocery store down the street." Ty opened Brooke's door for her. "Why don't we head there and pick up a few supplies."

Brooke nodded.

"Tell me what happened?" Ty returned to the conversation about Brooke's job.

"They're under staffed." Brooke pulled onto the road and got into a turn lane. "I did use your line though."

"How'd she respond?"

"She told me I had two options. Take the schedule she gave me or quit." Brooke's eyes were on the red light, but they didn't look sad.

"Did you actually quit?" Ty asked.

"Not really. I told her I couldn't be there and she said, 'Okay then. I guess you quit.'"

Ty mumbled a few frustrated words. "She trapped you into quitting to make it more difficult for you to collect unemployment!"

"I don't care, Ty." Brooke glanced up and grinned. "I'm almost relieved." The light turned green and Brooke pulled into the parking lot. "I should have quit this job a long time ago."

■ ■ ■

As they stepped into the grocery store, cool air met them both with a blast. Brooke let her eyes travel over the new environment.

Ty grabbed a cart. "Do you need anything?"

It hadn't yet occurred to Brooke that she'd run out of her house with nothing but her purse and her computer. She needed a lot of things. But at this moment, Brooke was still trying to process their current situation. “I’m sure I do, but I just can’t think right now.”

“They have little congratulations cakes.” Ty motioned toward a bright blue cake with balloons all over it and grinned. “The balloons could represent freedom of being in that work environment.”

“I’m not sure I’m ready to celebrate. I’m still in a bit of shock.” Brooke knew he was joking, but Glenna’s sharp words and hostile tone still rang in Brooke’s ears.

Ty grabbed some bottled waters and threw them into the cart. “I need to find the phones.” His eyes scanned the aisles.

Brooke followed Ty to an end cap and watched as he tossed several low-end phones into the cart and read the policy regarding buying minutes.

“You’re buying multiple phones?” Brooke watched Ty make his selections.

“I’ll explain later.” He led the way to the cashier and paid with cash.

“This one is yours.” They walked outside and Ty handed Brooke one of the phones. “Don’t use it unless you have an emergency.”

“I don’t understand. We just threw away my cell phone.”

“These numbers can’t be tracked. Your phone could. Although, once we use these phones, there are ways for a person with the right access to track us.”

Brooke and Ty walked back to her car.

“Do you want me to drive?”

Brooke nodded. “So, we’re going to New York City?”

Ty opened the passenger door for Brooke and walked to the driver’s side. “Actually, the FBI agent I know and trust won’t be back in ‘til Wednesday.”

“What should we do?”

“I was thinking of calling Wyatt Longstreth. I don’t know who he is, but he gave me his cell phone number.”

Ty dialed the number and Brooke just listened.

■ ■ ■

“Officer Longstreth?” Ty asked when the voice at the other end answered.

"Yes."

"You spoke with me earlier."

There was a pause at the other end. "The man from Cincinnati. You need to tell me who you are so that I can help you."

"I was instructed by Officer Pratt to only report to him."

"I understand. But he's not available. The house you made your call from this morning was broken into by the time the authorities arrived." Wyatt cleared his throat. "I sincerely hope this Brooke Dunbar is not in danger. Is she a friend of yours?"

"Sir." Ty was not about to disclose any information until he understood what happened to his contact. "My identity has been compromised and I'm trying to figure out who is after me. I need to know why I'm expected to suddenly trust you with my information."

"Because, Matthew Pratt is not available."

"Not available? What does that mean?" Ty's tone was firm.

The voice at the other end paused for a moment. "Officer Pratt has been missing for five days."

Ty's mouth went dry. "Missing?"

"Yes. I can't tell you anything else." The man hesitated. "Can you please tell me who you are? I want to help you."

Ty leaned his head back on the driver's seat, conscious of Brooke's eyes on him.

"Give me your identification number," Wyatt pushed.

Ty blew out a resigned sigh. "Okay." He recited the number from memory.

Wyatt was quiet for a moment. "Can you repeat that?"

Ty repeated himself clearly.

Wyatt cleared his throat. "Are you sure that's the correct number?"

"Absolutely sure." Ty sat up and placed his free hand on the steering wheel. "Why? Is there a problem?"

There was a long silence on the other end of the phone but Ty could hear fingers tapping on a computer.

"Your number is not in our database."

Ty glanced at Brooke who was obviously hearing everything Ty was saying. Ty opened the car door and began pacing in the parking lot. "What does that mean exactly?"

"I'm not sure. Let me try your name…"

"No." Ty shook his head even though he was on the phone. "I'm not giving you any more information until I understand what's going on."

"Listen," Wyatt urged. "I want to figure this thing out too. The number you gave me is not in our system. Maybe I can find you by name."

Ty's mind raced. Obviously someone already knew his name—they'd found him. He'd already been compromised. "Ty Westgate."

More computer key clicking could be heard at the other end followed by a long pause. "Your name is not here."

Ty felt the wind escape from his lungs. "What does that mean? What do I do? I'm in witness protection. I've been in hiding over four years."

"I don't understand this either. Our database is secure."

"Yeah, well obviously it's not," Ty spat sarcastically. "I'm done here."

"Wait!" Wyatt blurted out before Ty hung up. "I'm going to keep digging. How can I get in touch with you?"

"I'll call you in a few days." He turned off the phone and slammed it on the ground with such force that pieces of plastic shattered across the pavement. Ty picked up the fragments and disposed of the phone. *Now what?*

Ty returned to the car. "We need to go."

"What happened?"

"They don't have my information in their database and my contact at the marshal's office is missing." Ty started the vehicle and scanned the parking lot for anything unusual. "He may have tracked that phone—I don't know. I just don't want to be here long enough to find out."

Brooke's eyes showed her concern. Deep pools of dark brown helplessness drew Ty's hand to her arm. "We'll figure something out."

"Ty, why would this man be missing?" Brooke spoke the question Ty was struggling with.

"I don't know. Something's not right." He shook his head. "I can't help but wonder if it's related to the phone call I made to my parents. That was three months ago."

"Are your parents alright?" Brooke asked.

Ty stared out the windshield and tried to decide which direction to go. "I don't know."

"Where do they live?"

"Maine."

"How long do you think it would take us to get there?"

"Fourteen or fifteen hours." Ty glanced at Brooke. "What are you suggesting?"

"We could drive there and check on them," Brooke said softly. "They already know you're alive."

Ty glanced at Brooke curiously. "You'd be willing to drive to Maine?"

"Let's do whatever you need to do."

Chapter 5

Brooke drove through the night. She was surprised Ty actually took her advice and slept. The hours of quiet in the car gave her time to process the events of the past twenty-four hours.

She was supposed to be at work now. Elisha's schedule was midnight to noon. Had Glenna found a replacement for Elisha yet? It was a relief not to be there. Brooke didn't regret being fired. It felt good.

But was she really fired?

Brooke glanced at Ty who was sleeping somewhat uncomfortably in the passenger seat. When had she ever met a man so intuitive about her feelings? She'd known him one day and he'd already picked up her insecurity. He wanted her to have a voice.

She was about to meet his parents. What would they think of her? What kind of woman would run off to Maine with a man she barely knew? If Ty's parents were half as nice as him, they would understand.

It was hard for Brooke to imagine Ty being a dirty lawyer. How bad had he been? What kind of things had he covered up and for what kind of people? The whole thing felt like a dream. *I'm just a nurse.*

Ty tried to roll over onto his sore arm and let out a quiet moan.

Brooke hoped it was healing well. He hadn't let her look at it since the morning. It was raw and red all those hours ago. She'd forgotten to ask him when he'd had his last tetanus shot.

Ty moaned again.

She placed a comforting hand on his shoulder. "It's alright," she whispered.

Ty opened his eyes and turned to face her. "Hey." He sat the seat up and glanced out the window.

"Good morning." Brooke smiled at him. His blue eyes were puffy and tired.

Ty glanced at the clock. "Wow. It's almost six."

"Yes. And we're in Massachusetts." Brooke pointed to a road sign.

"You've made good time." Ty rubbed his chin. "I need to shave." He pulled down the mirror and studied his stubble. Brooke wondered if he knew how handsome he was.

"No you don't. If I have to show up at your parents' wearing jeans and a sweatshirt while you're in a suit, you can be unshaven."

"We can stop somewhere and get cleaned up." Ty suggested. He shifted in his seat. "Are you hungry for breakfast?"

"Not really. Although I could probably handle a fruit smoothie."

"I could go for a strong cup of coffee." Ty closed the visor and leaned back.

"I saw a sign just before you woke up. There's a coffee shop coming up at the next truck stop. Then you can shave and I'll let you drive for a while."

"Sounds good. What clothes did you bring for me to change into?" Ty reached behind him and unzipped his bag. After a little digging he pulled out his Bible. "You brought my Bible!"

Brooke figured he'd appreciate that. It was lying opened on his bed when she went into his room to find clothes. Any person who kept their Bible opened on their bed must genuinely care about it.

He turned his light blue eyes on Brooke and studied her. "Thank you."

"You're welcome."

"I meant to ask you, but so much was going on." He ran his hand over the leather bound Book. "I've got a lot of my favorite verses highlighted in this one, I would have really missed it."

Brooke tucked a hair behind her ear and nodded quietly.

"Do you have a Bible?" Ty asked.

"Yes." Brooke clutched the steering wheel and watched the taillights of the car in front of her.

Ty watched her closely as if waiting for her to say more.

Brooke reached for the stereo and turned it on search, hoping to find something to tune out their conversation before it got started. "Do you like country?" Brooke found a song she was familiar with.

"I can appreciate country."

"Let me guess." Brooke glanced impishly at Ty. "Jazz and classical."

"I do enjoy jazz and classical. How about you?"

"Both." Brooke shrugged. "It all depends on the mood I'm in. I enjoy classical guitar, contemporary jazz, blues, you name it."

"Contemporary Christian?" Ty threw her off by naming it.

"I'm familiar with it." She turned on the blinker and moved toward the exit. "Here's our truck stop. Good coffee and a place to get cleaned up."

Brooke found a place to park not far from the entrance.

"Don't get out yet." Ty glanced behind him.

Brooke looked in the rear view mirror. A black SUV parked behind her. Should they leave?

A young couple exited the vehicle and unbuckled their children from the back seats. Brooke's shoulders relaxed.

Ty smiled. "I think we're good." He opened his door and grabbed the clothes he planned to change into. "Thanks for packing a razor."

Brooke clicked the lock on her car and they walked inside.

■ ■ ■

Ty stood outside the coffee shop waiting for Brooke. She was an interesting woman. He had to admit she was very attractive. On more than one occasion he'd had to steer his thoughts away from her athletic figure, stunningly dark eyes, and beautiful smile.

As attractive as she was, Ty sensed a timidity born of some deep hurt. He noticed that she changed the subject every time he ventured to talk about spiritual things. But she remembered his Bible. Brooke was thoughtful of others… considerate. But she lacked consideration for herself. Why?

"You beat me?" Brooke met Ty at the coffee shop and smiled.

Ty walked with her through the line and paid for their drinks. "We can stop at a mall before we get to my parents' house and get you a change of clothes if you'd like."

"Could we?" Brooke sounded relieved.

“That’s fine. It’s another three to four hour drive to my parents’ house,” Ty said as they carried their drinks to the car. He opened the passenger door for her and waited for her to get in.

As they pulled away, their conversation turned to what to expect at his parents’ house.

“My parents don’t know me as Ty Westgate,” he began. It felt strange talking about his true identity with someone.

Brooke was quiet as Ty continued.

“They know me as Blake Kendall.” Ty shook his head. “Wow. I haven’t said that name in a really long time.”

“But it’s your real name…” Brooke studied his face intently.

“Are you trying to see if I look like a Blake?” He caught her expression.

“Yes.”

“Well?” He turned to her for a moment.

“I can see it.” She turned her face back toward the window. “So who are you? Blake Kendall or Ty Westgate?”

Ty let out a chuckle. “Honestly?” He leaned back and let his eyes follow the road. “I think I’m Ty.”

“Why?”

“After I became a Christian, my old life, my old identity, it all disappeared. The Bible says I’m a new creation. The old is gone. The new has come. My new name kind of solidifies that new identity in Christ.” He took a deep breath. “Blake Kendall was a fraudulent lawyer. Ty Westgate is a follower of Jesus Christ.”

“And you think it makes that much of a difference?” Brooke asked.

“The new name or becoming a Christian?”

“Becoming a Christian.” Brooke pulled her legs up on the seat and wrapped her arms around her knees.

Ty considered her question. “It’s made all the difference.”

Brooke cleared her throat. “You mean you don’t think you would have been an unethical lawyer had you been a Christian?”

“Absolutely not. The Spirit of God who dwells inside of me would never have allowed me to live that way.” Ty glanced at Brooke. This was the most he’d been able to say to her about God.

Brooke shook her head and stared out the passenger seat window. Her whole composure changed and Ty sensed a huge brick wall going up between them.

"What?" Ty didn't want the conversation to end.

"Nothing."

"You know," Ty began, "I'm the one in witness protection, but you know far more about me than I do about you."

Brooke blew out a sigh. "Yeah."

Ty glanced her way and saw that she'd closed her eyes. Was she going to sleep? She'd not slept all night. *Father, please give me more opportunities to talk to her about You.*

■ ■ ■

Ty wondered how his parents would react when he and Brooke showed up at the door. Would his parents even be home? What if something happened to them?

The gas gauge told him it was time to make a stop. Ty pulled off the exit in New Hampshire and Brooke woke up.

"Good afternoon," he greeted her.

Brooke cleared her throat and glanced at the stereo. Ty was playing contemporary Christian music on the radio. "So are you trying to preach to me subliminally?" She turned down the music.

Ty grinned. He appreciated her sense of humor. "That's a really good idea." Ty reached to turn it back up. "The driver picks the station. That's always the rule."

"This is my car." Brooke left the volume where he'd put it.

"I like your car." Ty ran his hand over the steering wheel. "German engineering."

"What do you drive?" Brooke asked.

"A Beemer."

"German engineering at twice the cost." Brooke's eyes twinkled.

"I like my BMW." Ty wondered if he'd ever see it again. When he'd lost his first identity, he walked away from everything. He'd left it all to his parents and sister, so maybe they'd still have a few of his old things. It was a strange thought.

He pulled into the gas station and filled up the tank. "Good thing you grabbed all my cash." Ty climbed back into the driver's seat.

"Was that only yesterday?"

"Hard to believe, isn't it? It's been a crazy twenty-four hours." Ty pulled back onto the highway. "So where did you get your nursing degree?" It was time to learn more about this woman who'd just dropped everything to help him.

"Cincinnati." Brooke ran her fingers through her hair and sat her seat up.

"Very good. Are you an LPN or an RN… or what?"

"I have my bachelor's degree, so I'm an RN." Brooke explained.

"What made you chose nursing?"

Brooke cleared her throat. "It's what my dad wanted me to study." She lowered her eyes.

This was clearly another sore subject. Ty wasn't sure he should push. He didn't want her to clam up again. "I understand."

"I wanted to study art," she offered. Her eyes were on the quickly passing countryside and she once again pulled her legs up and wrapped her arms around them.

Ty thought it made her look little and vulnerable to sit that way. Like she was trying to ball up and disappear. "Your paintings are beautiful."

"Thank you." She gave a slight smile. "I took as many art classes as I could while in college. I figured if I couldn't major in it, I could at least take some classes."

"Did you get a minor in art?"

"No." She let out a soft chuckle. "There wasn't enough time for that. I just took a few classes where I could. It made my major more bearable."

"If you loved art so much and you knew you didn't want to go into nursing—"

"I didn't have a choice," Brooke interrupted. "At least I didn't think I did."

Ty glanced at Brooke for a moment. She held her forehead in her hand and closed her eyes.

"So your parents chose your major?" He attempted to clarify.

Brooke sighed. "Please, Ty." She wiped her face. "Let's not talk about me." She turned her dark brown eyes toward him and gave a wan smile. "Where did you get your degree?"

Ty wondered what this lovely young woman was hiding. "I got

my undergrad in Boston and my law degree at Yale."

Brooke studied him for a moment. "Wow," she chuckled. "A true Yale lawyer."

Ty shook his head. "No. Not anymore. I was disbarred."

"Can you ever be reinstated?" She asked.

"In most states after a period of at least five years, if a lawyer can prove himself to have been rehabilitated and represents no threat to the public, a lawyer may apply for reinstatement." Ty fell back into his legal speak.

"Do you think you ever will?"

"Well," Ty began, "Ty Westgate doesn't have a law degree."

"Does he ever want one?"

Ty considered this thought for a moment. "I don't think so. I like what I do now. In fact, Ty Westgate would like to write a book on wise financial management."

"A writer." Brooke smiled approvingly. "Are those in witness protection allowed to be in the limelight?"

Ty shrugged. "Not sure. I'm supposed to keep a low profile. Authors sometimes put their pictures on their books."

"You could have a pen name and not put your picture on your book."

Ty nodded. "The problem is, I like public speaking. I'd want to do seminars, promote my books, counsel people with their finances. I'm not a low profile kind of guy." Ty was surprised how much he was telling this woman. It had been a long time since he'd been able to talk openly about himself and it felt nice.

"I'm sure you're good at it." Brooke's lips curved into an attractive smile and Ty glanced at her long enough to catch it.

"Have you done any public speaking since you've been in witness protection?"

"I have. I did a business seminar in Texas last year and I've spoken on financial wisdom at a few churches around the Midwest. My U.S. Marshal told me to stop, however, and made me shut down my website."

"You had a website?" Brooke turned to face him.

Ty shrugged. "Like I said, I'm not a low profile kind of guy." He sobered and blew out a deep sigh. "There are a lot of things I'd love to do. But it's not easy to start over. People aren't as forgiving as God. As you saw, there are those who'd like to see me dead."

"They still think you're Blake." Brooke's tone was compassionate. "It really is hard to escape the past."

Ty figured Brooke was speaking from personal experience, but he wasn't about to push.

■ ■ ■

They found a mall off the highway and Ty offered to make a stop so Brooke could stock up on a few things.

She was anxious to change her clothes and freshen up.

He opened the door for her and let his eyes scan the mall entrance. "Get whatever you need."

Brooke wasn't sure what to say. Her quiet, simple life had taken an abrupt change. Part of her was scared. She wasn't sure what to expect. But there was something about it that felt like an adventure.

It wasn't too difficult to find a store she was familiar with.

"Grab enough clothes for a few days," Ty handed her a wad of cash. He seemed to realize her need for privacy in purchasing personal items. "I'll meet you back at the mall entrance in thirty minutes."

Brooke watched his back as he walked toward the men's department. Thirty minutes to shop for three days worth of stuff. Brooke tried to think of the things she would need for a few days—shirts, socks, underwear, a fresh pair of jeans, a hairbrush, toothbrush, deodorant. He'd given her quite a bit of cash. How much of it should she spend?

She took the full thirty minutes and found Ty waiting for her at the doors.

"All done?" He glanced at the few bags she carried.

"We'll probably need to stop at a drugstore for a toothbrush and stuff." Brooke tried to hand him the rest of the money but he waved it off.

"You hang on to it. There's a coffee shop across the street. Would you like to run in and change? I'll grab a couple drinks for the road."

They drove to the coffee shop and walked inside together. Ty got in line, while Brooke slipped off to the ladies room to change.

She stood in front of the bathroom mirror and studied her new outfit. The jeans were the same brand she already had at home, but the pink shirt was one she simply selected quickly. She pulled on her new, beige cardigan, and threw the tags away. With a quick brush of her hair, Brooke was ready to continue on their journey.

CHAPTER 6

"Welcome to Maine. The way life should be." Brooke read the sign as they entered the state.

"This was home." Ty's tone warmed to the word.

Brooke's eyes were on the scenery. It was early autumn. The trees were just beginning to change. She imagined the colors would be brilliant in another few weeks. "Did you grow up here?"

"I did." His eyes held the view.

"How long has it been since you've been home?"

"It's been almost five years. I came home for a week the summer before everything went down." Ty reached for his empty coffee cup and gave it a shake. "I think that trip home was instrumental in my decision to come clean."

"Do you think anyone will be watching your parents' house?" Brooke asked.

"They can't be everywhere." Ty switched lanes and let a truck pass. "But just to be safe, I was thinking I could drop you off at their house and you can call me if the coast is clear. Is that okay?"

"I would meet your parents alone?" Brooke wasn't sure how she felt about this idea.

Ty nodded. "Yes. That way you can find out if anyone is there and explain the seriousness of the situation. My dad will understand. My mom… she'll be really excited."

"They haven't seen you in almost five years?"

"No." Ty sighed. "I went into hiding almost immediately after coming clean with the FBI. If they hadn't faked my death, someone else would have made sure it really happened."

"What should I say? They don't know me and I hardly know you." The whole situation was intimidating.

Ty was quiet for a moment. "Talk to my dad first if you can. He's got a lot of wisdom. He'll know if it's safe."

"If it's not?"

"Have my dad drive you to the park in Camden. I'll meet you on the tower."

Brooke assumed Ty's father would know what that meant. She licked her dry lips. They were still a couple hours from his parents' house, but Brooke was apprehensive. She wondered how her parents would react if she showed up at their home after her years of being away. It would not be a welcome reception.

Ty's parents' house in Rockport, Maine, was more beautiful than Brooke ever imagined. Her eyes took in the grand two-story, stone and cedar-faced mansion on the bay. A long covered porch ran along the front of the house and various windows of unique sizes gave the house charm. It looked like something from a magazine. "This is home?" She glanced at Ty.

Ty shrugged and grinned humbly. "Yeah."

Brooke contrasted Ty's parents' house with her parents' house in Indiana. Their modest two story brick home located in a middle-class suburban neighborhood was no comparison. "I suddenly feel underdressed."

Ty reached over and gave her hand a quick squeeze. "They're just people."

"What does your dad do?"

"He's a doctor." Ty smiled. "You'll have lots to talk about."

Her eyes widened. "Are you going to show him the stitches?"

"I plan to. I'll drop you off here. Follow the driveway to the side door. They never use the front," Ty explained. "I won't drive away until I know you're in. You've got that cheap cell phone. My number is the only one in there. Call me in an hour."

Brooke tried to steady her trembling hands. She was about to step outside in the middle of Maine and watch Ty drive away with her car. It was surreal. "Be careful." She felt a strange attachment to this man who was only person she knew in Maine.

"You too." Ty's blue eyes lingered on her face. "And remember, don't call me Ty."

Brooke stepped from the car and walked toward the house, uncertain what she was about to find.

■ ■ ■

An attractive older woman, fashionably dressed, answered the door. "May I help you?"

"Hi." Brooke did her best to smile. "I'm looking for Blake Kendall's parents."

"I'm Anne Kendall. How can I help you?"

"I'm a friend of your son." Brooke cleared her throat. "Can we talk?"

"Who is it, dear?" A man called from another room in the house.

"Perhaps you should come inside." Anne held the door open.

Brooke glanced down the driveway and watched her dark blue Jetta drive away.

Anne led Brooke toward a room off the kitchen where an older man was assembling golf clubs into a large, black golf bag. He glanced up and gave an inquisitive smile. His eyes, as blue as Ty's, studied her curiously.

"George," Anne began. "This young lady said she is a friend of Blake's."

"Sir, have you ever checked your house for bugs?" Brooke asked the first question Ty had instructed her to.

His eyebrows shot up. "Should we?"

"It's probably a good idea."

"Do you golf?" George asked.

"I've played a little."

"Let's step outside and we'll hit a few balls. I have a small putting green out back." George lifted up his bag. "In a few weeks I'll be raking leaves off my green."

George led Brooke outside and talked about the weather. Once they were far enough from the house, he stopped and set down the bag.

Brooke zipped up her jacket and waited for the older man to speak.

"There are no bugs out here. Although we have the house exterminated throughout the summer." He pulled out a putting iron and turned to Brooke.

"Blake's identity has been compromised," Brooke blurted out.

"You've talked to my son?"

"He drove me here."

George took a step back. "Blake's in Maine?"

"Yes." Brooke could see the longing in the older man's eyes. "He wanted me to make sure it was safe for him to come."

"Why wouldn't it be?" George let his eyes travel the horizon. Was he worried about them being watched?

"He contacted you almost three months ago. Two days ago someone tried to kill him."

"Dear God," George lifted a prayer. "Is he okay?"

Brooke nodded. "He wants to meet with an FBI agent in New York. But the man is out of the office until Wednesday. His U.S. Marshal contact is missing."

George shook his head. "How was his identity compromised?"

"Blake wondered if anyone asked about him…"

"No… I mean, no one has said anything to me. I can't imagine Anne talking to anyone about him." He glanced toward the house. "She knew the seriousness of Blake's situation, although she's been a new woman since learning that Blake's alive."

"Would anyone you know suspect anything from her happiness?" It was a confusing question, but Ty wanted her to weed out any possible leak before he returned. "Blake doesn't want to put you or your wife in danger by showing up here. He needs to know it's safe."

"I'll check the house for devices." George shrugged. "But I can't imagine anyone bugging our house." George returned the putter to his bag. "We'll do a quick inspection and then we can talk freely inside."

They walked back to the house while Brooke explained Ty's plan.

George held the door open for Brooke and signaled for her to take a seat in the kitchen. He placed a finger to his lips and motioned for his wife to be quiet while he did an assessment of the house.

"Nothing appears unusual." He returned to the kitchen. "I

checked the phones, light bulbs, mirrors—every place I could imagine hiding a bug. He turned to his wife. "Did you ever tell anyone that Blake was alive?"

"No. I promised him I wouldn't." Anne fidgeted nervously with her hands as they sat in the Kendall's huge, updated kitchen. She glanced toward the window and blew out an apprehensive sigh. "But when we went down to D.C. to visit Olivia and Clayton last month—"

George turned his blue eyes toward Anne. "You didn't…"

"No. But remember how she and Clayton commented on how happy we were?"

George nodded. "We told them it was because we finally came to understand what it meant to be followers of Christ."

"That's right." Anne shifted uneasily. "Remember when Clayton asked us how we found this new understanding?"

"Yes."

"I started to say Blake—remember?"

"I didn't catch it." George paced across the hardwood kitchen floor.

"Maybe neither of them did," Anne shrugged. "But Olivia made a comment while we were there about how she hadn't seen me so happy since before Blake died. Then, that night, Clayton asked if I was totally convinced Blake was dead."

"You didn't tell me this." George leaned against the kitchen island and watched his wife.

"I didn't think much of it," Anne confessed. "I avoided the question by asking him why he would suggest such a thing."

"And…"

"He said it seemed like a strange coincidence that Blake was in that accident right after all that evidence against his clients was presented."

George let out a heavy sigh. "How did you respond?"

"I tried to change the subject. I couldn't lie to Olivia and her husband…"

Brooke glanced at her watch. It was almost time to call Ty. "Do you think it's safe for Blake?" She asked Ty's dad.

George nodded. "I think the house is safe. What car is he driving?"

"Mine."

"Let's park it in the garage to be careful. Tell him to pull right in." George went to move his own vehicle to the driveway.

■ ■ ■

It was difficult to watch Ty's reunion with his parents. Brooke had a hard time keeping her own emotions at bay as she watched Ty's parents engulf their son in hugs and warmth. When had she seen that kind of love?

Ty's blue eyes were wet with tears as his mother wept on his chest.

"I'm so sorry," Ty choked out.

"I never thought we'd see you again." Anne pulled away from him to study his face. "My son."

Brooke turned away and crept to the room where George kept his golf clubs. Ty and his parents needed some time to themselves.

An overstuffed chair beside a large, sunlit window seemed like the perfect place to curl up and ward off memories. Brooke glanced outside at a small bush of purple asters nearing the end of their blooming season. Asters grew well in Ohio. It was nice seeing the familiar flowers growing in Maine. As cool as it was, they would not be blooming for long. The cozy chair and quiet of the room calmed Brooke's nerves and before she knew it, she dozed off.

She was alone for quite some time before Ty came looking for her. "Are you okay?" he asked.

Brooke blinked a few times. How long had she been asleep? "I wanted to give you and your parents time together."

Ty reached for her hand and pulled her from the chair. "Come on, they want you in there."

"Me?" Brooke felt strangely out of place. "They want to see you. They have no idea who I am."

"Dad said you did a great job on my arm." Ty cocked an eyebrow. "He followed it up with a shot of penicillin."

"He can also take the stiches out."

Ty motioned for her to follow him to his parents' living room where Anne and George were waiting.

"Thank you for taking care of our son." Anne's face was wet with tears and her eyes shone with unspeakable joy. She studied Brooke for a few minutes and grinned at Ty. "Are you two dating?"

Brooke almost choked. Was he going to tell his mother they only met two days ago? How would that look?

"No." Ty winked at Brooke. "We're just friends."

"Too bad," George said. "Anyone who can stitch a man up like that is worth keeping."

Brooke could tell George was teasing, but she blushed anyway.

"You know," Anne directed her attention to Brooke. "I feel terrible that I did not offer you a drink. Would you like anything?"

"Water would be nice. Thank you."

Anne got up and took Brooke's hand. "Come with me. I want you to help me pick out what to make for dinner."

Brooke let herself be led by this sweet older woman. There was something very natural about Anne's show of warmth.

"I figured I'd let George have a few minutes with Blake and that way you and I can get acquainted."

Once in the kitchen, Brooke took a seat on a high stool at the island and accepted the glass of water Anne handed her.

Anne began digging through her refrigerator. "I was planning on making meatloaf. Do you like meatloaf?"

"Yes. Meatloaf sounds good." Brooke was anything but hungry, but it was better to be polite.

"How long have you and Blake known one another?" Anne asked as she pulled down a large bowl and began getting out her spices.

"Not long." Brooke didn't want to be deceptive, but what would Anne think if she knew the truth? What kind of woman runs off to Maine with a man she hardly knows?

"Are you from his church?" Anne dumped ground beef into the bowl and began measuring ingredients.

"No." Brooke glanced toward the door. How long would she have to endure the personal questions?

"But you're not dating?" Anne sounded disappointed. She let her eyes linger for a moment on Brooke's.

"No." Brooke forced herself to smile.

Anne shrugged. "Blake is a good man." She seemed intent on explaining. "He made some wrong choices, but he accepted the consequences and made himself right."

This was not the conversation Brooke expected to be having with his mother.

"He had a beautiful place in New York City. It was a large studio apartment with a view of Central Park. I'd been there several times." Anne worked the meatloaf with her hands. "He said he thought God was working on his heart even back then. I believe it. Blake didn't seem happy in New York."

Brooke offered to help.

"No need. I love to cook. You can just keep me company until the boys come in." Anne smiled. "George was telling Blake about how we both put our faith in Jesus after Blake called us. Since that time, we found a good church and got baptized."

"That was fast," Brooke blurted out.

Anne nodded. "We were both ready. It was like God was preparing our hearts. Blake's call was the pivotal point."

Brooke nodded. She hoped "the boys" would rescue her soon.

"When did you become a Christian?" Anne asked before Brooke could think of a good question to change the subject.

Please Ty... rescue me... Brooke glanced toward the door and wished she could call for him. Anne was watching her and Brooke squirmed under the older woman's soft, gray eyes. Her own dark brown eyes blinked back emotion and she cleared her throat to stall. "Well… I'm not a Christian, Mrs. Kendall." There. She said it. The disappointed look in Anne's eyes made Brooke wish she'd have just made something up. She could have thrown out a few words about Bible camp or Vacation Bible School. Brooke knew how that whole thing worked. She'd gone to church growing up.

"I'm sorry," Anne stopped working on the meatloaf and washed her hands. Suddenly, making dinner was no longer important to the woman.

Brooke sucked in a deep breath. Would it be tacky to say, 'just kidding' and make up a good story? She shrugged. "No problem. But I'm happy for you and Mr. Kendall."

"Please call us Anne and George." She reached for Brooke's

hands. "You brought Blake to us. You're family."

Brooke feigned a smile and squirmed internally at the warmth in Anne's soft hands. Is this how other people's mothers really were?

"George and I were late in coming to the Lord. It's still very new to us. We've been reading the Bible together every night and we're learning a lot. We both have so many questions." The compassion in Anne's voice was almost Brooke's undoing. "I don't have all the answers, sweetheart, but if you have any questions, I'd be more than happy to tell you all I can."

"Thank you." Brooke heard the tightness in her tone. "I don't have any questions right now."

Anne nodded and reluctantly let go of Brooke's hands. "George and I did our best to explain it to Olivia when we went to D.C. That's why we went. Olivia and Clayton rarely come up and my daughter hardly ever calls. She's a very busy woman."

Brooke listened quietly. She was curious about Ty's sister.

"I wish I could see her more." Anne put the meatloaf in the oven to cook and began peeling potatoes at the kitchen island. "More than anything, George and I wish we'd have raised our children in a Christian home."

"Didn't you ever go to church?"

"Christmas and Easter sometimes," Anne confessed. "But rarely more than that. George was cynical about Christianity when we were a young couple, and I was too busy with worldly things to see my spiritual need."

"What changed?" Brooke figured she should at least sound interested to be polite.

"After we were told Blake died, it gave us a different perspective on life. George has a colleague who is a Christian. He and his wife had a few pointed conversations with us about the Lord over the past couple years. Neither of us admitted our interest in the idea until after Blake called."

Brooke offered to help cut the potatoes and place them in a pan.

"Thank you so much, dear." Anne placed a loving hand on Brooke's arm. "Do you enjoy cooking?

"I do," Brooke confessed. "But I don't have much opportunity for it." It was good to finally change the conversation.

■ ■ ■

"How long will you be able to stay, Blake?" Ty's father asked during dinner.

"I'd like to get to New York by Wednesday morning." He glanced at Brooke. "I sincerely hope my coming here has not put your lives in danger."

"Son, we know where we will spend eternity," George said confidently. "Nothing could have brought me more joy than to have you here right now."

Ty lowered his eyes. He was glad he came. Hearing about his parents' newfound faith was worth the shot though his arm. But he didn't want to put them in danger. From his conversation with his parents, Ty wondered if somehow Olivia and Clayton linked his parents' joy with Ty being alive. Would they have mentioned it to someone in D.C.? Who in D.C. would care? All of Ty's old contacts were in New York, weren't they?

"You look deep in thought," Anne interrupted Ty's mental questions.

"Just trying to figure things out." He took a bite of his mother's meatloaf and savored the taste. "This was worth coming home to."

"You are a wonderful cook, Anne." Brooke interjected.

"Thank you. It's been too long since I've gotten to cook for my boy." Her smile warmed her face. "Please, take more meatloaf." She passed the plate to Brooke who complied.

Ty took note of it.

"She keeps me well fed." George patted his stomach and kept the conversation going.

Ty glanced across the table at Brooke. She'd been extra quiet since arriving at his parents' house. She must feel out of place. Overwhelmed.

"After dinner, perhaps we can take a walk along the harbor," Anne suggested.

Ty gave his mother a disappointed shake of the head. "I could be recognized."

Anne set down her fork. "I didn't think of that. This is frightening."

Brooke glanced up from her food. "You mentioned that my condo was broken into after we left," her eyes were serious. "Do you think there is any kind of search going on for me?"

"I wondered that." Ty nodded.

"If there is, wouldn't they be looking for her car?" George asked.

"I would think so." There could be all kinds of searches going on by now. Would her parents have been notified?

"When you two leave on Tuesday, take the Mercedes." George told his son.

"That's a good idea. We can leave Brooke's Volkswagen in your garage."

"So you're a German car lover too, huh?" Anne smiled at Brooke.

"I wouldn't put my car in the same category with a Mercedes."

"Do you mind us keeping your car in my dad's garage?" Ty made a point of asking. Decisions were being made about Brooke's car without her voice. Was she okay with this?

"I don't mind at all."

After dinner, they convened in the living room to talk more about the events in George and Anne's lives for the past four years. Ty explained to his parents that he needed to keep any information about his past four years vague.

■ ■ ■

Brooke listened quietly to the friendly banter of a healthy family reconnecting after a long separation.

There was something about Anne and George that Brooke really liked. They were nothing like her parents.

Her eyes roamed the room and found an assortment of family photographs in unique frames scattered around. None of them were close enough to see the details, but she could tell from the photos that they represented years of family time and probably vacations.

A photo on the table beside her of George with a teenaged girl caught Brooke's eyes. The young woman's face could be clearly seen. This must be Olivia. She had one arm around her dad and another on her skis. They both looked happy. Olivia looked safe. What kind of relationship did they have?

"Are you getting tired, Brooke?" Anne asked.

"Maybe a little, but please don't trouble yourself. I'm fine."

"If you'd like to go to bed, I can take you upstairs to the guestroom," Anne offered.

Perhaps Ty would like more time with his parents alone. Brooke was willing to give them space. "That's fine." She said a quick goodnight to Ty and George, and followed Anne upstairs where her shopping bags had already been taken.

"You're welcome to use the shower or anything you need. Please make yourself at home." Anne patted Brooke's shoulder. "We're so glad you're here."

Brooke thanked Anne kindly and found herself alone in one of the Kendall's lovely guestrooms.

It was a spacious room with a queen sized bed and a full bathroom attached. Brooke opted to take a long hot shower and curl up in bed for the night. It was good to snuggle down in a clean bed, but it also made everything more real. She'd quit her job. She was in Maine with some man she'd known less than two days—and someone wanted to kill them!

CHAPTER 7

In the morning, Brooke was the last one downstairs. Even though it was Sunday, Ty's parents stayed home from church.

"After breakfast we will have our own church service," Anne told Brooke when she arrived at the table.

A large assortment of food covered the dining room table, and the smell of maple syrup filled the room. Breakfast reminded Brooke of a bed and breakfast she'd stayed at once with a group of friends from college. Anne prepared apple maple French toast, fresh fruit, carrot cake muffins, and goat's milk that Anne said she got from a local farmer.

George led them all in a prayer of thanksgiving and began passing the food around.

"You'll appreciate my mother's coffee," Ty told Brooke. "It meets the standard."

Brooke was happy to allow Anne to fill her cup. The fresh aroma of coffee warmed her senses. Brooke added cream and took a sip.

"How long have you been a nurse?" George asked Brooke.

"Five years." Brooke took a bite of her French toast and thought she'd just gone to heaven. "This is amazing!"

"Thank you. I got the recipe from a friend of mine in Vermont. She has her own maple trees and has dozens of maple syrup recipes." Anne started telling Brooke about some of the wonderful meals her friend prepared using maple syrup.

"They make chocolate maple ice cream," George interjected.

"That sounds terrific. I love maple syrup," Brooke offered. It was one of those safe things she could say about herself.

"I'd be happy to write out some of the recipes for you," Anne rattled on.

Brooke enjoyed Anne's talking. It was better than Anne's questions.

"Did you sleep well in the guest room?" her hostess asked.

"I did." *Once I finally fell asleep.* "Thank you."

"You know, George." Anne turned to her husband. "While I was getting Brooke's bedroom ready, I realized that I've had a window opened in that room for who knows how long. We've been wasting heat." She shook her head repentantly.

Brooke glanced at George. Would he be angry?

George shrugged. "Guess the room was all nicely aired out for Brooke then." He grinned. "I love a freshly aired out room."

"I'm just glad no rain seemed to have gotten in." Anne took a sip of her orange juice.

His reaction caught Brooke off guard. No argument? No flying off the handle? This family was a different breed. Or was hers the unusual one?

"I'm sure pastor John will call this afternoon to ask where we were," George said. "We haven't missed a Sunday since we started going to Grace Community."

"What will you tell him?"

George glanced at his wife. "I guess that we had unexpected guests show up last night and weren't able to get out this morning."

"You know I don't mind if you go," Ty said.

George shook his head. "We can worship with you and Brooke this morning."

Brooke took another sip of her coffee. Was there a way to opt out of their family worship service? She found Ty's eyes on her and wondered if his mother mentioned anything to him about her not being a Christian. *Hopefully not.*

■ ■ ■

An hour later, Brooke sat next to Ty with a Bible in her lap. It was a new Bible. Ty had his. His parents shared another. They began their family worship by having Ty read several of his favorite Bible verses.

Ty was eager to share with his parents what God had been teaching him from the Word.

"Rejoice in the Lord always; again I will say, rejoice!" Ty read. "Let your gentle spirit be known to all men. The Lord is near. Be anxious for nothing, but in everything by prayer and supplication with thanksgiving let your requests be made known to God. And the peace of God, which surpasses all comprehension, will guard your hearts and minds in Christ Jesus."

"Where is that found?" George asked.

"That was Philippians 4:4-7." Ty smiled at his father. "I love the book of Philippians."

"I definitely needed to be reminded not to fear," Anne confessed. "The idea of someone being after my son…" She turned her eyes to George and wiped away tears. "I can't bear the thought of losing you again, Blake."

Ty breathed out a steadying breath. "I understand, Mom. That's why we need to pray."

Brooke ran her hand over her unopened Bible, allowing herself to feel the soft leather and textured surface.

"There's a lot to pray about. And a lot to be thankful for." George turned to the place in his Bible. "These are encouraging verses."

"We've been praying for Olivia and Clayton ever since we became believers," Anne said.

"I have too." Ty nodded.

"We need to pray that whoever is after you be brought to justice." George steadied his gaze on Ty.

"What about you, Brooke," Ty turned to her. "Do you have any prayer requests?"

Brooke shook her head. "No. I'm good." She turned her face toward the window and looked out at the bay behind the house. A lone sailboat drifted by, silhouetted by the blue sky and sunshine. *But I'd sure love to be on a sailboat.*

The family took a few minutes to lift up their concerns to the Lord and Brooke listened quietly. When had her family ever prayed like that?

After the family ended their worship time, Anne asked Brooke if she would like to run into town to pick up food for the evening meal.

"No one should recognize Brooke," Anne said.

Ty asked Brooke if she wanted to go. "I'm probably trapped here for the next few days, but you're welcome to run off with Mom."

Brooke figured Anne wanted her to go, so she consented politely.

■ ■ ■

Brooke enjoyed her quick trip to town with Anne. Ty's mother was one of the sweetest women she'd ever met. They ran into a couple of Anne's friends at the small Camden grocery store and Anne introduced Brooke as a family friend.

"What would you like for dinner tonight?" Anne asked as they neared the meat department.

"Anything's fine." It was nice to be given so much consideration for a family meal.

"Do you like ham?"

"Yes."

"They have a wonderful all natural ham with no phosphates," Anne selected one large enough for leftovers. "George loves ham. I didn't used to buy it as much because of all the preservatives. But when our grocery store started carrying this, I was hooked."

Brooke pushed the cart while Anne loaded it and talked.

During their short drive back to the Kendall's house, Anne pointed out all the sights and told little stories about Blake and Olivia growing up. Camden was a quaint little harbor town nestled along the rocky coast of the Penobscot Bay. The streets were dotted with charming New England houses of all sizes and shapes. Brooke took in the scenery with interest.

"Where did you grow up, Brooke?" Anne asked curiously.

"Indiana."

"How nice. Do you have a big family?"

"Not really."

"Are you and your mother close?"

It was an honest question. Brooke appreciated Anne's desire to know her better. When was the last time someone showed that kind of interest in her life? High school? College? Brooke grabbed a couple grocery bags when they pulled up to the house. "Not really." She said as she followed Anne to the door.

Ty rescued her from the conversation by asking how their trip to the store went.

He helped carry bags inside and threw an idea at Brooke. "My dad suggested that since I can't be seen around town, I take you out for a cruise around the bay."

Brooke's eyes lit up. "On a boat?"

Ty chuckled. "Yes. My dad has a small schooner." He shrugged. "I thought you'd enjoy a tour of Penobscot Bay."

"I would love that." Brooke couldn't hide her enthusiasm. "Will we all be going?"

"Dad's got to help me navigate, since I've got this bum arm." Ty motioned to the arm he still kept close to his side for protection." He turned to his mother. "Do you want to come?"

"Its too cold to go out on the bay." Anne wrapped her arms around herself. "And I want to get this ham in the oven. How long will you be?"

"A few hours."

"Make sure you bundle up though. These autumn days are getting cooler," Anne said.

Ty grinned and turned to Brooke. "Why don't you put on your warmest clothes and I'll meet you downstairs."

Brooke was more than happy to comply.

■ ■ ■

It didn't take Ty and his father long to get the schooner ready for a short sail around the harbor. George had the boat out the week before so he felt confident that it was ready to be out again.

"Welcome to the Kennebunkport Kiss." Ty reached out a hand to steady Brooke as she boarded the vessel.

"It's beautiful." It was hard not to smile at the name of the boat. She wondered if the name held any special significance.

Ty handed her a life jacket and donned one of his own. "It's Dad's policy that we all wear one of these lovely bright orange vests." He glanced down at the buckles and snapped himself in. "At least these aren't as bulky as the ones we had as kids." He grinned.

Brooke sat at the front of the boat and watched Ty and George ready the boat for departure. She ran her hand over the sun warmed surface of the deck and let her eyes travel over the two large masts.

Ty had explained that a schooner was a sailboat with more than one mast. She felt small underneath the huge sails towering overhead.

The boat moved slowly at first and Brooke could hear Ty's father call out instructions to his son as they coasted away from the shore. In only a moment, the Kennebunkport Kiss began to pick up speed as the wind filled her sails with power. The boat skipped across the white crested waves like a puppy running through a field of daisies. An invigorating cool spray misted up and touched her face. Brooke closed her eyes to breathe in the salty smell of the bay.

Glancing over her shoulder, she found Ty's eyes on her. He smiled and made his way to the bow where he could sit near her. Brooke moved over and they sat quietly, watching as the boat cut through the water. There was something freeing about setting sail into the wild blue—leaving the responsibilities of the world behind them. Brooke's eyes were expressive as they took in the scenes around her. "I love it."

"Dad used to threaten to sell the boat." Ty's voice broke through the sound of the wind. He glanced back at the helm where his father was steering the craft. "I'm glad he didn't."

"I'm glad too," Brooke agreed.

George's eyes were on the horizon. Brooke could tell the man was miles away in his thoughts.

"When I went off to college, Dad thought the Kennebunkport Kiss would be too much work for him and Mom. It does require a fair amount of maintenance. But they learned to handle it." Ty glanced back to Brooke. "Dad always said the water called to him. I think sailing is his escape."

"It's a pretty awesome escape." Brooke did her best to control her hair as it blew in spirals from the gentle wind.

The boat moved at a steady pace through the bay. The concept of time seemed lost on the water. Brooke watched as they passed dozens of parked boats and lovely houses along the shore. What would it feel like to call this place home?

■ ■ ■

"Have you ever sailed?" Ty asked.

"No." Brooke leaned back on her arms and watched as the sky

moved past.

"You would love it in the summer. My sister and I used to dock out in the middle of the bay and swim."

"I love it now," Brooke confessed. "I've always loved the water. While we were doing the church thing this morning, I noticed a sailboat go past. I wanted to do something like this… but I never dreamed."

Ty held back a chuckle at Brooke's definition of their family worship time. "Church thing, huh? I guess God heard your heart." Ty dodged a breaking wave as it splashed onto the boat.

"I didn't ask."

"That doesn't mean God didn't hear." Ty said.

"You have very nice parents." Brooke changed the subject. She spoke soft enough to keep their conversation private.

Ty nodded reflectively. "I've missed them." He watched his father sailing the boat. George loved captaining his little rig. Strong hands gripped the wheel as he stood at the helm. He even wore a captain's hat while driving the boat. Ty spent the time while his mother and Brooke were at the store talking deeply with his dad. It was a wonderful conversation and Ty was convinced that God led him to Maine, if nothing else, but to have a short time of fellowship with them before going back into hiding.

Brooke seemed to need the quiet time. Ty leaned back and left her to her thoughts. It was good to be able to be in someone's company without feeling pressured to talk just to fill the silence. It was the first down time he'd had since he'd been shot.

Was that only three days ago? So much had happened. Ty's arm was still sore, but on the boat he felt completely removed from the events that brought him here.

George was a good sailor and had the boat moving at a moderate, steady pace. The only real motion was a gentle rocking from the slight wake.

Sailing the bay, it was hard to imagine that they were in any kind of trouble. Life seemed good right now. Was this the calm before the storm?

Ty glanced over and noticed a tear running down Brooke's soft, delicate cheek. Impulsively, he reached to wipe it away.

Brooke turned to look at him but didn't offer an explanation for her quiet display of emotion.

"Are you okay?" Ty asked softly.

"I am." Brooke smiled in spite of her wet lashes. "It's so nice to be away."

"You were supposed to be at work today."

"I'm glad I'm not." She confessed.

"Even though you're now unemployed, and possibly in danger because of me?" Ty brushed a stray hair away from Brooke's face.

"I needed the change."

"I don't know what I would have done without you," Ty expressed his gratitude. "You probably saved my life."

Brooke met his gaze.

There was so much Ty wanted to say. This was the first time in four years he was free to be himself. It felt good—even if it was only for a couple days.

"Maine is beautiful." Brooke sighed. She looked out the rocky coast dotted with colors of autumn. "I wish we never had to leave."

Ty watched Brooke's long hair as it lay across the deck of the boat. It was like an exquisite frame for her lovely face. He swallowed hard and turned his face away. *Watch it, Ty. There's no point in letting yourself feel something for this woman.*

■ ■ ■

"Thank you so much for taking me out on your boat." Brooke expressed her gratitude after helping the men dock the boat and secure the ropes.

"It was a pleasure," George said. He stepped from the rig and put a friendly arm around her shoulder. "You're welcome on my boat any time."

Brooke wasn't used to George's show of kindness. It took her a moment to recover from the awkwardness of having his arm around her. He only had it there for a moment, but Brooke tried to process the friendly touch.

They returned to the house to find a wonderful meal waiting for them in the kitchen. Anne pulled homemade rolls from the oven and waved the pan under her son's face so he could smell the aroma.

"Mom, you're going to pack pounds on me if I'm not careful." Ty walked to the sink to wash his hands.

"You have plenty of room for a few pounds."

"But then none of my suits will fit me." There was a twinkle in Ty's eyes.

"I saw the one with the bullet hole." Anne carried a steaming hot ham to the table. "It was truly sobering." She glanced up at her husband.

"Just throw that suit jacket out." Ty sat down at the table. "And the shirt too. I don't want them."

After a quick prayer of thanksgiving, the family enjoyed another meal together. The conversation stayed light. No one seemed to want to talk about looming threats and secret identities. Ty told his parents about the book he hoped to write and how much he was enjoying teaching financial wisdom. George and Anne listened attentively to all their son had been doing these past few years.

"Can I help you clean up?" Brooke asked after the meal.

"That would be wonderful." Anne accepted Brooke's offer.

"I'll help too, Mom." Ty picked up his plate and gathered the silverware.

George joined in and gathered the cups.

What an unusual family. When had her father ever helped clean dishes? With four workers, it didn't take long to rinse the dishes and put them in the dishwasher.

"Did your father tell you he's found someone to buy his practice?" Anne wiped down the counter and dried her hands on a towel.

"Really?" Ty grabbed a bottle of water and offered one to Brooke. "That's wonderful. When are you retiring?"

"Not for several years still," George explained as they walked into the living room. "Robert is a good doctor, but he's swimming in college debt. It will be a few years before he can pick up a business loan."

"It has taken a lot of weight off your father to have him there though," Anne added.

"It truly has," George confessed. "But we're making the transition slow, which I like."

Brooke listened to the small talk and felt herself dozing. Her many nights working late at the hospital and the long drive to Maine were finally catching up with her. "I think I need to make this an early bedtime." She stood up. "Thank you, again, for the boat ride, and the wonderful meal."

The others wished her a goodnight and Brooke slipped away to catch up on some rest.

■ ■ ■

"She's quiet," Anne said after Brooke left the room.

Ty's eyes lingered on the door. He didn't know her well enough to know whether she was feeling quiet due to the strange circumstance, or if she was quiet by nature.

"She said you haven't been friends for very long." Anne got up and carried a cup of herbal tea to her husband.

A grin spread across Ty's lips. *That's an understatement.* "We never told you exactly how we met did we?"

George and Anne waited for Ty to continue.

His explanation wasn't long. They'd known one another for three days. How much could he say? But what he did tell them was that she probably saved his life and lost her job for him.

"So you hardly know this lady," George reiterated.

"I've known her a day and a half longer than you have."

"She's a very attractive woman." George took a sip of his tea. "And very intelligent." He motioned toward his son's arm. "She did a class act job on your arm."

"I told her you'd be impressed."

"Had she ever given stitches before?" Anne asked.

Ty shook his head. "No. I had to talk her into it. Especially since it was a gunshot wound."

"She took a big risk for a total stranger." George shook his head. "I don't know that I'd do the same."

"She was a perfectly-timed answer to prayer," Ty said reflectively. "God knew exactly who I needed. I have no doubt His hand was on the whole thing."

Anne glanced toward the door where Brooke had exited. "She told me she's not a Christian."

"That's more than she's told me about her relationship with

God," Ty confessed. "She clams up whenever I ask anything personal about God or her past. She's more private than the man in witness protection."

"I practically had to drag it from her," Anne said. "And she didn't tell me anything else."

Ty wasn't surprised.

The phone rang and Anne hurried off to the kitchen to answer it.

"Maybe God has His hand in this for more than just saving your life," George suggested.

"I'd thought of that." Ty leaned his head back on the leather recliner and let his eyes roam to the window. It was dark outside, but Ty could see the lights dotting the harbor. "How do I get her to open up about Him though?"

"That's God's job. You just continue trying," George said.

Anne was slightly flushed when she returned to the living room a few minutes later. "That was Olivia."

George's face showed surprise. Ty knew his sister was not in the habit of making frequent calls to their mother. Maybe she was beginning to realize the need to cherish the time she had with them.

"She said that her and Clayton have a few days off and wanted to come see us." Anne's expression was torn between a smile and perplexity.

"When?"

"This week." Anne returned to her seat. "She mentioned arriving Wednesday night and staying through Friday. She's scheduled to speak at a benefit on Saturday, so they only have a couple days."

"Both children in one week." George crossed his arms and shook his head with a grin on his face. "What did you tell her?"

Ty wondered the same thing. He prayed that his mother didn't give anything away.

"I played it off. It was easy to sound surprised and excited, because I am." She glanced at her husband. "How long has it been since they've been up?"

George blew out a heavy breath. "Maybe two Christmases ago."

"Mom." Ty's expression showed his concern. "You'll to have to be careful."

"We will be," Anne pulled her feet up under the couch pillow.

"But in all seriousness, who would your sister tell? She and Clayton would be so happy to know you're alive."

"I'm sure they'd be happy, but they can't know." Ty hoped his mother fully grasped the seriousness of this situation.

George echoed his son's words. "The more people who know, the more dangerous it is for our son."

"Olivia and Clayton know a lot of people, Mom." Ty didn't have to explain this. His sister was running for senator. Her name was all over the place. "It's also dangerous for the people who know." Ty hated that he'd put his parents in this position.

"I understand," Anne furrowed her eyebrows to both of the men in her life. "I think I did a pretty good job playing it off just now and I can keep up the act while they're here."

Ty gave his mother a sympathetic smile. "I'm sorry I put you in this position."

"We're not sorry, Son." George spoke up. "You led your parents to Christ. We know where we will spend eternity." George got up and moved to the chair next to his son. "If something happens to us, you can't blame yourself."

That was easier said than done. Ty was glad he was able to point his parents to the Lord, but if something happened to them…

Chapter 8

Ty moved Brooke's car to the far side of his father's garage. "I seriously hope they don't notice." He clicked the lock and handed his father the keys.

"The thing they would notice is my Mercedes missing." George walked back into the house with his son. "Take the SUV. I hardly drive it."

Ty liked his father's Toyota 4-Runner. He only wished it got better gas mileage. "I'll call you next week. Only use the cell phone number in an absolute emergency."

"We'll be praying for you, Blake." George handed Ty a credit card and patted his hand. "Use this to book your hotel."

"Thanks, Dad." The younger man hugged his dad and forced back his emotions.

Brooke met them downstairs with her bags. Ty gave his mother a final hug and led Brooke to the Toyota. His parents followed them to the garage and helped Ty and Brooke load up their few belongings.

Anne took Brooke's hand before she climbed into the SUV. "I will be praying for you, dear."

Ty was proud of his mother's boldness. She wasn't a bit afraid to talk about her faith.

"Thank you." Brooke smiled tenderly at Anne.

Anne gave Brooke a gentle hug and stepped back so Brooke could get into the vehicle.

Ty pulled out of the driveway and watched his parents with a sentimental lump in his throat.

"Do you think they'll notice the car." Brooke leaned back in the large leather passenger seat and made herself comfortable.

"My sister is pretty self-absorbed." Ty glanced over his shoulder before pulling onto the main road. “I doubt it.”

“Which one of you is older?” Brooke asked.

“Olivia. By ten years.”

“Ten years?” Brooke sounded surprised. “That’s quite an age difference. I guess when I pictured you and your sister on the boat together I thought you were close in age.”

Ty shook his head. “I was just a little guy, about eight. It was before Olivia went off to college.”

“Did you stay connected after that?”

“As much as we could. Olivia studied law as well, so she had some influence in my life.” Ty pulled the vehicle onto the highway and set his cruise control. He glanced at Brooke. “How about you? Any siblings?”

Brooke shrugged.

“You do this every time.” Ty grinned.

Silence penetrated the car for several minutes. Ty figured he’d let Brooke drift away to the safe place in her mind.

“I have a brother,” Brooke finally said quietly. “We’re very close.”

Ty could see those words carried with them a lot of emotion.

“He’s a ski instructor in Colorado.” Her lips curved into a smile. “Believe it or not, where we lived in southern Indiana there was a ski place.”

“Perfect North Slopes,” Ty interrupted. He knew the place well.

“Yeah.” Brooke ran her hand over the smooth surface of the leather seat. “Cody practically lived there growing up. He’s amazing on skis. He can go backwards, front ways, do jumps, flips, snow board. Cody can do it all.”

Ty listened intently.

“We still talk, although he’s pretty busy in the wintertime.” She rattled on. “I usually go out to see him for a week every summer.”

“That’s awesome. Who’s older?”

“Me, by three years.” Brooke ran her fingers through her hair and let out a nervous sigh. “Okay, so… I told you quite a bit.” She grinned.

“Thank you.” Ty reached over and gave her shoulder a quick

squeeze.

Brooke turned toward the window.

Ty left her to her thoughts. He was glad to know there was at least one person in Brooke's life who she was close to. He was curious to know more, but for whatever reason, Brooke was protecting her privacy. He would respect that.

■ ■ ■

Ty knew New York City well. He drove them to a nice hotel not far from the FBI office and allowed the valet to park the Toyota.

"Isn't this hotel a little expensive?" Brooke glanced at the bill.

"It's a safe location. That's more important." Ty pushed the elevator button and the doors opened. "We'll take a taxi to the FBI office tomorrow."

Ty and Brooke had adjoining rooms. Ty insisted that under the circumstances, he wanted her to have easy access to him in the event of an emergency. "We'll keep the doors closed but unlocked."

"Thank you." It was nice that he considered her safety Her eyes traveled over the large hotel room. She'd definitely been staying at the wrong hotels. The large king sized bed, piled high with pillows and covered with a thick, down comforter, hardly filled up the space. Windows overlooking the city took up one side of the room. A craftsman style desk and chair sat against another wall like high-end furniture in a catalogue. Brooke set her purse down on the leather loveseat and glanced up at the crown molding around the ceiling.

Ty knocked on the other side of the door that joined their rooms and Brooke opened her side.

"How's the room?"

"I suppose it's adequate." She tried not to start laughing. Was this really normal for him?

Ty arched an eyebrow. "I suppose a suite would be more to your liking." He grinned. "Are you hungry? I thought we could grab a bite to eat and then I'll take you shopping."

"Shopping?" Brooke showed interest.

"I want to buy you a suit."

"A suit?"

"I plan on wearing mine tomorrow and thought you'd blend in a little more if you've got one." A smile tugged at his lips. "I told you, when you're wearing a suit, people listen."

"I'll give it a shot."

"Get freshened up and we'll leave in fifteen minutes." Ty slipped back into his room and closed the door.

Brooke wasn't sure what to expect. New York City was a little overwhelming to the small town Indiana girl. Cincinnati was big enough. She put on the nicest clothes she had and knocked on Ty's door to let him know she was ready.

Ty straightened his tie and they walked out of his hotel room together.

"How many years did you live here?" Brooke asked as he led her down the road toward the restaurant where he insisted she just had to eat.

"Three." Ty wrapped his arm through hers. "Keep your purse between us and stick close."

They crossed the road at a crosswalk and Ty motioned toward the restaurant.

"Will you be recognized?" She allowed him to hold the door opened for her.

"In a city of this many people? No. Not likely. Anyway, I'm dead. People tend to forget you after you die."

Ty and Brooke were seated at the far back of a quiet, dimly lit, Italian restaurant and waited to be served. Soft instrumental music played in the background and the smell of Italian food permeated the air. Brooke's eyes traveled over the new environment, conscious of the many well-dressed women. No one else was wearing blue jeans.

"Have you been to New York City?" Ty leaned forward to talk.

"No. I'm not a big city kind of person." Brooke shrugged. "This is a totally different world to me. Everyone here is so fashionable and refined."

"They don't hold a candle to you."

Brooke glanced down shyly. His compliment embarrassed her. Something told her that encouraging people was natural for Ty. There was nothing flirtatious in his words. He was just being kind, but when was the last time a handsome, sophisticated man paid her a compliment?

"Thank you for telling me about your brother earlier today." Ty reached for his glass of water and took a sip."

Brooke lifted her eyes to Ty's blue ones and felt them searching her thoughts. *I've told him so little about myself.* "I'm sorry I'm so secretive."

"You've been hurt deeply." He reached a compassionate hand to hers.

Brooke's eyes shifted to his hand on hers. It wasn't the first time Ty had touched her as a show of tenderness. He took after his parents that way. It was a safe kind of touch. Brooke wasn't afraid of it. But it wasn't something she was used to. "I have," she answered honestly. "I guess that's why it's difficult for me to open up to people."

"I won't push you for your story," Ty continued. "But I want to be your friend if you ever want to share."

"Thank you."

The waiter arrived and Brooke let Ty make a suggestion for her.

"Has the menu changed much since the last time you were here?" Brooke watched the waiter walk away.

"Not really." Ty let his eyes travel over the large room. "I've only been here a few times," Ty confessed. "But I always enjoyed it. It's not nearly as expensive as some of the restaurants along this road."

When the meal arrived, Brooke took in the lovely presentation—a square white plate covered with a bed of fresh lettuce, a variety of vegetables, and two large pieces of marinated grilled chicken. "It looks too pretty to eat." Brooke's pink lips revealed a pleasant smile.

Ty paused to pray and Brooke closed her eyes while his soft words found her ears. He prayed for the journey they were on and asked for God's blessing on each step they made toward learning the truth. He also prayed for Brooke. "Please heal her hurts, Lord. Help Brooke find joy in You."

He's praying for me. She let his words linger in her mind and opened her eyes to find him watching her. "Thank you."

She took a bite of her dinner. "I don't know when I've ever eaten at such a nice restaurant." It felt good to change the subject.

Ty told Brooke about some of his favorite places in New York City.

"Did you have a lot of friends here?" Brooke asked.

"I knew a lot of people, but I don't know how many friends I actually had. I have more real friends in Cincinnati than I ever had in New York."

"Even though you were in witness protection?" Brooke took a sip of her iced tea and waited for him to continue.

"Yes. Even though there was a lot I couldn't tell them, they genuinely cared about me. They were real friends. Does that make sense?"

It did.

"How about you? Do you have many friends in Cincinnati?"

"When I was in college, I had some wonderful friends." Brooke glanced off toward a large painting hanging over several tables. "Although… there was a lot they never knew about me." She turned her eyes to Ty. "Once I graduated, several of my friends got jobs in other cities and moved. Other friends got married and our lives went in different directions. Once I started working at the hospital, it was difficult to really have time for friends."

"You didn't have any friends at work?"

"Just acquaintances. The environment was stressful. I always felt like I was walking on eggshells." Brooke considered how similar it was to her home environment. *Maybe that's why I'd put up with it.*

Ty studied her for a few seconds. "The store I'd like to take you to closes at eight." He glanced at his watch. "We should probably head out."

"How far away is it?"

"Just a couple blocks. We'll walk." Ty left a generous tip and took Brooke's arm.

Brooke recognized quality as soon as they stepped into the department store. High-end brands hung along the walls while wooden shelves of neatly folded sweaters, shirts, and shoes stood in organized displays throughout the store. Leather sofas and chairs offered shopping comforts in every department, and easy jazz music played softly in the air.

They walked to the ladies apparel department and Ty told the clerk what they wanted.

After trying on several suits, Brooke and Ty agreed on a soft gray that fit her slender curves and moderate height. Ty helped her select a couple blouses that would flatter the suit and the clerk suggested a pair of low black pumps to complete the ensemble.

Ty paid with cash and Brooke gave him a questioning glance. "You just happen to have that kind of cash on you?" she asked as they walked toward the door with their new purchases.

"Well, I didn't think I should use my dad's credit card." Ty winked.

"If I'd have known it was going to cost anywhere near that amount, I would never have let you buy me those clothes." Brooke wasn't sure she'd have the nerve to wear a suit of such expense. "What if I spill something on it? What if I snag it?"

"Then you get it washed or repaired." He held her arm and looked both ways before following a small crowd across the street. "The bullet hole was really a first for me. I've never had to throw out one of my good suits before, and trust me, I've spilled coffee."

It was well after eight by the time they reached the hotel, but the city streets were still busy with people. Brooke longed for the solitude of the sailboat.

"We'll leave at eight tomorrow, grab some coffee and a pastry at the coffee shop across the street, and head over to the FBI office," Ty said as they reached their hotel rooms. "If you need me, just knock."

Brooke nodded and watched Ty slip into his room through their adjoining doors.

Alone in her room, Brooke glanced at her new suit, still hanging in the plastic. What would it feel like to walk down the streets of New York City wearing this gorgeous suit?

She glanced in the mirror and brushed her long brown hair behind her back. Could she really stand tall in a suit like that and exude confidence? Brooke wasn't confident that she could.

Taking a seat on the bed, Brooke opened her laptop computer. She wanted to check her emails. Ty warned her not to go onto any social networking sites, but Brooke only laughed at that. Who would she social network with?

She had several emails from various stores and her college alumni news—nothing worthy of opening. An email from her brother caught her eyes. *Where are you?* Was in the heading. Brooke's mouth felt dry as she opened the email.

I got a phone call from the police today asking me if I've talked to you. The man said your apartment was broken into and that you've gone missing with some fugitive. What in the world is going on? I've tried your cell phone but it goes right into voice mail. I'm tempted to call Mom and Dad—and you know I'd have to be desperate to do that. Please, sis, if you get this, let me know you're okay! -Cody

Brooke's eyes filled up with tears. The email was sent on Friday. *Poor Cody.* She hated that he was worrying about her. Should she return his email?

"Ty," she knocked at his door, hoping he wasn't already sleeping.

Ty met her at the door, wearing a pair of athletic shorts he'd gotten from his parent's house and a t-shirt. "Is everything okay?"

"Did I wake you?"

"No. I was reading my Bible."

Of course you were. Brooke lowered her eyes. "My brother emailed me."

Ty followed Brooke into her room and read the note.

"Can I write him back? I don't want him worried sick."

"Keep it cryptic. Don't tell him where you are and urge him not to trust whoever that policeman was who called."

Brooke typed a quick message in return.

Cody—I'm sorry you have been worried. I'm perfectly safe. Please do not be in touch with the man who claimed he was a police officer. I can't explain right now, but things are not as they seem. For now, email will have to be our only contact. Please tell no one that you've been in touch with me. Trust me with this. I love you, little brother. -Brooke

Ty read the reply and nodded. "Will he trust you?"

"I think so. I wish I could call him."

"Now's not a good time."

Brooke shut down her computer and put it away. "Why would they be contacting my brother? How did they even get his name?"

Ty sat at the edge of her bed. "I don't know."

"Is he in danger?" Brooke asked. What would she do if they hurt Cody?

"I hope not." Ty ran his fingers through his hair. His blue eyes were wide with concern. "It's sad how the consequences of one man's sin can be so far reaching."

Brooke waited for him to continue.

"This is my fault. All of it. It started seven years ago when I compromised what I knew was right to get ahead as a lawyer. My sin." Ty looked discouraged. "I know I'm forgiven, but that doesn't erase the consequences." He glanced at Brooke. "I'm sorry I dragged you into this."

Brooke sat beside him and touched his shoulder. It wasn't in her comfort zone to touch someone to show warmth, but this was Ty's love language. "It's okay, Ty."

Ty turned to face Brooke. "I don't know how far these people will go to get me, Brooke." Ty's expression was grave. "If they think you're helping me and they've been in contact with your brother…"

"I don't blame you. I chose to help you." Brooke sat up straight and steadied her gaze. "Remember? I told you, I would help you as long as nothing we were doing was illegal."

A slight grin formed on Ty's lips. "You did say that, didn't you?"

"Yes." Brooke considered that for a moment. "And you let me."

"I didn't have anyone else." He reached for her hand. "Thank you."

They were quiet for a moment.

"Oh no…" Ty's face showed alarm. "Write your brother back. Tell him you won't be checking your emails and won't be able to contact him until this thing gets straightened out."

"Why?"

"It just hit me. If they figure out you've contacted your brother, they could use that against you." He stood up and paced the room. "I don't know why I didn't think of that before."

"Is it too late?"

"No. You just sent it. Email him right now."

Brooke hurried to turn on her computer. She already had a reply from her brother.

Thanks for letting me know you're safe. I talked to Mom and Dad over the weekend. It wasn't good. Someone's been in touch with them too, but they haven't changed. Do you have a phone number where I can reach you? Who is this man you are with?

Ty read over her shoulder. "Write him back. Then shut down your email account."

"Shut it down?" Brooke glanced up at Ty.

"Just to be safe. Whoever is looking for me needs to know that it is impossible for Cody to reach you."

Brooke's fingers danced over her computer keys.

Cody—I'll be shutting down this email account and won't be able to contact you until everything is straightened out. Please know I'm safe. Don't tell anyone you've talked to me and don't trust the "police." Love you!

She glanced at Ty.

"That sounds good."

Brooke hit send and watched her message disappear into cyberspace. Before she could change her mind, she closed her email account. *Goodbye world.*

"Now you're in witness protection."

CHAPTER 9

The next morning, Brooke stepped into the hallway wearing her new suit, red blouse, and black pumps. There was something nice about dressing up. If only she felt as confident as she looked. She glanced at Ty, who'd been standing outside her door waiting for her.

"You look great." His eyes lit up.

"Thank you." Brooke smiled. How did he know she needed encouragement?

They walked across the street, ordered mocha lattes, and carried their beverages outside where Ty waved down a taxi.

The FBI office was not far, but the drive gave Brooke a few minutes to observe New York City in the daytime. Her eyes scanned the towering skyscrapers, bumper-to-bumper traffic, and shoulder-to-shoulder people. How did people find their way around this busy place?

When the cab stopped in front of the FBI building, Brooke walked with Ty through the double doors.

Ty seemed to know exactly what he was doing. He made his way to the fifth floor and led Brooke into a busy office. He scanned the area for the man he wanted to see.

"May I help you?" A middle aged blonde woman stopped him and gave both Ty and Brooke the once over.

"I'm here to see Owen." Ty gave her the brush off and led Brooke past the woman to a glass door with the man's name printed across the front.

Brooke remembered what Ty said about acting like you belong somewhere and people believing you do.

Ty knocked on the glass and nodded at the man who looked up from his desk.

■ ■ ■

"Blake?" Owen Vance opened the door and ushered Ty and Brooke inside. "I thought you were in witness protection." The tall, middle-aged man glanced curiously at Ty and motioned for them to take a seat.

"I am." Ty watched Owen close a file he was working on and sit across from them at his desk.

"What in the world are you doing in New York? You look like Blake Kendall." Owen leveled his eyes on Ty.

"I need your help, Owen." Ty blew out a heavy sigh.

Owen listened while Ty explained the situation. He didn't leave anything out.

"Let me get this straight." Owen ran his fingers across his forehead. "You wanted to tell your parents that you're now a Christian?" He blinked a couple times and stared curiously at Ty.

Ty nodded. "And I don't regret it. They don't regret it."

"But you've opened Pandora's box."

"It was time. Owen, we've got to drive out the last of those crooked politicians and if you need me to do it, I'll help."

Owen glanced at Brooke. He pulled up his computer database and glanced over a few recent reports. "Your apartment has been broken into and you're reported as missing."

Brooke nodded. She handed the FBI agent the business card of the "policeman" who'd visited her house the day they left.

Owen ran the name and it came up blank. "The phone number is an unregistered cell phone."

"I figured." Ty cleared his throat. "We think the guy has been in touch with Brooke's brother, Cody, as well as her parents." They explained that she cut off communication with Cody and never established it with her parents.

"Good moves." He studied Ty. "You know I haven't dropped this case."

"I hoped you hadn't. But it's been over four years."

"I've run into some red tape. There are gaps I can't seem to fill in." Owen buzzed for one of his agents and requested a case number.

"Do you trust that guy?" Ty watched the agent leave the room.

"Absolutely." Owen nodded. "This U.S. Marshal that's gone missing—when is the last time you've talked to him?"

"It's been several months." Ty did a quick mental assessment. "He made me pull down my Wisdom Financial website."

"You had a website?" Owen attempted to drain his empty cup of coffee into his mouth. "Why did you have a website?"

"I was growing my business." Ty shrugged. "It was a Christian site. I doubt anyone would have linked it to me."

Owen's assistant walked in carrying the files Owen requested. "Thank you, Nathan." Owen glanced over a few details and cleared his throat. "I'd like a few minutes with Ms. Dunbar." He lifted his empty coffee cup to Ty. "You remember where we keep the coffee machine in this place."

Ty knew he was being excused. He placed a reassuring hand on Brooke when he saw her look of concern. "I'll be right back."

■ ■ ■

Owen watched Ty walk from the room and studied Brooke for a moment. He glanced at his computer screen and sniffed. "The U.S. Marshals have issued a search for you."

A search? For her? It was a bit overwhelming. "Am I in trouble?" Brooke's eyes grew wide.

"No. I think they want to make sure you're safe."

Brooke nodded and took a deep breath to steady her nerves.

"What is the relationship between you and Ty?"

Brooke let her eyes travel to the door where Ty just disappeared. "He's a friend."

"You do realize you've placed yourself in danger by your association with Ty?"

"Yes." Brooke sat up a little higher in her seat in her attempt to appear confident.

"Do you trust him?"

Brooke considered his question. She'd known this man less than a week, and yet, he'd been nothing but kind and respectful to her. Ty was a man of character. She'd met his parents and found warmth and acceptance from them in just a few short days. "Yes." She watched Owen for his response. "Is there a reason I shouldn't?"

Owen's eyes softened. "No. I believe Ty is a good man." He glanced at the stack of files his assistant left on his desk. "Before he came to me, over four years ago, I'd been gathering information that would have put him away for several years. I knew something was going on, but I had no idea how deep the roots went into the system. Ty came on his own initiative. He was surprised we'd been watching him. But he was genuinely disgusted with himself and with the system he'd allowed to drag him down. He was willing to serve time in order to bring these people down." Owen patted the files. "Instead he gave up everything and went into witness protection. All his assets were distributed as if he were deceased. He walked away from his whole life and helped bring down over a dozen high profile people whose crimes far exceeded his own."

There was something in Owen's voice that made Brooke believe he respected Ty.

"I will notify the Marshal's office to discontinue their search so that we can concentrate on who else is searching for you. They're our best lead on who shot Ty."

"What if there is someone in the Marshal's office who can't be trusted?" Brooke's dark eyes showed gravity. "I mean—Ty said his profile was wiped from their database."

"We'll do our best to keep you both safe."

Brooke smoothed her skirt and pushed a strand of long hair behind her back.

"We'll also keep an eye on your family," Owen promised.

Ty returned with Owen's coffee and stood outside the door.

Owen motioned for him to enter. "Where did you go for my coffee?" Ty was clearly not holding Owen's coffee mug.

"Across the street. I got one for Brooke and myself as well." Ty's expression said that he was clearly pleased with himself.

"I see you haven't changed."

A smile shone in Ty's eyes. "There have been some changes."

Brooke caught the reference to his faith. She accepted the coffee and watched Ty sit across from Owen. Could God really change a person that much?

■ ■ ■

Owen called his assistant, Nathan, and another trusted agent into a private meeting room with Ty and Brooke. He reviewed the events and issued certain plans be put into place.

"Because this is such a high profile case, potentially affecting people in power, it is important to report only to me." Owen took a sip of his coffee, furrowed his eyebrows, and set down the cup. "Next time just get me black coffee from the break room."

"I'm not sure you can actually call the stuff in the break room coffee, but I'd be happy to save the five bucks." Ty shrugged and took a sip of his drink.

Owen laid a large pile of folders in front of Ty and placed his hand on the stack. "Most of these are your files. I know it's been over four years since you've seen them, but I want you to pour over them. See if there is something we missed. Someone we didn't investigate. Anything that seems off."

Ty nodded.

"Miss Dunbar." Owen crossed his arms at the table. "I need the names and addresses of your parents and your brother."

"I've not been in contact with my parents in over six years," Brooke told Owen.

It was one more piece of Brooke's life that Ty didn't know.

"Nonetheless, the man who contacted your brother also contacted them. We need to keep an eye out for activity."

Brooke nodded. She wrote out the requested information and slid the paper across the table. "What else do you need from me?" She glanced up at the man for direction.

"I need you to lay low. It may take Ty the rest of the week to peruse these files," Owen explained.

Ty glanced at the boxes of file folders. More than a week… he hadn't seen these folders in over four years.

Reading through his past cases was a stark reminder of the dark path he'd been headed down. Why did he allow himself to compromise what he knew was right? Was the money really that alluring? Was it for power?

His sister had been convinced that Ty would have made a wonderful politician. "People are drawn to you, Blake," his sister had told him. "You've got those baby blues that every woman is attracted to and a smile people trust."

Ty shook his head. *You can't lead people with your looks.* Ty recalled a scripture he read about God's perspective of physical appearance. "But the Lord said to Samuel, 'Do not look at his appearance or at the height of his stature, because I have rejected him; for God sees not as man sees, for man looks at the outward appearance, but the Lord looks at the heart.'" Ty knew 1 Samuel 16:7 from memory. It was his prayer that his heart was pleasing to the Lord.

He glanced quickly at Brooke. Her delicate features and feminine figure made her quite pleasing to the eyes. But where was her heart? Ty recalled another verse he'd read. It gave advise about what to look for in a woman. "Charm is deceitful and beauty is vain, but a woman who fears the Lord, she shall be praised." Proverbs 31:30. As lovely as she was, Brooke needed the Lord.

"Hey, Ty." Owen slipped into the chair beside him and let his eyes follow Ty's to Brooke. "You seem a little distracted."

Ty sensed a hint of suggestion in Owen's voice. "No, Owen. It's not like that."

"I hope not." Owen's tone was soft. "You know the risks."

■ ■ ■

"Mom! You look great! Have you lost weight?" Olivia greeted her mother with forced enthusiasm.

"You say that every time." Anne placed her hands lovingly on either side of her daughter's face. "And you know I love it." She gave her daughter's cheek a quick peck.

"How are you?" Olivia's husband greeted George with a professional handshake.

"Good. It was quite a surprise to have Olivia call and suggest a visit." George welcomed his son-in-law. "Come on inside. Let me get your jackets."

"We would have arrived earlier but got stuck in traffic just outside of New Jersey this morning. We lost at least two hours."

"That's not a fun way to start off a trip." George led them into the living room. "Do you have your bags?"

"Out in the car. Clayton can get them." Olivia motioned for her husband and sat across from her mother. "The house looks great. I saw the little garden bench out in the yard."

"Actually, we got it right after Blake died." Anne's face reddened. "We planted a little garden in his honor."

"Oh. I don't remember it." Olivia scanned the room with her large, gray eyes. "Did you and Dad paint?"

"We painted last summer. But I guess you haven't been up in a while. We also remodeled one of the guest rooms upstairs."

"I hope it's the one that had ducks all over it," Olivia laughed.

"It is. That wallpaper was severely out of date. Your dad stripped it and we went all out Pottery Barn."

Olivia nodded. "Nice! That's the room I want."

Clayton returned to the house carrying their bags.

"Take our stuff to the Pottery Barn room." Olivia stood up. "Come on, Mom, show me."

George and Clayton carried the bags upstairs while Anne and Olivia followed. "It looks like you redid the hallway!" Olivia was delighted.

"This is why you need to come around more often," George said.

"Oh my goodness!" Olivia walked into the recently remodeled guest room and did a three hundred and sixty degree turn around. "This is beautiful. I love the color. It's so muted and trendy. Good job, Mom."

"Your dad picked the paint color," Anne put her arm around her husband.

"Good job, Dad." Olivia patted her father's back. "You two are moving into the new decade."

"I need to hang up my dress shirts." Clayton stood just inside the doorway.

"There are hangers in the closet." Anne walked toward the bathroom with Olivia. "Wait until you see the color in here."

George followed them and assisted his wife in pointing out all the new features of the remodeled guest bathroom. "Even the faucet is new."

Olivia was the first one back out of the bathroom and saw her husband holding up a soiled suit jacket. She licked her lips and ran her hand over the sleeve. "Is this one of Blake's old jackets?" She turned around and found her parents only a few steps behind her.

Anne's face grew ashen and she glanced quickly at George.

"Yes," George took the jacket from Clayton and held it up. "We just hadn't parted with it yet."

"What did you do with most of Blake's stuff?" Olivia asked. She touched the jacket again and watched her father's expression.

"Donated it."

"But this one was in pretty bad shape. It needs thrown away." Anne shrugged. "I guess we forgot."

"I'll take it out to the garage." George hurried the jacket from the room.

Olivia and Clayton followed Anne back to the living room where they could catch up on life.

"It was a wonderful surprise to have you show up so soon after our visit to you." Anne changed the subject.

"Well, this might be our last chance for a while. Once the elections draw closer, my life will start spinning out of control."

George returned to the living room and sat beside his wife. "We kind of hoped you were coming to make an announcement." His blue eyes twinkled.

Olivia let out a dry chuckle. "Oh no, Dad… no kiddos here." She tugged at Clayton's shirtsleeve. "I'm not maternal."

Clayton agreed.

"Maybe you can live vicariously through the people in your new church." Olivia suggested.

"Did you get the A. W. Tozer book I sent you?" George asked. "It's got a powerful Christian message."

Olivia gave Clayton a knowing glance. "Yes, Dad. Thank you. That was so sweet." She flashed her pearly whites and nodded.

"Have you read it?"

"No. I haven't had time. But it is on my to do list." She cleared her throat. "It's been encouraging to see this new interest in your lives."

George nodded knowingly. "About thirty or forty years later than I wish."

"Oh, Dad… religion is one of those things that finds everyone at a different point in their lives. I think it's sweet that you and mom found it together."

Clayton pulled out his phone and checked his messages.

"Now, you know that Clayton and I want to treat you to dinner tonight, right?"

Anne nodded. "I didn't cook."

"Good. Not that I don't appreciate your cooking, Mom, but we're here to visit, not be served."

"Did you leave Mrs. Calvin a key to the house?" Clayton interrupted his wife. "She just texted me that she wanted to feed Cleo but can't find the key."

"She wasn't home when I stopped by this morning. Tell her I put the key in the planter next to her front door." Olivia sighed and shook her head. "Our neighbor is watching our cat."

Anne nodded. "Pets can make it difficult to travel."

Olivia agreed. "You have no idea." She sat up in her seat and changed her expression to that of delight. "But I'm so glad we're here. It will be wonderful to catch up."

■ ■ ■

Brooke rubbed her eyes and looked up from her computer. She'd been searching for nursing jobs all day, but nothing appealed to her. Why was she even doing this?

"Any luck?" Ty glanced up from his files and watched her close her laptop.

"Nothing that remotely appeals to me." She sighed. "But something has to pay the bills." She stood up and brushed the wrinkles from her suit skirt. "Maybe I'll just sell the suit and live off of that for a few months."

"Funny."

"How about you?" She reached for her water bottle. "Any leads?"

"No." Ty shook his head. "This seems hopeless."

"Don't get discouraged." Owen joined in. "We haven't even scratched the surface yet. Let's call it a day. Take that young lady out to dinner."

Dinner sounded great. Brooke put her laptop in her computer bag and zipped it shut.

"We'll see you in the morning." Ty left his files sitting where they were.

Owen was getting a phone call so he gave a quick wave.

"Where would you like to eat tonight?" Ty asked.

They walked toward the elevators together and Brooke turned to Ty. "Can we leave the city?"

"Where do you propose?"

Brooke didn't care. "Anywhere outside of New York City."

Ty was thoughtful for a moment as they rode the elevator down to the first floor. "Why don't we find a nice place on the waterfront?"

"The waterfront sounds good. Your father's sailboat is my new ideal."

Ty waved down a cab and opened the door for Brooke. "I think I know just the place." He gave the driver directions to a small café on the water.

"This is the best I can do on short notice."

Strings of lights hung over the tables and a jazz band played on one side of the restaurant. They were seated near a window, and Brooke looked outside at the moon over the water. "This works."

The service was surprisingly quick. Brooke glanced at the menu and ordered grilled salmon. She squeezed a lemon into her water and enjoyed the atmosphere.

"So, did you search out every nursing job in Cincinnati?" Ty asked.

"And Covington, and Columbus, and Maine."

"Maine?" He eyed her curiously. "It must have made an impression on you."

"I liked it."

"Is there anything or anyone keeping you in Cincinnati? Some boyfriend back home you forgot to mention?"

Brooke chuckled. "No, not at all. I went to school there and got a job right out of college." She shrugged. "There's really nothing keeping me in Cincinnati."

"It is a nice city."

"It is. I like Cincinnati, but I guess it's people that make a place feel like home." She glanced out at the lights on the pier. "How about you? Any grieving widow going by the name of Mrs. Blake Kendall?"

Blake grinned. "No. Blake didn't have a wife. He dated a little—nothing serious."

"And Ty Westgate?" Brooke pressed.

"No. Ty Westgate knows it's futile to pursue a relationship while in witness protection." He shook his head. "I'm surprised you haven't made a catch yet."

"I don't fish much."

"No?" Ty sounded surprised.

"I've dated a little, but…" she shrugged.

"I understand. My mom always told me I'd know when I found the right one."

The waiter brought their food and Ty prayed. Brooke was getting used to it.

They were both hungry and ate quietly for a few minutes.

"I've missed this place." Ty took a sip of his iced tea. "I used to come here in the summers. They open up the patio and put tables outside."

Brooke glanced at the large patio doors and imagined it would be nice to sit outside on a warm summer evening. Maybe she should try waitressing. "Do you suppose it's the same with career choices?"

"You mean knowing when you find the right one?"

Brooke nodded. Her eyes lingered on the flowers in the middle of their table. Fresh yellow daisies and a small bunch of baby's breath filled the simple yellow vase.

"I think God has given us all gifts, and it's our job to use those gifts and talents the way He created us to." Ty pulled one of the daisies out of the vase and placed it in Brooke's hair. "It looks prettier there."

Brooke left the flower in place and blushed. "How do we know what our talents are?" Her eyes searched his.

"I believe God works within the desires of our hearts."

"Art?" Brooke asked softly.

"If you love art and you've been given artistic talents, which I believe you have, then yes, Brooke, I would say that's the direction you should head."

"But there's no money in art."

"Who says? There are many avenues for art. You just have to

look for a niche. Do you like teaching? Do you like working with children?" Ty began. "I know many parents who are willing to invest in their children's education through art camps or art classes." He glanced around the room. "Then, there are places like this. Notice the walls? It took a serious artist to paint those designs."

Brooke glanced around the room. The walls were painted with a variety of swirls and shapes using bold, bright, colors.

"This artist found a niche." Ty said. "And you can too. There are many places that hire artists to do various types of work. There is also canvas art like you have at home. Get in with a good interior decorator and you could have a steady flow of business."

"I never thought of all those possibilities. You're so full of ideas."

"I like to dream." Ty placed the napkin on his plate and took a drink of his iced tea.

Brooke lowered her gaze to the table. "I don't think I have any dreams."

Ty placed his finger beneath her chin and gently raised her head. "You do, Brooke. You just need to find them." He studied her sad, brown eyes. "And the best way to find your dreams is to know the One Who gave you your gifts."

Brooke took the flower from her hair and studied it. She spun it around in her fingers and ran her fingers over the petals.

"He's an artist, you know," Ty added.

Brooke didn't move her eyes from the flower, but her lips curved into a smile. "I guess I would have to agree with you there."

Ty paused for a moment. "So, then I guess that means you don't deny His existence?"

"What is that supposed to mean?" Brooke glanced at him.

"Well, I'd like to understand your starting point. Every good lawyer seeks to understand the starting point. We can build on it from there."

"Hmm."

Ty accepted the bill from the waiter and paid with cash. "Sometimes a starting point needs to be washed clean, meaning I'd have to destroy false speculations. Other times we can build on what you already have. I was just curious if you actually believed in God."

Brooke pondered his statement for a moment. "I suppose in my case you'd have to destroy some speculations."

Ty raised his eyebrows. "You're giving away knowledge—that's helpful. Can you tell me what speculations we need to destroy?"

"I don't want to make it too easy on you, Ty. We wouldn't want your lawyer skills to get rusty, now—would we?"

"I told you, Ty's not a lawyer. Blake was a lawyer."

Brooke's eyes twinkled. "Well, Ty should have been one too because he is quite a talker."

Ty pulled out another flower and threw it at her. "Not funny!"

The waiter returned with Ty's change and Ty apologized for throwing the flower. "I'll include clean up in the tip." He smiled at the man.

As they rose from the table, Brooke noticed her purse hanging opened from the back of the chair. *No! This can't be happening.* "Ty—my wallet is gone."

■ ■ ■

"Let's get back to the hotel." Ty took Brooke's arm. "We need to cancel all of your credit cards before anyone uses them. If they get used all over New York City it will be obvious where you are."

"Even though I'm not the one using them?"

"If someone is watching for action on your cards, it will turn on a green light."

Brooke fidgeted with her hands.

"What was in your wallet?"

"My drivers license, social security card, Discover, Visa, a few random department stores…"

"How much cash?"

"None. I kept my cash in a separate compartment of my purse."

"That's good.

"But this is terrible." Brooke watched Ty wave down a taxi. "I'm scared."

"We'll take care of it. I'll help you. For that matter, we'll get the FBI on the case. We need to notify them immediately." He glanced at Brooke and saw the worry in her eyes. Their spiritual conversation was cut short and now she seemed miles away.

Brooke was quiet the whole way back to the hotel. Ty tried to think about the people who walked past their table in the short time they'd been at the restaurant. He'd not noticed anything strange. But a professional pickpocket could be discrete.

When they finally reached the hotel, Ty paid the driver and they hurried to Brooke's hotel room. She rushed to the bed and dumped her purse of its contents. "So, my Kohl's card was in the bottom of my purse."

"And your J.C. Penny." Ty pulled it from the pile.

"But my Visa and Discover are gone." She ran her fingers through her hair. "And my driver's license. Where am I going to get my driver's license replaced in New York City?"

"It will all work out."

Tears filled Brooke's eyes. "I haven't even let myself think about my condo and what may have been taken from there." She covered her face. "And now my wallet."

Ty placed a comforting hand on Brooke's back. *This is my fault. I dragged her into this situation.* He wished there was a way to take away her fears. "Let's start making phone calls."

It didn't take long to phone the various credit card companies.

"We will need to report your stolen social security card to the federal trade commission and your bank." Ty said. "We're also supposed to report it to the police, but I think we'd better go through the FBI since you're in hiding."

Brooke leaned over and placed her head on the pillow while Ty phoned Owen.

"Owen, it's Ty. We have a situation."

CHAPTER 10

The next two days, Ty worked with Owen, pouring over files. Brooke was encouraged not to worry about any of the items stolen from her purse. Owen had an agent working to stop any possible identity theft and to reissue her an Ohio driver's license without making her return to Ohio.

"If everyone who had their wallet stolen had their own personal FBI agent working on their case, it would make this country a much nicer place to live." Ty sat beside Brooke and handed her a thick slice of lemon bread.

Brooke gave him a weak smile. "That was pretty funny."

"But it didn't wipe that look of worry from your face."

"Owen said my Visa was used before we had the chance to cancel the cards." Brooke shifted nervously. "And what makes you think lemon bread will make it better?"

"It always does." He broke off part of it and popped it in his mouth. "We're almost done here and tomorrow is Sunday."

Brooke sighed.

"They said you should have your new driver's license by Monday."

"What are we doing tomorrow?" She asked.

"I was thinking about visiting a church and was hoping you'd go with me. I don't want to be alone in this big scary city."

"So, you need a woman to keep you safe?"

"I do. Will you go with me?" Ty took another piece of the lemon bread and stood up. "I told Owen I'd work another hour. We've found a couple discrepancies."

"Is that good?"

"It could be. Either that or my secretary was a terrible note taker." He winked. "We're actually missing a couple of files that I remember having. I know I gave Owen everything I had. But what we don't know is whether those files went missing before I gave them to the FBI or after. There were too many to notice at the time, and things moved pretty fast once we started knocking down the dominos."

"You mean someone may have tampered with your files before you got them to the FBI?"

"Maybe. Or else they tampered with them here. Either way—something's not right."

"Do you know what files are missing?"

Ty chewed on his lower lip. "Yes and no. It's complicated."

"Kind of like not knowing exactly what was in my wallet but knowing there was stuff there."

"Exactly."

■ ■ ■

"How did you find this church?" Brooke smoothed her skirt after Ty helped her out of the car. She glanced up at the large, brick building and white painted cross. The sign out front said, "Let's get real—Faith Bible Church."

"The internet." He reached for her arm. "I did a search for solid, Bible-teaching churches in the suburbs of New York City. This one came up."

"That's quite a specific search."

"It is. They gave a few sermon notes and even a video of last week's message. It sounded good."

Warm friendly faces greeted Brooke and Ty as they walked through the door. Brooke put on her own churchy smile and returned the friendliness.

The service began with contemporary worship songs and Brooke did her best to follow along. Ty seemed to know them all by heart. She glanced at him several times and noticed that his eyes were closed as he stood singing.

After a few announcements, someone led the congregation in a hymn. *At least I know this song.*

The sermon was on genuine faith and Brooke sat back and listened skeptically.

"For I determined to know nothing among you except Jesus Christ, and Him crucified. I was with you in weakness and in fear and in much trembling, and my message and my preaching were not in persuasive words of wisdom, but in demonstration of the Spirit and of power, so that your faith would not rest on the wisdom of men, but on the power of God." The pastor read from 1 Corinthians 2:2-5 and asked the congregation to bow their heads in prayer.

Brooke listened as the pastor talked about the passage. He discussed the difference between faith built on the wisdom of men and faith that rested on the power of God.

"As true believers, we should be living our faith in the power of God," he said.

The pastor gave a few examples from his own life, some of which were quite vulnerable. This was different than the sermons she'd heard as a child.

"Church," he said, directing the word to the people not the building. "We need to be the real thing. We need to live our faith. The world needs to see it in our actions, not simply our words."

Brooke glanced at Ty. He was taking notes.

The closing song was unfamiliar to Brooke, so she read the words rather than try to sing along.

There was a light in Ty's eyes when the song ended and he turned to smile at Brooke. "Thanks for coming with me today."

"I only did it because you were afraid to be alone," Brooke reminded him playfully.

"How did you like it?"

"It was different." Brooke noticed a man and two women hurrying toward them. "Here comes the greeting committee," she whispered.

"It was so nice to have you here this morning." A friendly woman in her mid-fifties shook Brooke's hand. "I hope you were blessed."

"Thank you." Brooke returned the friendliness with forced sincerity and listened while Ty told the man how much he loved the sermon.

"Do come back again," the other woman urged. "You two are an adorable couple."

"Thank you." Brooke slipped her arm through Ty's and smiled.

"Wonderful service. Thank you for stopping over to say hello." Ty gave the women a brief greeting.

After the greeters left, Ty and Brooke worked their way through the hospitable crowd to the door where they were given one final greeting from the pastor.

He shook Ty's hand. "Thank you for joining us today."

Ty nodded. "Thank you. I enjoyed your message."

Brooke did her best to slip past.

"And thank you for coming as well." The man extended his hand to Brooke.

"Thank you." She gave him a quick handshake and shot Ty a look that said, "let's go."

Once in the car, Ty stared at her for a minute. "You're used to church, aren't you?"

"Not that kind." Brooke cleared her throat.

"Was this better?"

"I didn't know any of the songs." She pulled down the sun visor and leaned back.

"You knew the hymn."

Brooke shrugged. "Okay, let's get lunch." She watched the cars pulling out of the church parking lot. "Since we're in the suburbs, I bet we could find one of my kind of restaurants."

"What's your kind of restaurant?" Ty pulled out onto the main road.

"Something with soup, salads, and sandwiches that cost under ten dollars a meal." Brooke scanned the buildings along the road looking for such an establishment.

"Can they have coffee too?" Ty asked.

"Yes."

"Panera Bread?" Ty saw it before she did.

"Yes! Look at that. A little piece of familiarity right here in New York." She leaned forward in anticipation.

"I sense some serious sarcasm. Did going to church put you in this mood?" Ty winked when she glanced at him.

Once inside, Brooke knew just what she wanted and ordered. Ty took a few minutes longer.

After a quick prayer of thanks for the food, Ty looked up at

Brooke. "So, did you like the sermon?"

"Ty, I made you promise not to ask me how I felt about the sermon if I went to church with you." Brooke took a bite of her salad.

"No you didn't."

Brooke shrugged. "Well I meant to." She glanced across the restaurant and spotted one of the women who'd greeted them at church. "Oh my goodness, she's here," Brooke whispered. "And I think she saw us."

"Hello." The woman smiled as she walked the full length of the restaurant with her husband in tow. "This is my husband, Donny. Honey, this is the couple I was telling you about from church today."

Donny greeted them both warmly.

"Can we join you?" She motioned to the two empty seats beside Ty and Brooke.

Brooke cleared her throat and smiled as she looked at Ty for help. *No. Please no.*

"Sure." Ty nodded.

"I don't think I caught your names this morning." She reached out to shake Ty's hand. "I'm Judy."

"Ty. Nice to meet you."

Brooke introduced herself and devoted her attention to the salad.

"Are you new to the area?" Donny asked.

"No. We're visiting." Ty took a bite of his soup.

"I forgot to order a coffee. Did you want one, dear?" Brooke placed a hand on Ty's back. She averted Judy and Donny's eyes.

"Sure. Get me the iced thing you mentioned."

Brooke grabbed her purse and got back in line. It was much easier to stand in line again than have to talk to the church people. Why did they annoy her? Maybe it was Judy. She reminded Brooke of someone from the church she'd attended as a child. Maybe it was Donny. He gave her the creeps.

After ordering their drinks, Brooke carried them to their seats and listened to the conversation Donny and Judy were having with Ty.

"My alcohol problem almost destroyed our marriage." Donny let out a burdened sigh. "I played the game every Sunday morning and drank away my problems the rest of the week."

Was he really saying this to a couple of strangers? Brooke glanced up at him curiously.

"But I loved my husband," Judy interjected. "I wasn't going to let the enemy win. I started praying and fasting and praying some more."

Brooke tore off a piece of her bread and dunked it in her soup.

"Then one Sunday, Donny said something had to change. We'd been going to church all our married life but he admitted he'd been faking it. He wanted a fresh start, so we started going to Faith."

"I went forward that morning and gave my life to the Lord." Donny's eyes lit up his face.

"I went with him to show him my support, tears falling the whole way."

"So, you're saying you went to church all those years and you weren't really a Christian?" Brooke wanted clarification.

Donny nodded. "I thought I was. I thought being a Christian was a title you were born with. Kind of like being German or Swedish."

Brooke crossed her arms.

"But it's a relationship," he added.

"And of course you stopped abusing alcohol after you became a Christian?" Brooke shot him a stern gaze.

Donny nodded. "I did. But, it didn't happen all at once. I had several setbacks."

"Were you abusive when you were drunk?" It was a fair question. He obviously wanted to tell them his whole life story.

Donny glanced at his wife with misty eyes. "I was a lot of things."

Brooke clenched her teeth. No wonder she didn't like this man. She turned her face away and stared out the window.

"But sin is sin." Ty placed a comforting hand on the man's arm. "We all sin and fall short of the glory of God. Thank you for sharing your testimony with us."

"Thank you for allowing me the privilege."

"I do hope the two of you will come back to our church some time," Judy invited sweetly.

"Thank you." Brooke turned on the same smile she'd used at church. "We should probably get going, Ty." She stood up and grabbed her tray. "It was a joy meeting you."

Ty spoke to the couple a few minutes longer and caught up with Brooke outside the restaurant.

She walked quietly to the car and noticed that he wasn't smiling. That's okay. She didn't feel like smiling either.

Ty was quiet as he pulled onto the main road. Was he mad at her? She crossed her arms and turned to face the window.

"Why were you so rude to them?" Ty broke the silence.

Brooke blew out a couple of heavy sighs. "They rubbed me the wrong way."

"And so you treated them like that?" Ty's tone carried with it all the disappointment she knew he was feeling for her at that moment.

"They didn't notice." Brooke crossed her legs and wished she were wearing blue jeans instead of her suit.

"I disagree. Judy is a discerning lady. She didn't stop being kind, but she could read your sickeningly fake sweetness."

Brooke kept her eyes focused on the passenger window.

"That man shared a very personal testimony with us. He obviously still grieves over his past."

What about the people he hurt? Brooke blinked back hot tears and clenched her teeth.

"I've never seen this side of you." Ty held both hands on the wheel and kept his gaze on the road.

"You've only known me a week and a half. There's a lot you don't know." Brooke wanted to get back to the hotel. She wanted to be alone.

Ty drove the rest of the way in silence. As soon as he parked, Brooke opened her own car door and walked toward the elevators without Ty.

"Brooke," Ty called out and hurried to catch up.

It took all her strength to keep her emotions at bay. Neither of them spoke as they rode the elevator to their floor. She hurried ahead of him and walked into her room.

Brooke locked the door that joined her room to Ty's, closed the large window curtain, and turned out the lights in her hotel room. Her heart was heavy with all the memories that flooded her mind.

She missed her little brother. The only other person in the entire world who knew what she'd lived through.

Great tears welled up in her eyes. Brooke sat on the floor with her back against the bed and gave into the pain. Ty could never understand. His family was perfect.

■ ■ ■

Ty left Brooke alone the rest of the day. She turned down his offer of dinner when he'd knocked on her door.

Reluctantly, he made his way to the hotel café and ate a small, over-priced meal.

Why had Brooke reacted so rudely to that couple? Was it in response to Judy mistakenly calling them an adorable couple? Brooke could have simply corrected the woman. Instead, she played along. *How was I supposed to correct that misunderstanding after Brooke played it up like that?*

Why was she so hard on Donny? Ty recalled the way Brooke's eyes flashed at the man when she asked him if he'd ever been abusive. The man was obviously repentant.

Ty finished dinner and returned to his room. He turned on the television and flipped through a few channels. After watching fifteen minutes of political talk, he turned it off. He was glad he was out of politics. Grabbing his Bible from the nightstand, Ty ran his hand over its smooth surface. What made her think to pack his Bible?

She was so close lipped when it came to spiritual conversations. Ty reflected on their conversation at the waterfront restaurant. She was finally opening up. Why did it have to end so abruptly? That was definitely the enemy. Ty shook his head. When would they have another opportunity like that?

He opened his Bible and tried to read a few chapters from the book of John. He glanced up at the wall that separated his room from Brooke's. *Why won't she talk to me?*

It was probably a lot to ask. They'd known each other less than two weeks. Why did it feel so much longer?

He closed his eyes and lifted her up in prayer. "Lord, how can I help her?"

■ ■ ■

"Where's Brooke?" Owen glanced up from the table when Ty

walked into the office the next morning.

"She didn't want to come today." Ty set down his coffee and pulled up a chair.

"Were you able to rack your brain for what pieces are missing from your files?"

Ty shook his head. "Not really. I think if I lay my files out the way I would have organized them in my office I might be able to visualize what's missing."

Owen liked the idea.

Ty spent most of the afternoon organizing his files. He let his mind drift back to the people that each file represented and what their cases were about. Some of them were simple clients with basic lawsuits. Others hired Ty to write up their legal and financial documents. Ty was forced to remember some of the compromises he'd made as a lawyer.

"I was a terrible lawyer." He glanced up at Owen with regret in his eyes.

"We all make mistakes," Owen said. "But not all of us have tangible files to remind us."

Ty grinned. "Thanks, Owen. I'm glad God doesn't keep files on our sins."

"You're really taking this God stuff seriously, aren't you?"

"It's the best thing that's ever happened in my life." It was good to be reminded. "I knew I messed up and the weight of it was all consuming. Learning that Jesus died for those sins and that He would throw them as far as the east is from the west was healing."

The conversation was deep, but Owen listened. Ty prayed that his FBI friend would come to the same knowledge of Jesus Christ.

When they returned to the files, Ty studied one grouping in particular. "The campaign files." He glanced up at Owen.

"What campaign files?"

"I had a whole section on them. They're gone." Ty scanned the stacks of files once more.

Owen called Nathan into the room. "Double check everything we have on Blake Kendall. We're looking for files specifically labeled campaign files."

Nathan nodded and went off to do as he was told.

"What were these files, Ty?" Owen sat across from the younger man and laid his hands on the table.

"They were documents about financial gifts and donations." Ty tried to recall everything in the files. "One of my clients asked me to make the evidence disappear." Ty sighed. "I hadn't accepted the case. I was swamped. That's why the files were all together. It happened right before I came clean with you about Anderson.

"I don't remember ever seeing those files."

Ty shook his head. "They may have been gone before I gave the FBI access to my office."

"Who would have been affected by those files?

Ty blew out a breath. "I'd have to really think. I only skimmed them."

"Do you remember who gave you the files?"

"One of the office assistants working for Jasmine Greenwich." Ty remembered that much.

"Who is Jasmine Greenwich?" Owen asked.

"She's a high profile lawyer. Worked for several politicians in D.C. at the time."

"Why would a lawyer from another office want to hire you to make something disappear?"

"Maybe she wanted out of it. Maybe she was in over her head. I'm not sure. I never talked to her." Ty ran his fingers through his hair and tried to think if he'd ever actually met her in person.

"Let's try to figure this out. Can you brainstorm? Who was running for office around that time?" Owen handed Ty a blank sheet of paper. "Let's roll with this."

■ ■ ■

Brooke wanted some alone time. She told Ty when he knocked on her door that morning that she preferred not to spend her day at the FBI. Ty didn't seem happy about it, but she stayed at the hotel.

Her heart was still heavy. Why did she let herself get worked up by that man and his wife? What must Ty think of her now for treating them that way? She'd been rude. Donny and Judy didn't deserve to be treated that way.

It was after lunch before she finally felt hungry enough to want to leave for a little while. The coffee shop across the street had wonderful blueberry muffins. She could venture that far by herself in this overwhelming city.

When she returned to her room, Brooke turned on her computer and went on-line. The solid oak craftsman style desk wasn't as large as the table where she'd been working in the FBI office, but it was comfortable, and working was a good distraction from her loneliness. She pulled up a national job search site and inserted her education and experience.

She looked good on paper. Brooke scanned over her answers. Nothing about this job search excited her. She had the skills of a nurse, but it wasn't what she loved. She shook her head and closed the site. What did she hope to find? Another job like she'd had in Cincinnati? What was the point?

How to make art your career... Brooke's fingers tapped across her keyboard and she waited to see what would come up. She was surprised at the selection of articles that appeared on her screen. One blogger even titled her article, *From Biologist to Artist. When pursuing what you love is more important than money.*

Brooke was soon pulled into her search and began reading articles written by people who shared her desire to make a living from art.

A knock at the door pulled her from a business site for artists. Assuming it was Ty, Brooke walked across the room and opened the door without looking through the eyehole.

A man wearing a ski mask pushed himself through the door and pointed a gun directly at her chest. "Don't scream."

Cold fear spiraled through her body and her mouth went dry.

He pulled the door closed and moved toward her. "I brought you something."

Brooke stepped backwards and almost tripped over her shoes. She stared at the gun in his black-gloved hand.

The man held up a bottle of vodka. "Thirsty?"

"I don't drink." Brooke heard herself say. It felt like someone else was talking. Brooke's hands trembled.

"Sure you do, Brooke," the man said. "I read the police report. Seven years ago, you were so drunk you fell down the stairs, got into an argument with your father, and caused your brother to get arrested. Remember that night?"

"It's not true."

The man set the bottle of vodka on the dresser. "This is expensive stuff. Imported from the Balkans. It's 176 proof." He motioned toward a hotel glass. "Bet you've never had anything like this before. Fill the glass."

Brooke shook her head.

"Fill the glass." The man motioned toward the alcohol.

"No." Brooke's eyes grew wide with fear and wet with tears.

"Do it, Brooke, or I'll send a bullet right through your heart."

Brooke stared at the man for what felt like a full minute, wondering what would be worse—to let him shoot her or to drink the alcohol? *Ty... where is Ty?*

"Maybe threatening to kill you isn't enough. Would you like me to get in touch with your brother?" The man motioned for the drink. "Colorado is a beautiful place to live. I hear Cody is quite the ski instructor. I would hate for him to have an accident."

At the mention of her brother, Brooke's heart sank. *Not Cody...* Brooke shook her head. Who was this man? How did he know so much about her? "Please—"

"Fill up your glass," The man ordered.

With unsteady hands, Brooke opened the bottle and filled the glass with the clear liquid.

"Now drink it."

Steadying her hand around the glass, Brooke lifted it to her lips. The smell of alcohol met her senses. She couldn't do it. She quickly turned the glass and splashed its contents into her assailant's face. While the man wiped his eyes Brooke made a run for it. He grabbed her arm and threw her to the floor.

"I was going to make it easy." He smacked her across the face with the backside of his hand. His eyes were red from the fiery liquid and he blinked a few times, but he straddled her on the floor and held the bottle to her lips. "Drink it!"

Brooke tried to resist. She dug her fingernails into the man's skin, but he clutched one hand around her throat while he forced the bottle into her mouth. She had to swallow in order to breathe.

She'd consumed half the bottle before he finally pulled it away.

Her face and hair were covered with the strong smelling liquid.

The room spun. Brooke did her best to blink back the blur. Her attacker laughed triumphantly and pulled Brooke to her feet. "Maybe now you'll drink it like a civilized person." He dragged her across the room. Brooke could hardly walk. He shoved her toward the bed and picked up the glass from the floor.

Brooke couldn't think. "Please no." She clutched the bedspread hoping it would keep her from sliding off the bed. Brooke was sure she was sliding.

The masked man wiped the glass and handed it to Brooke. He wiped the bottle and filled the glass. "Drink it."

Brooke was too dizzy to refuse. She forced down the liquid while tears slipped down her frightened dark eyes.

The man handed her the bottle and made her pour another glass.

"No more," she tried to say, but the words wouldn't come out. There was no refusing. Her assailant was determined to watch her drink the whole bottle.

Minutes passed but they felt like hours. Brooke felt sick. She felt herself slide off the bed. The man made her sit back up and fill her glass. Brooke couldn't even think clear enough to know what was happening. How much had she drunk? She felt like dying. *Oh God, please help me!* Brooke was sure she'd said the words out loud. The man told her to finish the glass. Brooke held it to her lips and felt herself sinking.

"No Cody! Don't hit him!" Was that Cody standing beside her?

She raised the glass to her lips and the world went black.

Chapter 11

Ty glanced at the clock and stretched. "I should get back to the hotel. Brooke's been there alone all day."

Owen nodded. "Where are you guys staying? The Waldorf?" he teased.

"Yes." Ty put on his suit jacket and brushed off the sleeves.

"You're too predictable." Owen shook his head. "You do realize that's where I would look for you if I were trying to find you in New York City."

"I trust the Waldorf. They're good at protecting privacy." Ty walked toward the elevators and thought he heard thunder. He hoped it wasn't raining outside. He'd forgotten to grab his umbrella.

It only took a moment to wave down a taxi, and Ty climbed in before the rain broke free.

Ty was at the hotel in minutes and hurried inside to avoid getting soaked. He hoped Brooke was ready to talk to him. He missed her.

Brooke didn't answer when he knocked on her door. Ty couldn't imagine Brooke going anywhere alone. He knocked again and called for her.

"I'm going to unlock the door myself if you don't answer." Ty gave one final knock and slid the key reader into the door.

The smell of alcohol met Ty's senses as soon as he opened the door. Brooke lay lifeless on the floor. "Brooke!" He ran to her and tried to wake her up, but her body was completely limp. "Brooke!" His hands trembled with fear. He made sure she was breathing and dialed 911.

Ty lifted her to the bed and brushed the hair away from her face.

When would the paramedics get there? What was taking them so long?

Ty's eyes moved wildly around the room. An empty bottle of

vodka lay on the floor where he'd found her. A half eaten muffin and a cup of coffee were all indicators that she'd been out that day.

Ty rubbed her hands and tried talking to her. Brooke lay motionless.

"Why did you do this, Brooke?" Ty clenched his teeth to ward off tears. "Brooke, why?"

The paramedics finally arrived and began working to revive her. Ty heard one of the paramedics mention alcohol poisoning another said something about a coma.

They hurried Brooke to the ambulance and made room for Ty beside her limp body. He held her hand and prayed. *Why Lord? Why did she do this?*

The hospital wasn't far and Ty stayed with Brooke as they ushered her into the ER. He felt helpless. What good was a law degree or a business degree? Somebody save her life!

"Sir, we need you to step outside." A nurse motioned him toward the door. Was this one of those tired over worked nurses?

Brooke...

Ty sat on a waiting room chair and stared blankly at the wall. A painting of the well at Bethesda took up one portion of the wall. Brooke could paint the well at Bethesda.

People asked him questions. A policeman arrived. Ty's head swam. He walked away from them and called Owen.

The FBI agent promised to be there right away. Ty leaned forward with his face in his hands. *Your rod and your staff they comfort me...* Ty wished he could remember the whole Psalm, but those few words refreshed his mind.

Was this because he'd brought her to church yesterday? Was she under spiritual attack? Why didn't he make her talk to him last night?

The clock seemed to stand still. Ty watched each second and wondered when Owen would arrive.

"Ty," the familiar voice greeted him with concern. "What happened?"

"I found her unconscious on the floor of her hotel room with an empty bottle of vodka."

"Why on earth?" Owen shook his head.

"There's a policeman over there who wants to take down a report." Ty motioned to the man who'd been bothering him for the past half hour.

"I'll take care of him." Owen placed his hand on Ty's back. "Just sit tight. I'll be right back."

Ty leaned his head back and relived the terrible image of Brooke lying unconscious on the floor. What if she died? People died from alcohol poisoning.

God, please don't let her die. Ty put his face in his hands and felt a rush of emotion overtake him. *Why did she do it, Lord? Why?*

Hours passed. Ty paced the room, sat on his chair, and paced some more. Owen went to their hotel to investigate and returned with information he said might shed some light on the situation.

"This was seven years ago. The police report says she was so drunk she fell down the stairs and hurt herself. She evidently argued with her father, her brother got involved, and he was arrested." Owen scanned the report to make sure he wasn't missing anything.

Ty rubbed his temples. His head ached.

"She must have a drinking problem." Owen leaned forward on his knees.

"I wish they would tell me something." Ty got up to pace some more.

"You really care about this woman, don't you?" Owen asked.

Ty stopped and sat down. "I brought her into this, Owen. This is my fault."

"You can't blame yourself." Owen put his hand out to stop Ty's tirade.

"She's my friend, Owen. She laid down everything to help me." Ty leaned his head against the wall. "I don't want her to die."

■ ■ ■

It was afternoon of the next day before Brooke was coherent enough for a visitor. Her eyes met Ty's and filled with tears.

"I was so scared." She held her hands to her face and let her emotions wash over her.

Ty sat beside her on a chair and reached to take her hand. "I was scared too."

Brooke's head ached and she felt dry in the mouth, but at least she could think again.

"Why did you do it, Brooke?" Ty finally asked. His eyes were misty and the dark circles under them were evidence of his lack of sleep.

Brooke tilted her head to one side. "What?"

"Why did you drink yourself into an oblivion? The doctors said it's a miracle you aren't dead. The amount of alcohol in your body was enough to kill a person twice your size."

It took a moment for Brooke to process his question. He thought she did it by choice? She shook her head. "I didn't do it."

"Brooke, don't… I just want to know why."

"Ty," Brooke's eyes filled with tears. "I didn't do it. Some man came to my room…"

Ty took a few steadying breaths and tightened his grasp on her hand. He touched a bruise on her wrist and rubbed it gently. "We can talk about it later."

Brooke's dark eyes took on a new kind of pain. "No. Ty, you need to hear me. I didn't do this to myself. Yesterday afternoon, someone came to my room. He was wearing a dark ski mask. I opened the door because I thought it was you—"

Ty placed his fingers over her lips. "Stop Brooke. You're not making any sense."

Brooke pulled her hand away. "I'm not imagining this. I remember everything up to the point when he held the bottle to my mouth. I could hardly breathe. I had to swallow. Then everything is a blur."

Owen knocked on the door outside the room. "How's she doing?"

Ty got up, walked to the FBI agent, and shrugged.

"Tell him, Ty. Please…" Brooke's tone was desperate. "Owen, someone came into my room yesterday and forced me to drink."

Owen gave Ty a sympathetic shake of the head.

"Please." Tears filled Brooke's eyes. "You've got to believe me. The man knew my name. He knew my brother's name and that Cody is a ski instructor in Colorado."

"Brooke," Owen interrupted her. "You were drunk, alone in your hotel room."'

Ty turned his back to her. "I can't listen to this."

Brooke's stomach heaved at the thought that they wouldn't believe her. It was just like her childhood. It was just like high school. *They don't believe me.* "He knocked me on the floor and forced the bottle into my mouth." Brooke ran her tongue along her teeth to make sure none of them were chipped. "I remember him grabbing my wrist. We struggled…"

Ty turned around and reached for the hand he'd held when he first came into the room. Her wrist was bruised in a circle. "Look at this bruise."

Owen studied her wrist.

"What else did he do?" Ty searched her face. He brushed her hair away from her cheek and exposed three distinct red lines across her face. "Did he slap you?"

"Yes. I splashed the first glass into his eyes. He threw me to the floor and slapped me. I remember that much. He had a gun… with something on the end of it—a silencer."

"Do you have any other bruises?" Owen asked.

"I don't know," Brooke shook her head.

Ty glanced at Owen. "Look at the marks on her neck."

Brooke winced at his touch.

"Did the man try to choke you?" Ty placed a comforting hand on her arm.

"He held me down with the bottle in my mouth. One of his hands held my throat. I fought him as best as I could." Brooke trembled.

Owen walked toward the door. "I'll order prints on the room."

Ty sat beside her on the side of her bed. "You promise you're not making this up?" His face was strained with emotion.

Brooke stared at him in disbelief. How could he ask that? "I don't drink, Ty. Ever."

"Owen found a police report…"

Tears rushed from her eyes. "That police report is a lie, Ty. The man who came to my hotel room—he mentioned the police report." Brooke shook her head. "It was my dad who was drunk that day. My parents lied." Sobs shook Brooke's body and Ty leaned forward to hold her.

■ ■ ■

"We need to check you and Brooke out of these rooms." Owen met Ty at the hotel later that afternoon.

"What did you find?"

"We're having the bottle and the glass checked for prints," Owen began. "The man at the front desk is certain Brooke only left the hotel once after lunch and she carried back a coffee and a small pastry box from the café across the street. We're running video footage of the hotel entrance to see if it shows anything else."

Ty's eyes traveled around the room.

"We also found broken fingernails on the carpet." Owen held up the evidence bag. "They were dug into the fibers."

"Like she was fighting to get up."

"Perhaps." Owen nodded. "We'll need to see if these are hers."

Ty tried to remember if her fingernails were broken. "I plan to return to the hospital soon."

"Well, we're taking your stuff and Brooke's stuff to the office until you and Brooke can find another hotel. If what Brooke said is true, the two of you have been found."

"Were they trying to kill her or send a message to me?" Ty licked his dry lips.

"After hearing what her blood alcohol levels were, I'd have to say this was attempted murder. And for whatever reason, they tried to make it look like she did it herself."

Ty told Owen what Brooke said about the faulty police report. "She claims it was her father who was drunk and that her parents accused her to make an excuse for her bruises." Ty wished he knew more about this story. "Was an alcohol test ever done on her seven years ago?"

"I don't remember seeing anything mentioned about it. The only arrest was her brother, Cody. Evidently he attacked his father in front of the policeman. It was assumed he was drunk, too."

Ty tried to process it all. "Confirm that detail on the report, will you?" he asked Owen.

Owen nodded. "I'll let you know when we get the reports back."

■ ■ ■

Brooke's eyes opened when Ty walked into her hospital room.

"Hi." His tone was soft.

Something lit up on her face when she saw him.

Ty pulled a chair close to her bed and took her hand. There was a long awkward pause. Brooke wondered what he was about to say. She'd wrestled with all kinds of emotions since she'd woken up. What if no one believed her? What if the man who'd attacked her yesterday came back to finish the job?

"I'm sorry I didn't believe you." Ty broke through her thoughts. "I feel terrible." He shook his head. "I didn't know what to think. I was so worried about you… but the bottle of vodka… I just assumed."

Brooke felt a rush of relief. He believed her. If nothing else, at least he believed her. Tears filled her eyes. "I forgive you."

Ty turned her hand over in his and studied her fingernails. They were broken. "The FBI found your fingernails in the room."

Brooke glanced at her free hand. "I'm not sure how I did this."

Ty blew out a heavy breath. "Someone tried to kill you, Brooke."

She lowered her eyes.

"And it's my fault." There was moisture in his eyes.

"Please don't…"

Ty smoothed the hair away from her face. "I can't even imagine what you must have been going through. You must have been terrified," he said with emotion. "I should never have left you alone at the hotel."

"It was my own stubborn fault." Brooke reached up and touched Ty's hand on her face. "And I'm sorry too."

"Brooke—"

"Don't I get those words?" She gazed into his eyes.

"I forgive you." Ty's lips curved into a sad smile. He steadied his eyes on hers and lowered his hand. "I have a lot of questions, Brooke."

She knew he would. But telling people only left her hurting more. No one ever believed her. There were all those lies to cover things up. "I don't know—"

"Not right now." Ty tightened his hand on hers. "You need to rest. Owen is finding us a new place to stay. The doctor said you'd be released tomorrow morning." Ty glanced at the clock. "And I'm not going anywhere."

Brooke closed her eyes. The hospital bed was nowhere near as comfortable as her huge, pillow-filled bed at the Waldorf, but Ty was here and she was safe.

■ ■ ■

Ty handed Owen a piece of paper and pulled out a chair for Brooke. Owen and Nathan sat across from the couple and scanned the list of names.

"This is a good list." Owen glanced up.

"But it's all speculative." Ty opened a bottle of water and made himself comfortable in the FBI office chair. "I'm just going by memory."

Owen pointed to a few names and Nathan got up to get something. "It's a starting point. If any of these people had something to hide four and a half years ago, chances are they have something to hide now." He patted the list. "We simply need to start digging."

It sounded good. Ty wasn't sure what more he could do at this point. He'd exhausted his resources. He'd gone through his files so many times he practically had them memorized. "What did you find out about Brooke's assailant?"

Owen glanced at Brooke apprehensively.

"It's okay. I want to know." Brooke crossed her legs and laid her hands on the table.

"There was DNA in her fingernail fragments." Owen opened a file and pulled out a crime photo. "It belongs to this man."

Ty took the picture and Brooke leaned over to study the face.

"You must have dug your fingernails into his flesh pretty deep because you drew blood."

"Who is he?" Ty hoped she dug deep enough to make it really hurt.

"He goes by the name Mike Rider." Owen pulled out a rap sheet. "He also has a few other aliases. He spent some time in prison for armed robbery and was accused, but never charged, of murder." Owen studied Brooke's frightened expression. "Someone hired him and I want to find out who." He took the picture from Ty and returned it to the file. "Does he look like the man who called himself Vince Gearhart?" he asked Brooke.

Brooke shook her head. "No. I don't recognize him."

"We're running hotel video monitoring to see if we can find out when he arrived and left."

"Did you find out anything else?" Ty asked.

"The bottle and glass were both wiped clean of all prints but hers."

Brooke lowered her eyes.

"But that's okay," Owen reassured her. "In what world does a bottle of alcohol only have one set of prints?"

"What do you mean?" Brooke asked.

"There were no other prints," Owen reiterated. "What about the store proprietor? What about the alcohol distributer who put the bottle on the shelf? Where are those prints? The bottle you had was intentionally wiped clean before it was given to you."

Ty reached over and placed a comforting hand on her back.

Nathan knocked on the door and motioned toward the outer office.

"Is he here?" Owen asked.

"Yes."

"Ty," Owen leaned forward. "Wyatt Longstreth from the Marshal's office is here to see you."

Ty wasn't sure what to expect.

"I've already talked to him and verified his position. He's on our side, Ty." Owen stood up. "He'd like to talk to you for a few minutes," he said to Ty. "Brooke, why don't we go get a cup of coffee across the street?"

Brooke was safe with Owen. Ty watched her leave the room and waited to meet Officer Longstreth."

■ ■ ■

Ty stood up to greet the U.S. Marshal and felt incredibly short. Wyatt's hands practically swallowed Ty's and he couldn't remember ever feeling so small around a person since he was in junior high.

"Glad to finally meet you." Wyatt took a chair and motioned for Ty to sit. "Although I'm still not sure you exist." He tossed a computer sheet to Ty.

Ty read the words "Not in system" under his witness identification number and looked confused.

"I, of course, see now that you are indeed a real person and I realize there is something wrong with our system and not you." Wyatt pulled the computer sheet back to himself and tapped the paper. "I was hoping to meet you on Tuesday, but Owen let me know what happened."

Ty nodded.

"We're going to hide you in Maryland for a little while." Wyatt leaned back in his seat. "Matthew Pratt is dead."

Ty felt the wind leave his body. "What happened to him?"

"We found his body last week." Wyatt scratched his face. "We know his computer files have been tampered with but so far yours is the only one we know has been deleted. Until we can retrieve the files, we won't know who else is missing unless they call us." Ty ran his fingers through his hair. "Do you have any leads?"

"None. I'm going to go over the stuff you and Owen have been working on and see if I can find any links." Wyatt shook his head. "Matthew was a good guy."

Ty agreed. "I trusted him completely."

"He left a family." Wyatt blew out a heavy sigh. "I aim to catch these people."

"I couldn't agree more."

"Tell me about Brooke Dunbar." Wyatt crossed his strong arms across his barrel chest. "How is she involved?"

"She saved my life," Ty began. He gave Wyatt a brief overview of the events that led to where they were now.

"So, she's not your girlfriend?"

"No. I've only known her for two weeks."

Wyatt attempted to hide a smile. "Well, I've got the two of you staying at a little ranch house in Maryland as Mr. and Mrs. Duncan."

"Mr. and Mrs.?"

Wyatt grinned and scratched his head. "It's a three bedroom house so… I'll let you both figure it out."

"What are our first names?"

"You're Carter and she's Jessica." Wyatt handed Ty his Maryland driver's license.

"Carter?" Ty raised his eyebrows. "Really?"

"It should only be for a few weeks."

Ty glanced toward the window. "I kind of like Ty."

"We'll try to bring these guys down and then you can be Ty or even Blake Kendall again if you want."

"What about my dad's car?"

"We'll take care of it. We got you a Toyota Camry." Wyatt handed Ty two sets of keys, two cell phones, the address of the safe house, and credit cards in both of their new names. "This is for groceries, gas, and necessities." He glanced over Ty's fine suit. "Make sure you lay low."

"I assume you'll be in touch with me?" Ty picked up the phone.

Wyatt nodded. "You can call Owen and myself. Don't call your parents."

Both men glanced up when Owen knocked on the door. "Can we come in?"

Wyatt nodded and motioned for Brooke to take a seat beside Ty.

"Are my parents safe?" Ty fidgeted with the new keys and concern showed in his blue eyes.

"I think so. Does anyone else know you were there?" Wyatt pulled a few more things from his briefcase.

Ty couldn't imagine his parents telling Olivia and Clayton.

"Ty's sister visited the day after Ty and Brooke left." Owen passed Ty a mocha cappuccino and sat beside Wyatt.

Wyatt glanced over Ty's profile. "Olivia Davis is your sister?"

Ty nodded.

"Was your sister ever one of your clients?"

"No." Ty shook his head. "We never mixed family with work." He caught the look Wyatt gave Owen. "No! My sister would never have tried to kill me." Ty fought the unsettling feelings in his stomach. He hoped Olivia was not going to be dragged into this. She was right in the middle of an election campaign and did not need a scandal. "Leave Olivia out of this, please. I don't want more people I care about getting hurt."

"I understand." Owen placed a calming hand on Ty's arm. "We might look into things, but we'll make sure we're quiet."

Ty blew out a frustrated breath. Look into Olivia? What was the point? If this leaked out to anyone it could taint her career. This is why politicians shouldn't have criminals in the family.

Wyatt directed his attention to Brooke, who was waiting to be given her instructions.

"Ms. Dunbar." Wyatt handed Brooke her Maryland driver's license. "You are now Jessica Duncan and… this is your husband, Carter." He glanced at Owen.

"You made them a couple?" Owen's eyes grew wide.

"I didn't know. I thought she was his girlfriend." Wyatt gave an apologetic shrug. "It's just temporary. You're not really married. You said they needed to be hidden together." He glanced at Brooke. "The safe house is a three bedroom in the suburbs. You can each have your own room."

Brooke took the license.

"Upon your initial disappearance you do need to know that your parents were notified." Wyatt continued. "They too had been contacted by this Vince Gearhart, who we still have not identified. Your parents admitted that they had not seen or heard from you in over six years."

Brooke nodded.

"Owen told me that the man who assaulted you Monday night made threats concerning your brother. Have you been in touch with Cody?" Wyatt glanced over the file to make sure he'd gotten the name correct.

Brooke explained the email and told them she'd deleted her email account.

"That was a good move."

"I've had someone get in touch with Cody, and we are keeping an eye on him to make sure he's safe," Owen explained.

Ty took a long sip of his coffee and reached to place a comforting hand on Brooke's back. "When do we leave?" he asked the two agents.

"You can go now." Wyatt rose to his feet. "I'll take you to the Camry and you can head directly to your safe house."

CHAPTER 12

Brooke released a breath of relief as they left the city and headed toward Maryland. It didn't matter that the car was small and the seats weren't leather, she was glad to be out of New York.

"So we have to pretend we're married?" Brooke pulled her new license out of her purse and studied her fake name. "Why did they choose Jessica?"

"Why did they choose Carter?" Ty glanced at her from the corner of his eyes. "Please still call me Ty."

"The house looks cute." Brooke glanced over the photo and description. "One thousand, four hundred and seven square feet, three bedrooms with two full bathrooms." She glanced up and grinned. "It would fit in your parents' living room."

Ty laughed. "It would not. It's a nice-sized house."

"Where is Glen Burnie? Will we be near the water?"

"Check the map. I think Glen Burnie is near Chesapeake Bay."

Brooke found it on the map. "How did you know that? I've never even heard of it."

"I've seen the exit signs when I've traveled between New York and Washington D.C." Ty switched lanes and set the car on cruise.

"Have you been to D.C. very often?

Ty shrugged. "My work took me to D.C. once in a while. I've also gone down to visit my sister."

Brooke studied Ty curiously. "You're sister is running for senator?" She'd been surprised when the Marshal said it, but had kept her questions to herself.

"Yes." Ty's facial expression showed stress. "I sincerely hope this doesn't cause any problems for her. She's in the middle of a campaign."

"Wow. I didn't realize she was so high up." Ty's wealthy, high profile family was a bit intimidating. "What about her husband?"

"Clayton is her behind-the-scenes guy." He glanced quickly at Brooke. "He's her campaign manager, her schedule keeper, and the one who brushes her cat."

"The one who brushes her cat?" It sounded disrespectful. "Are they a cute couple?"

"Cute?" Ty chuckled. "Olivia looks good. She's… well, she became a blonde while I was in college and it suits her. She keeps herself in shape and dresses almost, let me say that again, almost as well as me."

Brooke slapped his arm playfully. "I don't even want to know what you think of the way I dress."

"Well, I've only seen you in about five different outfits. Although, I'd say you look lovely in all of them. Which one is your real style?"

"I like them all."

"Especially the suit though, right?" He winked at her. "We'll get some more clothes when we get to Glen Burnie. I'm sure there's a mall around there somewhere."

They were both in need of clothes and Brooke was happy to comply.

"We also need to buy wedding bands." Ty steered the car into the slow lane so another car could pass him. "Do you think the U.S. Marshals office would pay for platinum?"

"Doubtful." Brooke leaned back and looked out the window. "How long will we have to pretend to be married?" she asked.

"You want a divorce already?" Ty cleared his throat.

"No. I mean…" she blew out a sigh. "How are we going to do this?"

"You can have the master bedroom and I'll take the next largest."

"Can we get a dog?" Brooke tried to be funny.

"No dog. I think Carter is allergic."

"What does he do for a living?"

"He keeps a low profile," Ty chuckled. "Wyatt made that very clear and did you see the abs on that guy? I don't want to make him angry."

■ ■ ■

The house in Glen Burnie was a newly built ranch in a neighborhood of moderate-sized houses. The inside was completely furnished with clean, new furniture. A long, black kitchen island extended into the great room where a plush gray couch and matching loveseat filled the space beside the fireplace. A dining room table and six chairs were placed beside a set of double patio doors overlooking a fenced in back yard.

"It looks nice." Brooke glanced at Ty to gauge his response."

"Not bad."

"Do we have Wi-Fi?" Brooke set her bag down on the kitchen counter and walked around to the cabinets to peek inside.

"Doubtful. And chances are the phones are monitored." Ty carried her suitcase to the master bedroom and Brooke followed. "It's clean. That says a lot."

Brooke nodded. The master bedroom was as large as the living room. A king-sized bed covered in a dark blue comforter and piled high with colorful pillows filled the center of the room.

"Did you see the sun room?" He opened a French door on one side of the bedroom and motioned to the enclosed porch. "We should find an art store, buy some supplies, and set up a little studio for you."

"Ah, so Jessica is an artist?"

"Yes. I'm her behind the scenes guy. Her agent."

"You brush my cat." Brooke sat on the bed and hoped her joke didn't offend Ty.

Ty chuckled and walked to his own bedroom to hang up his suit. "I figure we'll run out and get some dinner, do a little shopping and explore our new town," Ty said to Brooke as she walked passed his door.

She glanced inside. Ty's room was smaller, but had a walnut desk under a window and a skylight over the bed. "Can we swing by the bay tonight?"

"Why don't we get our supplies tonight and find a park along the bay tomorrow? We can spend the day there. I haven't taken my wife out on a nice date for a while. What do you think?"

"I think Jessica would enjoy that."

■ ■ ■

Brooke sat on the sand, overlooking the water, and breathed in a deep, satisfying breath. The familiar smell of autumn leaves flooded her senses. The sound of water rolling across the sand mingled with the sound of birds, readying themselves for their journey south. The Chesapeake Bay Bridge stretched across the horizon, taking travelers over the Chesapeake Bay to the peninsula. It was a peaceful place—a sharp contrast to the craziness of New York City.

"So what do you think of Sandy Point State Park?" Ty asked. He took a seat beside her on the sand and handed her a bottle of water.

"I think it's just what I needed." Brooke lay back and let the sunshine warm her face.

"Kind of like a vacation from our adventures." Ty leaned back beside her and lifted his hand in front of his face to study his new ring. "I like yellow gold."

Brooke held out her hand and studied her matching band. "But I got cheated out of an engagement ring."

"Hey, it was a short engagement. Give me a break."

Brooke dug her fingers into the cool sand and let herself enjoy the moment. "Remind me again how you proposed—and make it sound romantic."

"Well we were on my father's yacht." Ty played along.

"A yacht?" Brooke glanced over at him and scowled.

"You like the sailboat better?"

"Yes. I love the sailboat." She smiled.

"Okay. We were on the sailboat. Just the two of us." Ty glanced at Brooke. "I took you out of the harbor to a small island where I used to go as a child."

"Did you really?" Brooke sounded excited.

"Did I really take you there, or did I really go there as a child?"

"Sorry, go on."

"Yes, I really went there and let me finish my recollection of our engagement story." Ty cleared his throat. "We both sat on a rock and put our feet in the water. It was cold, but we didn't mind."

"Were my toenails painted?"

"Pink. Very soft pink. Like your lips." Ty winked at her and continued. "It was there that I took your hand and held it close. I told you that I didn't have much in the way of the world, but that I love you. I told you that I'd prayed ever since I gave my life to Christ that God would send the right woman for me. 'Charm is deceitful and beauty is vain, but a woman who fears the Lord, she shall be praised.'" Ty quoted. "I told you that I respected your talents, your intelligence and your heart for others. You told me that you respected my great taste in clothes and incredible wit."

Brooke caught the smirk that crossed his lips.

"Then I kissed each one of your fingers and I brushed your long brown hair away from your face and asked you to spend the rest of your life with me."

Brooke swallowed hard and sat up in the sand. "And then I dropped the bomb that I'm not a Christian and that you had no place marrying me."

"No, you didn't. I made sure you were a Christian before I asked."

Brooke threw a handful of sand at Ty.

"Hey, that's the way I remember it!" Ty threw a handful of sand back at her. "How do you remember it?"

Brooke brushed the sand off her lap and sniffed. "Well, I remember the boat. It was a beautiful day. The sky was blue and the grass was green. You sailed the boat out of the bay to your little island." Brooke glanced at Ty to see if he was listening. He smiled and sat up next to her. "We did put our toes in the water and I was wearing pink nail polish just like you said. But you also had your phone with you and turned on some country music."

"Oh, yeah, I remember that." Ty grinned.

"You said all those nice things to me and kissed my fingers. That was a nice touch." Brooke glanced playfully at Ty. "But then..." Brooke was quiet for a few moments and her face grew pensive. "Then I told you that you wouldn't want me." Brooke's eyes grew misty and she watched the water splash against the rocks. "I'm damaged goods, I'm a mess... you're from such a nice, normal family. Mine..." Brooke swallowed a lump in her throat. "There are too many dark secrets." She shook her head.

Ty studied Brooke's face intently and waited for her to gather her emotions. "Did you tell them to me?" he asked softly.

"No. I couldn't tell anyone. It's one of those things you struggle with alone."

Ty reached for her hand. "You don't have to be alone."

"But I am." Brooke pulled her legs up close to herself and wrapped her arms around them.

"That's your choice."

"I don't have choices." Brooke's dark eyes flashed painfully at Ty.

"You do about this." Ty steadied his gaze on Brooke. "You choose how you will respond to the things that happened in your life. You choose whether or not you're going to let God take your hurts and wash away the past. You choose—"

"God?" Brooke spat. "Really? Ty, you have no idea."

"Tell me then."

"I've never told anyone." Brooke wiped away her tears. "Not really." She lowered her face into her knees and let her sorrow wash over her.

■ ■ ■

Ty prayed for the right words to say at the right moment. Brooke was obviously dealing with a heavy burden and he figured it was wrapped up in the relationship she had with her parents.

When Brooke finally lifted her head, she took a sip of her bottled water and wiped her eyes on her sleeve.

"You don't have to tell me," Ty began. "But I'd love to be your friend."

Brooke was quiet for a few minutes. " I grew up in an abusive home."

Ty let the words sink in. "What kind of abuse?"

"Every."

A lump rose in Ty's throat.

"My father was an alcoholic," she continued. "We went to church on Sunday and he drank the rest of the week."

"Like Donny…"

"Yeah." Brooke nodded. "He was usually just angry. Cody and

I did our best to avoid him and Mom kept busy with her job. The sexual abuse only happened a couple of times. Cody doesn't even know about that. I was ten. I tried to tell my mom but she told me I was making things up."

"She didn't believe you?"

"No. She said a few touches didn't mean I'd been sexually abused."

Tears filled Ty's blue eyes and he let them flow freely.

"The physical abuse was the worst." Brooke kept her eyes on the water. "He actually broke my arm once."

"Didn't the authorities step in?" Ty's anger mounted and he wanted to beat this man to a pulp.

"The authorities didn't know." Brooke explained. "I tried to tell on my dad a couple times, but my parents always found a way to discredit me. Sometimes they blamed the bruises on Cody, other times they told people I was a klutz."

Ty wanted to hug her, to comfort her, to take away her pain.

"From the outside we looked like a normal family. Dad had a good job. Mom had a good job. We lived in a nice house in the suburbs. But my dad was controlling and my mom wanted to keep up appearances." Brooke sighed. "When my dad told me I should study nursing, that's what I did. They paid for my school and I moved to Cincinnati. It was a relief. I was finally free from his control, his angry words, and the back side of his hand."

Ty couldn't bear the image of some man causing pain to this sweet young woman.

"I managed to stay away the summer after my freshman and sophomore year. But Cody graduated from high school the summer after my junior year. I went home for his graduation. I'd missed Cody. We were always close."

Ty did the math and figured out this was the year of the police report.

"After Cody's graduation party, my dad was totally drunk. He got on me about the art classes I'd taken at college. He knew about them and didn't approve. He said they were a waste of my time." Brooke shook her head at the memory. "I think being away for a couple years gave me a little more courage. I told him I hated nursing and taking art classes was the only thing making school bearable."

"How did he handle that?"

"I'd never seen him get so violent." Brooke turned away. "He unleashed three years of pent up anger that he'd not been able to release while I was away at school. It was Cody who called the police, but he couldn't stand by and watch my father beat me up. He attacked my dad with all the vengeance of an eighteen-year-old who was tired of all the injustice."

"The police arrested your brother…"

Brooke nodded.

"My dad smashed a half empty beer can on my head when he first started abusing me that night. When the police arrived I smelled like I'd been drinking—and that's what my mother told them."

"Your mother?"

Brooke nodded.

"She said I was wasted and fell down the stairs. She told them that Cody beat up my dad and then she stood and watched while they arrested her own son."

"What did you guys do?" Ty couldn't imagine the scene Brooke just painted for him.

"Cody spent the weekend in jail and moved in with a friend until the court rulings were over. After he attended anger management classes, he moved to Colorado and started working at a ski resort." Brooke rubbed her hand over the sand. "I moved back to Cincinnati and finished my schooling. I had to take out a loan for my last year, but I paid it off pretty quickly after graduating. I've been working ever since."

"How often do you see your brother?"

"We spend Christmas together every year and I usually go to Colorado at least once in the summer." Brooke brushed away a tear. "We've stayed really close."

"But Cody never knew about the sexual abuse?" Ty hated to press, but wanted her to work through the pain.

Brooke shook her head. "I couldn't bear him knowing. Anyway, he was only seven when it happened… and my dad didn't do much..."

"It doesn't matter how much he did. Any kind of inappropriate touch is wrong! Your mom was wrong to belittle it." Ty placed his hand on her back. "Brooke, you're not damaged goods."

Tears coursed down Brooke's face and Ty pulled her to him and engulfed her in his arms. She let him hold her close while she cried against his chest. Ty wept too, as he let the pain of her burden sink into his heart.

■ ■ ■

Ty held Brooke for quite some time. Praying for her while he held her was the best comfort he could provide. When she finally let go of him, her eyes were red and her face was wet.

"I didn't mean to unleash all that on you," she said softly.

"It's okay. I wanted to help you." Ty wiped her face with his hands. "It feels better to talk about things, doesn't it?"

Brooke nodded. "You're the only person I've ever told some of that to."

"And the only one I'll talk about it to is God."

Brooke ran her hand over the sand, making a swirling pattern on the surface. "Now do you understand why I don't want to talk to God?"

Ty smoothed Brooke's hair away from her wet face.

"Where was He while I was suffering?"

Ty was quiet for a moment. "Right now I just keep thinking of one little verse.

Brooke waited to hear it.

"Jesus wept," Ty said softly.

"That's a verse?"

"John 11:35," Ty cited it.

"What does it have to do with me?" Brooke wiped her face on her sleeve.

"Jesus was there, Brooke. He saw everything and He wept. To use a human term—it broke His heart."

"Then why didn't He stop it? I asked Him! I begged Him! There wasn't a night when I was a little girl that I didn't plead with Him to make my dad stop. I even asked God to strike my dad down. I prayed he'd drive drunk and kill himself!"

Ty could feel Brooke's pain, and from a human standpoint, he understood the desire for vengeance. But he also knew that vengeance belonged to the Lord. "Brooke," Ty held her hand tenderly in his. "When God created this world, He created us with freedom to choose right or wrong. That's the only way we could be truly free to love Him. If we didn't have a choice it wouldn't be love. But along with that choice to obey God comes the choice to disobey. It's when we disobey that we cause pain to ourselves and others."

Brooke looked exhausted. Her sad dark eyes were drained of all tears. "But where was He? Why didn't He help me?"

"He was there, Brooke. He was there to carry that burden for you. He was there to restore your joy. He was there to be the Father you didn't have." Ty prayed he was saying the right things. "He still is."

Brooke buried her face in her hands and her body shook in silent sobs.

Ty watched the colors change in the sky and prayed that God would restore Brooke and touch her heart.

It was getting dark when Brooke was finally ready to leave. Ty took her hand and led her to the car. Neither of them said much. Brooke obviously needed to think. Ty prayed she would take her thoughts to God.

Even though Ty didn't have all the answers, the one thing he was certain of was that "Jesus wept."

CHAPTER 13

Ty let Brooke sleep in while he made a delicious smelling breakfast of orange pancakes, with real maple syrup, and fresh fruit. He knocked on her bedroom door and called to her when everything was ready. "Are you hungry?"

Brooke opened her eyes and squinted against the sunshine that streamed through her bedroom skylight. She sat up and dressed before joining him in the hallway. "It smells good. I didn't know you cooked."

"I have a few recipes up my sleeve." Ty pulled out a chair for her and sat across from her at the table.

Brooke waited while Ty asked for God's blessing on the food.

"These pancakes are amazing." She said after taking her first bite.

Ty agreed. "It's my mom's recipe."

"How did you do this?" Brooke wanted to know.

"You simply replace the milk with orange juice." Ty gave away the secret. "But you have to make your pancakes from scratch and can only use real maple syrup."

"I am so glad my husband can cook." Brooke took a sip of orange juice.

"Would you like coffee?" Ty rose to get her a cup.

"Yes, please. Thank you."

Ty poured the coffee and added the amount of cream he'd noticed she used. "I thought maybe today you'd enjoy just sitting in your art studio letting your creative juices flow. What do you think?"

Brooke thought it sounded amazing. "A whole day with nothing to do but paint?"

Ty nodded and handed her the coffee. "Did you sleep well?"

Brooke nodded. "You even made my coffee just right."

Ty grinned. "Thank you for opening up to me yesterday."

"I regretted it a little this morning." Brooke confessed. She let her eyes rest on the pot of pink chrysanthemums in the center of the table.

"I figured you would." Ty took a few bites of his pancakes and let Brooke compose her thoughts.

"Thank you for listening." Brooke looked up into his blue eyes. "It was good to finally let it all out." She pushed a strawberry around on her plate. "It was also good to finally have someone believe me."

Ty's face showed compassion.

"When that man forced me to drink and you thought I'd done it myself," Brooke began. "I felt like that little girl who told her teacher that the bruise under her eye was from her dad… and the teacher didn't believe her."

"I'm sorry…"

Brooke shook her head. "You didn't do anything wrong. As soon as you put the pieces together, you believed me. Both you and Owen believed me. It meant so much."

"But your teachers never put the pieces together…"

"And eventually I stopped telling them." Brooke lowered her eyes.

"I'm glad you told me."

■ ■ ■

The next morning was Sunday and Brooke agreed to let Ty "drag" her to church again. This time she had a better attitude, but enjoyed teasing him about it.

They pulled up in front of a large, pole barn style building. "This is an unusual looking church." The large, wooden cross out front drew her attention and she appreciated the lovely landscaping.

Friendly faces and warm greetings met the couple inside. Brooke glanced down at her wedding band. "Will we have to lie to anyone about being married?" She whispered.

Ty reminded her that they were technically under witness protection and were ordered not to disclose their identity. "I think God knows our hearts, Brooke," Ty told her. "According to witness protection, you are Jessica Duncan and I am Carter Duncan. And you could say that legally, Jessica and Carter are married."

It was a strange thought for both of them.

This church was smaller than the one in New York, but it was similar in many ways. They opened the singing with hymns. Brooke sang along with those songs. After announcements and prayer request, the praise band came out and the music became more upbeat. Brooke glanced at Ty and noticed his peaceful expression as he sang.

After they sat down, the pastor approached the pulpit and welcomed everyone to the service. Then he slammed his hands on the podium, shook his head, and let out a pathetic moan. "I've got a confession." It caught Brooke's attention.

"I was angry at God this week."

Brooke's eyes grew wide. Was a pastor allowed to say that? She glanced momentarily at Ty, but his eyes were on the pastor.

"See, we got a letter from the Internal Revenue Service saying that we'd done our taxes wrong and that we were going to get audited," the pastor continued. "I know what you're thinking... what a stupid thing to get mad at God about. And it was! My wife reminded me of that." The man glanced down at his wife who was sitting in the front row. "But I was mad. I told God it wasn't fair. I shouldn't have to waste my time getting audited when I was busy doing His work."

There were a few chuckles in the congregation.

"Then God had something to say to me." The pastor smiled. "Open your Bibles to Job 38."

Ty opened his Bible and placed it between himself and Brooke. She read along.

"Then the Lord answered Job..." The pastor began his sermon by reminding the congregation who Job was. "The man was upright before God. He'd done nothing wrong. But Satan asked permission from God to throw a few wrenches at Job to see if the man would crack."

Brooke listened curiously. She'd never heard a preacher explain things quite like this.

"Job got pretty bummed out. I think I would have thrown in the towel long before Job finally started whining. But Job never cursed

God… he was understandably discouraged and had some serious questions, but he didn't turn away."

Brooke followed along in the Bible.

"Job 38 starts God's response to Job concerning Job's questioning. God reminds Job of who He is. We get a pretty good painting of the majesty and power of God. This is the Creator of the universe."

Ty took notes on the back of his bulletin and Brooke listened intently.

"God didn't have to explain Himself. He's God. But here's the great part. He did." The pastor gave that thought a moment to sink in. "God took the time to talk to Job. I'm sure God did not enjoy watching Job suffer. God loved Job. Job was faithful and righteous. I'm reminded of the words of John 11:35 where the Bible tells us Jesus wept. I bet God wept for Job."

Brooke tried to process the fact that the pastor just quoted the same verse Ty quoted the night before.

"But God used the situation. He did a work in Job's life that stretched Job beyond what we can comprehend. It's powerful." The pastor slapped his Bible. "And then, what did God do?" The pastor glanced around at the congregation. "Come on, someone tell me…"

"He blessed Job!" someone spoke up.

"That's right! He restored all that Job lost and gave him more than he'd ever had! Job 42:10 tells us that 'The Lord restored the fortunes of Job when he prayed for his friends, and the Lord increased all that Job had twofold.'" The pastor let out a whoop. "That's awesome! The dude got to live to 140 and see his sons and grandsons—four generations. Wow!"

Brooke tried to force herself not to smile at this man's enthusiasm.

"How dare I whine?" The pastor paced the stage for a moment. "I know taxes are really a lame example of true suffering. But you've got to see it. God loves you and wants to take all the terrible things in your life and talk to you, and help you, and bless you." He stopped in front of the podium again. "In that passage where Jesus wept, remember why He was crying? His friend Lazarus just died and his friends Mary and Martha were grieving. Jesus knew He was going to raise Lazarus from the dead—but it hurt Him to see His friends suffering. Jesus cried not because Lazarus was dead, but because Mary and Martha were sad."

He paused and looked out at the congregation. "Some of you are sad." He paused. "Jesus knows. He loves you and He cries when you're grieving."

Brooke tried to stop the tears from filling her eyes.

"Let Him comfort you." The pastor's voice softened. "Understand that my reaction to God this week was sin. That's why I told you all that I had a confession. We all sin." He glanced around. "But the Bible tells us in Romans 10:9-10 'That if you confess with your mouth Jesus as Lord, and believe in your heart that God raised Him from the dead, you will be saved; for with the heart a person believes, resulting in righteousness, and with the mouth he confesses, resulting in salvation.'"

A few of the band members quietly crept on stage and played a soft melody while the pastor continued.

"If you've got a burden to lay at the Lord's feet today, won't you come up to the altar and leave it here?"

Brooke swallowed back the lump in her throat and watched as a few people walked forward with tears in their eyes. It was unlike anything she'd ever seen during a church service.

"Or maybe you've never turned your life over to Him. Maybe you're holding on to that hurt and haven't surrendered yourself, confessed your own sins, and experienced that transformation of heart that only Jesus can give you. If that's you, I invite you to come to the altar and someone will pray with you."

Brooke's heart pounded in her chest. This was crazy. This was like church camp. She glanced around and saw that Ty was kneeling beside his chair, obviously deep in prayer. The music continued and the pastor walked around with some of the other members of the church and prayed with those at the altar. Brooke couldn't hold back any longer. Her heart was breaking and she knew she needed what Ty had. She knew she needed to accept the love that God had for her. She needed to surrender the hate and bitterness that she'd been harboring all these years and experience the forgiveness and new life that Jesus wanted to give her.

Brooke slipped from her pew and went to the altar. It was time.

■ ■ ■

It was a very different Sunday for Brooke and Ty. After the service, the pastor and his wife invited them to their home for lunch.

Brooke's eyelashes were still wet from all the crying she'd done at the altar, but she sat beside Ty in the Camry as they drove to the pastor's home.

"Have you ever been invited to a pastor's house for lunch?" Brooke asked Ty as they followed the minivan in front of them.

Ty glanced at her and smiled. "He's just a person."

"Okay, I understand that. But growing up, our pastor seemed to be otherworldly and unapproachable."

"Kind of like a movie star?" Ty asked.

"Yeah. Kind of." Brooke leaned back in her seat.

"Or maybe a doctor or a senator."

"Okay, you're laughing at me." Brooke crossed her arms. "Look, I didn't grow up around royalty like you obviously did. Even my doctor seemed superior." She glanced at him out of the corner of her eyes. "And your dad *is* a doctor."

Ty reached out and touched Brooke's hand. "We're all created by God. He's the King of Kings—and now you're one of His children."

What a beautiful feeling. He is the King and we're His children. Brooke's lips curved into a smile and she let her eyes linger on Ty for a moment. His encouragement in the morning service meant so much. When she'd gone to the altar, Ty was right there, praying for her with the rest of the group. When had she ever met such a wonderful man?

They pulled into the driveway of a modest two story and Ty gave her hand a squeeze. "Are you ready?"

"What did the pastor's wife say her name was?" Brooke asked.

"Linda." Ty reminded her. "And his name is David."

Brooke repeated the names softly. She watched as Linda unbuckled her youngest child from a car seat and smiled as the child bounded after her siblings to the front door. They looked like a nice family.

Inside, Linda explained that she already had a pot roast cooking in the slow cooker and that it would only take her a few minutes to set the table. The young wife had a slight twang to her voice that reminded Brooke of a friend she had from West Virginia. "Would you like to help?" she asked Brooke.

"Absolutely."

The men went into the living room with the children, and Brooke followed Linda into the kitchen. It wasn't much larger than Brooke's kitchen in Cincinnati. The cabinets and appliances were clean and neat. A few toys and an opened children's book lay on the round kitchen table, and a cat bowl sat beside the back door. Everything felt warm and homey.

"Thank you so much for inviting us to join you today." Brooke's eyes misted.

"I'm excited that you were willing to come."

Brooke carried the silverware to the dinning room while Linda poured water for everyone.

"How long have you and Carter lived in the area?" she asked.

"We just moved here." Brooke laid out the napkins. "Where are you from? I detect a slight accent."

Linda chuckled. "Slight? Now be honest, David tells me I sound like a cowgirl." She set out the children's plastic plates. "I'm from Texas."

Brooke smiled. There was something very real about Linda.

When the table was set, the men and children met them in the dining room. David asked Ty to pray.

Heads bowed and Ty's voice broke through the quiet. "Father, thank You so much for bringing us all here together today. Thank You for this table full of food and these brothers and sisters in Christ. More than anything though, thank You that Brooke put her faith in You today…"

Brooke glanced up when she heard her real name. He forgot to call her Jessica. Did the others notice?

Ty closed the prayer and opened his eyes. "This food smells great!"

"So is 'Brooke' your nickname?" David asked.

Brooke peeked up at Ty to gauge his reaction.

Ty glanced at Brooke. "Uh. That's what I call her, yes. It's a really long story."

"Jessica… Brooke… I get the connection." David smirked.

Linda patted her husband's arm. "David, don't tease them." She pretended to scold her husband.

"My name is Hannah Grace," the oldest daughter announced.

"Hello, Hannah Grace." Ty smiled at the seven-year-old.

"I go by Hannah," she explained. "Are you going to a funeral?"

"A funeral?"

David and Linda laughed.

"You're wearing a suit," David explained. "No honey, you don't have to go to a funeral to wear a suit."

Ty chuckled. "Your dad's right. I actually wear suits a lot."

"I have a suit," the middle child spoke up. "I wore it when I was in my Aunt Kathy's wedding. She made me wear a green tie that Dad said looked like a squished Kermit the frog."

Linda gave her husband one of those looks. "See David… you have to be careful what you say." She glanced at her son. "It was a nice tie, Andrew."

The pastor shrugged and Ty and Brooke chuckled.

"It did!" David passed the peas and told his wife he'd behave.

"So, how long have you two been married?" Linda asked the couple.

Ty turned toward Brooke and raised his eyebrows. "Less than a week actually."

"Awesome!" David's tone held approval. "How did you meet?"

Brooke was curious how he would handle this one.

Ty reached out and clutched Brooke's hand. "Brooke is a nurse and she saved my life. I've been falling in love with her ever since."

Brooke turned curious eyes on Ty. Falling in love? Ty was usually so good at keeping things honest.

"That is so sweet," Linda gushed.

"I like to play nurse." Hannah turned the subject back upon herself.

"You do?" Brooke was thankful for the shift of attention. "Do you have a nurse's kit?" Brooke took a bite of her pot roast and let Hannah take off with a whole dialogue about her nurse's kit with a stethoscope and bandages and everything else the seven-year-old knew the technical names for.

"Hannah did surgery on the cat once," Andrew interjected.

"You're not supposed to tell that story!" Hannah grew instantly defensive. "Mom!"

There was a little bit of chuckling at the table and Brooke was sure there was a funny story to go along with it, but David and Linda hurried to protect their oldest from embarrassment.

"Miss Kitty is just fine, Andrew." Linda cleared the air. "Would you like more water, Carter?"

■ ■ ■

After dinner the children entertained the adults for another twenty minutes by showing Ty and Brooke everything they could do with just about every toy in the house.

Brooke enjoyed their banter and wondered in amazement at how David interacted with his children. He laughed with them, tickled them, played with them, talked with them, and encouraged them. It was what Brooke thought a real father should be like.

"Okay, crazy kids." David finally called a stop to their play when Andrew brought out his drum set and said they were going to play praise band. "Its time for all good preacher's kids to go have rest time. Mommy and Daddy want to hang out with our new friends, now."

Hannah stuck out a sulky lower lip, but her mother reminded her that her best friend Molly was having a birthday party this week and that Hannah still hadn't made the card. The seven-year-old skipped off with a bag of markers and a pile of colored paper from the craft drawer.

Andrew followed his sister up the stairs and Linda carried a very tired three-year-old behind them.

"Those are three amazing kids." Ty expressed what Brooke was feeling.

"We'll keep them." David leaned back on the couch and rested his arm on the back where his wife would be sitting. His eyes twinkled and he shook his head. "Married less than a week. That's... that's cool."

Brooke shifted in her seat and noticed a unique piece of pottery on a bookshelf. "What a beautiful bowl." She stood up to inspect it.

"Linda made it." David turned around so he could see it.

"She made this?" Brooke turned it over in her hands. It was a unique piece of stoneware, delicately painted with snow-covered trees, a spattering of snow flurries, and a few cardinals.

"Yeah. She's artsy that way." David chuckled. "Me, I'm lucky if I can accomplish a stick figure."

"Stick figures can be very artistic, David," Linda said as she walked down the stairs. "And thank you." She stood next to Brooke and touched the piece fondly. "I love working with clay. It's kind of my outlet."

"She definitely needs an outlet," David spoke up.

"Thanks, Darling."

"I paint," Brooke offered. "I guess you could say that's my outlet." It felt good to be open with this couple. She liked them.

"You'll have to show us your work some time," David said.

Brooke nodded shyly and glanced at Ty.

"So, I have to ask because I'm one of those kind of people," David said. "But I'm really curious. Jessica was your nurse so that's how you met, you just got married, and Jessica just gave her life to Jesus today. How about you, Carter? When did you surrender your life to the Lord?"

"A year and a half ago," Ty answered honestly.

Brooke and Linda both took a seat and waited to hear Ty's story.

"It's a really long testimony so I'll try to keep it under and hour," Ty teased. "I did not grow up in a Christian home. After college, I made some wrong career choices that got me into trouble. I tried to start over, got a new job, moved to a new town, but the guilt of my sin and my total emptiness followed me." Ty paused for a moment to form his thoughts. "While working as an accountant I was invited by one of my clients to a men's breakfast." Ty grinned. "I thought it was going to be a good business opportunity, maybe make a few new contacts, get a few new angles. But when I got there I found out it was a Bible study."

"You mean your friend didn't tell you that part?" David laughed.

"No." Ty shook his head. "But I liked the men. They were friendly and interesting and… real. I needed real in my life. I didn't have a lot of close friends in my new town and was very lonely."

Brooke understood that feeling. She'd felt lonely for the past five years.

"These men didn't push me but they kept me intrigued. We read the Bible, talked about it, and prayed together once a week from six in the morning until eight and I couldn't get enough of it."

"That's what I like to hear." David clung to the conversation eagerly.

"Finally, one morning I told the guys that I wanted what they had and they walked me through what it meant to be a follower of Jesus Christ. I put my faith in Christ, was baptized, and got involved in my friend's church. The rest is history."

"That's a beautiful story." Linda leaned back into her husband's arm.

"What about you guys?" Ty asked.

David glanced at Linda and Linda shrugged. "I'll go first," she said in her Texas drawl. "I grew up in foster care."

It wasn't the beginning Brooke expected to hear.

"I came from a very destructive home life filled with all kinds of abuse and pain." Her eyes were sober with the memory. "For about four years I bounced around the system until I ended up with a sweet little Christian couple named Don and June Parsley." Linda's lips curved into a smile. "The Parsley's children were all grown, and the couple decided to take in foster kids as a ministry. They were amazing. They took the broken, angry little girl I was and showered me with the love of Jesus. They eventually adopted me, and soon after that I was adopted into God's kingdom when I gave my life to Christ."

Brooke held her lips together to keep her emotions at bay. How easy it seemed for Linda to share that story. Would she ever be able to talk about her abuse like that? Brooke couldn't imagine it. Linda seemed so well adjusted. Her children adored her and her husband obviously loved her very much. Brooke felt Ty's hand on her shoulder and wished she could snuggle up close to him the way Linda was with David. Ty understood her.

"Thank you for sharing your story, Linda." Ty spoke softly.

David blew out a heavy sigh. "Is it my turn?" He did his best impression of their seven-year-old when she was about to do something she didn't want to.

Linda slapped his arm playfully.

"Alright." David grabbed her hand and kissed it. "I was a pastor's kid. Grew up in the church and got saved really young." A mischievous grin graced his lips. "But I was a stinker."

Brooke didn't find that hard to believe.

"My dad was a great preacher. Still is actually. But he's the serious hit your fist on the pulpit and yell them all into repentance kind. I'm glad he was, because it was one of his fire and brimstone sermons that scared me to my knees," David confessed. "But I'm not like my dad. Never was and never could be. Dad told me that was okay." David's face held a look of peaceful reminiscence. "He told me God could use me and my style of telling people about the Lord. He was sure there were enough other people with ADHD who would appreciate me and that I should consider being a pastor, even though I'd never be offered the pulpit at his church."

Ty chuckled. "You are teasing right?"

David shook his head. "Not one bit. He used those very words about people with ADHD. I've never been diagnosed, but my parents are convinced that I am."

Brooke smiled and shook her head. "You do have a very unconventional preaching style, but I like it."

"Thank you." David nodded and tightened his fingers around his wife's hand. "I guess this little lady likes it too." He gazed lovingly at Linda.

"Every once in a while he has been asked to preach at his father's church though," Linda confessed.

"I tell Dad it wakes them up." David laughed. "My dad's a good preacher, he's just a little more traditional."

The couples talked through part of the afternoon, and Ty finally said they needed to go home before they would have to stay for dinner.

"I can't thank you enough for your message today." Brooke shook David's hand. "It was just what I needed to hear."

David's eyes warmed to her encouraging words. "I just preach what the Lord tells me to."

"Well, thank you for obeying."

Linda gave Brooke a long hug and told her she would love to visit with her again. Brooke wanted to ask when and actually get a date on the calendar, but resisted.

By the time Ty and Brooke walked out to their car, they were both feeling refreshed and encouraged.

■ ■ ■

"I feel like I just lived a fairy tale that I didn't want to end." Brooke leaned back in her seat.

"Why a fairy tale?" Ty asked.

"It was unlike anything I ever experienced. This whole day has been."

Ty was glad. He was still in utter amazement that Brooke turned her life over to Jesus. Was it only a week ago that Brooke gave him the silent treatment after church?

"I did feel awkward about lying to them though," Brooke confessed.

Ty understood. "I tried to keep it as honest as possible."

"You played it off pretty well when they asked you how we'd met." Brooke pulled her legs up on the seat.

Ty wondered what she thought of his explanation. As soon as he mentioned falling in love with her Ty began doing inventory of his heart. Why did that roll off his lips? Why didn't it feel like a lie? He caught Brooke's profile out of the corner of his eye.

Charm is deceitful and beauty is vain, but a woman who fears the Lord, she shall be praised. The verse ran through his mind. Brooke now feared the Lord. Would their friendship change now that she was a believer?

CHAPTER 14

"Did you get my text message?" A cool voice asked over the phone.

"Yes. Glen Burnie. Got it." Mike Rider held his phone close to his head. "Want me to take them out?"

"No. It'd be too obvious." The other man said. "But I want you to watch them. I think Ty's doing some research of his own and I want to know what he's learned."

"What about the girl?"

"She's good leverage. We might need her to jar his memory again."

"Alright." Mike carried his phone to the hotel window and let his eyes scan the street."

"Make sure they don't see you."

"They never see me."

There was quiet on the other end of the phone. "They know it was you in the hotel room. They found your blood under her fingernails."

"Can you take care of that?" Mike asked.

"I'm doing my best."

Mike reminded the other man of his price.

"You got it. Keep in touch. I'll let you know when it's time."

■ ■ ■

Brooke spent the morning raking leaves in the front yard. It was nice to be outside in the sunshine doing something productive. She knew the house wasn't hers. She knew she probably didn't need to rake the leaves. But it felt good.

They'd been at their safe house for almost two weeks and Brooke was enjoying the change of pace. They returned to David and Linda's church on Sunday and visited a mid-week Bible study—funny how she actually wanted to learn more about God now.

It was getting close to noon so Brooke rose to put lunch together.

Ty used her laptop to research people from the campaign files. He'd kept a copy of the list for himself to conduct his own investigation.

"How is the Wi-Fi in this house?" Brooke walked inside with dirt all over her hands.

"I think I'm using the neighbor's Wi-Fi," Ty confessed.

"Is that safe?"

Ty shrugged. "As safe as it can be, I guess. So far no one has complained."

After washing her hands, Brooke took a seat beside Ty and asked him how his investigation was going.

"At this point, I'm just searching old newspaper articles, conference itineraries, public political events, and anything else I can find floating around out there on the web."

Brooke glanced at the computer scene. "Are you finding anything?"

"There's an awful lot of information about these people. I'm amazed how much I've actually learned just reading various blogs."

Brooke watched Ty put hash marks next to a few names.

"This tells me when I see the same individuals at the same event."

"It looks like several of them run in the same circles." Brooke got up to start cooking.

"That's typical for people in this line of work." He made another hash mark and moved the curser down the screen. "I used to run with some of these people myself."

"So is Blake Kendall in any of those write ups?" Brooke started peeling potatoes and glanced at Ty from the kitchen island.

Ty cleared his throat. "I've seen his name a couple times. But I'm sure I'd find more if I did a search for him individually." He blew out a sigh. "And I'm not sure I'd like what I'd find."

Brooke understood. She left Ty to finish his searching while she devoted her full attention to making lunch. It was nice to have someone to cook for. Usually, she only prepared meals for herself. She remembered her conversation with Ty's mother. It was nice of Anne to change the subject from spiritual things to cooking when she noticed Brooke was growing uncomfortable. Brooke appreciated Anne's sensitivity. *I wish I could tell her that I am a believer now.* Brooke knew Anne would be excited by the news.

The smell of chicken corn chowder was enough to lure Ty away from the computer as Brooke carried his bowl of soup to the table.

"This looks amazing!" Ty closed the laptop and moved his papers over.

Brooke sat across from him and waited for Ty to pray.

"This is fabulous." Ty dug into his soup with pleasure. "Did you just make this from memory?"

Brooke shrugged. "I don't usually measure things, so I just throw together what ingredients I remember and hope for the best."

"Are you and Linda still going out for coffee this evening?"

Brooke nodded. "You think we'll be safe?" Brooke had not been away from Ty since her terrifying experience at the hotel.

"I think you'll be fine."

Brooke took a bite of her soup and tried to consider the question she had for Ty. "I was thinking of telling Linda a little bit about my childhood." She glanced down.

"That's a wonderful idea." Ty's eyes showed pleasure. "I think Linda will understand and she can probably give you some good counsel."

"I'm a little scared. I'm usually not very vulnerable with people, but I feel like Linda will understand." Brooke marveled at how easily Linda shared that part of her life when she shared her testimony. Linda seemed free from the pain of her past. Brooke wanted that freedom and hoped Linda would help her find it.

■ ■ ■

The little coffee shop along the bay was quaint and cozy. Brooke and Linda sat at a small table near the back of the café with a view of the water.

"I'm so glad you invited me to get together." Brooke wrapped her fingers around her mug and let the warmth of the cup sink into her hands.

"I'm glad you said yes," Linda confessed. "I don't get very many nights out."

The two women small talked for a while, but Brooke wanted to go deeper. Linda's story was burned into Brooke's mind and she wanted to talk about it. She glanced at the clock on her cell phone to make sure they had enough time.

"Would you mind if I talked to you about something kind of personal?" Brooke finally mustered the courage to ask.

Linda leaned forward in her seat and steadied her gaze on Brooke. "That's fine. What did you want to talk about?"

"Your testimony." Brooke swirled the chocolate around at the bottom of her mug. "You talked about… abuse." She forced out the word.

"Yes." Linda nodded. Her face sobered. "My birth mom had a lot of boyfriends. One of them in particular mistreated me for many years.

"Did she know?"

Linda blew out a heavy sigh and nodded. "She did. That's what finally got me taken away from her."

Brooke stared into the coffee cup for a few minutes. "How did you overcome it?" It seemed like a crazy question. Had Linda overcome it? Could anyone ever really overcome that?

"It's a process," Linda began. "It started with talking about it. I also met with a Christian counselor. She taught me to work through my feelings and surrender the hurts, anger, and insecurities… all of it to God. I had to learn to forgive. That was vital to my healing. Un-forgiveness is sin—therefore holding on to un-forgiveness only gives the enemy a foothold in our lives." Linda spoke with conviction. "Forgiving was a pivotal point in my healing." She paused and studied Brooke's face tenderly.

Brooke glanced away and brushed a tear from her face.

"You've been there too," Linda said. "Am I right?"

Brooke nodded. She opened up and began unloading that deep, dark secret that for so many years she'd only bottled inside. It felt good to finally let it out.

"Your secret is now in the light," Linda explained. "When it's in the light, the enemy can no longer control you with it. Have you surrendered it to God?"

"Yes. Several times."

Involuntarily, Linda reached across the table and clutched Brooke's hands. "Brooke," she began. "You are not alone in this journey of healing. Not only is the Lord Jesus right there with you helping you through this, but I want to be there as a friend who can pray for you, encourage you, and even council you if you need it."

"I want that very much!" Relief spread across Brooke's face. "Thank you."

The two women talked for hours. Linda gave Brooke some very practical advice to begin her journey of healing.

"Write a list of everyone who has ever hurt you, ask God to dig it out of your memory if He has to. Then, go through that list and ask God to forgive you if you have been holding un-forgiveness in your heart toward them. Ask Him to help you to forgive them and then choose to do so. After that, pray for those individuals. When you are done, give it to God and destroy the list."

Brooke listened intently.

"It's amazing," Linda said. "It's so freeing to forgive."

"I can imagine it is."

"Remember though, forgiveness doesn't mean you won't still feel the hurt. That's why you need to ask God to help. We can't do it in our own strength."

Brooke walked away from her evening with Linda with some practical steps toward healing. Linda also gave her several scripture verses that were crucial during her own recovery.

"I will be praying for you," Linda promised as she pulled up in front of Brooke's house.

■ ■ ■

Ty was noticeably worried when Brooke arrived home. "You ladies were out late." His tone showed concern, not anger.

"I'm sorry, but it was wonderful." Brooke had a feeling Ty would be pleased with their conversation. "Linda was very helpful and gave me lots of advice."

"That's good." Ty shut down the computer. "I guess I'm just

protective of you."

Brooke poured herself a glass of water and sat on the sofa across from him. It felt good to be protected.

"Were you able to share your heart?" Ty asked.

Brooke nodded. "Completely." Brooke shared some of the advice Linda gave her. "It gave me a lot of hope." She ran her hand along the smooth water glass. "There's a lot I still need to deal with, but I can see God walking me through it and I know He is already healing those hurts."

"I prayed it would go well."

"How was your research?" Brooke noticed the papers scattered across the table.

Ty glanced down at his chicken scratch and sighed. "I learned that my sister worked very closely with Brad Bronowski for about two years."

"Brad Bronowski?"

"Jasmine Greenwich was his lawyer when he was in Washington. I can't be certain, but I think his name was in those files." Ty reached across the coffee table and picked up his water bottle. "Unfortunately, I didn't pay much attention to those files because Greenwich approached me around the same time I came clean with the FBI for my other involvement."

"Do you know what the files contained?"

"I have a pretty good idea what they were about, but without the files I have no evidence." He leaned back on his chair and placed his arms behind his head. "I also don't have a concrete list of everyone who was represented in the files."

"And you have no idea who took them?" Brooke asked.

"No." Ty cleared his throat. "I didn't even realize they were missing until I started going through my old files with Owen. My guess is they were taken from my office before the FBI moved in and seized all my documents."

"How can we get them back?"

Ty paused for a moment and his lips curved into a smile. "You said, 'we.'"

She had. And it felt right. Her heartbeat quickened. "We're in this together."

"Thank you. That means so much." Ty's face sobered. "I really don't know what I'd do without you."

"I feel the same way." She chewed lightly on her lower lip. Did he have any idea how much his friendship meant to her? She took a sip of her water and tried to keep her thoughts from running wild. "So, what's the plan?"

"I'm not sure. I guess part of me wishes I could talk to Olivia."

"Your sister?" Brooke knew very little about this political woman, except her husband was the cat groomer and personal appointment manager.

"She might know about the files. Even if she was not directly involved in any of the misuse of campaign funds, she knew Bronowski quite well."

"Where is Bronowski now?"

"For whatever reason, Bronowski pulled out of Washington about three years ago." Ty raised an eyebrow. "He's working as a divorce lawyer in Miami."

"Interesting."

"Yeah. I guess he either felt the need to leave the political rat race or he was encouraged to leave by some kind of damaging information."

"Would Olivia know?"

Ty's face grew pensive. "I'm not sure."

■ ■ ■

"It's time."

Mike heard the voice on the other end of the phone. "Would have been nice if you'd told me a couple days ago. She was out for coffee with a friend. First time they've been away from each other since they got here."

"I didn't promise you an easy job. Just do it. I want them both alive."

Mike crushed his cigarette in a full ashtray. "You take away all the fun."

"You'll get your fun. Do you need another man on this?"

Mike carried his phone to the counter and picked up his gun. "Don't insult me. When do you need it done?"

"Two days."

"No problem."

■ ■ ■

Brooke and Ty sat with the pastor and his family during the worship service. Linda asked her oldest daughter, Hannah, to move over so mommy could sit by her friend.

Since putting her faith in Christ, the hymns and worship songs took on meaning in Brooke's life that they never had before. She closed her eyes and let the words minister to her soul.

Brooke felt Linda reach for her hand. It was good to have a friend who understood.

David got up to preach and Brooke leaned forward to listen. His sermon spoke right to her heart.

At some point during the sermon, Hannah asked if she could move back into the middle of them so she could sit by Brooke. Linda complied. Brooke placed an arm around the seven-year-old and smiled at her. When had Brooke ever had such special friendships?

After the service, Hannah told Brooke and Ty that they were going to see their grandparents that afternoon.

"That will be fun." Ty greeted all three children. "Are you going to play praise band with them?"

"No. Grandpa doesn't really like the drums," Andrew explained and crossed his arms.

Linda smiled at her middle child. "Maybe you can just sing for him."

"I'm going to go see Daddy!" Hannah waved and skipped down the aisle to stand beside her father as he greeted people from the congregation.

"Enjoy the rest of your day." Linda set down her youngest and gave Brooke a hug.

"We will. Thank you."

Ty and Brooke greeted people as they walked from the sanctuary. "Did you want to get lunch somewhere or go home?" Ty asked.

"Let's just head home." Brooke suggested.

■ ■ ■

"I'm making lunch." Ty told her as he parked the car in the driveway.

"Oh yeah? What are we having?"

"Green chicken chili." Ty opened his door and climbed out. He waited for her to come around to his side of the car. "It's just a little spicy, but I think you'll like it."

Brooke followed him to the front porch. "Sounds good. Another one of your mom's recipes?"

"No. It's one I found on my own." Ty opened the front door and they stepped into the house. Something didn't feel right. Who closed the blinds? He put out his hand and stopped Brooke from walking any further.

Brooke glanced at Ty and he put a finger to his lips.

She remained frozen in the doorway to the kitchen while Ty checked the back door. It was unlocked. Ty motioned for her to back up. Brooke stepped backwards while Ty crept quietly toward the bedrooms at the back of the house.

"Let's go." Ty ran back, grabbed her hand, and practically dragged her through the doorway.

Brooke didn't have time to wonder what was going on. Ty clicked the unlock button on the Camry and told her to get in. Brooke complied.

Ty just started the car when someone appeared at the front door, running toward them with a gun.

"Get down," Ty ordered and peeled out of the driveway.

Bullets struck the side of the car. One broke the taillight, but Ty put his foot to the gas and peeled out of the neighborhood.

"They're behind us." Brooke watched out the rear window.

"Stay low." Ty sped through stop signs and tore through an intersection with a black SUV hot on his tail.

Brooke crouched low and clung to the door.

Ty whipped their car onto the interstate and zipped past cars and trucks, unconcerned about speed laws. A policeman would be a refreshing sight in this situation.

The SUV was several cars behind them. Ty weaved in and out of traffic and pulled off an exit at the last moment, leaving the SUV on the interstate. "Hang on!" He made two lefts and got back on the highway headed the opposite direction. "I think we lost them."

Brooke sat up and glanced over her shoulder. "How did they find us?" Her eyes showed fear.

"That's a good question."

"How did you know?" she asked.

"The blinds were drawn. You opened them this morning and commented on the sunshine. When I went into your room, one of the French doors was open and I could smell cigarette smoke."

Brooke leaned back in her seat and stared out the windshield. "They were waiting for us."

Ty reached for her hand.

"What does this mean, Ty?"

"I'm not sure exactly." He shook his head. "Your computer…"

"Where was it?"

"I'd left it on the table next to the sofa. I didn't see it when I checked the back door. How much personal information is on your laptop?"

Brooke's eyes showed concern. "I deleted my email account, but all my contacts are in my computer."

"All my research is in the internet history." He smacked the steering wheel. "I don't even have the list of names." He glanced at the sign headed toward D.C.

"Should we call Owen?" Brooke asked.

"Probably." Ty glanced in his rear view mirror. "Can you pull up his number for me?" Ty handed Brooke the phone the marshals gave him.

Brooke found Owen's number and handed Ty the phone.

"We've been discovered," Ty said as soon as his friend's voice came through the line.

"How?"

"I have no idea. We kept a low profile, no contact with anyone from our pasts, no emails, nothing." Ty switched lanes and finally slowed to the speed limit.

"What happened?"

"There was someone at the house when we got home from church." Ty explained the whole scenario.

"Was there anything to find?"

"We both had our identification with us. But they got Brooke's computer and all my notes about the campaign files."

"You've still been working on those?"

Was Owen scolding or impressed? "I've learned quite a bit."

"Ty, we have to get you and Brooke somewhere safe."

Ty paused. "I want to go to my sister's."

"She doesn't even know you're alive. You can't just show up unannounced."

"My parents handled it. Olivia can too." Ty glanced at Brooke to see how she was responding to his idea.

"What's your motivation for going to your sister?"

Did he really want to explain this to Owen? "I didn't realize how closely my sister worked with Brad Bronowski around the same time I went state's evidence."

Owen was quiet.

"Jasmine Greenwich had been Bronowski's lawyer before she came to me. I'm fairly certain his name was on that list. I want to find out what Olivia knows about the campaign files." *Hopefully nothing.*

"Ty, if she was involved, you could be walking into something dangerous," Owen's tone held concern. "Do you remember her name in the files at all?"

"No, but like I told you, I didn't do much with the files. They were brought to me right before I got out." Ty cleared his throat, hoping his conversation wasn't causing more stress to Brooke. "I know my sister, Owen. She would never try to hurt me. We'll be safer with her than anywhere. If my identity has been compromised, the last place they'll look for me is at my sister's house at the height of her campaign."

Owen seemed to be thinking. "I should probably get the okay from Longstreth."

Ty paused. "Longstreth's the only other person who knew where I was."

More silence on the other end. "I don't want to jump to conclusions."

"Well, something is going on at the Marshal's office. Unless the FBI has a leak—"

"It's not the FBI." Owen was quick to reply. "I'm the only one here with your information.

"Alright. But I'd rather you not tell Longstreth."

"I need to let him know what happened. However, I won't tell him where you're going."

"So, I have your support going to Olivia's?"

"Just stay in touch with me."

Ty promised he would. When he hung up he reached a hand toward Brooke. "Are you okay?"

"I'm scared."

"I understand." He didn't know what else to say. Once again Brooke's life was in danger because of him.

CHAPTER 15

Olivia's house was a large, brick estate, set back from the road, and lined with a row of high bushes, giving it a cover of privacy. It was more pretentious than their parent's house in Maine, but it fit Olivia. Ty pulled the car up close to the house and they both got out.

"Should I be intimidated?" Brooke's eyes traveled over the house and back to Ty.

"Not at all. She's my sister." Ty led the way up the brick lined walk to the ornately carved walnut door. There was a long pause after he rang the doorbell and Ty listened for movement inside.

One of the large doors finally opened and Olivia stood, glaring at Ty. "What in the world are you doing here?"

"You don't seem surprised."

"Get inside before someone sees you." She glanced around the porch and noticed his car. "You parked right in front of my house?"

"What else could I do?" Ty stepped inside with Brooke.

"Let me have your keys. I'll pull it into the garage." Olivia pushed the garage remote and walked outside to put the Camry into hiding.

Ty watched as Brooke's eyes traveled over the high ceiling, elaborate trim work, and the large ostentatious light fixture that hung overhead.

"I don't understand her response," Ty confessed. "She obviously knew I was alive."

"Are you sure we should be here?" Brooke licked her lips and followed Ty further down the marble tiled hallway into the kitchen.

Ty nodded. "There's got to be an explanation. I trust Olivia."

His sister walked through the garage door a moment later and threw Ty his keys. "Do you want some coffee?"

"Is it fresh?" Ty knew his sister was no cook and even coffee was questionable at her hand.

"I just made it." She grabbed down three mugs and poured the dark liquid. "Cream?"

"Yes." Ty pulled out a chair for Brooke and took the seat beside her.

"Why are you here, Blake?" Olivia used her brother's real name and handed him his coffee. She placed another mug before her brother's guest, but made no move to greet or introduce herself.

"I think you owe me an explanation first." Ty gave Brooke opportunity to use the cream and then added it generously to his own mug. "Weren't you at my funeral four and a half years ago?" He knew she was. "You don't seem surprised that I'm alive."

Olivia blew out a frustrated sigh. "Of course I knew you were alive, Blake. Who do you think got you off to such a good start in Cincinnati?" She sat across from her brother at the table.

Blake's blue eyes flashed unease. "You weren't supposed to know."

"Well someone had to look out for my little brother." Olivia took a long drink from her black coffee. "I only wish you'd have come to me first—before the FBI. I could have helped you."

Ty shook his head. "I did the right thing and I don't regret it. Who else knows I'm alive?"

"Just myself, Clayton, and Matthew Pratt." Olivia glanced toward Brooke for a split second.

"Matthew Pratt is dead." The words rolled off Ty's lips. He noticed the immediate look of surprise that flashed across Olivia's face.

"What?" She laid her hand down on the table. "Are you sure?"

"Absolutely sure." Ty leaned back. "How did you know Pratt?"

Olivia shrugged. "I know a lot of people, Blake. Matthew and I go way back."

"It was a breach of confidence for him to tell you my identity." Ty felt his respect for the U.S. Marshal contact waning.

"He knew that as your sister, I would do what I could to help you. I'm glad he told me." She ran her finger over the lip of her mug. "How did he die?

"He was murdered."

"Murdered?" She shook her head and furrowed her thin eyebrows. It was obviously not something Olivia expected to hear. "Are you sure?"

"Yes."

"Any suspects?"

"None that I know of."

Olivia was thoughtful for a moment. She got up to refill her coffee. "That doesn't explain why you showed up at my front door." She glanced again at Brooke. "Or who your friend is."

"This is my wife." Ty motioned toward Brooke.

Olivia's eyes flashed widely. "You got married?" She did a quick, visual assessment of this new "sister-in-law" and her eyes lingered on Brooke's wedding band.

Brooke glanced curiously at Ty.

"Okay, that's better. You owed me a look of shock." He smiled knowingly at Brooke. "I was found out, Olivia."

"What did you do?" Olivia's tone said she blamed her brother.

Ty shook his head. "I have no idea. I was leaving my office about four weeks ago and someone shot me in the arm. They chased me by foot all the way to Brooke's apartment where I hid out front until she got home."

"Is that when you went to Mom and Dad's?" Olivia sat back down.

"Did Mom tell you?"

"No. In fact, poor mom did her best to avoid talking about you. I figured it out, Blake." She stared into her mug. "Taking the plates off the little Jetta didn't work." She raised her eyes to her brother and sighed. "And you left your suit jacket in the closet."

"Mom was going to throw that away."

"Well, I guess she forgot. Anyway, I knew something was up. I don't understand why Mom and Dad kept this from me, though. So, let me guess, you got married and wanted them to meet the new wife?" She glanced at Brooke. "Excuse me if I'm coming off rude—I just feel kind of out of the loop and a little left out."

Ty reached forward and placed a hand on his sister. "We're not really married, Olivia."

Olivia glanced at his wedding band. "Oh really?"

"Let me explain what happened." Ty started from the beginning and ended with their most recent incident. "I had nowhere else to go."

"This is really not a good time. Elections are in November." Olivia's expression was stoic. "Why would anyone be after you now? I thought you got all your old cronies thrown in jail."

What a way to put it. "I don't know."

"Are you sure you weren't followed?"

"Positive. We just need a few days."

"You want to hide out here for a few days?" Olivia flashed her eyes at Ty. "I've got a busy week. I'm supposed to go to South Carolina on Thursday."

"We can be out of your hair by Thursday."

Olivia sighed. "I'm not saying you can't stay—it's just not a good time. Won't your U.S. Marshal contact be looking for you once he finds out your identity has been compromised again?"

"I'm a free man, Olivia. I can hide wherever I want. Witness protection simply provides me with assistance when I go through them."

"So, you aren't telling him you're here?"

"No."

Olivia picked up her cell phone. "I need to tell Clayton not to park in his usual spot in the garage. He should be home soon." Her fingers moved swiftly over her phone screen. "He was picking up Chinese. Do you want anything?" She glanced from Ty to Brooke.

Brooke shook her head.

"I'm fine. We had a big lunch." Ty waited for his sister to finish her text. "I'm going to need to run out and get some clothes. Everything we had was at the safe house."

"You can take the Lexus tomorrow. Just don't get pulled over."

■ ■ ■

An hour later, Clayton listened emotionlessly as Ty recounted the events that brought Brooke and himself to his sister's house. It was natural for Clayton to show little feedback, the man rarely cracked a smile and placed little value in talking. Ty wondered how his brother-in-law felt about his two surprise visitors.

"What purpose would there be in making an attempt on your life now?" Clayton asked dryly. "Have any of those individuals who served time because of you been recently released from prison?"

"None that should matter. They all think I'm dead, remember? Besides, none of them should know I sourced the FBI with my files."

"Information like that gets out." Clayton crossed his legs. "But I don't suppose revenge on you would serve any point. You were just a small piece in the whole game. There were far bigger engines driving the investigation."

Ty glanced at Brooke. She'd been sitting quietly beside him on the sofa. How was she handling this?

Olivia walked from the room and returned with a glass of wine. She sat in an overstuffed leather chair and watched Ty and Brooke. "I don't want you to take this the wrong way," Olivia directed her words to Brooke. "But would you mind terribly if we spoke with my brother alone?"

"Why? She knows everything." Ty placed a hand on Brooke's.

"I don't doubt that." Olivia glanced at her husband for support. "But I don't know this friend of yours as well as you do, and there are things I would like to discuss in private with you."

"It's okay." Brooke glanced at Ty. "I don't mind. Where should I go?" She rose from the sofa and turned to Olivia.

"Why don't I take you upstairs to the guestroom? I've got some old clothes in a closet up there, maybe you could dig through them and find a few outfits you'd like."

As good as his sister looked, Ty was doubtful anything Olivia owned would fit Brooke's slender form.

Ty walked with Brooke and Olivia to the guest room. It was a large room and everything was neat and clean. The walls were painted white and a thick gray comforter layered with black and white pillows covered the queen-sized bed.

Why did Olivia feel the need to exclude Brooke from their conversation? It must be part of Olivia's need to appear perfect to the public. She didn't know if Brooke was a potential voter or not. "Will you be okay?" Ty placed a hand on Brooke's back.

"I'll be fine." Her eyes traveled over the new environment. "I might just take a shower and go to bed. I'm pretty tired." She turned to Ty and gave him a simple, understanding smile.

Ty let his eyes linger on hers. *Brooke understands.* Olivia's less than welcoming welcome hadn't squelched Brooke's sweet, gentle spirit.

"The bathroom is ready for guests." Olivia cleared her throat and walked across the white carpet to a door at the other side of the wall and motioned inside. "There are clean towels hanging up. The little baskets on the shelf contain soap, shampoo, and conditioner. Feel free to use it."

"It's kind of like the Waldorf." Ty winked at Brooke.

Olivia flashed spirited eyes at her brother. "I know what you are implying." She snapped off the light and walked toward the door. "My house is not cold and sterile like a hotel room." She said it like a scold.

Ty feigned shock. "Is that what you thought I meant?"

Olivia waved him off. "If you need anything else, don't hesitate to ask." She said it but her tone wasn't convincing. Had his sister always acted this way?

"Thank you." Brooke answered.

Olivia stood at the exit to the room. It would have been nice if he'd had at least a minute alone with Brooke to say good night and to assure her they were safe now. He was sure there were lots of questions whirling around in her mind.

"For pity's sake, let the poor girl do her thing." Olivia rolled her eyes.

"We'll talk later." Ty gave Brooke's hand a slight squeeze as he walked past her.

Why did Olivia have to come off so intimidating? Under that show of cold professionalism was a fun sister who cared about people. Why couldn't she show it to Brooke? *At least Brooke has enough character to be polite.*

■ ■ ■

"Brooke is no threat to your political career," Ty said as soon as they reached the privacy of the living room. He sat down on the leather sofa and stretched his legs out in front of him.

"I realize that." Olivia sat across from her brother and picked up her glass of wine. "But I don't know her. I'm not as comfortable as you are talking to this cute little thing you've only known for a month."

Ty grinned. Brooke was cute.

"I'm not sure I like the way you look at her." Olivia set her glass down and crossed her arms. "Now start explaining. Why is someone after you?"

Ty shook his head. "I've been trying to figure that out."

"What might you know that makes you a threat to someone?" Clayton asked.

Ty glanced at his brother-in-law. "The only thing I can think of is linked to a situation I was asked to make disappear just before turning state's evidence."

"A situation?" Olivia sounded interested.

"It was unrelated to the other case." Could he discretely ask his sister if she knew anything about it without sounding accusing? "There were several politicians who accepted campaign money from a company with an agenda."

"They took a bribe?"

Ty shrugged. "It looks that way." His eyes shifted from his sister to her husband. "I'm fairly certain Brad Bronowski's name was on that list."

Olivia's face remained indifferent. "And that should mean something to me?" She wrinkled her forehead.

"Only that you and Bronowski worked together to push legislation for several tax incentives." Ty watched for his sister's response.

She seemed unmoved. "And this is relevant why?" There was sarcasm in her tone.

Ty chewed on his lower lip. He opted not to tell his sister the whole story.

Olivia shook her head. "Well I never took any campaign bribes so this really doesn't involve me." She let out a frustrated breath.

"Who else was on the list?" Clayton asked. He got up and walked to the wet bar to pour himself a drink.

"Unfortunately, I don't remember all the names. I was too wrapped up in the FBI case to care. I told the client I wasn't interested but she pushed. She said it was something I should be interested in." Ty ran his hand over his chin. "I barely read through the first few pages."

Clayton returned with a glass of scotch. "So your client was a she? Who was it?"

Ty shook his head. "It's best if I don't disclose that information." Olivia should understand. "Client confidentiality still applies."

"Just not to the FBI." Olivia let out a sarcastic chuckle.

"So why did you come here?" Clayton took a long drink from his scotch.

"I had nowhere else to go." Ty turned to his sister. "And I guess I hoped you'd know something about the campaign bribes. You knew Bronowski quite well. You probably knew some of the others. What can you tell me?"

"I can't tell you anything. Bronowski retired from politics a few years ago, and I have my own level of client confidentiality to uphold. Blake." She leaned forward. "I can't get involved in this. You may stay here a few days. I can probably get you a new identity. But I'm nearing the end of my campaign, I'm completely swamped, and this is the last thing I want to be involved in."

Ty understood.

"I still don't understand why you didn't come to me first." Olivia let her eyes travel to the kitchen door. "You had so much potential. You and I could be working in Washington together. That's what I always thought would happen. You've got that charm. You've got the image people love."

"Maybe if I'd made better choices earlier in my career."

"That doesn't matter. We could have wiped those things away. But you went to the FBI."

What is she saying? "I made the right choice to come clean."

"Seriously, Blake?" Sarcasm dripped from her tone. "I even heard you've been teaching financial wisdom at churches? What kind of angle is that?"

"You read my site?"

"Of course I did. Like I said, someone had to look out for my little brother."

"I enjoy what I do," Ty confessed.

"So are you the one who got mom and dad into their religious kick?"

Ty couldn't suppress a smile. "I did tell them about my relationship with Jesus, yes. But, I think the Lord was working on them both before I contacted them."

"Jesus? The Lord?" Olivia's tone was sour. "Really? I honestly can't believe I'm hearing you talk this way. Is your new girlfriend a religious nut, too?"

Ty chose to ignore Olivia's question. "I know it's probably strange for you to hear me talk about Jesus. But finding forgiveness for my sins through what Jesus did by dying for me and raising from the dead—it's the best thing that's ever happened to me."

Clayton cleared his throat. "This is new, Blake. Can't say I like it."

"But it's wonderful." Ty sat up and turned to his brother-in-law. "For years I carried my sin around like an incurable disease. Coming to Christ gave me the hope I longed for."

"Don't bother." Clayton waved his hand in the air. "I don't have time for this." He rose from his seat and told his wife he was going to do a few things in the office and head off to bed.

"Clayton had to put up with Mom and Dad talking to him for hours about God. He's pretty burned out." Olivia shrugged. "You got to them pretty good."

Ty wanted to explain that it was the Holy Spirit who got through to them. He wanted to tell Olivia that there was forgiveness available for her as well. But she was obviously done with the conversation.

They talked for another half hour and turned in for the night. Ty assumed Brooke was already asleep, so he slipped quietly into his own guestroom.

■ ■ ■

Brooke lay in bed staring at the ceiling. Olivia was nothing like her parents. The feeling of unwelcome was thick and Brooke felt it. How long would they need to stay?

She heard Ty's voice in the hallway. Would he knock on the door and say goodnight? If she weren't afraid of meeting Olivia in the hallway, Brooke would have stepped into the hallway herself.

It was strange how close she felt to Ty. They'd only known each other for little over a month, but it felt longer. They'd been together every day, they'd talked about everything, and they had fun together—despite the circumstances.

Ty's blue eyes and handsome face brought a smile to Brooke's lips. There was no doubt she was attracted to him. But there was more to Ty than his good looks. He was a gentleman. He was considerate. He treated her with kindness and respect that Brooke wasn't used to.

Quit thinking about him. She rebuked herself. *Ty Westgate is out of your league.* Olivia knew it. Brooke could tell Ty's sister didn't approve of her. *Olivia probably has some brilliant lawyer or debutant picked out for Ty.*

Brooke pulled the rich cotton sheets closer to her face and tried to snuggle down into the soft feather pillow. At the little safe house in Maryland, Brooke and Ty stayed up late talking. They always said goodnight before going off to bed. Brooke swallowed back a lump in her throat. *Good night, Ty.*

Chapter 16

The next day Brooke found Ty in the kitchen making breakfast.

"Did you sleep well?" he asked.

Brooke wished she could be honest and tell him the cold feeling of unwelcome permeated the walls and gave her a horrible night's sleep. Instead she shrugged and smiled. "As well as I could. How about you?"

Ty placed his hands on the counter and leaned forward toward Brooke. "I missed saying goodnight to you." His soft blue eyes peered into Brooke's and warmed the cold spot on her heart left there by Olivia.

Brooke smiled shyly. "Me too."

Ty seemed pleased by her answer. "I'm making scones."

"Scones? Sounds delicious. What kind?"

"Orange."

"Mmmm." Brooke reached into the bowl and took a taste of dough. "Good stuff!"

"Well, I hope they're good. I grabbed the recipe off the Internet this morning. I've never made them before."

"I guess you've made yourself at home." Olivia walked into the kitchen and gave her brother a forced smile. "Good morning." She glanced at Brooke. "Did you sleep well?"

"The bed was more than comfortable. Thank you."

"Those sheets are fifteen-hundred count Egyptian Cotton. I bought them at Nordstrom." Olivia walked to the coffee pot and poured herself a cup. "I won't buy my sheets anywhere else. Clayton and I can't stand low end sheets."

Brooke wondered what Olivia would think of the on-sale flannel sheets she had on her bed back in Cincinnati. Brooke liked them even more than Olivia's cotton sheets. Would she ever see those sheets again?

Owen assured Brooke that her belongings were safe. Brooke wasn't sure she'd still have a condo when she got back to Cincinnati, but she was told that her belongings had been taken to a storage unit in some obscure, safe location to be disclosed when she was ready to retrieve them.

"So you're going to let us borrow the Lexus this morning?" Ty asked as he placed the scones in the oven.

"You both need to go?" Olivia asked.

Ty wiped his hands on a towel. "We both need clothes."

"Did you look through my old things?" Olivia directed her words to Brooke.

"Brooke needs her own things." Ty didn't give Brooke the opportunity to reply.

Brooke was relieved. She'd looked at Olivia's pile of old clothes and it was all too big and severely outdated. Brooke wasn't sure how she was going to explain it to Olivia without sounding ungrateful.

"Why waste money?" Olivia argued.

Ty shrugged. "It's government money. Being a politician I would think you'd give your full consent."

"Funny." Olivia walked to the refrigerator and pulled out the orange juice. "I was just trying to help."

"Thank you." Brooke spoke up. "I appreciate the offer."

"Orange juice?" Olivia offered Brooke.

"Yes, please."

Olivia poured two glasses of juice. "There's not much left." She glanced at Ty. "I can see he hasn't changed. When he isn't drinking orange juice, he's using it in a recipe." She drained the last of it into her own glass and tossed the carton in the trash. "I'll need the Lexus back by three. Clayton and I are supposed to be somewhere tonight and I prefer the Lexus."

"No problem." Ty glanced at the kitchen clock. "We've got five hours."

"Five hours for you to shop hardly seems adequate."

Brooke grinned. His sister obviously knew him.

They chatted until the scones were done. Ty applied a thin orange glaze over them. "How long has it been since anyone has cooked in your kitchen?" He teased his sister.

"I'm not going to answer that Ty. You're only trying to show off for Brooke." Olivia turned to Brooke. "He's always been like this—shows off for the ladies." Olivia took a scone and waved. "The keys are in the ignition."

■ ■ ■

It was refreshing to be alone with Ty again. Brooke could finally be herself. What was it about Olivia that made Brooke feel small and weak? It reminded Brooke of the way her night manager used to make her feel. Why did she let people intimidate her? She tried to remember some of the verses Linda encouraged her to learn. Already Brooke was learning that God's Word was healing. *But You, O Lord, are a shield for me, my Glory and the One Who lifts my head.* The Psalms spoke to Brooke. She loved David's humanness and his passion for the Lord. He was like Ty. A smile spread over her lips. She wanted to be like that.

The drive to the mall wasn't long, but Brooke relaxed.

"You're not comfortable around my sister, are you?" Ty's tone was sympathetic.

Brooke turned her head so she could watch him drive. How much should she tell him? Had Ty noticed Olivia's subtle disapproving glances toward Brooke? Did he hear the insincerity in his sister's tone? "I just don't think she likes me," Brooke answered honestly.

Ty shrugged. "I think we just caught her at a bad time."

Brooke kept her thoughts to herself.

"I'm kind of glad Olivia and Clayton have plans tonight," Ty said. He pulled the car into the mall parking garage and pulled into a spot. "I'd like to take a look in Clayton's office."

Brooke waited for him to explain.

"I don't think Clayton or Olivia had anything to do with my identity being compromised or the people who tried to kill me. But I don't think they told me everything they know about Bronowski. I think they're holding something back."

"You're going to snoop in his office?" Brooke was almost frightened at the idea.

Ty shrugged. "I don't have a choice." The two of them got out of the car and Ty clicked the locks. "I think Owen has been doing his own investigation of my sister. He suspects something. Owen doesn't know her the way I do. I'm her little brother. Olivia wouldn't do anything to put my life in danger."

"What about Clayton?"

"Clayton wouldn't do anything to jeopardize his wife's career. He's sitting on too much money for that." Ty opened the mall entrance door for Brooke and walked in right behind her.

Brooke supposed Ty knew his sister better than anyone. Perhaps the woman was just impersonal to outsiders. Maybe Ty saw the side of Olivia that she didn't let the public see.

The large shopping mall was a welcome distraction. Brooke's eyes traveled over the marble floors and up to the high mall ceiling. Hanging contemporary art sculptures hung from the opened rafters and skylights invited sunshine into the mall. She and Ty glanced over a map of the mall and selected the stores they wanted to shop in their limited time.

Brooke looked up from the map. "You do realize that buying new clothes is becoming a regular thing for us."

"Soon we'll have wardrobes in every state." Ty joked.

It was good to laugh with Ty.

Ty insisted they shop for Brooke first and they walked to one of the stores on her list. He waited just outside the dressing room on a small leather sofa the store clerk called, "boyfriend parking."

Brooke tried on a few pairs of jeans and several tops. She stepped outside the dressing room wearing one of the outfits and met Ty's approving eyes. "Do you think I should go with the beige shirt or the blue?" She held up the beige one and let Ty form his opinion.

"You look beautiful in the blue one, but beige brings out your dark brown eyes."

Brooke bit her lower lip between her teeth for a second. He noticed her eyes? She smiled and started to turn toward the dressing room.

"Why don't you get them both?" Ty suggested. He stood up and pulled a scarf off a mannequin. "And get one of these." He handed her the scarf.

"Nice choice," one of the store employees said. "He's a keeper." She winked at Brooke.

He's not mine to keep. The thought hurt. Brooke hurried back to her changing room and tried to distract herself.

After they were done shopping for Brooke, they shopped for Ty. He found what he needed quickly and they stopped to enjoy a cup of coffee before heading back to Olivia's house.

"Are you ready to play spy?" A mischievous grin tugged at Ty's lips.

"I'm a little scared to play spy," Brooke confessed.

Ty chuckled. Brooke figured this wasn't the first time Olivia's little brother had spied on his older sister, but this time the stakes were higher.

After they finished their coffee, Ty carried most of the bags and popped open the trunk on the Lexus.

"I really like all these new clothes I've been getting, but I'd kind of like to keep them long enough to enjoy them." She smiled playfully at Ty.

"Yeah." Ty closed the trunk and they both climbed into the car. "I liked that suit on you."

Brooke had to admit she liked the suit, too.

When they arrived back at the house, Olivia and Clayton were rushed to leave. Olivia gave a critical glance at their bags. "It took you long enough."

"You said be back by three." Ty tossed her the Lexus keys.

"Keep the front of the house dark. I don't want anyone figuring out we have guests." She didn't even offer a smile.

■ ■ ■

Clayton's office was locked. Ty wasn't surprised. However, he wasn't willing to allow a locked door to keep him from getting inside. In a matter of minutes he found an adequate lock-picking device. "Do you think my sister will miss this?" He bent a Bobbie pin and worked the doorknob.

"It's too late now." Brooke watched him.

The door clicked and Ty looked triumphant.

Once inside, he did a quick scan of the room for a possible camera. “No camera,” he called to Brooke.

“What do you want me to do?” she asked.

“Look for a file on me.” Blake motioned toward one of Clayton’s tall, oak file cabinets. “I’ll look for anything else.”

Brooke crept across the thick, soft carpet and trembled at the idea that she was snooping in someone’s office. Family or not, this was totally out of her realm of experience.

The two of them searched for several minutes before Ty let a disgruntled sigh escape his lips.

“What is it?” Brooke walked toward him.

Ty held a manila envelope filled with graphic photographs of a man and woman. “This is Matthew Pratt.” He sighed and shook his head.

“And I take it that isn’t his wife?”

“No. It’s not. These are blackmail photos.”

“What does it mean?” Brooke turned her eyes away from the photos and Ty returned them to the envelope.

“It means my sister lied to me when she said Matthew Pratt was a friend of hers who volunteered my location because she’s my sister.” Ty slapped the file down on the table and paced the room.

“Why would she do that? How did she even know your death was faked?”

“Olivia is determined. She and Clayton probably figured out that my death, at that very opportune time, was a safe way out for me.” He leaned against the desk. “I can’t believe she blackmailed Pratt.” He shook his head in disappointment and frustration.

“Are you going to tell Owen?”

Ty contemplated that thought for a moment. “First, I want to talk to Olivia.”

“Are you sure?” Brooke’s eyebrows furrowed. “She’s not going to like that you explored Clayton’s office.”

“Well, I don’t like that she lied to me. I think she’ll find that we’re even.” Ty stood up from the desk. “Did you find anything on me?”

“Not a thing.” Brooke shook her head. “I looked you up under Ty Westgate, Blake Kendall, just Ty and just Blake. What about the computer?”

Ty shrugged and they both walked toward Clayton's computer.

"It needs a password." Ty sat down in Clayton's leather desk chair and put his fingers on the keyboard.

"Any guesses?"

Ty shook his head. "Clayton is an anomaly. I'd have no idea what kind of password he'd use." Ty glanced up at Brooke. "You're not by any chance a computer hacker are you?"

"Sorry, I never learned that art."

Ty stood up and grabbed the file. "But we have this." He kept the manila envelope and closed the file drawer. "I couldn't find anything on Bronowski or any financial campaign gifts, so I guess we're done here."

Brooke nodded.

Ty did his best to return the room to its original order and locked the door behind him.

"It would be a good night to find out what the FBI might have learned. I'll give Owen a quick call and then we can make some dinner."

Ty's call to Owen included the fact that he found something but wanted to dig a little deeper before using it as evidence.

"If your sister is involved in this—" Owen began.

"She's not," Ty interrupted.

"But if she is, you can't protect her."

"I know." Ty let his eyes travel to the window. The early evening sky was soft over the colorful trees behind Olivia's house. Tall oaks, poplars, and maples filled Olivia's back yard, reminding Ty of the trees his father had around their home in Maine. Why did everything have to be so complicated? Ty sighed and prayed his sister wasn't involved.

"Any news on our safe house in Maryland?" Ty asked. "I'd like to know how we got discovered."

"Longstreth is investigating. The Marshals don't take highly to being compromised.

"Any leads?" Ty paced the floor with the cell phone against his ear.

"None that Wyatt has told me. He wasn't too pleased when I told him you were keeping your whereabouts a secret."

"Does he know you know?" Ty asked.

"I didn't offer the information." Owen paused. "Just be careful, okay? If your sister is involved—"

"She's not going to kill me."

"Well, someone tried."

"It wasn't Olivia." Ty opted not to tell Owen that his sister knew his whereabouts these past four and a half years. That would place Olivia front and center on their suspect list. Once he got a little more information he'd talk. But he hoped to find something to prove she wasn't involved.

■ ■ ■

"Do you like gardening?" Olivia's question the next morning surprised Brooke.

"Yes." Brooke nodded. She watched Olivia cross the room and lean against the kitchen counter.

"I do too." Olivia finished her cup of coffee and set the gray mug down on the marble countertop. Her lips curved into a fake smile and she fixed her eyes on Brooke. "I like to work in the garden on mornings like this. It gives me a chance to collect my thoughts."

Brooke couldn't imagine this high-strung woman ever pausing long enough to garden, but she listened.

"Blake asked to use our weight room this morning, so I thought while he's working out maybe you and I could work in the garden together."

"Sure." Brooke tried not to sound as suspicious as she felt.

"Unless you'd like to work out with me in the weight room," Ty offered. "She's got a sweet treadmill." Brooke noticed the enthusiasm in Ty's blue eyes.

"Don't try to keep her from me, Blake," his sister scolded. "I've got extra gardening gloves, shovels, you name it. I have a whole box of bulbs I wanted to plant this fall." She seemed to really want Brooke's companionship.

"I'd be happy to help." Brooke much preferred working out with Ty than working in the garden with Olivia, but this was obviously what Olivia wanted so Brooke consented.

Ty refilled Brooke's coffee cup and added just the right amount of cream. "It's a trap, Brooke. She just wants to make you her slave. She used to do it to me all the time when we were kids. 'Hey Blake, do you want to help me organize my closet?'" Ty did a humorous imitation of his sister's voice. "'It will be so much fun…'"

Olivia shoved a short blonde hair behind her ear. "It worked didn't it?"

"Yeah. You got your work done."

Olivia waved her brother off. "I'll go get the gloves."

It was nice to be outside. The trees were alive with color and the sky was clear and blue. Brooke spotted a Baltimore Oriole on a nearby branch. Its bright orange chest and black wings stood out brilliantly against the blue sky. She would have pointed him out to Ty, but didn't feel comfortable sharing her observation with Olivia.

"I haven't been out here enough this fall," Olivia said casually.

"Your yard looks beautiful." Brook's eyes traveled over the flawless landscaping. It looked like someone raked it every time a leaf fell.

"I have a man who comes out once a week to help," Olivia confessed. "Although I find it rewarding to plant my own flowers." She finished digging a small hole and reached for a daffodil bulb. "You can plant a cluster of tulips right here." Olivia motioned to a spot a few feet from herself.

Brooke couldn't remember ever digging into such nice garden soil. It made planting easy. With as many bulbs as they were planting, the flowerbeds would be alive with color in the spring.

"I'm sure you've been pretty frightened having two attempts made on your life." Olivia dug another hole.

Brooke nodded. "It was a terrible experience."

"I can imagine." Olivia cleared her throat. "You know as long as you are with Blake it's not going to stop."

Brooke was quiet for a moment. *This is just a set up. She lured me out here to talk about Ty.* She tightened her jaw and placed a handful of bulbs in the hole. "I'm not afraid."

"Really?" Olivia patted the dirt over a daffodil bulb. "Then you're braver than me." She moved a few feet away and began digging another hole. "You do realize that whoever is after my brother will be looking for his weakness."

Brooke placed mulch over the newly planted bulbs and waited for Olivia to continue.

"I've seen the way Blake looks at you. He cares a lot about you." Olivia stopped and glanced at Brooke. "In fact—I'd say you're his weakness."

Brooke pushed a hair behind her ear with her gloved hand and steadied her gaze on Olivia.

"As long as you're with Blake, they have a way to hurt him." Olivia returned to her digging.

Brooke wasn't about to take the bait. This woman didn't like Brooke and wanted to take her out of the picture, but Brooke wanted to be there for Ty. He wanted her there—didn't he?

"How long are you going to run with him?" Olivia tossed down the shovel. "He's in witness protection. Are you ready to give up your entire life for this man? Are you ready to never talk to your brother again?"

Brooke wondered how Olivia knew about her brother.

"As long as he is hiding and as long as there is someone in his life who he cares about, Blake's life is in worse danger." Olivia flashed her eyes at Brooke. "He can't just leave at the drop of a hat."

"We've already done it once." Brooke gathered all the gumption she could muster.

Olivia sat back on her heels in the grass. "Look, Brooke…" Olivia seemed amused by the rhyme. "I know right now you're both in this emotional place where you feel a connection. That's common. You've experienced something traumatic together." Olivia shrugged. "But you're not right for each other."

Brooke set down her shovel. She glanced curiously at Olivia.

"He comes from a very different life than you." Olivia sat up just enough to look down at Brooke.

What is she saying?

"He's a Yale Lawyer. Our dad's a doctor. You have an alcoholic father who can't hold down a job."

Brooke's dark eyes flashed indignantly.

"Don't look so hurt. You have to see it. You're from totally different classes." Olivia paused to let her hurtful words sink in. "I know you care about Blake. It's only natural. But if you care about him, the best thing you can do is leave."

"How do you know about my father?" Did Ty tell her? Brooke had to know.

"Do you really think I'd allow you to stay in my house without having my husband do a little research on you?" Olivia gave a patronizing grin. "Your father has had two DUI's in the past five years and was laid off from his last job for showing up drunk."

Brooke didn't know about those recent events, but her heart was heavy. Olivia was making it clear to Brooke that she had no place in Ty's life.

"I can make this easy for you." Olivia removed her gloves and picked up a manila envelope she had underneath the box of bulbs. "I got you a job working for Children's Hospital in a nice city just an hour away from your brother." She held the envelope out to Brooke. "I gave you a new last name to help keep your identity a secret, and I've set up a bank account with fifteen thousand dollars to get you started."

A bribe? Brooke tried not to let her feelings turn to bitterness. She glanced at the envelope in Olivia's hands and shuddered at this woman's proposal. "Have you talked to Ty about this?"

Olivia laughed. "Of course not! My brother won't want you to go. He's taken with you. I can see it in the way he looks at you. He can't see straight enough to know what's best for him. But you do—don't you?" Olivia leveled her gaze on Brooke. "You know I'm right."

Brooke lowered her eyes.

"Every day that you remain with my brother, he cares deeper and deeper for you and consequently, you place his life further at risk. The more he cares for you, the more they can hurt him."

A dull pain gnawed at Brooke's stomach. "Whoever tried to kill Ty made their first attempt before I even knew Ty." She forced herself to speak.

"Yeah, but the next thing they did was to go after you." Olivia reminded her. "Now he won't let you out of his sight."

Brooke rose to her feet and Olivia rose with her. "I can give you a new life. After this blows over, you can reconnect with your brother." Olivia's eyes bore through Brooke's tears and into her soul.

"You won't have this chance again."

Brooke took a few steps backward. She wanted to run. She wanted to leave this hateful politician—this hateful woman. Was this really Ty's sister?

"And if you choose to stay… what do you think is really going to happen? Ty will be given a new identity and where will you be? Do you think he's going to marry you?" Olivia asked sarcastically.

Brooke hadn't thought about it. She lost her job in Cincinnati. She could never go back to her parents. Where would she go?

Olivia sensed Brooke's hesitation and passed her the envelope.

Brooke glanced inside and read the information.

"I've booked you for a flight today." Olivia confessed. "You'll be staying at a high end hotel not far from the hospital until you can find an apartment." She watched Brooke intently. "It's all been paid for."

"What about my things? Owen said everything from my apartment in Cincinnati is in storage somewhere."

"I can find it and have it sent to you. I'll even find your little car. But until then, fifteen thousand dollars should get you off to a good start—and the job itself pays quite well."

Tears threatened to spill from her eyes and her hands trembled as she held the envelope. She felt so alone—insignificant and alone. *Olivia is right. I'm not good enough for Ty.* Even as Brooke said the words to herself her heart ached. *I don't belong here. I'm just putting Ty's life more at risk... But to never see him again?*

"Clayton can leave whenever you're ready."

"What about Ty?"

"He's working out in the weight room. Blake loves my weight room. You and Clayton can be on your way before Blake knows you're gone."

Brooke knew this meant act fast. The lump in the back of her throat threatened to release an onslaught of tears. She tossed her gardening gloves to the ground and gave a resigned nod.

"You're making the right choice. Now hurry and get your things."

Chapter 17

Ty felt good. He'd worked out for over an hour and a half on some of the best home workout equipment available. Olivia had top of the line stuff and it was almost better than the equipment he used at the gym in Cincinnati. After a nice long shower, he was ready to find out how Brooke and his sister got along in the garden. He hoped Olivia hadn't intimidated Brooke too badly.

Olivia was on the deck reading when Ty found her. She'd changed out of her gardening clothes into a pair of gray slacks and a white blouse. "Have a fizzy water." She looked up at her brother and motioned to a closed bottle of sparkling juice.

"No thanks. I'll stick with the old fashioned stuff." He glanced out at the flowerbed. "Where is Brooke?"

Olivia set the paper down, shoved her reading glasses into her short blonde hair, and studied her brother for a moment. She cleared her throat. "Take a seat."

Ty caught the look in Olivia's eyes. "What does that mean?"

"It means take a seat. We need to talk."

Ty sat across from his sister on one of her teak patio chairs, wondering what she was about to tell him. This couldn't be good. Had Olivia's biting tongue cut into Brooke's tender heart? Ty knew Olivia was capable of being harsh and could say some unpleasant things.

"She's gone, Blake."

Olivia's words caught him off guard. Ty shook his head. "What do you mean?"

"She's gone." Olivia sighed. "I gave her a new identity and a good job where she'll be happy. You know it's what's best."

Ty sprang to his feet. "How can you say that? Where did you send her?"

"Away."

"Tell me!" Ty's eyes flashed wide.

"No." Olivia kept her tone calm. "It's better for her if you don't know where she is."

Ty clenched his fists. "You had no right to send her away. She's under witness protection with me."

"Protection that's been compromised—come on Blake, you've been putting that poor girl's life at risk since the day you met her. You should thank me for taking her out of the situation and giving her a fresh, new start. She'll be working for a nice hospital where she'll be well paid and can stop living in fear that someone's about to kill her."

Ty couldn't explain the feelings in his heart. Brooke was gone? "How dare you make that decision for us."

"For us?" Olivia's eyes seemed to find humor in the words. "You and Brooke are an 'us,' huh?"

Ty wanted to hit something. "What we are does not involve you. Tell me where she is!" Ty leaned forward with his hands flat on the table.

"No, Blake. I refuse." Olivia's tone was resolute. "To tell you will only endanger that poor girl again and even yourself."

Ty shook his head and tried to deal with his emotions. He was furious, sad, hurt.

"As long as there is someone you care about in the picture, the people who are after you have a playing card they can use to win. You know I'm right."

"Using that logic, are you going to hide Mom and Dad?" Ty challenged her.

"I don't need to. I've already got eyes on them. How do you think I knew you and Brooke were there? I didn't need to see your suit jacket or her car to know. Did you ever wonder why I showed up just days after you did?"

Ty slammed his hand on the table. "Do you really have to control all of our lives, Olivia?"

Olivia flashed Ty her most daring glare. "No, Blake. I do damage control. You controlled your own life just fine when you went to the FBI with all those files."

"I made the right decision," Ty said boldly.

"You lost your opportunity to soar!"

"I will soar some day—on wings like eagles."

Olivia's lips curved into a thin sarcastic grin. "That's precious." She pulled herself up from the chair. "Brooke's safe, Blake. I set her up with a new name and a nice bank account. Just let her go."

"Well, maybe I can blackmail someone into telling me where she is." Ty spat.

"What's that supposed to mean?"

"I was in Clayton's office." Ty figured Olivia would know what he meant.

"You broke into Clayton's office?"

Ty opted for the sparkling juice and opened the bottle. His mouth was dry and his heart was heavy. He decided to use the only card he had. "Wait here."

It only took Ty a moment to grab one of the photographs from the file. He kept the rest hidden in case he needed evidence. Olivia was still on the deck, waiting with her arms crossed and a scowl on her painted face.

"Does this look familiar?" Ty handed his sister one of the incriminatory photographs.

Olivia kept her face unreadable. "I've never seen this in my life."

"Well apparently Clayton has. It was in his office under the Matthew Pratt file."

"So, what are you saying?" Olivia clutched the photo.

"I'm saying you blackmailed Pratt." Ty's eyes flashed an angry blue.

"How can you say that?" Olivia shoved the photo back into Ty's hands with force. "I never blackmailed anyone! I knew Pratt. We'd worked on a case together right out of college. Check my records. Dig through my old cases, you'll see that I'm telling the truth. Clayton and I even got together with Matthew and his wife, Jill, socially a few times.

"Then why the pictures?" Ty jiggled the unsavory photo in the air.

"I don't know. Unless Clayton was trying to protect Pratt from something."

"You're saying you knew nothing about the photograph?"

"Nothing!" Olivia's eyes softened as if she was hurt. "I may be a politician but I don't play dirty politics."

Ty blew out a sigh. He didn't know what to believe. "You do realize these pictures make you a suspect."

"They're not my pictures!"

"Tell that to the FBI."

Olivia's eyes grew wide. "You're turning them in?" She reached for the crumpled photo.

"Unless you tell me where Brooke is." Ty couldn't believe the words rolled off his lips.

"Oh," Olivia's lips formed the word. "I see—little brother has a blackmail chip."

Ty wasn't sure it was right to use it, but he had to know where his sister sent Brooke.

"You have to trust me." Olivia's eyes grew somber. "I sent her where I knew she'd be happy. She's not far from her brother."

"She's in Colorado?" At least this was something.

"Yes." Olivia laid her hand flat on the table. "Don't press for more. She's safe. She's at one of the most reputable hospitals in the area. And I told her after all this blows over she can reconnect with her brother."

Ty thrust the photo back into her hands and turned to go. She didn't know he had several more hidden under the dresser in the guestroom.

■ ■ ■

The drive to the airport was painfully quiet. Unlike his wife, Clayton was not gifted in the fine art of speech. The man's emotionless expression mingled with the quiet of the car made the drive feel like hours.

Brooke glanced at Clayton and noticed his blank expression as he repeatedly glimpsed in the rearview mirror. How did a man like that win Olivia's heart? Did they love each other or was it purely a marriage of convenience?

She glanced down at the paperwork Olivia had given her. *Brooke Peterson. Denver, Colorado.* An Ohio driver's license was paper clipped to the information packet. How did Olivia have a driver's license made with this new name? The photo was the same as her old license but the Cincinnati address was unfamiliar. Would Brooke need to learn it? Was she supposed to pretend that was her old address? How far did Olivia go to give Brooke a new identity?

Brooke remembered going to Denver one summer when she'd visited Cody. It was a nice city and Brooke was sure she would adjust to life there. But what about Ty? She looked down at the small gold wedding band she still wore on her left ring finger. Somehow that ring made her feel like she and Ty were still connected.

She'd left without saying goodbye. Would he be hurt? Brooke sucked in a painful sigh. It was too late now. She glanced behind her as if letting her eyes travel to where they'd been would make a difference.

She'd only known him a little over a month. Why was this so difficult? Why did the thought of never seeing him again hurt so much? She thought back over the weeks they spent in Maryland. Their time there was short, but they'd made friends and enjoyed sweet time together. She'd shared things with Ty that she never told anyone. *And he believed me.*

Brooke thought about her new relationship with Christ. With Ty in her life, it was so easy to find Bible verses that applied to various situations and answers to questions. Now that she was on her own again, would her faith stand firm?

She'd have an opportunity to tell Cody about the Lord. Brooke tried to find the good in her situation. She wasn't sure when it would be safe to disclose her whereabouts to Cody, but with only an hour drive between them, she could do it somehow.

Clayton made a turn off on an exit and Brooke noticed the airport signs. "Gather your stuff together," Clayton instructed. "I'm not going in with you."

Brooke understood. It was probably best if no one saw her with the man. "Please tell Ty I'm sorry." She gave Clayton one simple request.

Clayton nodded and Brooke took it as a yes.

He pulled his car up to the passenger drop-off and glanced in his rear view mirror. "Be quick."

Brooke stepped out and grabbed the bag Ty purchased for her during their most recent shopping excursion. Clayton pulled away as soon as she closed the door.

The airport was crowded and Brooke glanced at her airline tickets to remind herself where she needed to go. Busy people bustled past but Brooke walked slowly, as if a heavy weight pulled her back.

Ahead of her, Brooke noticed a man she recognized as a Cincinnati Bengal. She'd know him anywhere. His black hair, dark skin, and friendly smile made Ben Williamson a Cincinnati favorite. His broad shoulders filled out his Bengal's jacket and he carried a large overnight bag as if it were a lunch sack. His eyes caught hers for only a moment and gave her a friendly smile as he walked toward his destination.

Walking alone through the unfamiliar airport, Brooke observed her surroundings. She glanced around trying to find the proper airline check in and noticed a man not far behind her with his eyes fixed on her. She picked up her pace and glanced over her shoulder. The man was right behind her.

You're just paranoid, Brooke. She turned toward one of the airline counters. Ben Williamson was in line signing an autograph. She headed toward him when she felt something hard and steely pressed into her side.

"Don't say a word." A familiar voice whispered in her ear. The man stood so close that the gun was hidden between their bodies. "Come with me, Brooke."

How did he find her? This was the man who broke into her hotel. His voice was forever burned into her mind. Brooke's hands trembled and her eyes scanned the airport for some way of escape.

"Let's turn around together. I've got a car waiting outside."

The football player moved forward in line. Before she had time to change her mind she called out his name. "Ben! Ben Williamson!"

At the sound of his name, Ben turned around and saw Brooke.

"Wait up, Ben!" She clutched her bag and broke free from the arm that restrained her.

Too startled to respond, her abductor hid his gun and moved away to a nearby wall where he could stand and keep an eye on

Brooke.

Boldness Brooke rarely exhibited broke to the surface. She hurried to the football player and threw her arms around his neck in a familiar greeting.

"Do I know you?" The man accepted the hug, but whispered in her ear.

"No, but please fake it. I'm in trouble."

Ben patted her back after their embrace and wrapped an arm around her. "What can I do for you?" he asked softly.

"I'm in witness protection. The man behind me is trying to abduct me."

As discretely as he could, Ben scanned the area. "The ugly white guy with the cheap business suit?" Ben asked. "So you want me to take him down?" His tone said he would only be too happy to comply.

"He's got a gun." As large as Ben was, she knew his strength was no match for a gun.

The airline counter personnel motioned for Ben to move forward. "How may I help you?" she asked.

Ben handed her his airplane ticket.

The airline worker seemed to recognize his name and looked up approvingly. "So glad you'll be flying with us today, Mr. Williamson. Do you have any bags to check?"

Ben glanced at her name badge. "Actually, Veronica, I don't. But I do have a request." He leaned forward at the counter. "My friend here is being harassed by that man in the dark suit standing against the wall."

Veronica glanced discretely toward the man.

"I think he's a reporter," Ben continued. "They're always trying to find some kind of juice on me. I honestly can't be bothered by the media—I'd like to have a personal life."

"I understand. I'll call security to take care of that." She smiled at Brooke. "Are you flying with Mr. Williamson today?"

"Actually, I'm booked for a flight to Denver, but I'd like to change it if possible."

"You can't actually change your flight, ma'am."

Brooke glanced at the ticket. What should she do?

“Just give us a minute.” Ben put a finger up and pulled Brooke back a step so they could talk in private. “Where do you want to go?” he spoke softly to Brooke.

“No one was supposed to know I was here. The fact that he found me says my destination has been compromised.”

Ben nodded.

“I’ve got a contact in New York City who I trust.”

“So you want to go to New York?” Ben made sure he understood.

“Yes.”

“Alright,” Ben winked. “She’d like the quickest flight to New York City,” he told the woman behind the counter.

The woman glanced at her computer screen. “We’ve got a flight boarding in twenty-five minutes, but you’d have to hurry.”

Brooke nodded. “I’ll take it.”

Veronica quoted the price and Brooke opened her purse to see what she had.

“Tell you what,” Ben stopped Brooke’s hand. “Just put it on my charge.” He handed the woman his credit card. “Don’t tell any reporters where she’s going.”

“I would never.” Veronica wrote down Brooke’s information and issued an airline ticket “No bags to check?”

“No.” Brooke clutched hers tightly. She was on her third set of clothes and wasn’t about to risk losing these.

Ben offered to carry her bag. “I’ll get you to your plane.”

They stepped away from the counter. Airport security had already driven the man away. Ben took Brooke’s arm and walked her toward the terminals.

“You didn’t need to pay for my ticket.” Brooke glanced up at the large man. “I have money. Please let me pay you back…”

“Now you stop it,” Ben said in a playful tone. “It’s not every day I get to play Good Samaritan to a beautiful woman in an airport. Don’t rob me of my blessing.”

They arrived at the terminal a few minutes before boarding. “Are you going to be alright?” Ben placed a friendly hand on her shoulder.

“Yes. I can’t thank you enough for helping me. I—”

“Don’t say another word,” Ben interrupted. “Just keep cheering for me.”

“I will.” Brooke was convinced she was a Bengals fan for life now. “God bless you.” The words slipped off her lips. It was a new thing for her to say, but she wanted to leave him with words that would let the man know Who she served.

“He already has.” A smile spread across Ben’s face. “I’ll stay until I’m sure the ugly white guy isn’t anywhere around.” He waved as she boarded.

CHAPTER 18

Ty sat on the edge of the bed in the room where Brooke slept the night before. He'd gone to the room in hopes of some kind of note. The only thing she'd left was her emergency cell phone.

Olivia's reasoning made sense. Brooke's life had been in danger ever since she met him. They'd had two close calls in only a few weeks and until they got to the bottom of this, Ty was sure attempts would continue.

But why didn't she say goodbye? Ty paced the room and wished the heaviness on his heart would disappear. Would he ever see Brooke again? He didn't even have a photograph. He let the image of her expressive dark eyes and her long brown hair flash through his mind.

Part of him was tempted to head to the airport and catch a plane to Colorado. The world suddenly felt so big.

He returned to his guestroom to call Owen. He wanted to know if there were any more leads.

"She's gone, Owen," he said to his friend after Owen updated Ty on their investigation.

"Who? Brooke?" Owen listened for an explanation.

"Olivia sent her to Colorado without my knowledge." Ty wasn't sure how Owen would respond.

"Olivia had no authority to do that."

Ty was thoughtful for a moment. "She said it was best for Brooke."

"Where in Colorado?" Owen pressed.

"She won't tell me." Ty blew out a heavy sigh. "I can't even call her. Olivia told Brooke to leave her phone. I'm done here."

"I'm sorry, Ty."

Ty was quiet. "I still want to get to the bottom of this case."

"Well, I've dug up some news." Owen offered. "Jasmine Greenwich is dead."

"What? When?" Ty's interest was piqued.

"A car accident about five weeks ago. Supposedly, she was drunk and lost control of her car. She went over a bridge." Owen cleared his throat. "Guess what they found in her car."

Ty waited for Owen to tell him.

"A bottle of vodka, wiped clean of all prints but hers."

Ty placed his head in his hand and clutched the phone. "Not a coincidence, I'm sure." He glanced at his sister's clean guest room carpet and shook his head. "I hope Brooke is safe."

■ ■ ■

Brooke stepped from the terminal at John F. Kennedy Airport and glanced around nervously for the man she'd seen in D.C. What if he followed her? She worked her way through crowds of people, watching for an exit. It was close to four. Would she make it to the FBI offices before Owen got off work? How would she reach him if he already left for the day?

Brooke motioned for a cab. How did Ty do this every day? She climbed into the back seat. "FBI headquarters please."

The cab driver whipped through traffic toward the FBI building and Brooke found herself in the lobby by 4:40. She made her way to the fourth floor and walked toward Owen's office.

"Brooke," Nathan greeted her just outside Owen's door. "What are you doing back in New York?"

"It's a long story. I need to talk to Owen."

Nathan opened his boss' door. "Brooke Dunbar's here."

"Come in." Owen motioned to a chair. "Close the door, Nathan." He sat up in his chair and waited for Brooke to take a seat. "I thought you were on your way to Colorado."

Brooke's eyes flashed surprise. "How did you know about Colorado?"

"Ty called me. He said Olivia created a new identity for you and set you up with a job not far from your brother."

Did he tell you I left without saying goodbye? Brooke struggled to maintain her emotions. “Well, someone else knew, too. The man who came to my hotel a few weeks ago was at the airport.”

Owen sat up in his chair. “What?”

“He talked to me. I’d recognize his voice anywhere.” Brooke described the scene that met her at the airport.

“Let me see the paperwork Olivia gave you.”

Brooke handed Owen her new identity profile.

He leaned back in his chair and looked over the papers. “This does not look good for Ty’s sister.”

Brooke agreed. Had Ty told Owen about the photos of Matthew Pratt? Something wasn’t right. “But Ty is convinced that his sister would never try to kill him.”

Owen nodded. “I know.”

“Did Ty say what he was going to do?”

“He’s headed back to New York. I’ll give him a quick call and let him know what happened at the airport.”

Brooke writhed her hands and waited while Owen made his call.

“No answer.” Owen hung up without leaving a message. “I’ll try him again in a little bit. He glanced at his watch. “Listen, why don’t you come home with me? I’ll call my wife and tell her to expect a guest. It’s not the Waldorf, but we can put you up in our spare room.”

An FBI agent was offering his home? Brooke could hardly believe it. “Thank you.” Relief showed on her face. “Will your wife mind?”

“No. She’s always telling me she wants to help on a case.” He dialed his home number and spoke briefly with his wife.

“She’s fine with it.” Owen hung up the phone. “Let me grab your bag.” He turned off the light in his office and locked the door. “Nathan,” he called to his assistant.”

“Yes, sir.”

“I need you to check out this information—every bit of it.” Owen handed Nathan the file from Olivia. “And you have not seen Miss Dunbar.”

Nathan glanced quickly at Brooke and let his eyes travel past her. “Haven’t seen her at all.”

■ ■ ■

Yolanda Vance met Brooke at the door with a warm welcome. "I'm Yolanda." Two hands reached out to take Brooke's in a friendly greeting. "Come on in. Are you hungry?" A warm smile lit up Yolanda's naturally tan face and tugged at the corners of her striking green eyes. "When Owen said you were coming I went ahead and made enough for the three of us for dinner."

"Thank you." It was a relief to feel welcome somewhere again. What a contrast to Olivia's reception.

"My husband has never given me an opportunity to help on a case," Yolanda admitted as she carried Brooke's bag to the stairs.

Owen greeted his wife with a light kiss on the lips and set his brief case beside the coffee table. They were a beautiful couple. A few grays scattered throughout Yolanda's dark hair made it obvious she and Owen were close in age, but Yolanda's naturally tan skin gave her a more youthful appearance. A colorful scarf that acted as a headband, kept her thick dark curls away from her face.

"What finally made you give in?" she asked him.

"I needed a safe place to hide her." Owen turned to smile at Brooke. "And I'm sure the two of you will get along."

Yolanda showed Brooke to the guestroom and gave her a few minutes to get cleaned up for dinner.

Brooke appreciated the simple charm of Owen and Yolanda's house. Owen had told Brooke the house was part of a series of remodeled row houses built in the early nineteen hundreds. The hardwood floors and wide oak trim was all that was left of its original interior.

She changed into one of the casual outfits Ty purchased for her on their recent shopping trip and walked downstairs to the smell of homemade lasagna.

"This looks great." She took a seat across from Yolanda at the table. Owen sat at the head and the couple began eating as soon as Brooke sat down.

Brooke was reminded of the sweet, simple prayers of thanksgiving Ty offered when they ate together. She paused for a moment to breathe a silent prayer of thanks.

"This is wonderful. I haven't had homemade lasagna in a long time."

"It was my grandmother's recipe." Yolanda explained. "My father is part Italian, part Irish and my mother is from Mexico. I've got family recipes from all around the globe."

Yolanda's unique family heritage explained her lovely features.

"Did you get through to Ty?" Brooke was anxious to know.

Owen shook his head. "No answer. He called me after you left D.C. and told me he planned to leave soon. He was going to try to drive to New Jersey tonight and meet me at the FBI office in the morning."

Brooke hoped Ty was okay. Would the man who tried to apprehend her at the airport make an attempt on Ty? *We need to warn him.*

"You seem lost in your thoughts." Yolanda broke the silence.

Brooke gave a wane smile. "I'm just hoping my friend was able to get safely out of D.C." She glanced at Owen and found his understanding eyes on her.

"I'll try his phone again after dinner," Owen said.

■ ■ ■

Ty pulled onto the interstate and merged into the northbound traffic. He rubbed his tense neck and replayed his sister's last heated words in his mind. "You're leaving? Why? Because I sent her away? Come on, Ty. Think about it. She's not one of us."

What was that supposed to mean? "Let my people give you a new identity and just start over." Who were "her" people and how did she have enough authority to create a new identity for someone? Apparently, Olivia had more secrets than he'd thought.

He had told her he planned to return to New York and help Owen solve the case.

"Stay out of it, Blake," she warned. "Whoever these people are, they've tried to kill you twice and they're obviously not going to stop trying."

Ty sensed genuine concern. She cared about her little brother. *But I'm not backing down from this.*

Ty switched lanes and noticed a vehicle trailing behind. He turned on the radio and hit the search button. It stopped on a country station playing a familiar song and Ty's lips curved into a smile as he recalled his drive to Maine with Brooke.

He wondered if Owen would help him find Brooke. Would it be wise to try to find her? Ty wasn't sure when he would be free to live a normal life again.

The few weeks in Maryland seemed so normal. He and Brooke both loved that little church and the nice friends they'd made. David and Linda would wonder why they disappeared.

The car behind him drew closer and Ty switched lanes quickly. His blue eyes flashed to the rear view mirror and he knew without a doubt he was being followed. In traffic, it was easy to put a few cars between himself and the other car, but the tail wasn't far behind. How had he been found again?

Making a last minute lane change, Ty hurried off the highway and dodged a few cars to make himself scarce. On his GPS, Ty searched for an alternate route to New York and hoped he'd successfully lost the strange dark car.

He'd been driving for over thirty minutes when he noticed the car again.

How is this possible? Ty sped up.

The car approached quickly and pulled up in the lane beside him. It crept closer in an obvious attempt to run him off the road.

With few other cars around him on this back route, it was difficult to lose the other car. Ty clutched the wheel and did his best to outrun the vehicle, but whoever it was stayed hot on his tail.

He uttered a soft prayer for help when he heard the first bullet ricochet off the wheel rim of his car. Another well-aimed shot hit its target and Ty felt his car pulling against its flattened tire. Another shot and Ty could hardly keep the car on the road. With two flat tires, he was forced to pull over.

Ty wasted no time. He opened the passenger side and made a run for the woods beside the road. Dodging trees and undergrowth, Ty tore through the woods without a thought of his destination.

With a fast beating heart, Ty scanned the environment and saw buildings on the other side of the woods. A fence. Could he scale it?

His assailants were close. Ty reached for the fence and pulled himself up as a hard object struck his side.

Ty fell to the ground and was met by a painful strike across his injured arm with a baseball bat. Grabbing his arm, he let out a pained moan.

In only minutes, Ty was pulled from the ground and found himself in a fight between two men in ski masks. He did his best to defend himself against his attack, using all his strength to put his offenders in their place. Two well-placed punches landed one of his attackers into the fence. Ty was about to hit the man a third time, but the other man struck Ty with the bat and brought him to his knees.

"You're not going to win this, Blake."

He knows my real name?

Ty was about to respond but the man struck him on the head.

■ ■ ■

When Ty woke up, his body ached with painful bruises. Plastic zip ties bound his hands and feet. He did his best to sit up on the dirty couch where he'd been laid and looked around trying to figure out where he was.

The room was dark and the blinds were drawn. It was so quiet Ty could hear his own breathing. He knew instinctively that he was alone. The faint smell of stale cigarettes lingered in the room, but it was too dark to make out anything more than the shapes of a few pieces of furniture.

His head throbbed and Ty reached his bound hands to the side of his head where he felt a nice sized lump.

How long had he been unconscious? For whatever reason they'd left him alive. Ty closed his eyes against the pain in his head. He lay back down on the couch and prayed God would help him find a way to get out of this and find Brooke.

■ ■ ■

Brooke sighed when she glanced at the clock. It was after two p.m. and she'd still not heard anything from Owen about Ty. The FBI agent promised when he left for work that morning that he would notify her as soon as he heard anything.

Yolanda placed a cup of coffee in front of Brooke and sat across from her. Her eyes followed Brooke's to the clock and she nodded knowingly. Owen had explained the situation to his wife the night before and Brooke shared more details after breakfast.

"This whole thing is really crazy, isn't it?" Yolanda said.

Brooke reached for her coffee cup. "I know Ty would have called if everything was okay. He trusts your husband. If he decided to stay in D.C. he would have let Owen know."

"Maybe his phone died." Yolanda added cream to her coffee. "Owen and Nathan plan to leave for D.C. if they haven't heard anything by four. I'm sure they'll get to the bottom of it."

"Can I go with them?"

"I don't know. You'll have to ask Owen."

Brooke's eyes expressed her concern.

"I understand your worry," Yolanda said. "For fifteen years my husband has worked for the FBI and trust me, there have been many times I didn't know where he was and worried that something happened to him."

"Did anyone ever try to kill him?" Brooke asked.

"On more than one occasion." Yolanda sighed. "But at least you've got your religion to help you. I never really got into spiritual stuff."

Brooke never really thought of her new faith in Jesus as a religion. During their morning conversation, Brooke had told Yolanda about becoming a Christian. "I have been praying."

"Well hopefully that works." Yolanda tried to sound encouraging.

"I struggled a lot before becoming a Christian because I've seen bad things happen even when we pray."

Yolanda nodded. "To be honest, that's what makes it hard for me to believe in God. Being a Christian doesn't seem to change anything."

"But it does." Brooke glanced up and tucked a few long hairs behind her ear. "Bad things still happen, but that's because of sin in the world. But when you know Jesus, He goes through the storms with you."

Yolanda listened quietly as Brooke explained.

"I grew up in an abusive home," Brooke began. She wasn't sure why she started at the beginning, but suddenly Brooke found herself telling her hostess how God got a hold of her heart and healed her past.

"I know that God never wanted me to go through those bad things, I'm sure He even cried when I cried. But once I finally surrendered all my hurts and my own sins at the cross, He helped me understand that even though the enemy meant it for evil, God could use it for good."

There were tears in Yolanda's eyes by the time Brooke stopped talking. "I've never thought about God crying for me," Yolanda confessed. "It seems kind of unreal."

"But if you think about it, it makes sense. He created us. Why wouldn't our Creator hurt when we hurt? He loves us."

Yolanda nodded.

The front door opening drew both of the women's attention away from the conversation.

"Honey, I've got to get my stuff together," Owen said as he stepped through the door. He stopped when he saw his wife in tears. "Yolanda? What's wrong?"

Yolanda dried her eyes and almost chuckled. "We were just talking."

"I'm not used to you crying when you talk. Is everything okay?" He placed a comforting hand on her back.

"It's fine, Sweetie." Yolanda stood up and kissed her husband.

"Okay." Owen seemed unconvinced. "Well, we haven't heard from Ty and I'm concerned. He's been in regular communication with me since this whole thing started." He glanced at Brooke and back to his wife. "The fact that someone was after Brooke at the airport tells me they knew where you were and they knew your schedule. I hope they haven't gotten to Ty."

Brooke felt her hands sweat.

"I've got to pack and head out. I'm picking up Nathan at his apartment."

"Can I go with you?" Brooke asked.

"No, Brooke. It's safer for you here." Owen placed a hand on her shoulder. "Ty would want you to stay."

He was right. But she wished there was a way to sneak into Owen's car.

■ ■ ■

"Get up." Ty felt a hand slap his head and he opened his eyes. He wasn't sure how long he'd been sleeping, but light streamed through the closed blinds. A husky built man wearing a red and gray striped ski mask stood over him with a baseball bat. Another man, in a black ski mask, sat across from Ty on an old recliner. He was larger, with broad shoulders and a well-defined chest.

"We need to talk, Blake." The man on the recliner said in a thick British accent. Something about his composure said this man was running the show.

Ty wasn't used to anyone outside of his family calling him Blake anymore. He sat up gingerly and moaned as pain seared through his side.

"I need some water." Ty felt sick with thirst.

"Maybe after we talk." The man leaned in close to Ty. "Do you know what we want?"

Ty took a pained breath and closed his eyes against his headache. "The campaign files?"

"Very good. Where are they, Blake?" The man's tone was cold.

"I don't know."

"Unacceptable answer." He struck Ty across the head.

"I'm not lying!" Ty blinked back stars.

"I don't believe you."

The man in the red and gray ski mask drew closer with the baseball bat.

Ty wasn't sure how many more blows he could take. "Listen," he backed away on the couch. "I was given the files just a couple weeks before I turned state's evidence. I only read the first few pages. I forgot all about them until recently. They must have been taken before I gave my files to the FBI."

Ty felt the bat strike across his shoulder. He doubled over with pain.

"We want those files, Blake."

"I don't have them!"

"Who does?"

"I don't know." Ty's head swam. The man with the bat stood a foot away, ready to hit him again.

"Please." Ty's eyes were red with pain. "I haven't seen the files in over four years."

"Well you need to find them," the man on the chair said dryly.

"How? I'm not even sure they exist anymore."

The man stood up and looked down on Ty. "They exist."

Ty was in too much pain to ask questions.

Crossing his arms across his broad chest, the man in the black ski mask walked to the window and peered out. "Start with the names you remember and find it." He turned around. "Because you can't hide from us, Blake. You can't hide your parents. You can't hide your sister. You can't even hide your little friend, Brooke, even if she did slip away from us at the airport. She might be clever, but we'll find her too."

Ty wondered what happened at the airport. A sickening feeling spread through his stomach—was Brooke okay?

"Take him to the car," the man ordered.

Ty was yanked to his feet and the zip tie was cut from his ankles. With a gun to his side, he was led outside to Brooke's Jetta.

"Brooke's car?" Ty turned to the larger man for an explanation.

"See, we know where your parents live. If we can take the car, we can take a lot more than that."

The man shoved Ty into the driver's seat and cut the zip tie from his wrist. "Your suitcase is in the trunk. You've got one week," the man said. "You can contact me at this number." He handed Ty a slip of paper with a phone number. "Find those papers or everyone you care about starts dropping like flies."

Ty tried to steady the throbbing in his head well enough to start the vehicle and drive away.

CHAPTER 19

After a third ring of the doorbell, Olivia made her way from her kitchen to the front door. She was really too busy to be bothered by anyone, but their persistence made her curious. Usually delivery people just left their packages.

Her eyes met Owen's when she opened the door and he flashed her his badge.

"FBI. We need to talk."

"Of course you do." Olivia let out an impatient sigh. "I suppose you want to come in?"

"It would be more comfortable," Owen confessed.

Olivia led Owen and Nathan to her living room. "Please make this quick. I've got things to do this evening."

"Of course you do," Owen said in return.

Both men took a seat across from Olivia. Owen did a quick appraisal of the room. "We've come to inquire about your brother."

"Let me guess. You put him into hiding again and want to announce his unexplained death." Olivia grinned.

"No, Ms. Davis. We want to know where he is."

"How would I know?"

"He left your house yesterday afternoon and no one has heard from him since."

Olivia rolled her eyes. "Maybe he got tired of people controlling his life. I can't say I blame him."

"This is no joke, ma'am. Another abduction attempt was made on Brooke Dunbar while she was at the airport and we have reason to believe Blake's in danger."

"What are you talking about? Brooke's in Colorado."

"I am aware that was your plan and we do need to question your authority in making such a decision." Owen narrowed his eyes. "However, an attempt was made to abduct her at the airport and Brooke is now safely under FBI protection."

"Oh, that will get her far." Olivia's tone dripped with sarcasm.

"Obviously, it got her farther than your attempt."

"Look," Olivia began. "I don't know where my brother is. I'm sure he will turn up. I'm also sure I have nothing to do with his disappearance. Do you have any other questions?" She crossed her arms.

"I have a lot more questions, but I have a feeling you may have to be brought in for them."

"Are you threatening to arrest me?" Olivia seemed to take it as a challenge.

"I'm surprised you don't have more concern for your brother."

"Of course I'm concerned," she shot back. "But Blake is a big boy and he can do what he wants."

"Then why did you feel the need to send Miss Dunbar to Colorado? Or was that ever really your plan?"

"I don't know what you're talking about. My husband drove her to the airport."

"We'd like to know how that leaked out. She was met at the airport by the same man who made an attempt on her life in New York."

Olivia shook her head. "That's impossible."

"How many people knew where you were sending her?"

"Only a few. But I trust them all."

"Then either you have some misplaced trust or you had something to do with it." Owen's eyes peered steadily into hers.

"I had nothing to do with it." Olivia met his challenge. "Someone must be watching the house." She glanced at her watch. "We need to end this meeting."

"There is going to be an investigation." Owen leveled his eyes on her. "I may have to pull some strings to authorize it. But I promise—we will talk again."

"Good luck with that, Officer." Olivia rose to her feet. "We're done here." She waited for them to stand. "Have my brother call me when he turns up."

■ ■ ■

Ty was exhausted by the time he reached Philadelphia. He'd driven for over two hours and needed to stop for pain medication.

A light rumbling in the clouds let him know a storm was brewing. The sun had already set and Ty wasn't sure how much further he could drive in his condition. He pulled into a large truck stop and practically stumbled through the doors, unconcerned about his disheveled appearance. The truck stop held several fast food restaurants and a coffee shop, but he searched the establishment for water and ibuprofen.

"Can I help you?" Thc cashier asked.

Ty held up the bottle of medication. "Just this." He felt the man's eyes on him as he checked out.

He carried his purchase to the car, took a couple ibuprofens, and leaned his head back on the headrest. Every muscle in his body ached and his head pounded. He needed to talk to Owen. Was Brooke okay? His cell phone was dead and he didn't have a charger, but he was too tired to think about it. In moments, Ty was asleep.

In spite of the thunderstorm outside, Ty slept through the night. He woke up as the sun streamed through the grey clouds and took more pain medication. He didn't intend to sleep all night. Ty swallowed back the dryness in his throat and decided to use one of the truck stop showers before trying to make his way back to New York.

It took all the energy he could muster to pull himself from the car and take his small clothing bag from the back seat. The clerk's curious eyes watched him from behind one of the store counters. Ty avoided the man and staggered to the back of the truck stop to get cleaned up.

The warm shower on his aching body eased the pain, and he paid for extended time. A hot shower, shave and clean clothes did a lot to improve Ty's appearance, although the dark bruises on his ribs and back, and thc knot on his head were testimony to the fact that he was still hurting.

When Ty finally felt ready to meet the world, he walked to the coffee shop.

"It's been parked there all night," he heard one of the employees telling another.

Ty's ears perked up. *Are they talking about the Jetta?*

A hush fell over the baristas. "Can I take your order?" One of them asked.

"I'll have a large mocha," Ty tried to appear casual. He watched while the other employee steamed the milk and prepared his espresso. The rich smell of coffee helped clear his head.

Ty paid for his drink and walked toward the door. He stepped into the sunlight and noticed several police cars surrounding Brooke's car. *This can't be good.* He took a sip of his coffee, strolled toward the newspaper stand, and purchased a paper. There were enough people wandering in and out of the truck stop that it wasn't difficult to blend in, but he knew better than to approach the Jetta. Brooke had been missing for over a month and here was her car in the middle of a truck stop. How could he explain that?

Carrying his newspaper, Ty strolled back into the truck stop, glad that he had his bag with him. But how was he going to leave? He tried not to show signs of the physical pain he felt. Ty figured one of the truck stop employees must have reported him when he came staggering in with blood and bruises on his clothes. Good thing he got cleaned up.

There was a pay phone and several well-worn phone books just inside the door. Ty wondered if he could find Owen the old fashioned way. It was still early and Ty doubted Owen would be at the office yet. Surprisingly, there was a New York City phone book in the pile and Ty found the name Owen Vance. Ty hoped this was the right Owen.

■ ■ ■

"The coffee was just made, so please have a cup," Yolanda instructed Brooke. "I hate running out on you like this, but they need me in the office." She quickly wiped off the counter and tossed the sponge in the sink.

Brooke poured the fresh brewed coffee into a mug and topped it off with cream. "Don't feel bad. I'll be fine." She watched Owen walk into the room. He was still tired from his late flight the night before.

"You look exhausted, honey," Yolanda greeted Owen. She leaned over the island and gave him a kiss. "Coffee?"

"Use the travel mug. I needed to leave five minutes ago."

"Do you have to go in so early? You didn't get home till after one." Yolanda rubbed her husband's arm and went to pour his coffee.

Owen watched his wife. "I've got to." He accepted the mug. "If I hear anything I'll call you," he said to Brooke. "I'll leave a message on the answering machine and you can just pick up if you hear me talking."

Brooke nodded.

"I'm ready to go too, honey." Yolanda grabbed her purse and checked her lipstick in the hallway mirror. "Why don't I drive you?"

Owen accepted the offer.

"Feel free to make yourself food, watch TV, whatever you like." Yolanda told Brooke.

Brooke nodded and watched the couple slip out the door. It felt strange to be left here alone, but it was far nicer than being in a hotel. Brooke shuddered at the memory.

She carried her coffee cup to the living room and sat comfortably on the sofa, pulling her feet up under her legs to keep them warm. The Vance's kept their house cooler than Brooke was used to.

It was hard not to be discouraged after last night's hopeless attempt at finding Ty. Owen called from D.C. as soon as he'd met with Olivia to let Brooke and Yolanda know that Olivia pled ignorance.

There was really not much to tell when he got home.

Why did I leave my phone in D.C.? Brooke scolded herself. Although if Owen couldn't reach Ty, she probably couldn't either.

Brooke leaned her head back on the sofa, took a deep breath, and tried to calm her fears. She took a sip of her warm coffee and prayed that they would find him soon.

What if those men found Ty? What if he's already dead? Brooke set the coffee cup down and rubbed her temples. Ty's strong, handsome face flashed through her mind and Brooke wondered how life could ever go back to normal for her. Ty would forever be a part of her life, even if it were only in her memories.

The sound of the phone ringing pulled Brooke from her thoughts.

Her eyes found the clock. Owen and Yolanda had only been gone fifteen minutes. Could Owen have already heard something?

The answering machine went on and Brooke waited for the beep.

"Hey, Owen… it's Ty…"

Brooke jumped from the sofa and pulled the phone off the receiver. "Ty!" she interrupted him mid sentence.

"Brooke?"

"Let me stop the machine." Brooke stopped the recording and clutched the phone as if it were gold. "Ty… are you okay? We were so worried…" Tears filled Brooke's eyes and her voice quivered with a mixture of relief and fear.

"You're at Owen's house?" There was relief in Ty's voice.

"Someone tried to abduct me at the airport," Brooke explained. "I came to New York instead. Owen brought me here because he didn't feel it was safe for me at a hotel." Brooke sat down on the sofa with the cordless phone and closed her eyes. Why did it feel so good to hear his voice? "Where are you? We've been so worried."

"It's a long story. I'm in Philadelphia. Can you come get me?"

"Yes… how? I mean… should I call Owen?" Brooke stood up and paced the floor. Her bare feet dug into the soft shag carpet. "He's already left for work."

"You're there alone?"

"Yes."

Ty was quiet for a moment. "This could be a good thing. There's a leak somewhere. I don't think it's Owen, but it may be in his office. If you and I can just get off everybody's radar for a little while we might be able to figure this thing out." He spoke softer. "Can you get a rental and meet me at the truck stop just north of Philadelphia? It's a really big one. I can get you the exit number."

"Where can I get a rental? I don't know anything about New York City." Brooke swallowed hard and listened while Ty gave instructions.

"You won't be able to call me. My cell phone's dead. I'll be in the coffee shop reading a paper." Ty paused. "Brooke." Ty's voice became a whisper. "I can't explain it all right now but your Jetta is here. The police are watching it like a hawk."

Brooke listened intently and tried to understand.

“Don’t park anywhere near it and don’t act like you recognize it.”

“Okay.” He’d explain it all once she got there. “I’ll call a cab. Should I write Owen and Yolanda a note? They’re going to wonder…”

“We’ll call them later. Just hurry. The longer I sit around the more suspicious I look. It should take you about an hour and a half from the rental place.”

“How should I pay?”

“Do you still have Jessica Duncan’s credit card and driver’s license?”

Brooke grinned. “I do. I forgot to give it back to Owen.”

“Use that. They’ll know you rented a car, but they won’t know where you took it.”

Brooke said goodbye and hurriedly called for a cab. As quickly as possible, she gathered her things and went to the door to watch for the taxi.

■ ■ ■

“Here you go, Ms. Duncan,” a tall, wiry gentleman at the rental agency handed Brooke a set of keys. “You need to have it back to us by next Monday at midnight. Make sure the tank is full.”

Brooke wondered what would happen if she didn’t return the car in time.

The small, blue Chevy Cruze was nothing fancy, but Brooke was glad to have a car. She did her best to follow the signs toward Philadelphia and prayed she could find Ty.

With traffic, the drive took almost an hour and forty-five minutes. She pulled into the truck stop and spotted her Jetta immediately. She parked at the other end of the parking lot and looked around for anything unusual.

Her heartbeat quickened at the thought of seeing Ty. How would he act toward her? Was he upset with her for leaving? They hadn’t talked about any of that.

Brooke stepped inside and noticed a couple police officers standing near one of the counters talking to a cashier. She looked around for Ty and spotted him near the coffee shop with a newspaper and a cup of coffee on his table.

His eyes lit up when he saw her.

Brooke approached his table and he stood up. "You have no idea how badly I want to just wrap you in my arms and hug you right now," Ty whispered.

Brooke placed a tender hand on his bruised cheek and looked longingly into his eyes. "Then do."

Ty wrapped his arms around her slender body and pulled her to him. "I was so worried." He spoke into her hair.

"So was I." She relished the security of his arms around her.

He released his hold and ran his fingers through her long dark hair, staring into her eyes as if he was looking at an angel.

She reached to his face and ran her hand across the slight bruise on his cheekbone. "Ty, what happened to you?"

"I got a little roughed up." He glanced around her shoulders. "We should go." There was concern in his tone. "Where are you parked?

"Close to the trucks."

Ty reached for her hand and lifted his bag. "Just pray they don't question us."

With Ty's hand in hers, Brooke let Ty lead her through the truck stop and out the doors, avoiding the police officers. "We're parked this way." Brooke led the way through the crowded parking lot to the small blue rental. "They just keep getting better." She smiled.

"Would you mind driving?" Ty was beginning to show his weariness.

"Not at all." She walked toward the driver's door but Ty stopped her. He stared into her eyes with emotion. "All I could think about was that I might never see you again." He brushed her hair away from her face and moved closer.

"I'm sorry I left." Brooke lowered her eyes. "Your sister told me—"

Ty pulled her to him and found her lips. Brooke's heartbeat quickened and she returned his kiss, relishing the tenderness of his touch.

When he stepped away, Ty's eyes were apologetic. "I'm sorry—"

"Don't be." Brooke wondered why his kiss filled her with such peace. Olivia's words about relationships built on a traumatic event ran through her mind. *I know that right now you're both in this emotional place where you feel a connection. That's common. You've experienced something traumatic together—but you're not right for each other.* Brooke tried to shake Olivia's words from her mind. This was more than an emotional connection, wasn't it?

"We should go." Ty ran his hands tenderly over her arms. "There are police all over this place."

Brooke nodded and Ty opened the car door for her. She slipped into the driver's seat and waited while Ty threw his bag in the back. The feel of his lips still lingered on hers.

They were both quiet as Brooke pulled the car toward the exit. Brooke wondered if Ty regretted kissing her.

"We need to take the 95 south." Ty turned around and looked out the back window. He grabbed his side and let out a soft moan.

■ ■ ■

Ty did his best to get comfortable in the passenger seat. His body ached from the beating he'd taken and nothing seemed soft enough.

"What happened to you, Ty? You've been hurt. We weren't able to reach you for two days." Brooke set the cruise control and glanced quickly at Ty.

"After I left my sister's, I was followed." Ty explained the events that proceeded. "There were two of them. They shot out my tires and pursued me on foot." He rubbed the lump on his head. "I was struck on the head and when I woke up I was in some filthy little cabin about fifty miles away. They want the campaign files and they're convinced I'm the key." He turned and studied Brooke's gentle features while her eyes were still on the road. Should he tell her about the threats? That would only frighten her more.

"So, why are we headed south?" Brooke clutched the steering wheel and let her eyes catch Ty's. "Where are we going?"

"It's a long shot, but I have one theory about who might have the campaign files."

Brooke waited for him to continue.

"Brad Bronowski." Ty blew out a sigh.

"Why him? You had several names on your list," Brooke reminded him.

"Owen told me that Bronowski's lawyer, Jasmine Greenwich, died about five weeks ago. It was believed to have been a drunk driving accident. She was found with a bottle of vodka in the car—the bottle was wiped clean of prints."

Brooke's eyes showed concern. "What does all this mean?"

Ty ran his fingers through his hair and closed his eyes. "The men who roughed me up want those files." He carefully turned to face Brooke. "They've given me a week to find them."

"Or what?" Brooke asked.

"They know who I am, Brooke. They know where to find my family and they know who you are." He reached a hand to her arm. "They took your Jetta out of my parents' garage… We need to get phones. I should call my parents and make sure they're okay."

"Why were the police checking out my car?"

"I looked pretty bad when I showed up at the truck stop last night. I slept in the car. I'm guessing someone called me in. I'm sure they've run the plates and are searching for you."

Brooke shook her head. "This is crazy." She glanced quickly at Ty.

"Now tell me what happened to you?" Ty wanted answers as well. "The thugs who roughed me up said you slipped away from them at the airport."

"It was the same man who came to my hotel room," Brooke began. She explained the whole story.

"We need to send Ben Williamson a huge thank you." Ty rested his weary head on the seat. "I think the Bengals just became my favorite football team." He watched Brooke for a few seconds. "You're an amazing woman."

Brooke reached over and touched his hand.

"This really doesn't look good for my sister." Ty wrapped his fingers through hers.

Brooke moved into the fast lane. "I don't know, Ty. None of it makes sense. Owen verified that the new identity your sister gave me, the job, and the bank account were all real."

"Do you have access to the money?" Ty asked.

"I have no idea."

"I'm just not sure how long our funds will hold out now that we're on our own." He was thoughtful for a moment. "You charged this rental to Jessica Duncan's credit card, right?"

"Yes, and I used her driver's license."

Ty nodded. "I've still got mine too, but if I use it they'll know we're together. Let's stop at a grocery store and stock up on gift cards using your credit card. Gift cards are untraceable and once we buy them we'll still have that money even if the Marshals cancel our cards."

"You've got great survival skills." She let go of his hand to pull her wallet out of her purse. "It's in there." She handed it to Ty. "Should we find a grocery store now?"

Ty motioned to a highway sign with a list of businesses. "Let's get off here."

Brooke switched lanes and pulled off the exit.

"Head east. It looks like there's a bunch of businesses that way." Ty wondered how much money they could put on the credit card without it getting refused. He knew they'd have to act fast once they started using it. The card might already be on alert due to the car rental.

Ty pointed toward a large grocery chain and Brooke moved into the turn lane.

There was an awkward moment when Brooke parked the car. Ty stepped from the vehicle and waited for Brooke. She was quiet. Should he reach for her hand? Did she regret his kiss? It wasn't like him to be so impulsive.

Brooke gave him a shy smile and grabbed the cart closest to the car.

She's so sweet. I don't want to hurt her. Ty tried to push his thoughts away and focus on what needed to be done.

Inside the store, Brooke and Ty did a quick search for cell phones, gift cards, and the few necessities they thought they'd need. Ty breathed a sigh of relief when Jessica Duncan's credit card was accepted. They pulled out as much cash as the card would allow.

Brooke pushed the cart back to the car, insisting that Ty needed to take it easy.

"I'm fine." Ty opened the trunk for Brooke and helped her load their supplies. He searched her face, wondering if she felt uncomfortable around him now. "There's an outdoor store across the road. I think Jessica should buy a gun."

"Are you serious?" Brooke stopped to stare at Ty for a moment.

"I'm thinking a Ruger or a Glock."

Brooke watched Ty walk to the car with one hand holding his ribs and her eyes sobered. "Ty, please let me look at you."

"There's not much you can do. I'm just bruised up, maybe a busted rib." Ty climbed gingerly into the car. "Ribs heal on their own, don't they?"

"Provided it's a nondisplaced rib fracture." Brooke followed him to the passenger side of the car and knelt down. "Can I see?"

Ty's lips curved into an amused grin. "It's good to have my nurse back." He pulled his shirt up and heard Brooke gasp.

"Ty… what did they do to you?" She reached her hand to his bruised body. "Does it hurt to take a breath?"

"No." Ty shook his head.

"Have you coughed up any blood?"

"No." Ty reached for her hand and held it.

"We should have it x-rayed." Brooke's eyes were serious. "If it is displaced, it could puncture a lung."

"Let's just pray it's not." Ty studied Brooke tenderly. "What would they do for a simple broken rib?"

"Pretty much just let it heal on its own, give you pain meds, tell you to take it easy." She tightened her hand in his. "But if it's not a simple fracture…"

"We can't risk the hospital, Brooke. Not if we're trying to disappear." He smoothed one of her long brown hairs from her eyes and stared at her. "I think I'm okay." He wished he could wipe the worry from her brow. "We should head over to that outdoor store and see what we can get before Officer Longstreth cancels this credit card."

Brooke stood up and made her way to the driver's seat.

Ty found a 9mm Glock and purchased the gun and ammunition using Jessica Duncan's credit card. They were both relieved that the card was accepted and walked out of the store with their small piece of self-defense.

"Have you ever shot a gun before?" Ty carried the bag as they walked to the car.

"Never."

Did buying a gun scare her or just make it all feel more real? "I had a 9mm almost just like this back in Cincinnati. I didn't think to have you grab it for me when you got my stuff."

"I'm not sure I would have." Brooke climbed into the car. "I didn't know you."

"Good point." Ty closed the door and opened the bag. "I'll teach you how to use it. Although, I hope you'll never need to." He glanced up at Brooke. "I'm sure Officer Longstreth will be closing your credit card down shortly." Would Wyatt be able to tell what they purchased?

CHAPTER 20

"Where is Brooke Dunbar?" Wyatt Longstreth's voice bellowed from the other end of Owen's phone.

Owen was quiet for a moment. "Is this a trick question?"

"Do you know the answer?"

"I know where she was at 7:30 am. What do you know?"

"I know Jessica Duncan rented a car at 8:15 and recently made several large purchases right outside of Philadelphia. I just ran a check on her card and one of those purchases included a gun." Wyatt did not sound pleased. "Where is she?"

Owen cleared his throat. "Let me look into this."

"I expected you to keep me in the loop, Owen. You said you knew where she was this morning."

"She was safe."

"Safe." The tone on the other end was sarcastic. "So safe that now she's off buying guns with her witness protection credit card? If indeed it's even her. What if she's been abducted? Who else had access to her card?" Wyatt punctuated his questions with a few swear words. "What about Blake Kendall? Where is he?"

"I still haven't located him."

"How do I know you're not keeping things from me? I want answers and I want them now!"

This was not a conversation Owen wanted to be having. "Let me do a little research."

"No. I'm doing my own." The angry tone on the other end bellowed. "You've been keeping information from me and now it's time for the Marshals to take control of this case."

"This is an FBI case."

"We'll see." Wyatt hung up.

A sigh escaped Owen's lips and he ran a hand through his salt and pepper hair. A quick phone call to his home confirmed Wyatt's theory that Brooke was not where Owen left her. Why would she leave? Owen could think of only one reason Brooke would leave. *She found Ty.*

Owen dialed Ty's cell phone but got no answer.

■ ■ ■

It was late when Brooke pulled into a truck stop in North Carolina. "I don't think I can keep my eyes open any more," she confessed.

Ty sat up and blinked back the tired in his eyes. "How long did I sleep?"

"A couple hours, but you needed it." She watched the discomfort on his face. "You really need a good night's sleep in a bed. I saw a few signs for hotels."

Ty opened the door and stretched his legs. It was dark outside and the moonless night made the stars even brighter. He glanced at the sky. "I wish we had sleeping bags and a couple tents."

Camping sounded nice. "You said you wanted to call Owen when you knew he was home from work." Brooke glanced at the dashboard clock.

"I should probably have called a couple hours ago." Ty pulled out one of the throw away phones. "I'll give him a try now."

"Please have him tell Yolanda that I'm sorry." Brooke glanced down into her hands. She'd enjoyed the spiritual conversations she'd had with Owen's wife and hoped that disappearing as she'd done wouldn't hurt her witness.

■ ■ ■

"Owen…"

"Where are you?" Owen didn't even wait for Ty to identify himself.

"I'm still in the continental United States." Ty glanced at Brooke and grinned.

"I assume Brooke's with you?" Ty couldn't read Owen's tone. Was his friend angry or worried?

"Yes. We're both safe." Ty closed his eyes. *As safe as we can be at this point.*

"Why did you disappear? I've been trying to find you for three days. Wyatt Longstreth is furious wanting to know where you are and why you purchased a gun." Owen rattled on. "I can put you both back in hiding. What are you trying to do?"

Ty gauged his reply carefully. "We've gone rogue." He glanced at Brooke and winked. "I've got to find the campaign files, Owen. That's what this is all about."

"I can help you."

"No, Owen. There appears to be a leak somewhere and I can't risk them finding us."

"I'm on that, Ty." Owen said. "We're working with the Marshals to figure out what happened to your information in their database. They're aware there is something amiss, even though they want to believe it is a computer glitch."

"This is no computer glitch."

"Why didn't you answer my calls? You said you were on your way to New York."

Ty knew his FBI friend wanted the story, but worried that their location could be traced. "A couple thugs got ahold of me just outside of D.C. They've given me a week to find the information they want before they start taking out everyone I care about." Ty glanced at Brooke.

Owen was quiet for a moment and blew out a breath. "You can't negotiate with criminals, Ty."

"I know."

"You might save those you care about, but they're still going to kill you." Owen's tone was serious. "Don't try to do this by yourself. You're a lawyer, not a detective. Why did you buy a gun?"

Ty could hear the genuine concern in Owen's voice. He'd been on the phone long enough for the FBI to run a trace on his location, but he didn't think Owen would do it. "I'll be in touch, Owen." He avoided the agent's questions. "And Brooke wanted to tell you and your wife she's sorry for how she left. She appreciates all you did for her."

"She's in danger now too, you know…"

"Nothing's changed, but we're not alone." A light shone in Ty's eyes and he glanced out the car window at the star filled sky. They were never alone.

■ ■ ■

Brooke reclined the driver's seat in their car and leaned back. She was exhausted and needed sleep. Ty reclined beside her, but the look in his eyes showed his discomfort. Brooke worried about him. Did he need medical attention? He was right though, if they went to a hospital, they'd be found.

She watched him as he drifted back to sleep. The sound of his soft breathing filled the car. It was good to be back with Ty. In spite of their situation, Brooke would rather be here with Ty than back in Cincinnati working the job she hated and existing in her empty life.

Brooke let her eyes travel to the window and stared out at the stars. Giving her life to Jesus was the best decision she ever made. She thought about Ty's parents and the risk Ty made to tell them about his Savior. What about her brother? Behind Cody's happy go lucky attitude, she knew he still hurt deeply over their family's past. His anger toward their dad went as deep as hers.

What about her parents? Brooke wondered if they would even listen to her if she shared her faith with them. Could she face them and tell them? Brooke wondered if she'd crawl back into her shell and cower just being in their presence. Did she really want to see her dad again? Could her mom ever be as sweet and happy as Ty's mom?

Brooke turned toward Ty again and studied his handsome face. He'd kissed her. Was it just a moment of emotion? What did it mean? Why was his kiss so sweet to her? Brooke blinked back tears and tried to bury her emotions. She could never have a man like Ty. *You're not right for each other...* Olivia's words rang in her ears. *He comes from wealth and class...* Brooke rubbed her forehead and sucked in a sob. *I come from an abusive, alcoholic, middle class home. I've got too much baggage for Ty...*

He probably regretted the kiss. How should she act around him now? She wished she could push the kiss out of her mind—pretend it never happened.

Brooke decided to forgo sleep. She sat up, started the car, and pressed on toward Florida.

■ ■ ■

"Where are we?" Ty straightened his seat up and glanced out the window at the shades of pink on the horizon.

"Almost through South Carolina." Brooke took a sip of her gas station coffee and returned it to the console.

"Did you drive all night?" He reached for her coffee and took a swallow. "Eww." Ty made a disgusted face. "That's nasty."

Brooke grinned. "Taste doesn't matter when you're only drinking it to stay awake and yes, I drove all night."

He leaned his head back and let out a deep breath.

"How are you feeling?"

"Like a steam roller drove over me a few times and then I was thrown down a flight of stairs." Ty glanced at Brooke and tried to make himself comfortable on the seat. "Of course that's just speculation as I've never actually had a steam roller drive over me."

"But you've been thrown down a flight of stairs?"

"Not thrown… I've taken the fall on my own a few times as a kid, though." Ty reached for his empty water bottle and drained it of the few drops that were left. "If there's a place to stop, I'd love to get something to drink."

Exits were readily available and Brooke assured him she'd take the next exit that looked promising.

"So you didn't sleep at all last night?" Ty studied Brooke's face.

"I tried." Brooke's eyes were fixed on the road. "I pulled over at a truck stop for about forty-five minutes, but I couldn't sleep."

"I think I can drive now." Ty massaged the back of his neck. "After we stop I'll take over."

Brooke was ready for a break when she finally took an exit that promised a few small restaurants and a gas station. They opted for the gas station and made the switch after a quick fill up.

■ ■ ■

Wyatt stormed past Owen's assistant into Owen's office and slapped a form on his desk. "You're required to give me any and all information you have on Blake and Brooke." Wyatt sat on the hard wooden chair across from Owen and crossed his arms. "Have you heard from either of them?"

Owen reached for the form and read. He chewed on his lip and set the form back down in front of him. "I've heard from Blake… or Ty as I've grown accustomed to calling him."

"And…"

"He's trying to figure this thing out on his own." Owen shrugged. There really wasn't much more to say.

"Do you have a number?"

"Ty's too smart for that. He called me from a throw away phone. He doesn't want our help right now." Owen wasn't sure how much he wanted to tell this pushy U.S. Marshal. "He feels pretty certain that the reason he and Brooke keep getting found is because there is some kind of leak."

An exasperated sigh escaped Wyatt's lips and his strong barrel chest filled up with a deep breath. "What kind of investigation do you have going on?"

"We're looking into a few leads we've gotten from Ty. I assume you've got people trying to figure out why Blake Kendall's name is gone from your database."

Wyatt picked up a pen from Owen's desk and tapped it rhythmically against his leg. "We think it was Matthew Pratt."

Owen's eyebrows drew together. "Pratt? Why would Ty's contact erase his name?"

"Not sure yet. I've got men looking into it." Wyatt set the pen back down and crossed his arms across his chest. "What about Brooke? Have you spoken with her?"

Owen shook his head. "No. I haven't talked to Brooke since yesterday morning." He opted not to clarify that he knew she was with Ty. There was no point in giving too much information to this U.S. Marshal. Nothing was documented and at this point, Owen wasn't sure where the leak really was.

Wyatt rubbed his chin. "Hmm… then I guess you haven't seen the security footage from the gun department at Outdoor Adventure." He studied Owen suspiciously.

"No. I haven't seen the footage."

Wyatt dropped a thumb drive on Owen's desk. "Pop that into

your computer."

Owen put the drive in his computer and pulled up the footage. It was a clear picture of Brooke with Ty at the gun counter.

"Did you know they were together?"

Owen licked his lips. "I suspected it." He shut down the video and handed Wyatt the drive. "So they're both safe."

"Why did they buy a gun?"

"Exercising their second amendment right, maybe?" Owen leaned back in his chair and put his arms behind his head.

"We found a gun in Blake's Cincinnati apartment as well. Apparently he likes guns."

"There's no law against that." Owen studied Wyatt curiously. What was Wyatt worried about? "The man has had more than one attempt on his life, I'm sure he's thinking of it as security. Let's hope he doesn't need to use it."

"You make sure you get a recording of the next call Ty makes to you. I want to know what he's thinking. We don't need any vigilante heroes." Wyatt rose to go. "Tell him to call me."

Not sure it will do any good. Owen nodded and watched the man storm from his office.

■ ■ ■

"We're almost to Savannah." Ty woke Brooke and smiled at her. "I thought we could have lunch here." He returned his attention to the road and followed the exit to Savannah.

Brooke opened her eyes and yawned. "Savannah?" She glanced out the window.

"It's a beautiful city. It's loaded with dozens of historical architectural treasures and has a strong art community. I think you'll love it."

"Do we have time to stop?" She ran her fingers through her hair and tugged at a few tangles.

"We'll make time." Ty tried to keep his eyes on the road. "You're even pretty when you wake up." He grinned.

Brooke didn't respond to the complement. "Can we get cleaned up somewhere?" She looked at the clock. "How long did I sleep?"

"A few hours. I figured we'd get you some real coffee in Savannah and we can sit by the water and enjoy a nice breakfast."

Ty pulled into the town and Brooke sat up to take in the architecture. Colonials, Victorians, and Greek revival buildings graced the tree-lined streets of Savannah. Ty knew the town well from family vacations and his own travels through the south. It was a favorite place to slip away to a slow paced, relaxing environment that still challenged the eye and gave him mystery to discover.

Spanish moss dangled from the trees and Ty leaned forward in the driver's seat to get a glimpse of its beauty. He found a place to park the car and gave Brooke a few minutes to freshen herself up.

"The Savannah College of Art and Design is here. We should swing by so you can see it." Ty opened her door and reached for her hand.

"I'm sure an art school would only make me resent my nursing degree all the more." Brooke accepted his hand and glanced around the cobble stone street.

"There are some restaurants along River Street where we can get a late breakfast and some coffee." Ty led the way, still holding her hand.

Brooke's expression showed her pleasure with the unique town. Ty knew she appreciated its beauty. With her artistic bent, Savannah seemed like the perfect place to stimulate creativity.

"Have you never been here?" Ty walked Brooke toward an old stone stairway leading to shops beside the water.

"Never." Brooke grabbed the railing and let her eyes get their fill.

"How about this place?" Ty motioned toward a coffee shop right on the water.

"I thought we're on a budget now."

Ty ignored the comment and opened the door. They stepped inside, met by the smell of fresh ground coffee.

Ty glanced through the pastries under the glass. "I'll take a large mocha," he began. "And one of those chocolate chip pumpkin bread slices."

Brooke's eyebrows lifted. "That sounds really good. I think I'll have exactly what he ordered." She turned to watch the barista. "Skim milk though, and a bottle of orange juice."

They took their breakfast to an outdoor table and sat down to enjoy a moment of relaxation. A few sailboats moved slowly past in the distance and Brooke watched them.

"Sailing really made an impression on you, didn't it?"

"Was that like six weeks ago now?" she turned to Ty. "Since we sailed together."

"A little longer I think." He took a long drink of his coffee and smiled. "Now this is what I'm talking about."

"So much has happened since then." Brooke tore off a piece of her pumpkin bread and lowered her eyes.

"Do you miss your life back in Cincinnati?" Ty watched her curiously.

"No." Brooke shook her head. "Although, I wonder what's going to happen to my credit if I don't pay my car loan." She sighed.

"Owen said they'd take care of all that." Ty shrugged. "He said they had my BMW in storage." He glanced out at the water. "I guess realistically, none of that really matters. It's just stuff." He turned to Brooke. "People are way more important than stuff."

Brooke reached up and touched the bruise under Ty's eye. "It looks worse today." She furrowed her brows.

A young couple walked past hand in hand and smiled at Brooke and Ty.

"When you finish your bread I want to take you to a couple art galleries along this road." Ty watched the couple as they continued their stroll and wondered if their lives were as complicated as his. Would he ever be able to have a lasting relationship? He glanced at Brooke and found her eyes on his. It would be so easy to love Brooke. She was smart, pretty, fun to be around and she loved God. Those were just a few of the qualities he'd seen in her over the past month and a half. There was so much more to Brooke. But as long as he was in the chains of Witness Protection, Ty wasn't free to be in a relationship. *When, Lord? When will I be free from the sin of my past?* Ty blew out a sigh.

"You seem deep in thought," Brooke said quietly.

Ty finished his coffee and nodded. "Lots to think about." He glanced at Brooke's empty plate. "Are you ready?"

Brooke nodded and Ty took their plates into the café. "Let's stroll." He reached for her arm and led her toward an art gallery.

■ ■ ■

Time stood still for Brooke as she consumed herself with various art mediums in the small gallery she and Ty explored. "Take a look at this watercolor." Brooke held it up for Ty to see. "I can't imagine getting so much detail into my watercolor."

The painting depicted an old house in Savannah. Trees covered in Spanish moss stood in the foreground, while a rising sun reflected in the old glass windows. Each board of the yellow Victorian seemed to have detail of its own and Ty stared at it as long as Brooke. "It's beautiful."

Hoping to score a sale, the gallery agent approached and began giving a history of the local artist who painted the house. "It's called 'Bexford House at Sunrise.' The house doesn't actually exist," she pointed out. "The artist combined a couple local houses and incorporated the moss covered trees to give it an authentic Savannah look."

"Where did the artist study?" Brooke couldn't help but ask.

"I believe he studied here in Savannah."

Brooke set the painting down and stepped back to study more of the artwork lining the walls.

Ty busied himself with the local handmade jewelry and paid for something secretively. His lips expressed a whimsical smile as he carried his small brown bag through the gallery.

"Okay." Brooke stopped to play his game. "You are obviously proud of yourself for something. What's in the bag?"

Ty raised his eyebrows. "You'll have to wait until we're outside for me to show you." Ty held the bag against his chest and grinned at her. "But take your time here. I'm enjoying the artwork."

Brooke scrunched up her nose and reached for the bag playfully.

"Alright, come on," Ty reached for her hand and led her toward the door. "I'll just have to show you." He walked her closer to the water and made her close her eyes. "Don't worry, I'm not going to throw you in."

Brooke felt something cold against her neck and felt Ty clasping something behind her. He pulled her hair out from behind the chain and gave her permission to open her eyes.

Brooke glanced down and saw the beautiful silver cross hanging from a simple silver chain. "Ty…" she glanced at him curiously. "You shouldn't have bought me anything. I know everything in that store was insanely expensive."

"But it looks beautiful on you." He smiled. "Do you like it? I thought it was symbolic of what has been going on in your life these past several weeks."

"It's amazing." Brooke clutched the cross in her hand. "I love it, Ty." She lowered her eyes. "Thank you." When she glanced back at Ty she found his eyes on her lips. Was he thinking about that spontaneous kiss in Philadelphia? Would he ever do it again?

"I'm glad you like it." Ty's eyes moved to hers and he took a step back. "I wanted to give you something from Savannah and the cross seemed fitting of everything that's happened in our lives. Jesus has never left us alone."

Brooke nodded. Her eyes misted. Did Ty have any idea how much his little gift touched her heart?

CHAPTER 21

They walked around Savannah for a couple more hours, enjoying lunch in a small restaurant called the Bayou Café. Brooke had never eaten Cajun food and enjoyed the spicy fish, fresh salad, and the lively atmosphere. Jazz music drifted through the restored building, echoing off the brick walls and stucco ceiling.

Ty picked up a brochure about some of the local vacation rentals available in Savannah. He was determined to find access to a computer so they could find out if there were any rentals available for the night.

Ty found a place to stay that did not require credit card or identification. It was a small house with three bedrooms. Ty insisted they needed one good night's sleep before heading to Miami.

"Is this just another quiet before the storm?" Brooke sat beside Ty on the house's small front porch and watched the wind blow through the Spanish moss in a nearby tree.

"It might be." Ty glanced at Brooke sympathetically.

"What if this Bronowksi guy doesn't know anything?"

A sigh escaped Ty's lips. "It's my only good lead. I guess if it's a brick wall then we'll have to let the FBI help us."

Brooke nodded. She leaned back on the wicker rocker and let the cool night air relax her. She was tired. It had been a wonderful day and she almost hated to go to sleep. Would tomorrow be as wonderful as today? She'd not expected Ty to take her to a beautiful, relaxing vacation spot for the day. It almost didn't seem real.

"You look tired." Ty's eyes were on her face.

"I am. I think I could fall right to sleep." Brooke closed her eyes for a moment.

With their all-nighter in the rental car, they were both ready for a good night's sleep.

"We should probably make an early night of it," Ty suggested. "It's six hours to Miami and I don't want to get there too late."

They said goodnight and headed to their separate bedrooms.

■ ■ ■

They arrived in Miami the next afternoon. Ty struggled with how to approach Brad Bronowski. Would Brad even remember him? Ty figured the divorce lawyer had no idea Ty was still alive. They stopped to change into nicer clothes before arriving at Brad's house.

They pulled up in front of a contemporary one-story house across the road from the beach. He got out of the car and pulled on his suit jacket. "Hopefully I won't melt in this Florida heat." He glanced up at the sun, partially hidden by a palm.

They rang the bell a couple times but no one answered. What if the man was out of town? Ty tried one more time and heard movement inside.

The door finally opened. "Look, I've told you Jehovah's Witness people to leave me alone!" Brad yelled at them. The smell of alcohol was heavy on his breath.

Although several years older, Brad still looked just as Ty remembered him—a thick head of salt and pepper hair, blue eyes, and a strong chin. Standing at the door wearing a pair of swim trunks and a tight t-shirt, Brad seemed fairly fit.

"Brad." Ty held up his hand. "We're not JW's. I'm Blake Kendall." Ty hoped for some recognition.

"Blake?" Brad chuckled after a moment. "It is you. What the heck? I thought you were in hiding."

"Hiding?" Ty narrowed his eyes. "You're supposed to have thought I was dead."

"Come on in." Brad widened the door and let his eyes scan Brooke shamelessly. "Whose the babe?" He mumbled to Ty.

"This is Brooke." Ty introduced them.

Brad reached out a hand to greet this new female guest. "You're delightful to the eyes. I hope you're not Blake's girlfriend."

Brooke accepted the handshake but took a step back.

"We need to talk." Ty pulled Brad's eyes from Brooke.

"Sure. Come on, I'll get you guys something to drink. I was just sitting out by the pool. I was hoping you'd go away if I ignored you long enough." He laughed. "The JW's have been here every Saturday for the past three weeks. Guess they think I'm a heathen needing the kind of salvation they're selling." He chuckled. Brad led the way through the kitchen. "What can I get you?" He waved his hand past several bottles of various wines, liquors, and other alcoholic beverages.

"Just water for me." Ty furrowed his brow.

"Ah, not a drinker huh?" He chuckled. "I've got some good sparkling mineral water. Want that?"

"Sure."

"How about the lady? Can I make you a daiquiri?" He winked at her.

"No thank you. I'll take the sparkling water too."

"Too bad." Brad handed them both an unopened glass bottle of sparkling mineral water and led the way to the back deck. "So, you're here to talk. What's on your mind, Blake?"

"First of all, I'd like to know how you knew I was still alive."

Brad motioned to a couple of teak chairs with bright green cushions and took a seat across from them with his bottle of hard lemonade. "You went state's evidence and then mysteriously died. Come on—we both know how that works. You ticked a lot of people off and had to disappear." Brad shrugged. "I figured it out a long time ago. Plus, your sister didn't deny it last time we talked. I can always tell when Liv is hiding something."

Liv? Ty was taken aback by Brad's seemingly casual familiarity with Olivia.

"When did you see my sister?"

"About a year ago," Brad said casually. "She came out to let me know she was getting ready to run for senator. Wanted to make sure I was on the same page as her."

"Why would it matter to her what page you're on? I thought you got out of politics."

Brad let out a fake cough and took a long swig from his bottle. "Yeah. A lot has changed. Why are you here, Blake?"

"I'm here because four years ago I was asked to take care of some files—make the information in them disappear. I never accepted the case, but I turned state's evidence before I gave them back to my prospective client. Those files disappeared and now someone's after me."

The heat of the sun shone down on Ty's dark hair and he watched Brad closely for a reaction.

Brad sized Ty up and grinned. "What does that have to do with me?"

"It was your lawyer who brought me the files and your name was all over the first few pages." Ty narrowed his eyes on Brad.

Brad crossed his legs and leaned back in the solid chair. "Do you know what those files were?" Brad's tone did not plead ignorance. He scratched his square chin and stared at Ty.

"I know they had to do with campaign money. I also know whoever wants these files has made more than one attempt on my life and may have possibly murdered your former lawyer."

Brad's eyes grew wide and he sat up abruptly. "What?" His face grew ashen. "Jasmine's dead?" He stared at Ty in disbelief. "You're full of it. Don't mess with me like this." Brad swallowed another gulp and set the drink down.

Ty was surprised by Brad's reaction. "I'm not messing with you. Jasmine's dead."

Brad stood up and paced the poolside. "Dear God." He placed his hand on his head but he wasn't praying. "How? What happened? How do you even know this?"

Ty began to explain. He told Brad about Brooke's own experience with the man at the hotel. "It was the same stuff—176 proof Vodka. Brooke could have died, too."

Brad sat back down and his eyes were noticeably red. "Look, man. I know how this looks. Jasmine and I… we'd been close at one time. Kind of like your sister, you know…"

No. I don't know. Ty shook his head. Did he hear that right?

"We had a little thing years ago. I really liked Jasmine. She was my exotic beauty."

"Aren't you married, Brad?" Ty interrupted.

Brad blew out a sigh. "Not anymore. Sheryl left me."

Blake wasn't surprised. "How long ago?"

"Six months." Brad finished his bottle of hard lemonade and offered Ty and Brooke another drink. "I need more. Can I get you anything?"

Both Brooke and Ty shook their heads no.

While Brad was gone Ty glanced at Brooke. "I'm thinking he's a little more chatty today and that's not his first drink."

"What was he saying about your sister?" Brooke leaned forward in her seat and studied Ty curiously.

A cloud moved in front of the sun for a moment, giving them a small break from the heat. "I'd like to find that out." Ty watched as Brad returned.

"This is crazy. Why would anyone want to kill Jasmine?" Brad sat back down. He was still recovering from the shock. "I haven't seen her in years." His eyes found Ty's. "You just don't forget people like her."

"It's about the files, Brad." Ty tried to bring the mourning man back to the present. "I need to find those files."

Brad stared at Ty for a moment. "How are the files even an issue? They're long gone. They shouldn't be a threat to anyone." He sounded almost annoyed.

"They're an issue to someone. I about got my ribs beat out of me with a baseball bat over those files just a few days ago," Ty said. "I've got the bruises to prove it." Ty pulled his dress shirt from his pants and showed Brad one of his worst bruises.

Brad uttered a swear word and widened his blue eyes. "There's no reason those files should be a threat to you. This doesn't make any sense." He took a swig of his drink.

"There is an FBI investigation going on concerning these files, Brad." Ty felt the need to explain.

Brad's eyes widened. "Who all knows about them?"

"Those working on the case. My identity was compromised and an investigation began. Your name was on a computer list I'd compiled and the computer was stolen by whoever's after me." Ty wondered if this would concern the man. "Whoever is looking for the files has that list."

Brad chewed on his lip for a moment.

"Do you know where the files are?" Ty asked.

"Of course I do." Brad glanced around as if he wondered if someone else could hear him. "I'm the one that tried to hire you to make them disappear."

"You?" Ty waited for Brad to continue.

"I wanted to go big, like Liv's doing now, you know. I wanted to soar. Figured I'd go for congress. I had enough friends—but that was the problem. Jasmine said there was too much garbage on me. I'd made too many wrong friends, taken money, and made a few votes that may have been in conjunction with that money—Jasmine didn't think she could erase it all. She said you were pretty good at making things disappear, but then you went clean." Brad shook his head. "When your sister told me what you'd done, I made sure we got those files out of your office."

Ty's heartbeat quickened. "Where are they?"

Brad glanced at the pool. "It's good that Liv is getting to live the dream, you know?" He took a long drink. "I told her she'd make it."

It was difficult to sit and wait for Brad to stop his reverie and get back to the point, but Ty listened. He glanced at Brooke and wondered what was going through her mind.

He was known for making things disappear—what a reputation to carry around.

"I first met Liv when she graduated from law school. She was beautiful. Still is." A smile formed on his lips. "She started working in my office and I told her we could make something of both our careers. Honestly, I worked better with her than I ever did without her." Brad held the bottle to his lips and guzzled. "Things with Liv—they were real, you know what I mean?"

"You were married."

"She wasn't married when she first came to work with me. But yeah…" Brad sighed. "I was. We'd been married about ten years at that time, but I loved your sister." Brad turned his eyes full on Ty. "I told her I'd leave Sheryl, but Liv didn't want the reputation." He shook his head. "Instead she started dating that egg head, Clayton." A resentful chuckle escaped his lips. "Short, bald, spineless little bore. Liv thought he would be the best thing for her career. I'm sure she doesn't love him."

Ty let Brad's words sink in. "Does Clayton know?"

"I doubt it. The man knows politics, but he doesn't know his wife." Brad turned his eyes on Brooke and studied her intently. "Liv and I kind of went our separate ways. She started her own political climb and I kept pursuing mine until a little more dirt was uncovered from my college years and I figured my political career was washed up. Sheryl and I moved out here and I started making real money."

"What happened to you and Sheryl?" Ty still wanted to know where the files were, but Brad's story was telling. There might be something in all this.

"Your sister called about ten months ago. We met near my place in Aspen. She told me about her run for senate and wanted to make sure nothing from her past would ever come out to haunt her. I assured her that it had all been taken care of."

"What does that have to do with Sheryl?"

"Sheryl didn't like my meeting with Liv. It was just a little weekend thing. Sheryl wasn't even supposed to find out about it but she did and she got jealous." He shook his head. "Sheryl forgave me for Jasmine, but she never quite let go of her bitterness about Liv. I guess our last get together was kind of Sheryl's undoing." Brad set his empty bottle on the table beside him and leaned toward Brooke. "She divorced me about six months ago, so I'm a free man."

Brooke scooted back in her chair and glanced quickly at Ty.

Ty studied Brad's face. There was something in the man's eyes that didn't look repentant about his relationship with Olivia or Jasmine. Olivia had an affair with this guy? It was difficult to get his mind around it. "Olivia was really part of those bribes?"

Brad almost snorted. "You really are naïve aren't you? How do you think she got that nice big house outside of D.C.? How do you think she paid off her school loans? Liv learned how to play the system to her advantage." Brad's tone was callous. "She also learned to play the people."

"So where are the files?" Ty pressed.

Brad was quiet for a few minutes. "Sheryl took care of them."

"Took care?" Ty wanted to understand. "She cleared up the history and destroyed the files?"

"She hired someone. Sheryl wanted to see me soar as badly as I did. She wanted to be a Governor's wife, to live in a Governor's mansion. It was all she dreamed about for a long time." He lowered his eyes. "She never forgave me that shortcoming."

Maybe she never forgave your unfaithfulness. "Would Sheryl know where those files are?" Ty tried to pull Brad back in. The slightly intoxicated man was being painfully honest right now. "They've made a reappearance and I've got to find them. I've got one week."

"She said they'd been destroyed."

"They haven't been." Ty took several sips of his mineral water to cool off from the heat. "According to the men who roughed me up, those files have reappeared and someone's not happy about it. Who else is in those files?"

"There were half a dozen other names. Chadwich, Langly, Pierce…" Brad shook his head. "A few of them were your old clients and are still sitting behind bars." Brad rubbed his chin. "Glad I wasn't one of yours."

"We need to talk to your ex-wife." Ty's heartbeat quickened. Maybe finding the files wasn't impossible.

"She's in Aspen. I got the Florida house and she got the ski cabin." Brad leaned closer to Brooke in his chair. "She got the mountains and the newer house, but I got year round sunshine."

"Can we get the address?"

"She won't talk to you." Brad grew more serious. "She's a bitter old hag now. Meaner than when I married her."

"Can we just try?"

Brad tapped his hand rhythmically against the patio chair and stared at Brooke for a moment. "You never did answer me about Brooke. Is she your girlfriend?" Brad arched a sly brow.

Ty struggled with how to reply. "No. She's not my girlfriend, but don't even think about her." He glanced at Brooke for a moment wondering what her expectations were. Had their kiss changed things? "Can we have Sheryl's address?"

Brad chuckled. "If that's what you want." He got up and strolled to the house for a pen and paper. "Here's the address. Good luck."

"You should probably watch your back for a little while." Ty wondered if Brad would regret all he'd told them once he sobered up.

"I'm a divorce lawyer." Brad grinned. "I always have to watch my back."

■ ■ ■

Ty was hopeful when they walked to the car. "I should let Owen know we've got a lead. See what he thinks our next move should be."

Brooke climbed into the passenger seat and watched Ty close the door for her.

It as after five and Ty hoped Owen would be done for the day. When he got no answer on Owen's cell phone, Ty tried his home.

"We've got a lead." Ty started right in as soon as Owen answered.

"Can you tell me where you are?"

"Miami. I just met with Brad Bronowski." Ty shared what he just learned. "Now we need to go to Colorado. Any ideas for getting us there?"

Owen was quiet for a moment. "You know I'm not supposed to be helping you do this." He cleared his throat. "Wyatt Longstreth has been hounding me every day to learn where you are."

"Don't sweat it. We'll think of something."

A heavy sigh escaped Owen's lips. "I've got an FBI friend in Miami who I think can help you. Let me give him a call and I'll call you back."

Ty wasn't sure how he felt about getting someone else involved. "Do you know this agent pretty well?"

"We worked together for about five years. He's a good guy."

"Alright." Ty hung up and glanced at Brooke. "He's going to try to help us get a flight to Colorado."

"We're really going to Colorado?" Brooke's eyes widened.

"We need to. Are you game?" Ty was on a roll. "Brad's ex-wife might be the missing piece. If we can get her to talk, we might find the files."

It almost sounded too good to be true.

"Can we visit my brother?" Brooke's eyes were hopeful.

Pulling onto the main road, Ty made a turn toward a coffee shop. "Would he let us stay with him?"

"That would be awesome! I'm sure he'd want us to stay. I've

missed Cody so much." Brooke's eyes sparkled with hope. "But will it put him in danger?"

Ty considered her question. "I guess it could. Although, only Owen and his friend should know we're going to Colorado."

Brooke nodded. "I'd love to see Cody. I'm sure he has a lot of questions for me."

Owen's return call took a little longer than they expected, but Ty answered from his seat in the coffee shop.

"Shane said he'd do it." Owen started right in. "He can meet you at the Miami International Airport in two hours. I'll take care of the flight costs."

"You're the man!" Ty sounded relieved.

After hanging up, Ty and Brooke headed to a store to purchase a special travel case for the Glock.

"I didn't know you were allowed to travel with a gun." Brooke watched Ty pack the gun in the special case and lock it.

"You have to declare it and it will undoubtedly get inspected. But, yes, you can actually bring your gun on a flight, just not near you." Ty packed the bullets in his clothing bag and made sure everything was secure. "We should head over to the airport. Do you want to give Cody a call to see if he's willing to have a couple guests tonight or should we surprise him the way we did my parents?"

■ ■ ■

With Cody's work schedule, it was too risky to show up at his place without a call, so Brooke dialed his number and waited anxiously to hear his voice.

"Hello?"

"Cody." Brooke clutched the phone and smiled at the sound of his voice.

"Sis?" Cody still sounded uncertain.

"Yes. I can't talk long. I was wondering if you'd mind a couple guests tonight."

"Tonight?" Cody sounded confused. "Where are you?"

There was so much to say, but there would be time to talk once they arrived. "I'm in Miami. We're flying into Aspen tonight. I'm not sure what time our flight will arrive, but we'll be getting a rental.

It may be late before we make it to Snowmass."

"I don't mind. I'm up late anyway." Cody paused. "I've been worried."

"I know. I'm sorry." Brooke clutched the phone. "I'll see you tonight and explain all I can. Just don't tell anyone that we're coming."

She hung up and handed Ty the phone. "He's game."

■ ■ ■

Ty and Brooke met the agent at the airport and made quick introductions. "Owen said to take good care of you," Shane said with a curious glance at the couple. "He didn't give me any details but assured me this was legal."

Ty nodded. "We really appreciate it."

"You said you've got a gun to check? Does Owen know about that?" Shane walked with Ty and Brooke to the check in counter.

"He knows. And trust me, I hope I never need to use it." Ty meant those words.

Shane shrugged and walked to the counter. The formalities didn't take long and Ty handed the woman the gun case to check in.

"Thank you." Brooke sounded as appreciative as Ty after the arrangements had been made.

"Owen's got you flying back to New York in three days. If you need longer you'll have to call him."

Ty thanked Shane and boarded the plane with Brooke.

CHAPTER 22

The flight from Miami to Aspen was long, but because of the time change, they didn't get in as late as it felt.

"Will Cody mind us knocking at his door at this time of night? Ty asked.

"Cody's so easy going, I doubt he'd mind us showing up at three." Brooke watched Ty pull her bag from the rental vehicle trunk and carry it up the flight of snow-dusted stairs to Cody's front door.

Cody's apartment was above the garage of an upscale home along a mountainside. Built in the same style as the house, the detached garage boasted large dark logs with white mortar peaking out between.

At the top of the stairs, Cody threw open the door and grabbed his sister. "Brooke!" he spun her around playfully. "Man, I can't believe it! This is totally cool!"

Ty watched the reunion, happy that Brooke had this opportunity to see her brother. Cody's blonde hair hung in curls just above his shoulders. His clothes fit his muscular form loosely and a Celtic tattoo wrapped around the center of one of his strong biceps.

"Come on in before the landlady thinks I'm having a party." Cody motioned toward the door.

The apartment was clean and newly carpeted, but Ty caught the faint hint of marijuana in the air. He glanced at the wide picture window with a view of the snow-covered mountains and star filled sky. A brown leather sofa and ottoman took up a portion of the living room, and an enormous suede beanbag chair filled up the other side.

"It's good to see you." Cody stepped back and looked over his sister. "You look great." He glanced at Ty and back to Brooke. "So, you said there'd be two of you." He reached his hand out to Ty.

"Um… You're not like a fed or something are you?"

"No." Ty grinned and shook Cody's hand.

"That's cool."

"Is it the suit? Because I've been called a Jehovah's Witness today and now a fed." Ty tried to lighten things up between himself and Brooke's brother.

"Dude, it's totally the suit." Cody motioned toward the living room. "Take a seat. Want a beer?" He went to the refrigerator and grabbed one for himself.

"No thanks." Ty answered

Brooke shook her head. "No, I'm good."

Cody popped the top and walked to the giant beanbag. "So, I want to know what's going on. Are you like in trouble with the law or something? Even Mom got worried."

■ ■ ■

Brooke looked at Ty for how much she should share. It was strange to think her mom called. How did Cody handle that?

"Go ahead." Ty nodded.

Brooke started from the beginning and explained how they'd gotten to the place they were now, leaving out names and specific details that it was better for Cody not to know.

"So the phony cop and the call from the FBI—this is crazy." Cody shook his head. "I seriously didn't know what to think."

"I'm sorry you got dragged into it."

"No problem, sis! It sounds like you've been on an adventure." He grinned at Ty. "Brooke's never been the high adventure type."

"He says that because I prefer to ski on the green slopes and not the black diamonds."

"So, you're into Jesus now?" Cody jumped topics.

Brooke's eyes took on the joy that she felt inside since becoming a Christian. "I am and its awesome, Cody."

"Hey whatever works you know—we all need that inner peace. If you're getting yours from Jesus, that's cool."

"It's not only about inner peace though. It's about forgiveness."

Cody took a sip of his beer. "I get ya."

"It's not just a religion like we grew up believing. It's a relationship with the living God who loves us enough to send His Son to pay the price for our sins." She leaned forward on the sofa. "It's so much more than we were taught. I'm a follower of Christ now."

Cody stared at her for a moment and nodded a few times.

"You don't know how bad I've wanted to tell you about my faith. Just like Ty wanted to tell his parents enough to risk getting caught. Cody, you need this too."

A clock, built into a slab of wood hanging from Cody's living room wall, sent out a quick chime. Cody glanced at it and shrugged. "You know me… I kind of go with the flow."

"The Creator of those slopes you love—He loves you." Brooke gazed on her younger brother tenderly.

Cody kicked off his flip-flops. "I've got to be into work at eight tomorrow." He glanced around uncomfortably.

"How was your conversation with Mom?" Brooke asked.

"It was alright. She was cool." Cody shrugged. "She said she misses us."

"Did you talk long?"

"No, but she told me to call sometime. I might."

Brooke would probably need to do the same at some point.

Cody finished his beer and tossed it into a can across the room. "Score!" He gave himself a cheer.

"I'm sorry we dropped in on you like this." Ty said.

Cody let out a playful chuckle. "Dude, don't apologize. I'm always cool with seeing my sis." He yawned. "I figured I'd let you two have my room and I'll sleep out here."

Brooke protested immediately. "Oh, Cody—no. Ty and I aren't like that." She shook her head. "Just keep your bed and I'll sleep on the couch. Ty can crash on your beanbag." Brooke's face was red with embarrassment.

"Oh, my bad." Cody laughed. "I just kind of figured." He glanced from Brooke to Ty. "Brooke, you can still have my bed. I'll crash out here with Ty."

Brooke appreciated her brother's willingness to give up his bed for her. "Thanks, Cody. You sure you don't mind?"

Cody waved it off. "Totally cool with it."

■ ■ ■

Cody had to leave early for work, leaving Brooke and Ty to fend for themselves until the evening. Since it was Sunday, they decided to visit a local church.

The sky was gray and it looked like they might get a dusting of snow. Brooke was glad they'd rented an SUV. Snow in mid-October was common in Snowmass and the ski resort town was already blanketed in a thin covering of white.

The mountain church had a fairly large congregation. Brooke did her best to keep her distance from Ty. He was just a friend. There was no point pretending there was more. She glanced at him. *If only I believed that.*

In such a large church, it was easy to slip into the pews barely noticed. Brooke enjoyed the singing and sat through the sermon, eager to hear what God might want her to learn in this Colorado church.

After the closing hymn, they were drawn into a conversation with the man who'd sat behind them. The man seemed bent on learning about Ty and Brooke and making sure they were true followers of Jesus Christ. It was commendable, but Brooke didn't feel like talking to anyone.

"Where are you from?" the man asked.

"Cincinnati." Ty answered. "We're visiting Brooke's brother here in Colorado."

"Ah, that's nice. It's always good to visit family. Do you and your wife have plans after church?"

Ty glanced quickly at Brooke and she lowered her gaze. Why did everyone have to assume they were married or dating? She glanced at her left ring finger where she still wore the little gold band. *That's why.*

"We're actually supposed to be somewhere this afternoon. We were just excited to visit a new church while we're here. It was great meeting you."

Brooke wished the man well before turning down the aisle and escaping any attempt Ty might make to hold her hand and play off the married couple thing. How could she handle it? There was so much safety and comfort in his hand. She couldn't let herself think about it.

Ty caught up with her in the foyer and asked if she wanted to get a bite to eat before trying to hunt down Brad's ex-wife.

"Sure. Food sounds great. I saw a Panera Bread on the way here." Brooke walked toward the car just a few steps ahead of Ty and tried to act normal.

Before she could reach for it, Ty opened her door and Brooke stepped into the rental.

■ ■ ■

"If she's not home we can just explore Aspen for the afternoon and try again tomorrow." Ty pulled up in front of Sheryl's large log and stone ski cabin. It was everything Ty would expect from a wealthy lawyer. The landscaping was perfect, the driveway was shoveled, the Lexis SUV out front was clean and waxed, and the house had all the charm of a Colorado mountain resort.

Sheryl was much quicker about answering the door than her ex-husband had been. She also appeared to be sober and unsure about who just showed up at her front door. "Yes?" she asked curtly.

"Ms. Bronowski?" Ty tried to remember if he'd ever met Brad's wife socially before. He'd rubbed noses with so many politicians while working in New York that he'd lost count, but she didn't look familiar. Her bleached blonde hair was short and neat. She wore plenty of makeup to mask signs of aging, but her pursed lips did little to help. Ty thought she might have been pretty if she would only smile.

"I prefer to be called Sheryl. How may I help you?" There was a sophisticated reserve about the woman—a stark contrast from Brad.

"My name is Blake Kendall. This is my friend, Brooke. We need to ask you a few questions about some files."

"I don't know about any files. Thank you." Sheryl moved to close the door.

"Please, ma'am. This is urgent. Threats have been made on our lives..."

Sheryl stopped herself and studied Ty closely for a moment. "Your last name is Kendall? Are you related to Olivia Kendall Davis?"

"Yes. She's my sister." Ty swallowed hard and hoped that wouldn't make her slam the door in his face. "Please, just give me ten minutes of your time. I promise what I have to say is of vital importance."

Sheryl stood there for a moment as if trying to consider her options and finally opened the door for them to come in. "I've got a pie baking in the oven and I don't want it to burn, so you're going to have to come to the kitchen with me." She watched them walk in. "Mitsy, down!" She scolded her small, white poodle.

Brooke reached down and let Mitsy sniff her hand before petting the small dog's soft furry head.

Ty's eyes roamed the wide-open floor plan. A cathedral ceiling leading to a skylight gave the living room a very large feel. Wood beams lined the walls and a fireplace with river rocks led to the ceiling.

Sheryl motioned to two bar stools beside her kitchen island. "Have a seat. I'm giving you ten minutes." She sat across from them on another stool. "That's how much time my pie has left on it."

"I'll make it quick," Ty began. In as short of time as he could, he summarized the reason for his visit, not leaving out the attempts on his life as well as Brooke's. "Your ex-husband said you hired someone to make the files and all the information in them disappear. Obviously, someone still has access to them. I've got less than one week to get those files to the person who wants them before he starts killing off my friends and family." Ty's expression showed his deep fear.

The timer went off on Sheryl's pie and she got up to pull it out. "Forget the ten minute thing." She set the pie on the stove and returned to her stool. "You're saying that someone is going after you to get the files? I don't understand. Why you? Why would the information in those files affect you?"

"Because I was the lawyer who was asked to make them disappear. After I went state's evidence the files disappeared. Brad confessed he had them removed from my office, but someone thinks I know where they are and expects me to find them."

Sheryl took a deep breath and blew it out slowly. She ran her hand through her hair and stared at the window on the other side of the room.

"You seem to know something." Ty was hopeful.

Sheryl massaged her forehead and shook her head. Her eyes looked almost apologetic as she leveled them on Ty. "I have them."

It wasn't what Ty expected to hear, but he listened carefully.

"Your sister and my ex-husband had an ongoing affair seven years ago. Olivia was trying to get ahead in the political world and did whatever it took." Sheryl's eyes showed pain. "I hated her for it." She stood up and paced the kitchen floor. "When Olivia got married things died down and I did my best to forget the affair and move on." She brushed a tear from her eye. "But about ten months ago Olivia and Brad took a little weekend trip together and I found out about it. I'm not convinced this was their first time together in those seven years. That was it for me. I decided to get my revenge."

She turned to Ty and glanced quickly at Brooke. "After Brad got the files back from your office four years ago, I'd hired someone to cover up any and all details of the campaign bribes and other unethical things my husband and some of his comrades participated in, but I kept the original files. I never knew if I'd need them again."

"Have you?" Ty's mind raced with questions.

"Olivia took many bribes. She was almost as bad as Brad." Sheryl clenched her teeth. "When I heard she was running for senator, I started sending copies of pages from the files to her office. I mailed them from various locations to make it more intimidating. I never planned to make them public. It would have tainted Brad too much for that—and I kind of enjoy my alimony checks. But I wanted to make her sweat. I wanted to scare her. I wanted her to question her decision to run. Maybe even drop out because of it. I figured my threatening little reminders of her past would make it difficult for her to sleep at night. That's what I wanted." She turned to Ty. "I never wanted to hurt anyone else."

Ty's head spun with what he was hearing. "Wait a minute… you're saying this all has to do with Olivia? That doesn't make sense. My sister wouldn't try to kill me." His heartbeat quickened. Would she? Learning that she'd taken bribes and had an ongoing affair was something Ty would not have expected from her. *Obvi-*

ously, I don't really know my sister.

Brooke placed a comforting hand on his shoulder.

"I only sent the files to Olivia's office. No one else." Sheryl's face showed sympathy. "Your sister is not who you thought she was, Mr. Kendall."

Ty's eyes were wide with confusion. He shook his head and tried to process everything. He'd been shot—but not fatally. He'd been beaten—but not killed. Olivia knew where he'd been all along. She had pull. She had power. But Jasmine was dead. Brooke could have been killed.

"I need to think this whole thing through." Ty's face was ashen and his stomach churned.

"Look," Sheryl said as she walked toward her kitchen desk. "I'll give you the files. Give them to her—tell her to stop. I have no intention of talking." Sheryl pulled the files from a drawer and handed them to Ty. "It's all here."

Ty glanced down at the familiar files. He'd not seen them in over four years and here they were.

"Are you okay?" Brooke finally spoke.

"I don't know. I just—I can't believe it was Olivia." He shook his head.

Sheryl watched Ty quietly. "It hurts. I know."

This couldn't be real. There had to be more to the story. Ty glanced up. "Do you have a fax machine?"

"Yes." Sheryl walked Ty and Brooke to a back room where she had bookshelves, a desktop computer, copier, and fax machine.

Ty dialed the number and started the faxes going. "Can you ladies make sure they all go through while I make a phone call?"

Brooke and Sheryl nodded.

Ty reached Owen on his cell phone and walked outside onto Sheryl's deck. There were flurries in the air, but Ty was too distracted to notice. "I'm sending you some faxes. I need you to get them a.s.a.p."

"Are you saying don't wait until Monday morning?" Owen asked.

"That's exactly what I'm saying. I'm sending you the campaign files. All of them."

"You found them?" Owen sounded surprised.

"Yes." Ty glanced up at the gray sky and let his eyes travel over the snow covered treetops.

"Ty—" Owen changed the subject. "Brad Bronowski's dead."

All the breath seemed to be sucked from Ty's chest. "What?" He shook his head and clutched the phone. He couldn't have heard correctly.

"Bronowski's dead."

"I was with him yesterday. He was fine. A little bit drunk, but in good health."

"He was shot, Ty."

Ty clutched the railing with his free hand and stared out at the mountains behind the house. "How? When?"

"Sometime yesterday. We haven't gotten the autopsy yet."

Ty held the phone in one hand and covered his face with the other. The fact that this man died without a Savior, mingled with the fear that it was somehow related to his and Brooke having been there was a heavy weight. "I should go."

Owen paused. "I'll call you to let you know I got the faxes."

"That's fine." Ty was too mentally exhausted to think. What was happening?

"We got it all faxed." Brooke glanced up as Ty walked into the office with an ashen face. "What's wrong?"

Ty glanced sympathetically at Sheryl. "Brad's dead."

Sheryl stopped tidying her desk and looked up at Ty. "What?"

"I just talked to my FBI agent in New York. They are doing an autopsy. Sheryl, I'm so sorry…"

Sheryl licked her dry lips and tears welled up in her eyes. "Oh my." She clutched the desk. "This is my fault." She shook her head. "Oh dear Lord—are they going to come for me next?" She wrapped her arms around herself.

"I think you need to disappear for a little while. Do you have a friend you can visit—somewhere safe?"

Sheryl sat down in her office chair and shook her head. "I hated him, but I didn't want him to die."

Brooke knelt beside her. "I'm so sorry."

"I should go. You should go. I—I'll pack." Sheryl fidgeted with her trembling hands.

"Do you want our help?" Brooke offered.

"No. I—I just want to be alone. I'll be fine. I'll leave right away. I don't need much."

Ty glanced at Brooke with concern. Sheryl was obviously in shock. "Are you sure we can't help you?"

"No. Just go." She lowered her eyes.

Ty clutched the files as they walked to the rental vehicle. He made Sheryl promise to be out of the house within the hour. This was crazy. Why would they kill Bronowski? Could his sister really be involved in this? Would she commit murder?

Brooke offered to drive and Ty consented. He was lost in his thoughts.

Following the road they'd taken to Sheryl's house, Brooke descended the windy mountain road. The snow was picking up. "Pray we don't get stuck in a snowstorm."

Still clutching the files, Ty leaned his head back and closed his eyes. "I just can't get my mind around this. Olivia?"

"Ty." Brooke called him from his thoughts. "That silver car has been following us since we left Sheryl's house—he's right on my bumper."

Looking over his shoulder, Ty saw the car just as a gun appeared from outside the passenger window. "Speed up!" Ty reached under the passenger seat for his gun just as the first bullet ricocheted off the back of their rental vehicle.

Brooke clutched the wheel and sunk down in her seat just enough to still see the road.

Another bullet bounced off the rim and Ty told her to weave. "They want to take out our tires." He put down the window and pointed his gun to set up his defense.

Two well-aimed shots broke the windshield of the car behind them, but it didn't stop the armed passenger. Ty fired again and saw the car swerve drastically, almost hitting a snow bank.

Brooke took one of the curves at a frightening speed and almost lost control of their SUV on the slippery road. "I can't drive this fast, Ty! What should I do?" Her tone was frantic.

"Stay focused. You're doing great." Ty changed the clip in his gun and aimed at the windshield. His best bet was to disable the driver.

A bullet just missed his arm. Ty steadied his gun and shot directly at the pursuing driver. The vehicle behind them swerved and drove off the road toward a steep, snow-covered embankment. Brooke turned another tight corner as the car behind them slid off the road down the mountain.

Ty leaned back in his seat and tried to calm his beating heart. "You can slow down now." He turned to Brooke. Her knuckles clutched the wheel so tight they were white.

She slowed down and pulled to the side of the road. She put her face on the steering wheel and unleashed a torrent of tears.

Ty placed a tender hand on her back and pulled her toward him. "You did great. We're okay—you did it."

Ty felt Brooke tremble in his arms and breathed a soft prayer of thanksgiving that they were okay.

"Did they already get Sheryl?" Brooke glanced up after a moment.

"We can't go back. I'll call her house." Ty reached for his phone and dialed the number Brad gave him. He listened as the answering machine picked up. "She didn't answer. Let's hope she left." Ty watched a snow plow drive past. "We shouldn't stay here. Police may have been called. Do you want me to drive?"

"Yes, please."

Ty got out and walked around the car while Brooke switched seats. She leaned back and covered her face in her hands while Ty headed down the mountain. *What should I do?*

CHAPTER 23

Ty parked at a café not far from Cody's apartment and glanced at Brooke. She'd been quiet the rest of the way down the mountain. They needed to talk—to figure out their next move. Maybe Brooke should stay here with Cody. Would she be safer with Cody? Was Cody even safe?

"We need to talk." Ty reached for her hand but Brooke got out on her own and walked toward the café.

Was that rejection?

At the counter, Brooke and Ty ordered coffee drinks. The barista smiled and greeted them as if life should somehow be normal. Shouldn't it be?

"I really like your necklace," the woman behind the counter said to Brooke. "It's so original."

"Thank you." Brooke touched the cross she still wore around her slender neck and smiled. Ty knew it was forced.

He paid for the drinks and walked with Brooke to a small table near a window where he could keep one eye on their car.

"How did they find us?" Ty took a sip of his drink and let the warmth and sweetness of his mocha warm the cold spot in his mind. After everything that just happened, Ty wasn't sure what was going on.

"It's like they're just two steps behind us." Brooke finally said. "There's nowhere to hide from them."

After this scare, Ty tried to place each incident in some kind of pattern. They found him in Cincinnati and they found him in New York. They found him in D.C., they obviously went to Miami, and now they found him in Aspen. "If it is my sister," Ty hated the words as soon as he said them. "We already know she knew where I lived.

She admitted to having an eye on our parent's house. She would have known you would be at the airport and she knew when I left her place in D.C. But who knew our location in Maryland and Florida? Who knew we were in Aspen?"

Brooke's eyes widened and she placed a hand on the table in front of her.

"Owen." It hurt to say it.

"You just faxed him everything from the files."

Ty closed his eyes and punched his fist on the table. "What a fool I've been." He clenched his teeth. "He's the only one who knew we'd met with Bronowski and he's the only one who knew we came to Aspen."

"Why would he want to kill us now?" Brooke glanced out the window.

The snow had slowed, but everything was dusted in white, giving it a calm, clean appearance.

"He's got what he needs." Ty sighed. "What an idiot I've been. Duped by the one FBI agent I believed was my friend and duped by my own sister." His heart felt numb. He glanced at Brooke and saw the fear in her eyes. *I dragged her into this impossible situation.* He shook his head.

Ty's phone began to ring and he recognized the number. "It's Owen." Ty's eyes flashed angrily. "I'll take the call outside."

■ ■ ■

Ty carried the phone outside the coffee shop and answered.

"Ty, I got the files—"

"Yeah! So now you can kill us, right?" Ty interrupted. "Surprised I answered? Your attempt at killing us in Aspen failed!"

"What are you talking about?"

"Who else knew about Bronowski? Who else knew we were here?"

"I don't know what you're saying."

"You knew." Ty squinted up at the cloudy sky. "I told you everything—you knew where we'd been, you knew where we were going." He clutched the phone and wished he could beat the man on the other end. "I don't know what hurts more, the fact that I trusted you, or that my sister was in on it with you. You're both sick!"

"Ty! Stop—I don't know what you're talking about." Owen interrupted. "Did someone make an attempt on your life in Aspen?"

"Don't play dumb. You insult me!"

"Listen to me," Owen's tone was serious. "I'm not working with your sister—I don't have a clue what you're talking about. Who tried to kill you? Did this just happen?"

It was futile talking to this man. Ty stared at the phone for a moment and threw it forcefully into the slush-covered road where it was immediately driven over by a passing car. "I've had enough." He ran his hand over his forehead and walked back to the coffee shop.

"What did he say?" Brooke held her coffee cup as if it was the only thing keeping the room from spinning.

"He denied it." Ty shook his head and took a long sip from his coffee. "He has the files now. I don't even have my bargaining chip."

"You still have the files, Ty." Brooke patted the envelope in front of him. "He only has a copy."

"But it's only a matter of time."

"So let's make more copies and make sure they can be easily made public in the event of an accident." Brooke widened her eyes. "Let me call Cody and see if he's got a copier or a scanner.

"I'm all out of disposable phones." Ty glanced toward the car. "They know what our rental looks like."

"I'm sure we can use the café phone. Cody should be home by now. He's probably wondering where we are." Brooke walked to the barista and borrowed a phone.

■ ■ ■

"He'll be here in five minutes. He said they have a copier and a scanner at the ski resort." Brooke finished her coffee.

"I need to get the gun out of the car." Ty stood up and walked outside with Brooke. He was nervous who else might be around. He didn't want to be seen with the gun.

Cody arrived in less than five minutes and they climbed into his beat up Volkswagen hatchback. Ty climbed in the back so Brooke could sit by Cody.

"So, what happened?" Cody wanted to know.

Ty filled him in on the events of their afternoon.

"Some dude called right before you did and asked for you." Cody glanced in the rear view mirror toward Ty. "I played dumb and just told him he had the wrong number."

"Did he believe you?"

"He pressed me a little, but I told him I didn't know what he was talking about."

"Thank you, Cody." Glancing through the files, Ty caught several key words that would be damaging to his sister's future career. How did he miss all this when he'd been given the files four years ago? He remembered giving them a quick glance through, but most of the information he saw then was concerning Brad Bronowski.

"If you want to make sure those files will be made public if something happens to you, you could set up an email that will go out in like one week unless you stop it," Cody suggested. "If you're the only one that knows the email address then only you can stop it."

"That's a great idea." Ty gave Cody an appreciative nod. "Do you know how to set it up?"

"Sure. I do emails like that for the ski resort all the time. My boss writes up ski news to customers on our email list and sends them out every Sunday. She's not real computer savvy, so she has me put it in every week."

It was their best insurance. "Can we do it from your work?"

"Absolutely." Cody gave a thumbs-up.

They were at the lodge in less than fifteen minutes and Ty walked beside Brooke as they followed Cody.

"Are you okay?" He placed a comforting hand on her back.

"I don't know." Brooke shook her head. "It's all so surreal."

Ty wanted to hold her hand. He wanted to pull her close and hug her, but Brooke seemed to have put up a wall. Maybe it was better that way. It was dangerous to be his friend.

■ ■ ■

Owen sat at his desk pouring over the campaign files when the door opened. He quickly set the papers inside his desk and watched Wyatt storm into his office.

"So much for your rogue witness." Wyatt set the coroners report in front of Owen.

Wyatt's word caught Owen off guard. "Rogue?"

"He's gone vigilante hasn't he?" Wyatt sat in the chair across from Owen. "And he's taken justice into his own hands apparently." Wyatt pointed to the cause of death on Brad's file. "Bronowski was shot with a 9mm. The same kind purchased by Blake Kendall in Philadelphia. All we need is the gun and we'll surely have a match."

Owen glanced up from the paper and stared blankly at the weapon report. "This isn't real. Ty would never have murdered Bronowski."

"It's right there!" Wyatt used an angry finger to pound on the paper.

"Ty didn't give up his career as a lawyer and go state's evidence four years ago only to murder the man who helped get him one step closer to solving the case."

"Then explain the weapon! Quit trying to defend this guy. He's a self-seeking lawyer who went state's evidence to cover his own butt." Wyatt puffed out a sarcastic chuckle. "Where is he?"

"Something's gone wrong." Owen shook his head, still trying to figure it out. "I know Ty. He would never do this." Owen stared at the autopsy report.

"Have you talked to him?" Wyatt tried the more direct approach.

"Only briefly." Owen handed Wyatt the report. "But I have no way of reaching him."

"No more hiding this guy. He's wanted for murder." Wyatt stood up and snatched the paper. "I swear I'll make trouble for you if you keep helping him." Wyatt pointed his finger threateningly at Owen. "I don't care if he helped you solve a case four years ago. He's a murderer."

Wyatt stormed from the office leaving Owen even more baffled than he'd been after he talked to Ty. Why did Wyatt use the word "rogue"? That was Ty's word—during a private phone conversation.

■ ■ ■

Yolanda was surprised to see her husband home from work early. He walked into the house with his assistant, Nathan. When did

Owen bring Nathan home with him?

"Hi, sweetie." There was a question in her eyes as she gave her husband a quick kiss. She glanced curiously at Nathan.

"Let's step outside for a moment, I need to talk to you about something." Owen took his wife's hand and walked out the back door with Nathan right behind.

"What's going on?" She glanced at the two men.

"We need to check the house for bugs." Owen placed a hand on Yolanda's shoulder. "Has anyone been here in the past week or two that you didn't expect? Did you have any deliveries? Any surprise guests?"

Yolanda was thoughtful for a few minutes. "The cable guy was here last Tuesday."

"Why was he here? Did you call the cable company?"

"No." Yolanda shook her head. "He said they were having problems in the area with several of the boxes and asked if he could see ours." She tried to remember more details. "I let him in and showed him the two televisions. He was done in just a few minutes."

"Did you stay in the room with him the whole time?" Owen asked.

"No." Yolanda's dark eyes showed concern.

Nathan turned to Owen. "That has to be it."

"We're going to do a little exploring." Owen took his wife's hand. "Don't talk about any of this inside."

Yolanda nodded and walked inside with her husband and Nathan.

It only took a moment to find the first wiretap. Nathan held up the telephone receiver and the small bug he'd found inside.

Owen moaned and pointed upstairs. They all went to the master bedroom and watched while Owen unattached the phone and pulled out an identical wiretap.

Owen took the bugs and carried them both outside where he found a large rock and smashed them.

"Should we check for other bugs in the house?" Nathan asked.

"Probably." Owen shook his head and swore. "This is insanity!" He slammed his fist on the table. "No wonder Ty thought I was the leak."

Yolanda asked what it all meant and Owen explained.

"I've got to report this to Rhodes." Owen hoped his higher up would give him clearance to do some digging. "I don't take to highly to being spied on." Owen's eyes were hot with anger.

■ ■ ■

"This isn't exactly how I expected the next visit from my sister to go, but I'm glad you came out." Cody sat on the floor with his back against the chair in his living room.

Ty leaned back on the beanbag chair and crossed his arms behind his head. "I appreciate all you did for me. Now I've just got to figure out what my next move should be."

"Since those dudes tried to kill you, I guess you don't want to call them and tell them you've got the files."

"It doesn't change the fact that they made threats to my friends and family." Ty glanced around the living room and rested his eyes on Brooke. "I'm not sure you and Cody are safe right now."

Brooke closed her eyes and rubbed her temples.

"I'm sure they know where Cody lives and they know I care about you." Ty glanced away. He wasn't sure how to explain it to Brooke. How could he care so much for a woman he'd known such a short time? He couldn't let himself. It would never work. Not while he was in witness protection.

"Since this Owen dude is bad, is there anyone else at the FBI who will help you?" Cody asked.

Ty glanced at the slip of paper he'd been keeping in his wallet since that day he and Brooke escaped her apartment. "I was thinking of calling Wyatt Longstreth." Ty explained who he was. "I'm supposed to be able to trust him—he's the agent protecting my identity, but something never felt right about him."

"What about Olivia. Should you call her and at least find out if she's really part of this?" Brooke crossed her legs beneath her on the sofa and watched Ty with concern in her eyes.

"Sheryl made it perfectly clear that she'd been sending copies of the files to Olivia. Who else could it be?" Ty shook his head. "I should probably just call Wyatt." He glanced at Cody. "Do you have a place to hide out if you need to disappear for a little while?"

Cody shrugged. “I’m sure I can find someplace. My boss loves me and she’d probably let me stay at the lodge.”

“Whoever is after me could easily find you at your work.” Ty sighed. “If Owen already called you here, he could be watching us right now.” Ty stood up and picked up one of the new disposable phones. “I’ll call the U.S. Marshal.”

■ ■ ■

Ty hoped he was doing the right thing when he heard Wyatt answer the phone.

“Where are you?” Wyatt asked from the other end. “I haven’t heard anything from you since you left Maryland. I know you’ve talked to Owen—why did you cut me out?”

“I didn’t know who to trust.” Ty was quiet. Something in his stomach still wasn’t sure this was the right person, but what else could he do? He walked outside, brushed the snow off a patio chair, and sat down. It was cold outside, but Ty didn’t mind.

“Well I’m glad you called. I’ve been worried about you and Ms. Dunbar.”

“We’re both safe right now, although we’ve had another attempt on our lives. I’ve got some important information that might blow open the whole case.”

“Great!” Wyatt sounded pleased. “What made you finally decide to trust me?”

“I’m still not sure I do, but I’m running out of options.” Ty walked down the steps and looked at the star filled sky.

“Where are you, Ty? I want to help you.”

“I’m in Colorado. I’d like to get to New York but I don’t have a viable ID.”

“I can get you here. Does Ms. Dunbar need a flight too?”

“Yeah. Both of us.” Ty sighed. “Keep this low profile,” he added.

“No problem. I’ll personally pick you up in New York.” Wyatt promised.

They made arrangements and hung up. Ty swallowed hard. Was Wyatt just a little too accommodating? Ty walked back to the house. What if there was more than one leak? What if he was about to walk Brooke back into more danger?

■ ■ ■

"You don't look at peace." Brooke watched Ty walk across the room and sit across from her on the floor.

"I don't see any other option, but I'm not sure about Wyatt." He shared his reservations. "Brooke, I don't want to take you right into another dangerous situation."

Cody leaned back and opened a beer. "What if I took Brooke somewhere else?"

"Can you get off work?"

"Sure." Cody glanced at his sister and grinned. "Ski season doesn't start back up for a few weeks and I've got some vacation time stored up. What do you say we take a road trip?

"Can you keep it low profile?" Ty asked.

"I got lots of camping gear. You game, sis?"

Camping? Brooke glanced at Ty. Without Ty? What would this mean for them?

Ty nodded. "It's probably a good plan."

He wants me to go. She turned away and sucked in her breath. "Sure. That sounds great, Cody."

"Sweet! I'll call my boss. I'm sure she'll be cool with me taking a little down time before things get crazy. I'm her favorite ski instructor."

How could she say goodbye? She'd been with Ty for almost two months. The few days they were apart were agonizing. Why did it hurt so much?

Brooke cleared her throat and stood up. "I should probably get to bed. I'm pretty exhausted." She turned her face away from Ty's concerned eyes. "What time did Wyatt say he would book your fight?"

"He said he'd try to get me an early flight. I'll call him in the morning to confirm."

Brooke nodded numbly and walked to Cody's bedroom. What was wrong with her? She loved her brother. They'd always talked about camping. But how could she leave Ty? Tears flooded her eyes. What if they put him back into witness protection under a different name and she could never find him again? Alone in the room, Brooke finally let her tears fall.

■ ■ ■

Brooke was quiet as they drove Ty to the airport the next morning. It was close to nine and his flight left at ten. The sky was gray and dreary. It looked how she felt.

Cody pulled up in front of the passenger drop off and reached to give Ty a handshake. "Good to meet you, man."

"Nice meeting you, too." Ty returned the handshake.

Brooke stepped out of the back seat while Ty gathered his things.

"I've put the number for this phone in the one I gave you." Ty held up a disposable phone. "Call me if there's any emergency."

"I will. You do the same."

Ty gazed into her eyes. "Please be careful."

"You too."

He reached up and touched her face. "I don't know what's going to happen from here."

Brooke fought tears. "I know."

"You have to know I care about you."

Brooke lowered her eyes. "Thank you." She licked her lips. "You've been a great friend." She stepped back, afraid he was going to hug her. She knew if he hugged her she'd come unglued.

"I'll call you. I promise."

Brooke feigned a smile. "If anything looks suspicious, please…"

Ty reached for her hand. He held her fingers for just a moment and let go to grab his suitcase.

Brooke turned as Ty walked away. She couldn't bear to watch. She missed him already.

Brooke climbed into the front seat and fastened her seatbelt. Ty was gone. She turned to the window and watched the scenery outside. Two months of non-stop adventure—and now he was gone. He pointed her to Christ. Was there anything more special than that?

"You really care about that dude, don't you?" Cody broke the silence.

Brooke gave her brother a wane smile. "Is it obvious?"

"Yeah. Both of you looked like sick puppies all morning.

"You think Ty was sad too?" Brooke needed assurance.

Cody laughed. "Seriously? Come on, that poor guy is totally

into you." Cody shook his head. "The only reason I think he left you with me is because he thought you'd be safer here. Man, he'd much rather be flying on that plane with you."

Brooke shrugged. She watched the beautiful landscape leading to Snowmass. Forests of snow covered Aspens lined the backcountry roads and Brooke opened her window a crack to breath in the cool mountain air. This was much better than New York any day—all that was missing was Ty.

"Let's get some food." Cody pulled off the exit toward his home. "We need to plan our trip. I assume you want to head east?" He grinned.

■ ■ ■

Ty boarded the plane and found his seat beside a young man wearing a hoodie over his head and a pair of ear buds in his ears. The last time he was on a plane at the Aspen Pitkin County Airport he'd been with Brooke. Was that only three days ago?

She looked so sad this morning. Was he right to leave her? Ty leaned back and looked out the small window as the plane started to move down the runway. She said he was a good friend. *Is that all?* He massaged his temples to ward off a headache. *Why didn't I talk to her about us? Is there an "us"?*

He tuned out the stewardess as she gave the usual flight instructions. Aspen and Snowmass were beneath him now. He pulled the manila envelope from his carry on and flipped through the pages. He and Cody had scanned every one of the campaign files the night before. They made physical copies and a cyber copy. If he did not log in and change the send date, the cyber copy would go out to dozens of newspapers in one week. Cody and Brooke also had copies they promised would be well hidden and used in the event that anything happened to him.

Would Brooke have more opportunities to talk to Cody about the Lord? Every time Ty and Brooke ventured to talk about Jesus, Cody brushed it off.

What about Olivia? Was she really behind all this? Brooke encouraged him to call her, but how? At this moment, he was so angry with her he couldn't think about it.

Ty leaned his head back and tried to rest. His mind raced with "what if's."

What if he was flying into a trap? He hadn't prayed about his decision to return to New York. What if that bad feeling lingering in his heart was a warning? Ty shook the thought from his head. He couldn't second-guess himself. This was his course. It was too late to turn back. *God, You know the whole situation. Lord, please help me.*

■ ■ ■

When Ty stepped off the plane he saw Wyatt immediately. He also saw three other U.S. Marshals. This didn't look good.

"Blake Kendall." Wyatt approached Ty with a dark scowl. "You're under arrest for the murder of Brad Bronowski."

Ty's head whirled. Three armed officers surrounded him and Wyatt put him in cuffs.

"I told you I'd pick you up," Wyatt said icily in Ty's ear.

Ty eyed him coldly.

"Where is Brooke Dunbar?" Wyatt watched the gate.

"She had other plans today." Ty let sarcasm drip from his tone. "I'm sure she'll be disappointed that she missed the welcoming party."

Wyatt gave Ty a little shove against the wall with his gun. "Don't think we won't find her. She's only got one brother and we know where he lives." He turned to one of the other Marshals. "Frisk him."

Ty wished he could be certain that Brooke and Cody planned to leave today. With his face against the wall and strange hands pulling things from his pockets, he knew there was no way of calling her now. He watched as his phone was thrown into a bag along with his carry on bag and the master copy of the campaign files.

CHAPTER 24

Cody's phone blinked with five messages made within the past hour. He was about to check the messages when the phone rang. "Man, someone wants to get a hold of me bad." He grabbed the phone before looking at his caller ID and clicked the answer button.

"Look, I know you said you don't know where Ty is, but this is urgent. You've got to let me talk to him. I know he's got to be there—please…" Owen sounded desperate.

"Man, I don't know what you're talking about."

"I didn't set them up. I promise! Let me talk to him. Please!"

Cody hesitated. He glanced at his sister and her eyes grew wide.

"Tell them my phone was bugged. That's how it leaked. I found the bugs—I'm on this case with them, not against them."

"Dude, you're… man…" Cody shook his head and handed the phone to his sister. "I don't know what to say."

Brooke's hands shook when she took the phone. Why did he give in so easily? "Hello?"

"Brooke. Listen. I know how it looks, but my phone was bugged. That's how the information leaked. Yolanda can tell you. She was right there when we opened up the phones. I promise, I'm on your side. I need to talk to Ty."

"He's gone." It hurt to even say the words.

"What? Where is he? Can you call him?" Owen's tone was urgent.

"He flew back to New York."

"How? I didn't have you scheduled until tomorrow."

Brooke wasn't sure how Owen would take her answer. "Wyatt Longstreth flew him back."

Owen swore. "Why'd he do that?" His tone was concern not

anger.

Brooke sat down with the phone and held her face in her free hand. “He didn’t know who to trust.”

“Does Longstreth know you’re there?”

“He knows we’re in Aspen.” Brooke ran her hand along the soft suede of the beanbag chair. “Why? Is Wyatt bad?” Brooke wasn’t sure what to believe anymore either.

“Someone tapped my phones and Wyatt is the only one who’s been hostile about being out of the loop. Something’s not right. I’ve got my boss investigating Pratt’s death and looking into Wyatt. You and your brother need to leave.”

“Cody too?”

“Whoever is behind this is going to figure out who you’re staying with real quick. I can fly you both to New York right away.”

“Cody?” Brooke glanced up at her brother who’d been straining to listen to the voice at the other end. “Owen wants to fly us to New York.”

“Ty said to stay low key. Can you trust this guy?”

“I don’t know. I think so…” She glanced up at the ceiling and lifted up a soft prayer. “Where is Yolanda?”

“She’s at home. I can have her call you from her cell. She’ll tell you, she saw the bugs in the line. She knows what’s going on. I’ve never included my wife in a case like this. Do you want me to have her call?”

Brooke took his willingness as honesty. “Cody, I think we should go.”

“I’ll grab my bag. I hate New York, but hey, why not? It’s with you.” He smiled and left the room.

“We’ll head out now. Call my cell phone to tell me what flight we’re on.” Brooke gave him the number.

■ ■ ■

Ty shifted uncomfortably in a cold metal chair and strained to look at a clock. He couldn’t move very well with his hands cuffed to the table in the interrogation room. It was close to four a.m. When were they going to interrogate him?

God, please… Ty laid his head on the cold hard table and wished he could get his arm into a position to use it as a pillow. He didn't even know what to pray. He was so tired his thoughts went everywhere. Was Brooke okay? Why was he being accused of Brad's murder? Had Sheryl gotten to safety? He closed his eyes and fell into a fitful sleep.

"Wake up!" A hard slap on the table pulled Ty from his confusing dreams. "Want coffee?" Wyatt set a latte on the table and grinned. "Oh, wait, you don't have your hands free. Guess I'll drink it."

Ty blinked back the tired blurriness in his eyes. "What time is it?" He tried to turn around to see the clock.

"It's eight a.m." Wyatt took a sip of his coffee. "Did you have a good night's sleep?"

Ty clenched his teeth.

"I'm sorry I couldn't question you last night when we got home from the airport. I had plans." He set his coffee down on the interrogation table. "We need to talk."

"I didn't kill Brad." Ty said the only thing he wanted this man to know.

Wyatt shook his head. "I'm not so sure. From the coroners report the weapon that killed Brad was a 9mm Glock, just like yours. In fact, upon inspection of your gun, we're pretty positive it was yours."

"It wasn't."

"Maybe Brooke did it. Did she kill Brad Bronowski?" Wyatt stretched his arms behind his head. "I bet you're feeling kind of cramped. How many hours have you been sitting like that?"

"You know you're not legally allowed to do this."

"Oh, do you need a bathroom break?" Wyatt chuckled. He motioned toward the camera and two of the same Marshals who brought him in the evening before unattached him from the table and led him at gunpoint to the rest room.

Ty's short break was not enough to ease the tension in his arms and legs. When he was returned to the interrogation room, Ty watched as the men walked away. He noticed the light on the audio-video devise was no longer lit.

Wyatt followed Ty's eyes. "Don't worry, I turned it off. That way we can have a real conversation." Wyatt crossed his strong biceps over his chest and leaned back in his chair.

Ty watched Wyatt curiously for a moment. There was something about the way Wyatt crossed his arms that triggered a memory. Ty tried to picture the two men who'd accosted him after he'd been abducted. The man in the black ski mask—his build, his mannerisms, they were like Wyatt's. But that man had a British accent. Could it have been Wyatt? An accent could easily be faked. Ty had been in so much pain that day that the similarities had not dawned on him.

"We need to know where your friend, Brooke, is hiding." Wyatt started in again.

"Your guess is as good as mine at this point." Ty hoped he was right. He decided to keep his suspicions about Wyatt to himself.

A chuckle escaped Wyatt's lips and he leaned back. "Cody's landlord told us he was going out of town for a little while." Wyatt studied Ty's expression carefully. "That means he will be home eventually. We can wait." Wyatt grinned. "But I found this in your stuff." He held up Ty's cell phone. "You seem to have missed a bunch of calls from this same number but the person isn't leaving messages." Wyatt sat the phone down in front of Ty. "Is this Brooke?"

Ty didn't answer.

"Why don't we call and see?" Wyatt pressed the call button and put the phone on speaker.

"Ty?" Brooke's concerned voice on the other end answered immediately.

"Sweetie," Wyatt spoke soothingly to Brooke. "Where are you honey?"

"Don't answer, Brooke, hang up the phone. Hang up now!"

Wyatt slapped Ty across the mouth. "Don't listen to him, Brooke. Ty's in some big trouble, you can help him if you tell me where you are."

"It's Longstreth, Brooke! Hang up! Hang up!"

Brooke hung up and Wyatt grabbed Ty's shirtfront. "You're not helping any." He gave Ty a shove.

"I want to speak with a lawyer." Ty could feel a trickle of blood on his lip.

Wyatt crossed his arms over his broad chest and watched Ty with a smug grin. "I have no doubt that you know the legal system, Ty.

Undoubtedly, you understand that when a murder weapon is proven to have killed someone and the person who owned the murder weapon was known to be at the crime scene it looks pretty bad for them."

"This isn't about a murder, Longstreth." Ty couldn't bring himself to use the man's first name. "It's about a set of files that point some powerful politicians to some unethical acts."

"You're talking about these files." Wyatt pulled them out of his bag. "Yes. I've read them. This is good stuff. Is this why you killed Bronowski? To protect your sister, maybe?" Wyatt set the files on the table and patted them a few times.

Ty stared at Wyatt for a moment.

"Of course that's what will be presented at your trial if you try to bring the files into this, Ty." Wyatt took another sip of his coffee and finished it off. "No matter how you cut it, you're looking at serious time. You'll either do time on your own or you'll do time and pull your sister's political career down with you. Your choice."

"What do you want from me, Longstreth?" Ty was trying to put it all together.

"I want Brooke's location. I was hoping you'd work with me on that, but I can see you're convinced your silence can help her in some way." He shook his head. "Trying to protect her and your sister, aren't you?"

"I have no reason to protect my sister at this point." Ty narrowed his eyes on Wyatt. "In fact, in less than a week all the information in those files will be at every major newspaper in America." He watched for Wyatt's response. "I'm not trying to hide anything. Are you?"

Wyatt's hands made an involuntary fist. "You're bluffing."

Ty shook his head. "Why bluff? I made copies. They're waiting in cyber space right now. Whether I go to jail for a crime I didn't commit or not, those files will go viral unless I have reason to delay the send date."

"Idiot!" Wyatt smacked Ty across the head and stormed from the room. "Take him out of there. We're going to have to deal with him another way." His voice carried from the hallway.

■ ■ ■

Brooke found Cody in the kitchen with Yolanda making his favorite breakfast. The smell of pancakes filled the air. "I only like real maple syrup, though," Cody explained. "I'm a purist all the way, you know what I mean?"

"Where is Owen?" Brooke glanced past the kitchen to the living room.

"He's about to leave for the office." Yolanda glanced at the clock. "I figured you'd still be sleeping. You got in awful late." She grinned at Cody. "I also figured he'd still be sleeping, but he said he was hungry."

"Pancakes?" Cody's eyes twinkled at his sister. "I used chocolate chips."

"I need to talk to Owen. I just got a strange phone call."

"What about a phone call?" Owen walked down the stairs and greeted his wife with a kiss.

Relaying the call as best as she could, Brooke told Owen that Ty specifically told her something about Wyatt and yelled for her to hang up the phone.

Owen sat down at the table and accepted the cup of coffee his wife poured him.

They'd been up late the night before and Brooke gave her statement about what happened at Sheryl's home and the attempt made on their lives on the drive down the mountain. Brooke's testimony shed a lot of light on the details of the case. The new information concerning information being sent to Olivia, as a threat, presented a whole new angle.

"Wyatt hasn't returned any of my calls and they're being tight lipped at the Marshal's office. They won't answer any questions about Ty without Wyatt's consent."

"Isn't the FBI above the U.S. Marshals?" Cody asked.

Owen grinned. "I like to think so, but we're actually just different agencies. The U.S. Marshals is an arm of the federal courts. The FBI is under the Department of Justice. We investigate federal criminals and serve as internal intelligence."

"They won't even tell you if they have him?" Brooke asked.

"Nothing. I've got Nathan on it right now. I'd also like to talk to Sheryl Bronowski and Olivia Davis."

■ ■ ■

Owen called Nathan into his office and told him about Brooke's strange phone call.

"I finally got through to someone at the Marshals' office." Nathan leaned back on the conference table. "They've got Ty in custody. They claim they have Bronowski's murder weapon and it's been confirmed." His face grew serious. "They said it was Ty's gun."

"I know Ty didn't kill Brad. He called me when he left. Why would he bother telling me he was there if he'd committed a murder?" Owen threw his pencil across the room.

"No doubt. I'd say whoever bugged your home murdered Brad. They'd have heard the same information you did and therefore known exactly how to set Ty up."

"Wyatt knew Ty purchased a Glock." Owen crossed his arms. "He pulled the purchasing report on their credit cards. He also knew what model and ammunition Ty purchased."

Nathan nodded. "He knew where Ty and Brooke stayed in Maryland." Nathan opened a manila folder and pulled out several documents. "And… I think you'll find this interesting. Wyatt worked as a body guard for several years before becoming a Marshal." He tossed the paperwork down in front of Owen. "See that picture?"

"Is that Wyatt with Clayton Davis?" Owen pulled the photo closer to see it better. "Where did this picture come from?"

"I dug it out of some old campaign photographs last night while I was online. I blew it up and cropped it. The original photo shows Olivia Davis on stage. I happened to notice Wyatt in uniform talking to Clayton down on the foreground."

Owen set the photo down. "This doesn't prove anything, but it convinces me."

"There's more." Nathan pulled out another photo he'd found of a different event. "Here's Clayton and Wyatt at another event."

Owen's forehead puckered.

"I also found out Clayton Davis helped Wyatt get his position at the Marshal's office. He pulled a few strings using blackmail photos." Nathan crossed his arms over his chest.

"Ty told me about the photos. He said they were stolen when he got abducted just outside of D.C."

"My contact at the Marshal's office said Matthew Pratt told a few people about the photos shortly before he disappeared."

"This is starting to add up." Owen paged his secretary. "Did you get through to Olivia Davis for me?"

"Yes. She said she'd take a call at ten thirty."

"Thank you." Owen glanced at his phone. "That's in half an hour." He was starting to gain hope. "I need to call the Marshal's office. We need to get Ty into our custody."

■■■

"I don't have much time to talk," Olivia answered curtly at 10:31. I've already told you all I know. I told my brother I'm finished with him."

"There have been more developments, Ms. Davis," Owen began. "Concerning some mail you would have received upon several occasions over the past couple months."

Olivia snorted. "I don't get mail."

Owen paused. "What do you mean you don't get mail?"

"I have a secretary that screens everything and then Clayton takes care of the rest. I can't be bothered with mail. Most of it's junk anyway."

Owen was quiet for a moment. "Are you saying then, that you were not made aware of any files containing information about campaign donations and how they might have swayed your voting choices?"

"What?" Olivia sounded annoyed at the question. "Never. Who would send such rot?"

"The person who held the campaign files which we've spent the last eight weeks looking for. I've seen them, Olivia. They're pretty damaging."

"Are these the files Blake mentioned to me?"

"Yes, the very ones. I think you need to take a look at them. I have them right in front of me."

For the first time in her life Olivia seemed not to have a sarcastic come back. "Clayton is away this afternoon and we have a dinner tonight with several area doctors concerning the local hospital."

"Can you cancel any of that or do I need to issue a warrant?"

"I can come. I—I should let Clayton know."

"Maybe you shouldn't." Owen advised. "If he's the one who gets your mail you may want to hear my story first."

Olivia cleared her throat. "I'll catch an afternoon flight. Have a car ready."

Owen made the preparations and leaned back in his chair. Now he just needed to find Ty.

■ ■ ■

"He's not under my custody any longer." Wyatt's voice on the other end of the phone annoyed Owen as much as it did in person.

"Where is he?" Owen did not want to be trifled with.

"The FBI has their secrets, I guess the Marshals have ours."

"Don't play this game. I want Ty—Blake Kendall—brought to our offices this afternoon."

"We have further questions for Blake. Perhaps tomorrow."

Owen was ready to punch someone. He slammed down the phone and called Nathan. "Find out where they're holding Ty. I'm supposed to pick up Ms. Davis at the airport at two o'clock, and I need you to come with me."

Owen worked with Nathan until the time they had to pick up Ms. Davis. He wanted answers concerning Matthew Pratt's disappearance and the relationship Wyatt Longstreth had with Clayton Davis.

"Look at this." Owen held up one of Ty's old documents. "It appears Wyatt Longstreth worked for more than just Olivia and Clayton Davis."

Nathan scanned the paper. "Why haven't we seen this before?"

"There's not much about him. His history has several gaps. I honestly think this one is a fluke." Owen walked to the stack of files Ty handed in four years ago. "I wonder if there are any more flukes in these piles."

"It's worth inspecting."

By the time Owen was scheduled to pick up Olivia, Owen and Nathan had found a few files that placed Wyatt in a questionable position with several of Ty's old clients.

■ ■ ■

Owen drove to the airport. He had dozens of questions for Ty's older sister, but what she said about never reading her mail stuck with him. If she didn't know there was a threat, she would have no reason to go on a hunt for the files. Could Olivia really be naïve to all of this?

Olivia Davis was already off the plane standing beside the gate tapping her foot when Owen and Nathan arrived. It was amazing how much she could say by simply tapping her three inch grey heel. She pursed her lips when they approached and pulled her cell phone out of her white wool blazer pocket to check the time.

"Sorry we are a few minutes late." Owen could see she did not appreciate it. "Traffic was horrendous."

"Yes. This is New York City. Traffic is horrendous. Where are you taking me? I have to be back by seven."

"I'll do my best, but I can't make any promises." Owen walked her to the car and opened the door for her. "You do realize, ma'am, the position you are in right now could warrant you an arrest."

"Your threats don't intimidate me." Olivia crossed her arms and stared out the window while Owen drove through traffic toward the FBI offices.

As soon as they arrived, Owen asked his superior officer to join them in the conference room. Officer Rhodes was following the case closely and doing some of his own digging into the phone taps at Owen's home. The older gentleman had an authoritative presence about him that Owen hoped to bring to the table.

Olivia took a seat, crossed her legs, and wiped imaginary dust off her white wool pants. "Now," She leveled her eyes evenly on Owen. "Show me the files." It was clear that Olivia considered herself in charge of this meeting.

Owen set the files in front of her and Olivia flipped through them. "These are faxed."

"Yes. The originals are with your brother." Owen watched her pursed expression.

Olivia went back to the beginning and began scanning the files slowly. The haughtiness in her eyes was soon replaced with somber uncertainty. "I had no idea this information was still out there." She closed the folder and let her eyes fall on the three men in the room. "Ty mentioned files but I didn't believe him."

"Are you aware, Ms. Davis, of the problems that have arisen as a result of these files?" Officer Rhodes asked.

"No." Olivia was ready to listen.

Owen explained the tragedies and attempts on Ty and Brooke's lives as they searched for the files. "In this whole process your brother has been accused of murdering Bronowski."

Olivia's eyes widened and her face grew white. "Brad is dead?" The news obviously affected her.

"Yes." Owen continued to explain. "His ex-wife claims she had the files all along and began sending them to you upon learning that you planned to run for senator. She also claims her motivation was your relationship to Brad while he was her husband."

Olivia rubbed her temples. "I never received any copies of these files." Olivia's voice was soft. "I—I need a few minutes alone." She dabbed the corners of her eyes. "Would you mind?"

"We'll give you ten minutes. No phone calls, ma'am." Owen was firm.

He motioned to the others and they left her alone.

Giving Olivia a ten-minute break gave Owen the opportunity to check his phone messages. He'd felt his phone vibrate on his hip a couple times during their interview with Olivia, but couldn't take the calls. Three missed calls? He furrowed his brows. It wasn't like Yolanda to call repeatedly. Something must be wrong.

"Thank God you called back." Yolanda's strained voice met him on the other end. "Brooke is gone."

"She disappeared again?" Where would she have gone this time? "Did she have information about Ty?"

"No, Owen. People broke in. They wore masks. The paramedics are with Cody right now. He was shot—" Yolanda's voice broke into a sob. "They took her." Yolanda had to stop talking for a moment to get her emotions together.

"Are you okay?" Owen paced the room and felt his blood pressure rising.

"I'm fine. They bound my hands with zip ties and threw me on the ground. Cody tried his best to fight them off. We were powerless—Brooke put up a fight and they roughed her up, too."

"How is Cody?"

"The paramedics are hopeful, but he's lost a lot of blood. They're about to take him to the hospital. I'm going with them."

"Babe, please be careful." Owen clutched the phone.

"You be careful. These men are heartless. The one was huge! He dragged Brooke from the house like she was nothing. Owen, I'm scared."

The fear in his wife's voice brought chills to Owen. This thing was way too personal. They'd tapped his phone and now they'd broken into his house. The one place he thought Brooke was safe.

The other two men were already in the conference room with Olivia when Owen walked in. His face was full of concern and both men noticed.

"What's going on?" Bob rose from his seat.

Owen was very aware that Olivia was there, but he didn't care. "They broke into my house. They've taken Brooke and her brother's been shot."

"Is Yolanda okay?" Nathan asked.

"She's a wreck, but they didn't hurt her."

Olivia asked for clarification. "This is all related to the files?"

Owen nodded. "I need to see my wife. Get a team to my house. We need anything we can get."

Nathan nodded.

"Ms. Davis," Owen stopped and looked at Ty's sister. "I need to cut this interview short."

"I'll cancel my evening plans and make arrangements to stay in New York." She wrote down her cell phone number. "Call me when you wish to continue this conversation."

Owen appreciated her cooperation. She was obviously humbled, but he didn't have time to think about it. He needed to see Yolanda.

Chapter 25

It was early evening. Ty sat in a cell waiting in anxious uncertainty. How long did they plan to hold him without giving him opportunity to call a lawyer? He paced the room and tried to find hope in the fact that God was with him.

Why didn't I listen to that still small voice, Lord? You were trying to warn me. Why didn't I listen?

"I just need him for about an hour." Ty could hear Wyatt's voice in the hallway.

"Almost everyone's gone home for the night," an unfamiliar voice replied back. "Are you doing this off the books?" The voice asked.

"They're moving him tomorrow and I have a few more questions I need answered."

Footsteps echoed in the hall and Ty watched as Wyatt and another man approached his cell.

"Time to visit the interrogation room." Wyatt stood back while the man opened Ty's cell.

Once again, Ty was ushered to the same small gray room where he'd spent a restless night. He watched Wyatt enter, carrying a laptop computer. Did Wyatt hope to get Ty to delete the email?

"Well, Blake, I hope your accommodations were a little better this time."

Ty watched as he was cuffed to the table.

After the other agent left, Wyatt sat across from Ty, and crossed his arms. "I'm sure you know why I brought you back." He grinned. "Funny how you decided to trust me. I'm sure you're questioning your judgment now."

Ty studied Wyatt closely. "It was you all along…" He shook his head. "You were the man in the black ski mask, weren't you?"

A self-satisfied grin passed over Wyatt's lips. "I thought I did a mighty fine Britt," Wyatt said in the same British accent he'd used when Ty had been abducted. "What gave it away?"

It was his huge arms and broad chest that gave it away, but Ty decided not to give Wyatt the satisfaction of a complement. How did he not see it before? Ty shook his head. "So who wiped my name from the database?"

"That was Pratt." Wyatt returned to his own voice. "I guess he was trying to protect you. But the call you made to your parents put you back on the radar. Pratt's one good deed failed." Wyatt chuckled. "As far as Owen—he is the real deal. I didn't even think about breaking your trust in him when I bugged his phones. I just wanted to know where you were. This worked out perfectly." He leaned forward and opened the laptop. "Are you familiar with live feed?" he asked.

Ty figured it was a rhetorical question.

"I thought you'd like to see Brooke." Wyatt turned his computer toward Ty.

Ty's heart sank. Brooke sat on a metal chair bound and gagged. He instinctively tightened his fists and a wave of sickness washed over his body.

"As you can see, she is still alive." Wyatt pointed at her, "but you don't know where she is." He smiled. "I've got a friend taking care of her for you. I believe he introduced himself to Brooke as Vince Gearhart the first time she met him. Then there was Colorado. He's recovered well from the gunshot wound you inflicted on him." Wyatt leaned forward. "Can you give Ty a greeting?" He spoke to Brooke's captor.

A masked man approached Brooke and smacked her with the backside of his hand. Her muffled cry rang out in the empty room where they held her. The man administered another blow and Brooke tried to protect herself with her bound hands.

"Stop it!" Ty pulled at his cuffed hands.

"You can't pull yourself free, Blake." Wyatt laughed. "Let me tell you how this works." He crossed his arms and paced around the room. "You delete your email and we let Brooke go."

He placed his hands on the table and leaned forward. "Or—show him—"

Ty watched the computer screen as Brooke took another strike across the head. "Stop!"

"It is painful to watch isn't it? I'm sure you remember what it feels like." Wyatt stood over Ty and gave him a hard blow to the ribs.

Ty moaned and tried to catch his breath while the pain traveled through his body. It took him a few minutes to recover. *Dear Lord... help us.* He swallowed back the dryness in his throat. "How do I know you'll let her go?" He asked through a strained breath.

Wyatt scratched his head. "Hmm—good question. You're going to have to trust me."

It was a hopeless situation. Ty lowered his eyes. What choice did he have? They had Brooke. He glanced up at the computer and ached to hold the woman on the screen.

"This isn't going to end well for you, Blake." Wyatt's tone dripped with sarcasm. "We've got you so wrapped up in Brad Bronowski's murder that no jury will believe you're innocent." He grabbed his water bottle and took a long sip. "Trying to bring the files into it will only give fuel to your guilt, but it doesn't have to end bad for Brooke. That's up to you."

Ty didn't respond.

"Blake needs a little more convincing." Wyatt spoke to Brooke's captor and the man pulled her to her feet and shoved her into a wall. With her hands and feet both tied, Brooke had no way of breaking the fall. "I don't know how much more you want us to rough her up. She was hard enough to bring in." Wyatt held up his arm and pointed to a bruise. "She actually bit me." He grinned at the computer screen. "That's where she got the busted lip."

Tears welled up in Ty's eyes. What had he done? Sweet, precious Brooke. This was his fault—all of it. He'd dragged her into this and now she was suffering.

"Are you crying Blake?" Wyatt laughed. "You really love her don't you?" He turned to the screen. "Break her arm!"

"No!" Ty almost jumped out of his seat but the cuffs stopped him. "Let her go. I'll delete the account." Ty couldn't take it any longer.

"Good choice." Wyatt leaned forward and spoke through the computer. "Cancel that. Take her away. I'll let you know when to drop her off."

Ty watched the man yank Brooke from the floor. She was terrified. What little resisting she did was fruitless.

"She doesn't even know they're taking her to safety. Look at that." Wyatt turned the computer to Ty. "I'll un-cuff you so you can log into your email."

■ ■ ■

Ty's head ached as he lay down on the small bed in his cell. He'd cancelled the email, so all he could do was pray Wyatt would keep his end of the deal and release Brooke.

If only he had a way of getting a hold of Owen. Why had he doubted Owen? It was Wyatt who bugged Owen's phone. Ty closed his eyes and wished he could hit a reset button on the past couple days. The only hope he had for the situation is that he'd successfully faxed the entire file to Owen. Maybe Owen would piece things together. *God please help him.*

Ty prayed hard on that little cell cot. He prayed for Brooke. He prayed for Owen. He prayed for every person that came to his mind. His heart was heavy and he felt almost hopeless.

"Ty." Owen's voice pulled Ty from his prayers. He sat up and hurried to the cell doors.

"Get him out of that cell." Owen was clearly calling the shots.

"They've got Brooke… did they let her go?" Ty's eyes were red with stress. "It was Wyatt."

"I know." Owen motioned toward the door. "Let's get you out of here."

Ty wasn't sure if he was being released into FBI custody to further question his murder charges or if the charges were dropped and he was being released. It didn't matter at that moment. All he could think about was Brooke.

"We've taken Wyatt in for questioning." Owen said as they walked to his car.

"Have you found Brooke?"

"No. At this moment, Wyatt is denying everything." Owen fastened his seatbelt and looked behind him. "He claims you're behind it all—said it's a cover up for the murder."

"They had her in a room. They were beating her up. Wyatt had her on live feed." Ty explained the whole scenario.

"And of course Wyatt did all of this off camera." Owen shook his head.

"I'm sorry, Owen." Ty apologized. "I was wrong to accuse you. Wyatt told me he bugged your phones."

Owen shrugged. "You had every reason to suspect me. I don't blame you."

"Except that I should have known your character better. I'm sorry. Do you forgive me?"

It was not the question Owen expected. He glanced at Ty and almost grinned. "Of course I forgive you."

Ty glanced out the window and wished he could apologize to Brooke. Wyatt was right—he did love her. Why didn't he just grab her in his arms before he left and tell her how he felt?

"We're about to make another move that should answer some questions." Owen interrupted Ty's thoughts.

■ ■ ■

Olivia sat in her hotel room and poured a glass of red wine. Her hand shook as she poured and she let out a shaky breath. Clayton was on his way there and she planned to get to the bottom of things. She'd dealt with the loss of Brad. Now she had to deal with her husband's obvious criminal activity. What was going to happen to her brother? What were they doing to his friend, Brooke? How far was Clayton willing to go to make sure Olivia's past would not be brought to light?

Clayton knocked and Olivia went to greet him. Her mascara was smeared, her eyes were red, and she'd cried off all of her foundation and blush. Olivia didn't look like the same woman.

"What in the world is going on here?" Clayton showed no real concern for his wife. "You begged me to come. Here I am. Why?" He glanced at the glass in her hand. "Is it so I can sit here and watch you while you drink a bottle of red?"

"How did you get here so quick, Clayton?"

"I had business in New York today."

Olivia walked to a chair by the window and sat down. "Was your business Brooke Dunbar? Or maybe my brother?" Her red eyes flashed at him angrily.

"What are you talking about?" Clayton sat across from her on the other chair and poured himself a glass of wine.

"I'm talking about the files. I'm talking about Jasmine Greenwich. I'm talking about Brad Bronowski. I'm talking about Matthew Pratt!" She picked up her wine glass and threw it across the room. "What have you done?"

Clayton's eyes widened and he watched the wine drip from the wall where her glass had shattered. He narrowed them on his wife and shook his head. "I'm trying to clean up your mess, Olivia. You made some stupid political moves early in your career and it's my job to make sure those mistakes disappear. I'm trying to make you a Senator."

Olivia sucked in a troubled breath. "Dear God…" she looked at the ceiling as if really trying to pray. "Then it's all true."

Clayton rubbed the top of his head and cleared his throat. "How do you even know all this? How did you figure it out?"

"I didn't!" Olivia got up and paced the room. "The FBI figured it out." She turned to face her husband.

"But how? Wyatt has the files." Clayton shook his head. "Ty deleted the ones from the internet."

"Did Ty tell you about the ones he faxed to Owen Vance?" Olivia clenched her teeth.

"The little idiot!" Clayton slammed his fist on the table and swore. "I didn't see that coming. But, don't worry. We'll take care of it."

"Take care of it?" Olivia shook her head. "No—I'm done. We're done." She took off her wedding ring and flung it the same direction as the broken glass.

"Olivia, stop. This is what we've always dreamed of. Your approval ratings tower above Evanston. There's only two weeks until the election. You're a sure win."

"Do you hear yourself, Clayton? You killed people to cover up a few stupid files!"

Clayton stood up and grabbed his wife's arms. "Olivia, listen to me—"

"Did you kill them?"

Clayton paused, forming his words. "Wyatt and his two men did most of the work. We can pin it all on them if you want. I've kept my hands clean."

Olivia grabbed his hands from her arms and thrust them away from her. "How can you say that? What about my brother? Did you frame him for murder?"

"You know your brother ruined his career anyway." Clayton sat back down and rubbed his bald head. "Pinning the murder on Blake was Wyatt's idea. Several of the men Blake turned in when he went state's evidence had connections to Wyatt. While Blake ratted out his clients, Wyatt had to scramble to keep his name out of the dirt. I was the only one who knew his connection. The whole thing was an ugly affair. Wyatt never got over it."

"Wyatt was the missing piece and you knew it?" Olivia was about to fly off the handle. "My brother could have been free from witness protection four years ago!"

"Wyatt has been a far greater asset than your brother ever would have been."

"He's my brother!"

"Since when does family mean anything to you?" Clayton laughed sarcastically and finished his glass of wine.

It took a few minutes for Olivia to let Clayton's words sink in. "They're my family." Her tone softened. "They mean the world to me."

"Well, so does being senator." Clayton refilled his glass. "That's why you married me, remember? I promised you I could do it and I almost have."

Olivia glanced at the clock. "Where is Brooke? Did you kill her too?"

Clayton let out a dry chuckle. "She's alive."

"Where is she?" Olivia pressed.

"She's in the old Hickory Weaver's warehouse off River Street. We just roughed her up a little."

Olivia sat down on the edge of the bed and covered her face with her hands. Her emotions were spent but she'd gotten the information she was supposed to. She opened her blouse and showed Clayton the wires. "Thank you."

Clayton's eyes grew wide. "You were wired?"

In a matter of seconds, the door flew opened and five FBI agents filled the room with guns pointed at Clayton.

Olivia lifted her face and wiped her tears. "I never asked you to do anything illegal for me."

■■■

Ty sat with Owen in the hotel room across the hall. He ran a trembling hand through his hair and waited for direction.

"They've got a location on Brooke." Owen turned to Ty. "We'll get a team out right away." He set down his headphones. "Did you want to see your sister?"

Ty nodded. He walked across the hall with Owen and saw Olivia sitting on the bed watching while they arrested her husband. She glanced up as Ty walked in the door and her eyes filled back up with tears.

As much as he wanted to comfort his sister, Ty ached to know that Brooke was okay. He took a few steps into the room and Olivia approached him.

"I'm so sorry." She looked down. "I'm so sorry." She buried her face in her hands.

Ty placed a comforting hand on his sister's shoulder and drew her to him for a hug. "I don't blame you for any of this."

Olivia's shoulders shook and she stepped back. "Not just about Clayton." Her voice trembled. "For everything I've done. What a disappointment I must be to you."

"We all screw up, Olivia."

She shook her head. "I took it too far. I wanted power more than integrity." She wiped her wet face on the back of her hand.

"We're ready to go." Owen placed a hand on Ty's shoulder and turned to Nathan. "Make sure you notify the Marshal's office. Have Wyatt charged immediately."

Ty glanced at his sister. "We've got to go find Brooke."

Olivia nodded. "Of course. I hope she's okay." There was genuine concern in her voice. "We'll talk more later."

■ ■ ■

A dark SUV in the parking lot of the Hickory Weaver's Warehouse was a good indication that someone was there. The building was up for sale with little interest. Broken bottles were everywhere and weeds had grown up between the cracked concrete drive. Ty insisted on going into the building with Owen and his team. Owen insisted he stay back at least ten feet.

It was quiet in the old building. Ty felt the hairs on the back of his head standing up as they approached the stairs. Owen motioned for Ty to wait when they approached the fourth floor.

It was all he could do to stay in the stairwell when a small commotion ensued just inside the hallway. Gunshots were fired and Ty heard yelling.

"Where's Brooke?" Owen's voice echoed across the empty warehouse walls.

Ty stepped from the stairwell, eager for the answer to that question.

"She's not here." A voice echoed back.

Ty hurried into the hallway and watched as a man was handcuffed at gunpoint. Another man lay lifeless on the floor.

"Where is she?" Ty faced the apprehended criminal.

The man refused to speak, but his fiery eyes glared at Ty.

Ty scanned the empty room. Where was the chair? She'd been sitting on a chair. "She's got to be in this building." He turned to Owen.

"We'll find her."

"Search the building." Owen called out. He placed a restraining hand on Ty. "Go back to the stairwell."

Ty shook his head. "No, Owen. I've got to find her." His eyes were wide with concern. He stepped back apologetically and hurried out to the dimly lit hallway.

Footsteps echoed through the building. Ty heard voices calling out as various rooms were checked. Where was she? The image of her frightened eyes flashed through his mind. How badly had they hurt her? He felt sick at the thought.

With each dark room he entered, Ty prayed he would find her. He scanned the corners with his flashlight, calling out her name. Would he find her laying lifeless on one of the cold, concrete floors? *Please Father, help me find her. Help her be alive.*

CHAPTER 26

Brooke lay in darkness on the cold floor. The echo of a gunshot tore through the walls and brought back the memory of someone shooting Cody. She'd only caught a glimpse of him going down before she was snatched from the house. Fear like she'd never known gripped her heart. Was he alive? She had no concept of time, but the hours of not knowing were torture. She'd prayed and prayed from her lonely prison.

She could hear faint sounds of voices and footsteps in the empty building. Brooke wasn't sure if those sounds were for her rescue, or if she was about to endure another terrible call to Ty. The fear in his voice and the sound of defeat was heartbreaking. When had she ever heard him sound so hopeless? She wasn't sure how they were ever going to get out of this. What if they killed him? Her heart broke at the thought. Brooke wished she could have told him how she felt. She loved him. Tears coursed down her face. She tried to scoot into a comfortable sitting position, but her body was so tired.

God, please... help us. She was too tired to pray anything else.

The footsteps grew closer and Brooke strained to listen. Was someone calling her name?

"Brooke!" She heard the voice grow closer. Was it Ty? She was almost afraid to hope.

She mustered all the strength she had and cried for help.

"Brooke..." She heard him again. This time he was closer.

"Help," Her faint voice replied.

Ty barreled into the room and shone his light on her small huddled form. With her hands and legs bound with zip ties, Brooke looked up and started to cry. In only a moment, Ty knelt down. He took a knife from his pocket, cut her zip ties, and pulled her into his arms. He held her as if his very life depended upon it. Her body shook with emotion and Ty cradled her against his chest. His eyes filled with tears and he whispered thanks to God.

"Are you injured?" He asked softly. "I saw the way that man abused you." He could barely choke out the words.

"I'm okay." It felt so good to be in his arms. Ty's arms. "Is Cody okay?" Brooke pulled away slightly so she could see Ty's face. "They shot him." Her voice shook with fear.

Ty nodded. "Owen just talked to his wife. Cody is out of surgery, they removed the bullet, no organs were injured, and everything looks good. Yolanda said he had just woken up and was still very groggy but in good spirits."

Relief spread across her face. "I prayed so hard for him." She relaxed in Ty's arms and gave a soft prayer of thanksgiving. "I prayed for you too." She sucked in a trembling breath.

"Oh, Brooke…" He held her tightly. "I thought I was going to lose you. I was so scared. I don't ever want to lose you." His voice trembled. "I love you, Brooke."

The words were like sunshine. She snuggled closer in his arms. "I love you, too, Ty." It felt so good to say.

"I don't ever want to be away from you again." Ty ran his hand over her hair. He moved so he could see her eyes. "Marry me." He wiped her hair from her tearstained face.

His words caught her off guard.

"I mean it. I love you. I know this is an unromantic place to ask, but I want to spend the rest of my life with you, Brooke." His voice was full of emotion and his eyes full of love.

Brooke's tired eyes lit up with a beautiful spark of joy and she nodded. "Yes."

Very gently, Ty kissed her bruised lips and wrapped his arms around her. Peace washed over her. She was going to marry Ty.

■ ■ ■

Voices in the hallway reminded them that they weren't alone. "We need to let them know you're safe." Ty kissed her head and asked her if she could stand up.

Brooke let Ty help her to her feet and worked to stretch her sore muscles.

Ty took her hand and led her to the door. “I found her.” He called to the agents. “Someone let Owen know.” Ty did his best to rub life back into her sore wrists.

“I’m so thirsty.” She swallowed hard and licked her dry lips.

One of the agents got Brooke a bottle of water and Brooke accepted it gratefully. They’d turned on emergency lighting to the building and a dim glow shone on their faces.

“Paramedics are waiting for her outside,” the agent said.

“Brooke!” Owen hurried down the hallway. “Where was she? I was searching all the way up on the top floor with a team.”

“She was in a small room off the end of the hallway.” Ty kept a protective hand on her back.

“Are you okay?” Owen asked.

“I am now.” A slight smile shown on her face and she looked up at Ty.

“Let’s get you downstairs so they can take a look at you.”

Brooke nodded and Ty led her down the hallway.

“I’ll meet you down there. We’re finishing up with her captors. We’ll go see Cody as soon as they check you for injuries.” Owen promised.

The paramedics did a thorough examination and bandaged the few cuts and bruises she had. They offered her pain reliever, but Brooke declined it.

“They said you checked out.” Owen approached the ambulance. “Would you like to see Cody now?”

“Can we?” Brooke’s eyes were hopeful.

“Both him and Yolanda will be eager to see you.” Owen looked at her lip. “That’s a nasty bruise.” He shook his head.

“Wyatt took the credit for that,” Ty said. “He showed me the bite marks you left on his arm.” Ty’s lips curved into a slight smile. “Way to go.”

Brooke shook her head. “I’ve never fought like that in my life.”

“Let’s hope you never need to again.” Owen led the way to his vehicle. “Do you need anything? Food? Drink?” Owen offered.

“I just want to see Cody.”

■ ■ ■

If Cody were a little bit more coherent Brooke was convinced he would have shown far more enthusiasm at seeing his sister safe and sound. He greeted her with a wane smile and reached up with his IV to give her a high five.

"They said your surgery went well." Brooke sat beside her brother and reached for his hand.

"Yeah, but they didn't save the bullet for me. I was kinda bummed." Cody's lips curved into a playful grin.

Brooke glanced up at Yolanda who stood right beside her. "Thank you for staying with him. I was so scared."

"You had us pretty scared, too." Yolanda hugged the younger woman. "Your bruise." She said softly. "Are you hurt anywhere else?"

Brooke touched her lip. "Just a few bruises, no broken bones. I should heal up in a few days. The paramedics checked me out."

"I hope you left some bruises on them, too." Cody looked up at his sister. "I'm proud of you for fighting back."

Brooke squeezed her brother's hand. "And I'm proud of you. Thank you for fighting for me." She leaned forward and kissed the top of his head. "For always fighting for me."

Her words carried a lot of meaning and Cody gave her a tired smile. "That's what brothers do."

"Well, I've got the best brother in the world."

"Where's Ty?" Cody strained to look over the pillow.

"I'm right here." Ty stepped forward and gave Cody a sympathetic smile. "I guess this isn't the way you were hoping to spend your vacation days."

"It was an adventure. I dig adventure." Cody smirked.

"They said it was a clean shot right through his side. Thankfully it missed his organs and didn't go through any bones." Yolanda explained. "He should be able to come home in a couple days."

Cody's eyes started to close. "Are we coming back to your house?" he mumbled.

"Of course." Yolanda glanced at her husband and back to Cody. "At least until you're well enough to fly."

"I hate New York." Cody said as he drifted off to sleep.

Owen looked at the clock over Cody's bed. "It's pretty late.

I think everybody's done in. Why don't we all head back to my house?"

"Don't we have to give our statements?" Ty asked.

"I think you need a little break. I'll tell Nathan we'll be there in the morning."

Brooke's eyes fell on her sleeping brother. Was it safe to leave him?

"You need to rest so you can pamper him while he gets better." Yolanda placed her hand on Brooke's shoulder. "I'll sit with him in the morning while you're giving your statements."

Brooke nodded. She was anxious for a good night's sleep.

■ ■ ■

"That had to be the longest shower anyone has ever taken at my house." Owen greeted Ty when he descended the stairs. "Did you save any hot water?"

"No. It was my goal to use the whole tank." Ty walked past Owen to Brooke. "I made sure everyone else was done showering first."

It was good to hear Ty and Owen joking with one another. Brooke looked up at Ty and he smiled at her.

"Your lip looks better already."

"It feels better." She touched the tender scab. "At least it's not swollen anymore."

Ty leaned over and kissed her. "I just can't wait to get done with all this business stuff and start planning our future." He reached for Brooke's hand.

They'd already told Owen and Yolanda about their marriage plans. Neither of them seemed surprised.

Brooke and Ty rode to the office with Owen and spent the morning wrapping up the case.

"Nathan spoke with Sheryl Bronowski this morning," Owen said. "She will be flying out in a couple days to give her statements."

"How is she?" Ty asked.

"She's okay. Thankfully, she got out before her house was ransacked, but she's not out of the water. She's been holding onto evidence for the past several years and attempted to use it as blackmail."

“What kind of charges will she face?” Brooke felt bad for the woman.

“It’s hard to say. Without a doubt she’s got a good lawyer.”

“Hopefully one with integrity,” Ty added.

“The puzzle finally fits together.” Owen leaned back in his chair and put his hands behind his head. “Since Wyatt was the missing link in the other case, you no longer need witness protection.”

Ty let out a quick breath. “Wow. It feels good to hear those words.”

“So, you won’t be Ty Westgate anymore?” Brooke wondered what she should call him.

Owen crossed his arms and tilted his head. “He’s the only guy I ever met who fits both of his names so well.”

“My parents will always think of me as Blake Kendall.” Ty glanced at Brooke. “But as to wanting my old life back, I’d say no thanks. I’m a new creation.”

“How about Ty Kendall?” Brooke leaned forward. “I don’t think I could start calling you Blake.”

Ty chuckled. “You can always call me Ty, but we’ll be sharing the last name of Kendall.”

“Your sister finished giving her statements.” Nathan popped his head into the room. “She wants to see you and Brooke alone if that’s okay.”

Owen nodded and stood up from the conference table. “I’ll run across the street and get what Ty calls ‘real coffee.’ What do you two want?”

Ty and Brooke gave Owen their order and waited for Olivia to make her appearance.

Nathan walked her into the room and she sat across from Ty.

She was quiet for a few moments after Owen stepped out. She looked tired and her eyes were red from crying. It was obvious that what she was about to say was not easy for her. “I owe you both huge apologies.” She tucked a blonde hair behind her ear nervously and fidgeted with her earring.

“I already told you I forgive you, sis.”

“I know, but it’s more than just what happened with Clayton and Owen. It’s everything.” She blinked back tears. “I’ve been a terrible sister and…" she turned to Brooke. "I've been a terrible person." She swallowed and sucked in a deep breath. "Brooke, I'm sorry I tried to send you away." There was a genuinely repentant look in Olivia's eyes that Brooke had not seen in Olivia before. "I said some terrible things to you and I was wrong. I'm sorry."

Brooke brushed her hair behind her back nervously. There was still something about Olivia that intimidated her but the words were healing. "I forgive you."

Olivia's face softened. "Thank you." She glanced at her brother for a moment. "My priorities have been messed up for a long time. I'm sorry you had to go through all of this."

"The enemy meant it for evil, but God meant it for good." Ty's eyes shone with peace. "God used it—all of it. If it took me having to go into witness protection to turn my life to Christ, it was worth it. Mom and Dad, Brooke, all of us—" He reached his hand to Brooke's. "Our lives are forever changed for God's glory and none of us would change that."

Brooke felt the warmth of his hand in hers and nodded.

"I'm glad you've found something like that." Olivia looked away.

"You can too, Olivia." Ty leveled his eyes tenderly on his sister.

"Maybe some day." She glanced down at her hands and ran her thumb over her smooth, red fingernails.

It was a start.

"You did hit the nail on the head when you recognized a relationship forming between us, though." Ty glanced at Brooke and back to his sister. "We're getting married."

Olivia gave what Brooke thought was a genuine smile. "I wish you both the best." It was a bittersweet wish considering Olivia's marriage was falling apart. "Mom and Dad will be overjoyed."

Ty nodded. "They are. I called them this morning."

"I've withdrawn from the campaign." Olivia sighed. "I think I'm just going to slow down and maybe do local politics." She turned her eyes to the window. "Or maybe I'll retire and get a little beach house on the coast of Maine. I don't know."

"Brooke and I have decided on Maine." Ty tightened his fingers around Brooke's. "I told dad this morning to start looking for property."

Olivia gave Brooke a wane smile. "The things I said about you not being right for my brother—I was wrong. Money and society don't make a marriage." She glanced at the two of them. "Love does."

Ty tightened his grip in Brooke's hand. "Love and Jesus." He grinned at his sister. "You know I'm going to start working on you now."

■ ■ ■

Two months later:

"Dude, that was the coolest wedding ever!" Cody patted his new brother-in-law on the back. "It was short, sweet, and to the point."

Ty and Brooke had a small wedding held at Ty's parents' church in Maine. Pastor David from Maryland performed the ceremony and his wife, Linda, was one of Brooke's bridesmaids. Ty and Brooke had been excited to reconnect with the Maryland couple and continue building that friendship.

The reception was held at Ty's parents' home. A tall balsam fir stood proudly in the entranceway, beautifully decorated for a Christmas time wedding.

Olivia was Brooke's other bridesmaid. Cody and Owen were Ty's groomsmen.

The couple couldn't have asked for a prettier day for the wedding. Ty glanced out his parent's cathedral window at the snow-covered pines against the clear blue sky.

"That view of the harbor is awesome!" Cody let his eyes travel to the icy shore. "Your parents have a sweet place here."

Ty grinned and straightened Cody's tie real quick. "You clean up well, Cody."

Cody glanced over his tuxedo. "I haven't worn one of these since I went to my senior prom." He chuckled and glanced over at his parents talking to Ty's parents in the dining room. Brooke was with them, laughing about something Ty's father just said. Ty's mother had her arm around the bride and Brooke looked happy. "I still can't believe our parents came."

Ty nodded. "I'm glad they did." He stood beside Cody and watched them talk. "My parents said they talked to your parents about their relationship with Jesus at the rehearsal dinner last night."

Cody nodded. "Yeah. They've preached to me, too." He grinned. "Between you, Brooke, and your parents I just might end up jumping into this Jesus thing."

"Don't do it to get us off your back. Do it because you sincerely want to be a follower of Christ," Ty reminded Cody.

"Brooke's talked to me a lot about forgiveness. Not just God's forgiveness but my own forgiveness of Dad and Mom."

Ty knew she had. They'd both been praying hard for Cody.

"Hi boys." Brooke finally slipped away from the parents and greeted her new husband. "It's good seeing you two together."

"I finally got a brother." Ty placed a hand around Cody's shoulders.

"Me too." Cody did the same and he high fived his sister with his free hand. "I really dig Maine. It's kind of like Colorado… but different."

Brooke and Ty laughed.

"When you're ready to move up here, we'll help you find a place." This time Cody chuckled. "Find me a ski resort and I just might take you up on it."

"I can do that." Ty started rattling off places to downhill ski in Maine.

"Sounds good to me." Cody sounded genuinely interested. "I'm gonna go grab more of that lobster stuff before your FBI friends take it all." He gave them a wink and walked to the food table in the kitchen.

Brooke and Ty had a moment to themselves. Ty wrapped his arms around her and spun her around by the Christmas tree. "You're the best Christmas present I could ever ask for."

"That goes both ways." Brooke's eyes lit up radiantly.

Ty pulled her close for a tender kiss and stepped back to admire his bride. "It was good seeing you talking to our parents."

Brooke nodded. "Having your parents around definitely helped." She took a deep breath. "But we still have a long way to go." Brooke leaned into his chest and hugged him. "I'm just glad I got you."

"I love you, Mrs. Kendall." Ty wrapped his hands around her waist.

Sunlight streamed through the window and sparkled on the sequins in Brooke's wedding gown, but it was nothing like the sparkle in her eyes. "I love you… Ty Kendall." Brooke grinned. "And Ty Westgate… and Blake Kendall… and Carter Duncan…" she moved to kiss his lips. "I just love you."

76669572R00174

Made in the USA
Columbia, SC
07 September 2017